Hosting the Kazimeer

by C.E. Sales

Fantasy
Forge
Press

Hosting the Kazimeer
By C.E. Sales

Published by
Fantasy Forge Press, LLC
P.O. Box 1
Cliffwood, NJ 07721
www.fantasyforgepress.com

© 2000 by Christine Sales
ISBN – 0-9741704-1-0
First Printing 2003
Second Printing 2016
Cover Art © 2016 by Mark Pinheiro

This book is dedicated to Mark, who helped me to see why guys laugh boisterously and have to mosey when they walk. His love and support are the reasons why this book has seen the printed world.

And to my family for their constant help and for being my biggest fans.

TABLE OF CONTENTS

PROLOGUE

Subdued, hushed, still; the forest was as calm as a sleeping babe held in its mother's protective arms. The breeze was refreshing and warm, gently stirring the leaves and bushes. Soft sounds came from the night creatures beginning to wake. The lack of nearby villages made this forest darker than most, giving it an awesome feel. Because of this, no one saw the man fall out of the sky.

He did not scream or cry out as he dropped to the ground. The only sounds made indirectly by him were the cracking of branches as he collided through them, and a hard thud when he hit the dirt. Having all the air knocked out of him, he inhaled laboriously until he could breathe again. He suddenly became aware that he could, in fact, breathe. It hurt but that was probably more from lack of practice than the fall. The fall? He looked up into the night sky. Where was the opening that released him from his prison? Where was he now? How long had it been?

Slowly he rolled onto his side, sat up carefully, and straightened his back. It felt odd to have a body again instead of the shapeless form he'd become used to. Perhaps he always had his body but his mind had been so trapped he wasn't aware of it. That didn't matter right now though. Did he return or was this some other foul nightmare? He often dreamed of returning and plotted his revenge countless times, but they were always dreams and he recognized them as such. This definitely didn't feel like a dream.

Again he searched the sky for the opening. It showed up out of nowhere and provided him with a way out. It appeared in that timeless, empty void he had lived in for so long...how long? As part of an old habit, he reached out with his mind to search the Land but withdrew immediately. Pain, too much pain. He had to give himself a moment to become adjusted to the liveliness of the Land once more instead of the barren darkness he called the Pit. It was a horrid place not because of what it contained but rather what it lacked. No sound, no sight, no touch, no people and no power - an infinite void. He didn't exist when he was there and yet he had been constantly aware. Aware that there *was* nothing...except for him.

He wondered if he was mad now but how would he ever know? If he were mad would he willingly admit such a thing? His mind wandered through his memories as he tried to recall what he knew about himself. He knew who he was, remembered his childhood, and his coming of age into the power. He didn't feel mad. What else did he know? He'd been one of the *Trislarns* and then he had been the only one except for...*him*.

Abbnar. He wanted to shout out the name to shatter the image in his mind. Abbnar put him into the Pit; Abbnar and that abomination he created. Abbnar trapped him and probably took the Land for himself. His anger fed his strength and he reached out again with his mind; he wanted to recoil but not from pain, from disgust. Oh yes, Abbnar had taken over the Land. It was crawling with morphers. A few - a controlled few - were enough and that was how it should be. But now the Land was infested with hundreds of those filthy, revolting morphers who sucked the Land's power dry. The worst part was he could sense the presence of those beasts, those things Abbnar created. He would rid the Land of them soon enough; of all these morphers who plagued the Land, and he would not, could not, be punished this time.

He was free now. His strength and power were increasing every moment but he had to be careful and ease up on his search over the Land. No need to let Abbnar know he had returned after... He searched for the specific information and this time did shout to the sky. Nearly a thousand years! Abbnar had trapped him in the Pit for almost one thousand years!

In a fury he released a large amount of his power to hunt down Abbnar. Was he still alive? He hoped so...he *truly* hoped so. He nearly sagged with relief when he brushed across Abbnar's essence and quickly released the connection. Let the old fool think he imagined it. Let him think he was becoming paranoid. Abbnar would not worry because, of course, *he* was still in the Pit, right?

He had to take his time now and slowly, carefully build up what was stolen from him; his power, his army, and his Land. He would take his time because what were a few years compared to one thousand in the Pit. Yes, Abbnar would suffer. He would make sure Abbnar suffered in the most horrific way possible. The hardest part was choosing from his many ideas already planned through centuries of waiting. When he finally decided on one, he allowed himself to smile. The motion hurt his face but he ignored it. His attack was beautiful in its simplicity. His plan would start as a small pebble rolling down a snow covered hill but when it gained enough speed and strength, it would have the most devastating impact imaginable and would crush Abbnar.

It would take some time for his attack to blossom completely but that was just fine with him. Besides he had other things to do in the meantime. He would wait patiently then strike like a viper. Like the true meaning of his name; Taj.

LANDON

The Water Count folded his hands neatly on the smooth, polished table before him and his beady, brown eyes regarded the young man sitting across from him. "Our investigation is complete."

Landon slowly directed his gaze to the plump man with the sour expression. His sharp green eyes held the Count's for a moment before he said levelly, "I am glad to hear it."

The Water Count glanced along the table at other three Counts present and then continued. "At this time, we find no sufficient evidence connecting you to the death of Kazimeer Natal, his wife, and his heir."

"I am glad to hear it," Landon repeated in the same smooth tone.

"Therefore," the Wind Count stated, "we will allow you to officially be instated as Kazimeer of the Land."

Landon's eyes widened slightly and a sly grin spread across his face. "Why, thank you. It's only a month overdue."

"You must understand," the Wind Count said. "Such investigations take time."

The Fire Count added, "We wanted to prove your innocence, Landon. Surely you can see how not investigating these matters thoroughly can lead to suspicions among the people."

"Yes, I can see that." He nodded solemnly. "Then since this investigation is now complete, I am clear to take the throne?"

The Counts nodded.

"Fine. The Document please."

"Excuse me?" the Wind Count asked. "What document?"

"The Document of Exoneration. The one we will all sign and stamp with our own personal seal. The one that is signed at the end of every investigation regarding the stability and birthright of the present Kazimeer. *That* document."

The Counts exchanged glances.

"I was unaware," the Water Count began, "that you would require such a procedure."

"Then you have not read your history, gentle sirs," Landon stated. "For if you had, you would be completely aware that such an agreement is needed. Without it, you could remove me from the throne at your fancy. Surely now, you were all aware of that?" The Counts stared at him in astonishment and Landon smiled pleasantly. "I was."

The Wind Count's eyes narrowed. "Of course we are aware of the necessary documents needed at an investigation of this nature."

"However," the Water Count continued, "the Document of Exoneration will need to be drawn up. It should be ready within two weeks. Until then---"

"Then how fortunate for you," Landon interrupted firmly and clapped his hands twice.

Instantly the door behind him opened and a young boy entered, carrying a tray with five freshly written agreements laid out on it, a stylus, a beeswax candle,

9

and the seal of the Kazimeer. Following the boy was a large, gruff man dressed in the complete formal attire of the Kazimeer's Second, and behind him were two armed Defenders. The boy placed the tray in the center of the table and stepped back behind the Defenders.

Landon sat patiently with his hands folded neatly on the table and waited for objections. The documents were scrutinized several times by each Count, but Landon knew they would find nothing wrong with them. He'd spent the last few sleepless nights working on the agreement himself, researching past records to find the proper wording. However, if there were any objections, he was more than prepared to answer them.

Finally, the Counts signed the agreements and made their personal seals next to their names. When they were finished, Landon took the documents and scribbled his own name at the bottom of each. He called out over his shoulder, "Second Brazet."

"Yes, my lord," the large man answered, taking a step forward.

"This is my signature, is it not?"

"Yes, my lord."

Landon held up his personal seal. "This is the seal of the Kazimeer?"

"Yes, my lord."

"Thank you." Landon placed his seal carefully onto each parchment. When he pulled it away, a dragon with its wings spread fully and its head arched back, as if it were going to roar, was imprinted; the Kazimeer's mark.

Landon took one of the copies and dismissed his Second and the others. He waited until they had left before looking over the four Counts. "With that unpleasantness finished, I can assume there are pressing matters you all need to attend to."

"But first," the Water Count said, "we need to discuss some matters involved with your installation."

"Such as?"

The Soil Count spoke, "Such as your Second."

"My Second?" Landon asked. "What about him?"

"We feel," the Wind Count began softly, "that perhaps you made an emotional decision when you named him. Brazet is a fine Captain. I respect him. He performed his duties for Natal exceptionally." He leaned forward and met Landon's stare directly. "But what experience does he have with diplomacy or castle procedures? He's a Captain, not a Second. He's had no training whatsoever in performing a Second's duties."

Landon smiled. "And yet he managed to keep the four of you from throwing me into the dungeon when you arrested me."

The Wind Count sat back but the friendliness had run out of his expression and now he stared darkly at Landon.

"What we mean is," the Fire Count added quickly, "that it might be wise to reconsider your choice. I mean, you made this decision just after hearing of Natal's death. It's only natural that under such stressful conditions, it may be difficult to make an unbiased choice. We understand that you had to name someone, but now may be the time to reevaluate such actions to see if they were the best ones."

Landon folded his hands on the table and met each of the Count's eyes as he spoke. "Brazet is a natural Second. He has already proven his intellect, skill, and loyalty to me." His eyes narrowed slightly. "I will not be choosing another."

The Counts exchanged quick glances and the Water Count spoke up. "Then perhaps we can suggest another way to easily guide you into the Kazimeer position."

"Guide me?" Landon asked. "I didn't know I needed to be guided."

The Wind Count smiled. "It can be a little harrowing for any new Kazimeer to accept the demands of the position. Especially when the former Kazimeer isn't around any longer to assist you."

"I was the Kazimeer's Second for five years, gentle sirs," Landon stated pleasantly. "I know what the demands of the position are."

"We understand," the Water Count said. "But there are many aspects to being the Kazimeer that you were not involved with while you were Natal's Second. Crucial decisions need to be made instantaneously. Treaties need to be reviewed on a daily basis as well as a dozen other reports that require immediate attention. And since your current Second has so little experience with any of this, we feel the Land itself might suffer."

"That is why," the Soil Count began, "we recommend you recognize and name a Chancellor."

Landon blinked slowly. "A Chancellor?" The four Counts nodded and smiled congenially, which immediately sent chills up Landon's spine. He continued smoothly, "There hasn't been a Chancellor in over four centuries."

"We know," the Wind Count said. "But in these difficult times, the Land does need to come first. You would need someone extremely qualified."

Landon allowed a small grin to play on his lips. "And I'm sure you know of such a person?"

"Indeed we do," the Soil Count stated. "Lord Hammel."

"Lord Hammel," Landon repeated flatly.

"Do you know him?" the Fire Count asked.

"Yes, I do, in fact." He glanced down at the table and laughed softly, "I do indeed know Lord Hammel."

"Then you know he is qualified for the position," the Soil Count said.

"I know he's a smug, greedy, arrogant bastard." Landon smiled at the four stunned faces staring back at him. He shrugged. "Sorry, too accurate a description?"

The Soil Count cleared his throat. "I am not sure of your interactions with him but---"

"My interactions with him," Landon interrupted, "have been brief. Largely because he refused to acknowledge me when I was a Second and since I was not destined to be Kazimeer, he couldn't be bothered with me. I do recall Natal's advice to me about him, though. He told me if I ever trusted him, I was a damn, bloody fool." He smiled at their expressions. "Natal said he liked to live in pockets and I'm sure he'd like to live in all four of yours, if he doesn't already.

I'm sure if he were Chancellor, coins would just flow in the direction of the four providences all in the name of progress or some other thing. I have a feeling we wouldn't see much progress but we would see a severe depletion of coins. And all of this would be done behind my back because, as Chancellor, he wouldn't have to have my permission to distribute funds."

He studied their expressionless faces and nodded slowly. "I want my reign as Kazimeer to be a bit more involved. There will be no Chancellor."

After a pause the Wind Count spoke up. "We are sorry you feel that way, Landon. However, it is within our power to appoint a Chancellor if we feel it is needed." He smiled thinly. "Which we do."

Landon returned the smile. "You all thought Natal was soft, that he was weak. You all thought you were getting away with so much and he never had the slightest idea what you were doing. He did. He just didn't have the time or the patience to deal with you. He felt it kept things running smoother if he let you take your handful of gold here and handful of workers there. That was how he operated and it allowed him to sleep at night."

He paused for a moment and then lowered his voice a level. "But I cannot sleep at night knowing this is how things are and I think the four of you know that I cannot allow such actions to continue. So appointing a Chancellor is a brilliant way to keep me in line and to keep the coins and workers flowing smoothly, and in your general direction."

"We are concerned about the wellbeing of the Land," the Water Count snapped.

Landon sniffed a laugh. "Since when? What I should do is dismiss all four of you. It is within *my* power to do that. I won't because I'm hoping beyond hope that there is still something in each of you that remembers your duty to the Land and why you're in the position to begin with." He met each of their gazes. "Do keep in mind, gentle sirs, I have documents on each of you. I know all about the bribes, all about the hoarding of funds, all about the stealing, the trading of workers without pay, I know everything. As I mentioned, Natal couldn't be bothered but I can. He had information on all of you and now I have it." He took a deep breath. "So, do you really want to push this Chancellor thing?"

The Counts huddled together and whispered amongst themselves for a moment before sitting back and staring at Landon like wolves about to pounce on their prey.

"Perhaps," the Wind Count began, "we were hasty with our decision to conclude this investigation. We feel it is necessary to continue with it, at least for a few more months. Until then, someone will need to be in command. We cannot allow the Land to go for so long without a leader. And since it has already been proven that your Second is not qualified to handle the position presently, we will exercise our right to name a Chancellor."

Landon's face was expressionless at first. Then he slowly held up the Document of Exoneration and it was his turn to smile wolfishly. "I don't think so. You've already named me Kazimeer and signed that this investigation is complete." He leaned forward. "If you decide to reopen the investigation at this point, it will extend to the lords in each of your providences. And I would thoroughly enjoy speaking with each and everyone one of them to share my abundance of information with them."

He calmly rolled up the document, while Counts quietly fumed. He finally stared back at them and spoke quietly. "You have one year. One year to get your affairs in order or at least hide them better than you have. One year from this date I will begin a thorough investigation of each of you. If I so much as find a scrap of information, a pittance of proof, I will have you stripped of rank, publically tried and convicted, and, in the case of some of you, executed."

He inhaled deeply to soothe his rising temper but when he spoke it was heated and short. "The death of Kazimeer Natal and his family is tragic for the Land, but you seem to have forgotten, they were *my* family; my only family. And if you wished to make a painful time for me perfectly miserable, then you have succeeded. Believe me, I won't forget it. Now, I would like to mourn my lost family and begin to focus my energy on matters concerning the Land."

When none of the Counts had anything to say, he rose to his feet.

"Good. Then with that unpleasantness finished, I must attend to many pressing matters. I hope you will understand that I do not wish to have guests in my home at this time. My *Second* will assist with your needs and escort you on your way. Pleasant day, gentle sirs."

He did not wait for their response and left the chamber abruptly. Once outside, the young boy, with the tray in hand, was still waiting for him, as well as two Defenders. He started down the hall and was followed by them immediately.

Landon marched through the corridors of what was now his castle, the signed document gripped firmly in his hand. He kept up his brisk pace until he reached the door to his private chamber and called out absently to the young boy, "Webben, after you've put that tray away, draw me a bath."

"Yes, ma'lord," the boy answered and hurried down the hall to carry out his orders.

Two Defenders stood on either side of his door, and one opened it for him a second before he walked straight into it, and then closed it softly. Landon stood in the center of his chamber alone for the first time in weeks. No more Defenders of the Counts looking over his shoulder every time he wanted to take a piss, no more questioning about his every movement, his every sigh, his every absent gesture. His rage shook him, making his body tremble, and he gripped the parchment even tighter.

The fact of the matter was he wasn't all that heart-broken over the death of his family. Granted, Natal had a hand in raising him after their mother's passing when he was only four, but Nat also had a son of his own, who was six months younger than he was. Nat's attention was never divided equally between them. It bothered Landon greatly when he was a child, but after he'd spent several years at the Morpher's Training Halls and away from home, he'd come to terms with his position and accepted it. In fact, he accepted it with pleasure.

He enjoyed being a Second; all of the prestige with none of the pressure. No matter how often his nephew taunted him about how he would never have the throne, it never bothered him as much as Segvature wanted it to. Why would he want the throne? He already had the respect, the gold, and the freedom, without the weight of the Land on his shoulders. It was an arrangement he was more than content to live with. Then two months ago it changed.

Nat, Seg, and Maura returned home from the Gathering Festival deathly ill. What the Counts never mentioned during his questioning was just how they were diseased. It wasn't as if they were coughing and sneezing, with a fever. No, their illness was one the Healers never saw before and had no idea how to cure. It didn't even kill them quickly but went on for a month before it took them, while it slowly ate away at their bodies. Their skin was horribly burned, their hair fell out in clumps, their eyes, ears, nose, and mouth bled spontaneously. Landon only saw them once when they first arrived home, but it was enough to give him the shivers every time he thought about it. After that he was kept separated from them in case the unthinkable happened, which it did, and ended up leaving him the prime suspect to investigate.

The Counts never bothered to point out just how he would be able to give them such a sickness. He was a morpher, not a Weaver. He couldn't perform spells the way a Weaver could. So just how he supposedly murdered them the Counts never addressed, even though he snapped that question at them many times. The fact was the Counts didn't want him on the throne and were looking for any possible reason to keep him from it. Unfortunately for them, they had to come up with evidence so damning that the people wouldn't stand for him taking his brother's place. They knew he was well liked, well respected, and most importantly, he was the last ivory dragon morpher. All Kazimeer's were ivory dragons, it was just the way it was, and the people would not be so willing to accept a change after a thousand years. But that wasn't the reason he fought so hard against the Counts. He did so for personal reasons, to prove a point. Now he'd won and almost wished he let them condemn him.

A knock at his door brought him out of his thoughts. It must be Webben. "Come!" he called out, not bothering to turn around. He heard the door open and close again but didn't see the lad scampering by him toward his bath chamber. He slowly looked over his shoulder and wasn't that surprised to see who was standing there.

"So? How did it go?"

"I'm still here, aren't I?" Landon stated. "My head's not on a chopping block."

"Is it over?"

Stiffly, Landon raised his hand with the document still clenched in his fist. "I suppose so."

Weaver Mazon looked up at the ceiling and breathed with relief. He'd been the Kazimeer's High Weaver when Nada, Landon's mother, was still a girl. He'd been through the family's triumphs and tragedies for over a century, but this particular episode left him feeling his age. The very idea that Landon would have murdered his own family was absurd but the Counts seemed determined to pin the blame on him and nearly got their way. The past month had been tense around the entire castle, servants afraid to breathe around Landon, Defenders jumping at any shadow moving in his direction, and Light only knew what gossip had leaked out to the people. Landon's reputation had been damaged by the Count's investigation, and it would take some time before he could win their trust back again. Not to mention that because Landon was locked away for a month the Land had suffered, and now there were new problems which had to be addressed that would make winning the people's trust all the harder. Mazon breathed with relief again and couldn't help being proud of Landon. If he could tackle the Counts, he should have no problem tending to the dilemmas currently disrupting the Land. Something Mazon was not looking forward to discussing with the young Kazimeer.

He took a deep breath and held out his hand. "Give me the document before you rip it." Landon handed Mazon the parchment and flopped onto his large bed, covering his eyes with his arm, while Mazon reread the document. "You did a fine job with this, Landon."

"You helped."

"I only showed you where to look. You did the rest." Mazon nodded in approval. "A fine job."

Landon gestured indifferently and sat upright, running his hands through his white hair, when another knock came at the door. A moment later Webben entered carrying a steaming bucket in each hand. Landon rose to his feet and glared hard at the boy. "What has taken you so long!" he demanded.

If anyone deserved the title of 'lord' after this whole ordeal, it was Webben. The lad was the only servant who had been allowed to interact with Landon on a daily basis throughout the Count's investigation. With Landon being so tense and short-tempered, the boy took much of his abuse. Never physical, Mazon knew he raised Landon better than that, but verbally Landon's words and tone could slice through steel. Mazon fought the urge to interfere. It wasn't his place to question the Kazimeer's attitude toward his servants; he was only there to advise.

Webben, obviously used to such reactions from Landon, bowed his head. "Forgive me, ma'lord." He waited until Landon jerked his head in the direction of the bath chamber then quickly scurried by him, careful not to spill a single drop of water.

Mazon waited until the boy was gone before he spoke. "Why is he not using the private entrance?"

"The door's still jammed."

"From the other night?"

Landon looked guilty. "I'm not sure. I don't think so."

Mazon studied Landon curiously. "That was the same night those two Defenders of the Counts witnessed your…accidental morph, wasn't it?"

"Perhaps," Landon muttered, but Mazon could see the small, sly smile flash across his face.

Mazon clicked his tongue. "Tub get fixed all right?"

"Yes. Yes it did."

"Didn't stub a claw, I hope."

Landon gave the Weaver a long stare. "No. Thanks for asking."

"I've never heard of an accidental morphing taking place."

"It must have been the stress I was under."

"Uh-huh." Mazon nodded, knowing perfectly well what the boy was up to that night. In all his time, he'd never seen two Defenders run so quickly. No doubt they were not expecting Landon to suddenly burst into his true shape. Unfortunately, the bath chamber was never designed to hold something as large as a dragon. "Well, now that everything has calmed down there should be no more accidental morphings."

"I suspect not," Landon agreed and eyed Webben harshly as he hurried by him. "Before I die, Webben."

"Yes, ma'lord," the boy threw back over his shoulder and left the chamber to refill his buckets.

Mazon held in a groan. "Relax a bit, wash up, and then come down to dinner. We have much to discuss."

"Do I want to hear this?"

"Probably not, but you must." Mazon turned to leave but stopped and looked back at Landon. "You should've invited them to stay."

"Who?"

"The Counts." Before Landon could express his outrage at such a thought, Mazon added, "It would have infuriated them to call you 'my lord' for the next couple of days. Probably would've been the best revenge you could've taken."

"I just wanted them out of here," Landon grumbled.

Mazon nodded with understanding but then added, "It also would've done you good to hear this news from them."

"What news?"

"Relax a bit first, Landon." Mazon smiled and left, just as Webben came crashing back into the chamber.

Landon sat on the edge of his bed, eyeing the boy sternly until the tub was filled. After he'd been bathed and dressed in casual attire, he strolled to the dining hall with an armed Defender on either side of him.

The dining hall was spectacular and huge. A long, beautifully polished, dark wooden table extended from one end of the chamber to the other. There were stained glass windows every two steps, each depicting a different pose of a dragon, and a row of silver candelabras were perfectly lined up along the table. This dining hall was normally reserved for important functions but tonight Landon wanted to be surrounded by beauty while he dined, although he hardly noticed or appreciated it. He simply wanted a different atmosphere outside of the small dining chamber he'd been eating in for a month under close supervision. Tonight he wanted to spoil himself.

Landon walked to the head of the table, where only two other people stood waiting for his arrival. Mazon and Brazet bowed their heads as he walked by them and waited until he sank down into the plush, velvet chair, before taking their own. Immediately the servants began bustling in; one poured wine, while others brought in the first course, and each piece of food or drink was tasted by yet another servant, whose job was to be sure the Kazimeer's food was not poisoned. When the taster didn't fall over dead, the Kazimeer was allowed to dine.

Hosting the Kazimeer

Landon hardly noticed them anymore, and began talking the instant he sat down. He addressed Brazet first. "Have the Counts been sent on their way?"

"Yes, my lord," the rough Second replied, reaching across the table for a warm roll. "Packed and gone."

"Good," Landon half sneered and shifted his eyes toward Mazon. "Now what news of the Land do you wish to discuss with me?"

Mazon hesitated, picking at his plate of fresh vegetables. "The condition of the Land to be exact."

"What's wrong with it?"

Again the Weaver hesitated and finally said softly, "It's dying."

Landon stopped mid-chew. "Dying? How is that possible?"

"That's the problem," Mazon said. "No one knows how it's possible. There is no cause for the problem and yet crops are still withering, wells are drying up, and live-stock are falling ill."

"Not to mention the morphers," Brazet added.

"What about the morphers?" Landon demanded.

The Second and Weaver exchanged glances. Mazon answered, "This odd plague has befallen them as well."

Brazet snorted loudly. "Odd plague, my..." He shifted his eyes toward Landon, who raised an eyebrow, anticipating the colorful remark the former Captain always inserted into his sentences. "...my foot." He resumed eating and talked with his mouth half full, while waving his fork. "It's a pack of twisted fools, that's what it is."

"How do you mean?" Landon asked.

"There's been no one to blame," Brazet stated. "With you temporarily locked away, people need someone to point a finger at. Morphers are the next closest things to blaming you. And fanatics can be quite mean once they have a target to lock onto."

"What is happening to the morphers?" Landon asked.

Mazon cleared his throat, cutting off Brazet before he could get started. "Perhaps such things would be best to discuss after dinner."

"I want to hear this now," Landon said sternly.

Mazon sighed to himself but didn't have a chance to answer. Brazet spoke up. "They're being butchered."

"Butchered?"

"Like cattle at the market. Some reports have found them chopped to shreds in alleys; others just found them dead. Light, I've even heard rumors that they *are* selling them in place of cattle."

Landon waved his plate away. He caught the Weaver's eyes, now understanding why he wished to wait. Still, he let none of his disgust show. "What's being done to stop this?"

"What can be done?" Brazet asked. "We're doing all we can as it is. It's not like these fools announce when they're going to strike or where."

"Have more Defenders been placed in the towns where this is happening?"

"As many as I can spare."

"Spare?" Landon snapped. "Defenders are enlisted to defend the people."

"And I'm having them do just that," Brazet said in his defense. "It's not just droughts causing crops to die. There are floods too. Massive floods that have already wiped out three separate towns and damaged several more. I've placed the majority of forces in those villages to try and stop the flood or if not to evacuate the town." He dropped his voice. "Things have not been going well, Landon."

"It would seem so," Landon muttered. "This is what happens when the leadership of the Land is put on hold for a month." He pushed out a sharp breath as the second part of the meal arrived. A steaming bowl of soup was first tested, then placed before him. "I want all..." He paused, glanced down at the bowl, and called out in a matter of fact tone, "Not hot enough." A servant immediately took the bowl away from him and rushed it back to the kitchen. Landon never skipped a beat with his orders. "...all available Defenders to be placed in every town. What about the locals? Are they doing nothing to defend themselves?"

"They are doing what they can," Brazet answered. "Things are happening too fast for the Defenders to respond or for the villagers to react. I've placed people where the most help is needed."

"And no one knows what's causing this?" Landon accused. "Not a single being can explain these occurrences?"

"Weavers have performed cleansing spells across the entire Land," Mazon said. "Nothing has worked so far."

"Has this sort of plague ever attacked the Land before?" Landon asked not only of the other two, but also of himself. After thinking for a moment he shook his head. "I don't recall any record saying so."

Brazet shook his head as well. "I've never heard of any."

When the Weaver didn't answer, both their eyes fell on him. Mazon shifted in his seat and blew out a short breath. "The last known occurrence of such a disaster hitting the Land was during the *Bloodshed of the Trislarns*."

Brazet snorted loudly and dug into his food while Landon leaned back in his chair, a small smile playing on his lips.

"The *Bloodshed* was ages ago," Landon said.

Mazon held up his hands. "You asked. That is the last known record."

"The *Trislarns* are long dead along with their battle," Brazet said. Mazon said nothing, merely held up his hands. The Second sniffed and muttered under his breath, "The next thing you'll be saying is that Taj has been renewed." He laughed at his own joke and looked to Landon and Mazon to join him. Landon chuckled softly and shook his head, but the Weaver never so much as snickered. Brazet's eyes grew wide and he leaned forward. "Old Weaver, don't tell me you actually believe such nonsense?"

"Did I say anything?" Mazon asked defensively.

"No, and that's what has me worried." Brazet sat back and rubbed his chin absently. "Taj is dead. He's just a legend now."

Landon snapped his fingers suddenly. "But that legend is strong." He looked toward Mazon. "Could this be the work of a corrupt Weaver? One trying to mimic that Dark Master, trying to recreate his actions."

"It's possible." Mazon nodded. "And I would agree with you if it weren't for Panasom."

Landon searched through his mental library on the locations of all towns and villages in the Land and came up with the appropriate place. "Small village located in the Wind providence, main export is spices, population less than five hundred."

"That's the place," Mazon agreed. "You see, they've been completely unaffected by this whole thing. Just before the Counts left, the Wind Count received word that Panasom has been thriving. It seems they have a new Presiding Officer and ever since he's taken charge there have been no problems with their crops or any illness."

Landon thought of something else. "They also have no morphers."

"I thought of that as well," Mazon said. "I can't see a logical connection, although many people don't look for one. They just take the obvious and run with it."

Landon nodded, turning several ideas around in his head. What could this Presiding Officer be doing that he hadn't thought of yet? Perhaps it was only a coincidence, or maybe this person knew of some spell or formula that prevented such disasters. Whatever the reason, Landon knew he should be humble enough to ask for assistance when he needed it. He'd been too far removed from these ongoing problems, and if this person had any answers it was vital that they meet.

While his thoughts were buzzing around in his head, a new bowl had been brought to him. It was so hot the taster burned his mouth before the liquid ever touched his tongue. Landon nodded absently in approval and regarded the other two. "I would like to speak with this Presiding Officer. Invite him immediately to the castle."

"Landon," Brazet asked cautiously, "is that wise? People may see it as a sign of weakness."

Landon stared levelly at him. "People may also see it as the Kazimeer being more interested in correcting the problems of the Land than with his own image."

"I'm inclined to agree with Brazet," Mazon said. "Perhaps you should seek an answer for yourself first. If none can be found, and if Panasom is still showing no signs of this plague, then you could speak to the Presiding Officer."

"I should waste more time in the hopes of finding an answer, when the one I seek could be on its way?" Landon leaned back in his chair and stared off at nothing. After a moment he spoke, "Send for the Presiding Officer. While he is journeying here, I will perform some research of my own. By the time he arrives, I may very well have an answer or a different solution than he has. If so, we will discuss them, if not, no extra time will have been wasted." He shifted his eyes toward Brazet. "I will have a letter composed by this evening. Have it sent out as soon as it is finished."

Brazet reluctantly nodded. "Yes, my lord."

Dinner was completed in awkward silence.

TAJ

Twenty years. Some would think twenty years was a long wait, but not Taj. Twenty years was a blink compared to the time he'd spent in the Pit, and he had used each year well. His army had taken nearly all that time to build up to its current strength, since he had no choice but to do it slowly or else risk catching Abbnar's eye. Still, it had been worth it. Every Weaver, every morpher, every fighter was loyal to him. He made sure he recruited only the best, the strongest, and the easiest to manipulate. The fact that he could step in and out of their minds whenever he wished always gave them incentive to behave, but very few did he allow commands of their own. He made certain that the ones who did knew he would not accept gross mistakes. They witnessed that for themselves when the two Weavers he'd sent to assassinate the three remaining ivory dragons failed horrifically by missing one. And one was all it took to prevent him from stepping in to fill the Kazimeer's place, as he originally planned to do. However, after releasing his fury on the Weavers and reevaluating the situation, he discovered a far more delightful method of removing the last and final ivory dragon from the Land.

Taj stared up at the castle and smiled broadly. How more perfectly could things be going his way? Not any better than they were now, he was certain. He looked down at the formal invitation in his hand, signed and sealed personally by the Kazimeer. No one had ever refused such an invitation and Taj wasn't about to be the first. He chuckled quietly to himself and shook his head in wonder. He never expected that it would be this easy.

When he first set his magic in motion, he knew he'd grab that little pale mutant's attention sooner or later. After all, only a complete, blind fool would miss the Land dying around him, and only an even bigger fool would pass up the opportunity to find out why it was not doing so in his town. How convenient that he took over as Presiding Officer of Panasom when he did. The people there adored him and with good reason. The plague had not touched their homes, their fields, and their families. Taj, or as he was better known in Panasom, Blasdon, made certain his people were out of danger from it. He was pleased with himself that it actually took very little of his power to accomplish, but he always made sure to shield himself when he did cast. Abbnar must not find out about him…at least, not yet. Oh, he was certain Abbnar was also becoming interested in the fact that the morphers were dropping like rain, and he may have even suspected that it was him, but he wouldn't have an easy time finding him. Taj covered himself too well this time to be tracked.

Taj glanced over to Dapp, his Second, who Taj found only a short time after he had returned from the Pit. Dapp was a young, failed morpher, who couldn't be bothered to get work doing menial tasks. Though his self-image had been at ground level ever since he was ejected from training, his ambitions were outrageously high. Taj immediately snatched him up. Dapp was strong in his morphing, although most of the so-called Masters didn't bother to spend enough time with him. He wasn't disciplined, but when he did finally learn something it stayed with him forever. And he filled his role as Second perfectly. He seldom disputed Taj's decisions and if he felt he had to, would only do so in private. Taj didn't mind having someone looking over his shoulder; it kept him from making stupid mistakes. Dapp would point out the mistakes quickly and respectfully, and had actually given Taj some decent ideas. The best part about him was he was an obedient assassin. On more than one occasion, Taj used him to make sure his fighters remained loyal or to remove some unwanted person. Dapp could be quite intimidating, effective, and clean, never leaving any tracks to follow.

Taj placed the invitation in his Second's hand. Dapp looked down at the letter and nodded once. He strolled up to the front doors of the castle, being immediately intercepted by two well-armed Defenders each with a large hound by their side. Taj waited on the steps below with most of his army and nearly the entire village of Panasom at his back. He wanted a large crowd when he made this call, and only his people would give him the reaction he wanted. There was much going on that these two Defenders could not see. One, his army was casually surrounding the castle and would move in the instant he gave the word. Second, he'd sent certain trustworthy people into Sevatzer who were at this moment spreading the word of the important message that would be announced at the castle this afternoon.

Taj watched as one of the Defenders called for a servant who instantly responded. The woman was handed the invitation and sent scurrying back into the castle. Taj knew what would happen over the next few moments. There would be frantic scampering in all directions by everyone, including the Kazimeer. He'd caught the Kazimeer off guard, which was exactly what he wanted. There was no way for the pale thing to know that he was a master of Transfer and could do so with large groups. No sooner had he given his response to the messenger than he packed up his army and people, and Transferred the lot to the castle's doorstep. Taj had shown up about three weeks prematurely. By the time the messenger arrived back with Taj's gracious acceptance of the Kazimeer's invitation, the Kazimeer would be long dead.

After a moment of awkward waiting, the servant returned, whispered something to the Defender, and then ducked back into the castle. The Defender spoke to Dapp, looked over the large crowd standing behind Taj, and then added one more sentence. Dapp nodded and returned to Taj, obviously fighting a smile.

"The Kazimeer was not expecting you to arrive so soon. However, he will receive you now."

"How kind of him," Taj said flatly under his breath.

"Also," Dapp added, "it is requested that you not bring in your entire party." He referred to the bulk of the army and towns people. "Only selected members."

"Then select them," Taj ordered.

Dapp pointed to four of the burliest of Taj's sentinels and snapped his fingers. Two immediately moved in front of Taj, two stayed behind, and Dapp led the way. The small entourage ascended the flight of stairs and were admitted into the castle.

Taj paused when he entered, not out of awe as the two Defenders may have thought, but out of nostalgia. It had been a long time since he'd walked through these front doors. The place had certainly changed and most of it was unrecognizable to him. No doubt the ivory dragon that sent him to the Pit redid most of it, but there were still a few things that remained the same and tickled his memory. He walked down the long, marble hallways looking all about him, already making mental notes of what changes would be needed to suit his tastes.

He and his party were led to a small receiving chamber. Taj's first reaction was that it was cozy; his second was nausea. Two overstuffed, off-white chairs were placed directly in the center of the chamber, separated by a round, polished, wooden table and elaborate dragon statues marked each corner. There were no windows, only two doorways, the one that Taj entered and the other on the opposite side. Standing directly before it, with a smile stamped on his face was the Kazimeer. Taj was surprised to find the beast dressed in formal state clothes and wondered how quickly the thing jumped into them. Still, Taj had to admit he was impressed with the way the beast appeared relaxed, as if his arrival had not caused a sudden frenzy. To the Kazimeer's right was an older man, his white hair pulled back neatly and steel gray eyes staring intently at him, as if trying to size him up in one glance. From the robe the man wore, Taj knew he was the Kazimeer's Weaver. A quick look around the chamber showed only four Defenders; the Kazimeer's Second was nowhere to be seen.

It was obvious to Taj the moment he locked eyes with the thing that he was waiting for him to kneel. Taj was not about to do any such thing and remained standing straighter than usual, holding those green eyes steadily, until the creature gave a small sigh of compliance. The Kazimeer then offered his hand. Taj remained perfectly still and continued to stare deeply into the thing's eyes. Finally the hand dropped, the annoyance bubbling to the beast's face, which was masked under that stiff smile.

"I must admit," the Kazimeer began in a tight tone, "your sudden arrival was unexpected."

"Yes. I know," Taj answered flatly. "I could not contain my enthusiasm." There was an awkward pause. Taj could tell this thing was uncertain how to treat his remark.

Instead, the Kazimeer shifted the conversation in a different direction and gestured to the older man beside him. "This is Weaver Mazon, appointed High Weaver of the castle."

Taj stared at the man but the Weaver didn't so much as blink at him, let alone nod or speak a word of greetings. Taj smiled a little, admiring the way the man used his own tactics against him. Very well, he could die with the Kazimeer. Since there was no one else for the Kazimeer to introduce, Taj took his cue and gestured to Dapp. "This is my Second, Dapp. These other men are of no importance so I do not know their names, nor will I learn them. Their duty is my protection. Surely you understand."

The creature seemed taken aback by his bluntness but nodded. "Of course."

Taj deliberately made a show of looking around the chamber. "And where is *your* Second?"

"Since your arrival was not announced in advance, he's been detained with important matters that cannot wait. He will arrive shortly."

"Battles are not announced in advance," Taj said. "Are you so unprepared for them?"

Those green eyes widened slightly but that smile never wavered. "Are you comparing a peaceful tryst to a battle?"

The corner of Taj's mouth curled up faintly. "You've never been in a battle, have you?" Before the mutant could answer, Taj continued. "Because if you had, you'd know that every battle begins with a tryst, very much like this one. You want what I have. I may not want to give it to you."

The Kazimeer's face darkened. "I seek your insight and your advice for the benefit of the Land. However, if you wish not to discuss such matters with me openly, then you are free to leave. I'm sorry you wasted so much of my time." He turned on his heels to depart.

Taj could feel his anger boiling but kept it under control and decided to approach this challenge calmly. Besides, not only was there another Weaver in the chamber, which he could handle without problem, but he couldn't shake the thought that this creature's ancestor had a hand in sending him to the Pit. If this thing figured out how to do the same…Taj had no intention of returning there. He had to bide his time and be sure to catch the beast completely unaware before it had a chance to morph. He called out respectively, "I was merely making a comparison. I did not mean to offend you."

Landon turned around, his pale face resembling carved, white marble. "It appears that being Presiding Officer of Panasom has gone to your head."

Taj grit his teeth into a smile. He'd skin this mutant alive, but for now patience. "Perhaps it has."

"Are we ready to discuss matters of the Land now?"

"Of course."

The Weaver cleared his throat respectively. "My lord, if I may suggest that I fetch Second Brazet. I know he would like to be present."

"Yes, do that." Landon nodded to him and then spoke to Taj, "While we are waiting, would you care for some wine?"

"Always," Taj answered, but his eyes watched the Weaver as he left the chamber. Something about that old man disturbed him but he couldn't figure out what. He let a part of his mind work on the problem, while he kept most of his attention focused on the creature, who sat down lazily. Taj preferred to remain standing, sitting had a way of dulling ones senses, and kept silent while awaiting the arrival of the wine.

**   **

Mazon kept up his calm facade until he shut the door behind him. Then he made a mad dash down the hall in search of Brazet. He nearly collided into the Second as the large man rounded the corner, buttoning up his uniform with one

Taj   23

hand while he tucked his tunic into his trousers with his other. Mazon grabbed him by his shoulders, forcing him to stop.

"What!" Brazet cried softly. "Landon is waiting for me to show up in this chicken costume."

"Don't go in there," Mazon warned.

"Why?" Brazet's dark eyes twinkled. "Trouble?"

"Yes, trouble." Mazon nodded eagerly. He searched for words to describe to the Second just who that man was, without Brazet thinking he was mad. He finally blurted out softly, "Taj is in there."

"Taj," Brazet said doubtfully and then smiled. "Have you all gotten to drinking without me?"

"I'm serious." Mazon held the Second's eyes until the placating grin fell from his face. "We have to move quickly."

Brazet took a step away, studying the Weaver carefully. "Why do you claim he is that demon?"

"Because when he walked into the chamber, I felt his power. It was overwhelming."

"We all know he's a Weaver."

"No, no!" Mazon snapped. "He's more than a Weaver. No one who's just a Weaver has that much power. And those eyes. Those pitch black eyes." He shuddered and met Brazet's stare levelly. "I only know of one other person with such eyes and he's no one to tangle with. Trust me, the man I just met is Taj."

"Taj was killed," Brazet began.

Mazon shook his head vigorously. "Taj was never killed. He was imprisoned."

"But the history record says---"

"Never mind the history. I'm telling you, Taj was never destroyed." Mazon growled impatiently at Brazet's unbelieving expression. "Would you tell a group of frightened people that their greatest nemesis was only imprisoned or would you tell them that he's gone forever?"

Brazet's eyes narrowed and he leaned closer. "If Taj is in this castle, why did you leave Landon alone with him?"

"Because Landon will be safe for the few moments it takes me to tell you to get your Defenders into position for an attack. I don't think Taj will kill him just yet. From what I've heard, Taj likes to play with his victims first."

"How have you heard?"

"Never mind that," Mazon stressed. "Just position the Defenders. Have them be ready for any type of assault and have them stay close to Landon."

"I don't believe you would leave Landon alone with such a demon."

"Do you think I'm making this up!" Mazon hissed. "It's either leave Landon alone for a few moments and prepare the castle, or stay with him and have no defense ready. The longer it takes for you to listen to me, the more danger Landon is in. Taj must want him alive or he would've attacked the instant he walked in." The Second's expression was still unconvinced.

"Look, old Weaver," Brazet said affectionately. "I think your mind is playing tricks with you." Mazon's expression hardened and Brazet quickly

24   Hosting the Kazimeer

continued softly. "Listen to what you're saying. Do you know how unlikely it is that Taj would be alive today? And even if he were, the man would be almost a thousand years old. I think he'd be pretty harmless."

"You don't understand," Mazon growled.

"I understand that you're worried about Landon and the problems with the Land. I think you're letting your imagination get the better of you." Brazet spread his hands and continued, "Let's just go to this announcement, hear what Landon has to say, and you'll see there is nothing for you to be so worried about." He began to walk around Mazon when the Weaver's hand clamped firmly onto his arm.

"What announcement?"

"The announcement Landon's going to make."

"He's not going to make any announcement."

"It's all over town," Brazet said. "Everyone's gathering outside of the castle for it."

"Brazet," Mazon said slowly, "Landon's not going to say anything. This was going to be a private meeting, you knew that."

"I thought he changed his mind. Then who sent the word about it?"

"Get your people in place," Mazon said urgently. "Have them guard every entrance, every window, and have several Defenders stay close to Landon."

"I'm not going to send the entire castle into a panic just because you don't know about some---"

"Damn it, Brazet! Just trust me on this!"

The Second stared hard at the Weaver and finally nodded reluctantly. "All right, all right, I'll do it. I think you're overreacting, but I'll get the Defenders in place."

"Thank you," Mazon snapped and watched Brazet stalk down the hall, unbuttoning the top of his uniform as he went. Mazon headed back to the chamber and paused outside the door. He wiped his suddenly sweaty palms down the sides of his robe and hoped he could keep up his calm outer appearance long enough to get Landon out of there. Taking a cleansing breath, he opened the door and nearly tripped over his feet when he entered. He could only stand frozen with shock.

** **

Landon rang the bell for the serving maid the instant Mazon left and sank down into the large, plush chair. He offered the man a seat with a gesture of his hand, but the man remained standing stiffer than ever. Landon fought the urge to growl irritably and forced himself to relax. Despite the fact that he didn't care for this man at all, he had to remain pleasant until the Land was discussed. Then he'd be more than happy to show this man and his people out of his home. Who did he think he was, trying to intimidate him? Which reminded him, he never even asked what this person's name was.

The serving maid entered with a bottle of wine and two goblets. She set the tray down and began pouring, while Landon stared at the Presiding Officer. Those black eyes drilled into him but he didn't let it affect his light tone.

"So, what do they call you?"

Taj 25

Without batting an eye, he responded evenly, "Taj."

The serving maid gasped, nearly dropping the bottle and clanging the end of it against one of the goblets. She recovered quickly and filled the goblets with shaky hands, while one eye remained on the Presiding Officer.

Landon's eyes widened slightly but he kept his pleasant, small smile. "That's an interesting name. I didn't think anyone was called that anymore. I mean, one can't help but associate it with the Dark Master."

"Yes, I know." Taj smiled tightly. "Tell me, how many babes are born each year with the name Abbnar?"

Landon shook his head, confused by such a question. "I'm not sure. A dozen or so, I suppose."

"That's what I thought." Taj nodded and stared up at the ceiling. He muttered under his breath, "My name is cursed, while his is praised." He hissed out a breath between clenched teeth and stared back at Landon.

Landon quickly changed the topic, not liking the hard face staring down at him. He noticed the necklace the man wore and gestured to it. "That's quite a stunning piece." It actually was. The necklace had a large black stone nestled in the center of an elaborate silver setting. There appeared to be writing engraved in the silver, but Landon couldn't make it out from where he sat. He held out his hand. "May I see it?"

"No," Taj said abruptly. When Landon's eyes grew wide with shock, he continued casually, "It's such a delicate, valuable piece, I'm afraid you'd damage it." Before the beast could express his outrage, Taj took a goblet of wine being held out to him by the serving maid and raised it to Landon, who stood and accepted his own goblet, awaiting the toast. "To silly superstitions."

"To the recovery of the Land," Landon offered instead.

"Ah! That's a better one." Taj took a mouthful of wine, swished it around in his mouth, then spat it out onto the floor with a series of gagging sounds. He caught the thing's wide eyes staring at him in outrage and gestured apologetically. "It tastes like…um…like…swill."

Landon firmly put his goblet down on the table and glared at him. "I see you're a difficult man to deal with."

Taj grinned. "You have no idea." He placed his goblet on the table as well. "Let's get this over with then."

"Yes, lets."

"You know, you could make this easy on yourself and just leave. Steal away into the night, no one would have to know where you went."

"Are you referring to *me* leaving?"

Taj pretended to consider the question. "Yes, I think that's what I was saying."

Landon chuckled, "I believe you are under some delusion. For you see, it is you who will be leaving." He snapped his fingers and the four Defenders moved in around Taj, while the serving maid carefully began to back out of the chamber.

"Upupupup!" Taj said quickly, raising his hands. "I'd call them off if I were you."

Hosting the Kazimeer

"Don't you *dare* threaten me!" Landon roared.

Taj blinked hard and smiled. He was surprised to find such a spark in the beast. It wouldn't keep him alive, but it would make Taj feel like he had a challenge ahead of him.

Landon took a step closer to Taj, the Defenders waiting on his command. He pointed a finger at him. "Be thankful I don't imprison you right here. And don't think you can walk into my home, insult and disgust me, and believe you'll walk out of here in one piece. You may carry the Dark Master's name, but you are not him."

Taj cocked his head to one side. "Really?" He flung out his hands to either side of him, sending five balls of condensed air, each enclosing around the Defenders and the serving maid. The air immediately engulfed them completely and kept them in a field of silence. Taj twitched his wrists and the five bodies went flying backward, each smacking hard against the stone walls and cracking their heads open like melons. Taj watched in amusement and smiled broadly as the creature stared in horror at each of the five dead bodies bleeding all over the floor. "You were saying?"

Landon whipped his head around and found himself moving away from the man. He was unable to take his eyes off of him, while his mind whirled with a hundred different thoughts at once. What if what he was saying was true? But that was impossible. The real Taj had been killed centuries ago by the first ivory dragon. That was why all Kazimeer's were ivory dragons. Since the first one did so well at keeping the Land safe, the people thought all ivory dragons could do so. Taj was long dead. This man was just a dangerous Weaver, nothing more. And certainly not Taj.

The Second snapped his fingers crisply and two of the Presiding Officer's men immediately advanced on Landon. He barely had time to register that they were moving before he was being held tightly in their grasp, one on either side of him.

Taj stepped closer and wagged a finger in his face. "Now, don't say I didn't give you a chance to leave on your own, thing."

"You're insane," Landon hissed.

Taj raised his brow. "Perhaps you're right." He jerked his head toward the door and the two large men pushed Landon out of the chamber.

Landon was shoved down hall after hall and wondered where his Defenders were. They suddenly were nowhere to be seen or heard, and what happened to Mazon and Brazet? Surely they would notice something was wrong when they discovered him missing. All his thoughts jumbled around in his head as he was pushed harder with each step. He didn't quite realize where he was being taken until he was given a final shove out onto the balcony overlooking the front of the castle.

Landon still found he couldn't move, but not because anyone was holding onto him. Below the balcony were hundreds upon hundreds of people waiting. Some of the faces Landon recognized as belonging to the people of Sevatzer, most he didn't know at all. It was those faces that cheered as soon as the man and he were visible. Only they weren't cheering his name, they cheered for one called

Blasdon. It took Landon a moment to make the connection. So this man called himself Taj to his face, but not to the people. Which meant that he obviously knew how unkindly the people would take to him if he announced that he bore the same name as the Dark Master. Landon had to find a way to let these people see the truth.

The Presiding Officer was obviously enjoying the cheers of his false name. After he let the crowd go on for a few moments, he raised his hands and brought silence to them. "My dear people!" he boomed. "I've brought before you the one responsible for the plague that destroys our beautiful Land. The one who calls forth the corrupt morphers to carry out his twisted bidding. The one who murdered his own flesh and blood to name himself Kazimeer. I bring to you the greatest traitor this Land has ever seen!" With that the crowd roared with praise for the Presiding Officer and curses for the Kazimeer.

Landon stared dumbfounded at the man accusing him of such lies and felt his whole body go numb. He wasn't completely sure how to react. If he ranted that this was all a bunch of lies, he'd be seen as desperate to cover up his actions. If he did nothing, it would be as if he were willingly admitting his guilt. He had to respond but carefully. It was clear he underestimated this man and had to keep his wits about him if he was to win the people back. For the moment, though, he let the man go on, hoping to find some slip in his words to use against him.

"I bring him before you for justice. It will not be me who decides his fate; it will be you. His deeds of corruption are clear; his foulness that spreads across the Land and touches your families must be stopped. Be firm but be fair. For the sake of the Land, be fair!"

The crowd roared again and Landon waited them out patiently. Just as their voices began to die down, but before this man could open his mouth, he began clapping slowly and loudly until he caught the man's attention.

"What a delightful speech," Landon said smoothly but made sure his voice carried. "How odd that you speak of fairness and yet condemn an innocent man."

Taj rounded on him. "You dare speak of innocence when the evidence is obviously against you."

"What evidence?" Landon asked. The people below fell silent and seemed to be waiting on the Presiding Officer to retaliate. "If there is proof linking me to such horrific deeds, I would be interested in seeing it."

Landon wasn't sure if he caught this man off guard or not. His face was unreadable and those black eyes continued to bore holes into his skull. "Such acts as you claim to have no knowledge of began occurring precisely the same moment when you named yourself Kazimeer." The crowd eagerly responded to the accusation.

Landon waited until they died down again. "As I understand it, you were named Presiding Officer around the same time I was named Kazimeer. Much the same could be said about you. Perhaps an investigation of your actions will be conducted." He leaned forward and met the man's stare levelly. "Notice how I said investigation. I will not condemn any person before I have unquestionable proof." He faced the people. "Do not be swayed by such easy answers. I understand the Land is facing a crisis but do not look for a target to attach all the blame to. It is merely coincidence that I became Kazimeer around the moment the Land faced such difficulties. The same could be said about any of you, though, couldn't it? How many of you found a new job, lost an old job, had a baby, moved to a new area, or a dozen other daily activities I could name at the time the Land began to suffer? Suddenly we're all guilty. Before blame is pinned on anyone and before justice is carried out, perhaps a reexamination of all our lives needs to take place."

No one so much as coughed once Landon was finished. He hoped desperately that this snapped these people out of their hate-filled daze and made them see sensibly again.

"Of course a morpher would say such things."

Taj's booming voice drew Landon's eyes toward him. He managed to keep his face neutral and his voice steady. "I do not say these things because of what I am. I say these things only because they are true."

"The truth claimed by a morpher can always be twisted," Taj stated. "I have seen what morphers can do." He spun around to speak to the crowd. "They can destroy you with a touch. They will suck the life from you to feed their own twisted power." He pointed a finger at Landon. "Why does he not touch you? Because he knows his wicked magic will come forward and show you the truth!" The crowd roared in agreement.

Landon began to feel nervous; he was losing them again. Where were his Defenders, Brazet, and Mazon? Were they even aware of what was happening? They must be, with all of this commotion, but then why weren't they coming to his aide...unless. Landon's eyes darted in all directions below the castle. Where were his regular Defenders that guarded the entrance? Landon's eyes slowly shifted toward the man standing next to him, who seemed pleased by his sudden apprehension. What did he do to his Defenders? Landon's anger stirred. He was not about to lose the Land to this madman and couldn't let the people believe him. He raised his voice to be heard over the shouts of the crowd.

"Good people! I will prove that what he says is a lie!" The crowd grew quiet and watched him carefully. He reached out suddenly and seized the Presiding Officer's wrist tightly. He held it up for all to see before Taj pulled away. Landon smiled smugly at him. "It seems no ill effects have befallen you."

"That is because I am warded against such attacks," Taj responded coolly and addressed the crowd. "Who among you is so trusting that you're willing to touch this befouled morpher?"

Silence answered and Landon felt his heart sink. The people were actually going to believe such nonsense. Even if he was to get out of this mess with his head still intact, how would he ever convince these people that what this man spoke of was lunacy?

"Me!"

It was a strong voice that broke through the silence. All eyes zeroed in on the young man who spoke. He stood way at the back of the crowd by himself and he stared defiantly back at anyone who looked in his direction. Landon could hardly make him out due to the distance but had the feeling that he was in more danger of catching fleas from this youngster than the boy was from touching him. Still, he was grateful and felt a bit of his uneasiness dissipate. Taj, however, seemed reluctant. His black eyes narrowed as he stared at the boy for a long moment.

Before he could object, Landon shouted, "Yes! Let him through!" Now if this man objected it would seem suspicious.

The boy began to make his way through the crowd when Landon heard the grunts come from behind. He spun around in time to see the four large men fall to the ground with three of his Defenders standing over their breathing, yet unconscious bodies. Landon felt relief but also panic. If the people saw his Defenders attacking this madman's people it would surely be used against him. Still, Landon was delighted to see the three faces coming through the doorway; Alpro, Olin, and Steph, three of his best Defenders, no doubt hand picked by Brazet himself.

Taj backed away and Landon didn't give him a chance to say or do anything. He immediately moved toward Alpro, who had already come along side of him, taking hold of his arm to lead him away, while the other two began to corner Taj. Landon took no more than two steps when he was stricken immobile, and watched in stunned silence as Alpro's skin began to fall off in clumps, with the muscle and fat still clinging as it peeled away from his body. His eyes melted down his face, his hair dropped to the floor, his lips curled back away from his teeth until the soft flesh also fell away. Within seconds the person Landon had known as Alpro was gone and standing in his place, in his uniform, with a hand still attached to Landon's arm, was a skeleton. And it was alive.

Landon was surprised that he watched the entire transformation and didn't scream once. He noticed briefly that the other two Defenders had also undergone the same transformation as Alpro and were no longer cornering Taj, but him. He also heard Taj's voice ring out clearly to the crowd,

"You see for yourselves! With his destructive nature exposed, his power is lost! He can no longer hide his evil behind pretty spells. Look! See how his own creations turn against him! Behold that which you call Kazimeer! Do you want such a creature to be in control of your lives?"

The crowd became more rowdy with each word Taj spoke until they could no longer be controlled. Some even began climbing the outer wall of the castle in a frenzy to reach him. Landon registered all that was happening around him but only had eyes for the skeleton Alpro as it lunged its sword into his gut.

Landon's first thoughts were, what was happening and why wasn't there any pain from the sword's penetration? Then he heard a scream, realizing a second later that it was his own combined with someone else's. The skeleton Alpro, along with the other skeleton Defenders exploded on the spot. The sounds from the crazed mob pounded in his ears and he discovered that the skeleton had been the only thing holding him up when he began to collapse. But someone caught him before he hit the floor.

Suddenly he felt the pain. It felt like his blood had turned into fire and shot through his body, causing him to shake, but his eyes focused long enough to see Mazon hovering over him. Landon shifted his gaze in time to see Mazon throw his hand out and a blast of orange air streaked directly for and collided with Taj, forcing him to stumble backward. Then he felt himself being lifted off the ground and screamed aloud as the pain tore through his body again. He desperately wanted to cough but simply trying to get enough air into his lungs made his whole body spasm. He managed to snatch a final glance at the Presiding Officer, Blasdon…Taj and found those black eyes staring directly at him. Landon looked away from those eyes and ended up staring at the unusual necklace the man wore. What caught his attention was that the black stone now was glowing white. A brilliant white light erupted from the stone and came straight toward him. It seemed to be aimed directly for his face and instinctively, Landon threw his hands up, though the movement made his wound scream.

Everything spun before Landon's eyes and then faded into darkness.

JARON

Mazon winced silently as Brazet kicked the stone wall with everything he had, then punched it repeatedly in a furious rage. The Weaver was surprised that the Second didn't shatter his hand. When he was through, Brazet didn't even shake out his fist in pain but the knuckles were bleeding. He faced Mazon and gave him a dangerous stare.

"Don't say it!"

Mazon kept his tone even. "I wasn't."

"Yes you were!" Brazet growled. "It was on the tip of your tongue. This is my fault!"

"It's not your fault."

"Burn me, it's not!" Brazet roared and punched the wall again.

Mazon flinched from the sudden outburst. "Are you quite through?"

"I'm just getting started," Brazet snarled. "I'm pissed!"

"You have a right to be. So am I, but direct your anger toward Taj, not the wall."

Brazet laughed without mirth, ran his hands through his sweaty hair, and looked up at the ceiling. "Taj," he sniffed. "Why didn't I listen to you?"

"It wasn't an easy thing to believe."

"But I should've. I should've known you and your poxed-up power were right." Mazon's eyes widened at the Second's remark but he said nothing. "But I thought you were old and fearful and…" He trailed off and stared beyond the Weaver, his eyes beginning to mist. "He's dead, isn't he?"

Mazon didn't need to turn around to know who Brazet was staring at. Landon's body was lying still and bloody behind him on a blanket of fur, forced to breathe and function by his magic alone. It was Landon's body, but it was not Landon. Mazon managed to keep himself calm. "No, not yet."

Brazet snapped his gaze back to him. "Not yet?!"

Mazon quickly changed the subject. "We have a lot to do."

"Agreed." Brazet nodded eagerly. "First, we take back the castle."

"We can't."

"What do you mean we can't? If we catch him off guard---"

"You can't catch him off guard!" Mazon barked. "He's Taj!"

Brazet blinked at him in disbelief. "I left a lot of good men behind."

"They're gone."

"You don't know that."

"I know that and so do you." Mazon leaned close to him and dropped his voice. "Do you want to lose the rest of them? They're all we have left and we must use them wisely. We can't afford to lose a single person."

Brazet threw his hands in the air. "Then what do we do? Stay in hiding?"

"We move slowly and yes, stay hidden until we're ready."

"I'm not a coward and neither are my Defenders," Brazet sneered. "I refuse to sit trembling in the shadows."

"Brazet," the Weaver began steadily, "remember, you are the Kazimeer's Second. It's your responsibility now to make sure the Land remains safe. You can't go charging into battles without thinking things through first. If you get yourself killed, who will be in charge? The Counts?"

"What about you?"

"I'm just an advisor. I have no real authority. Landon named *you* his Second."

Brazet grumbled under his breath, "I don't know why that boy chose to do that. I'm a Captain, for Light's sake! I'm no...Second." He spat the title out as if it tasted sour. "He wasn't thinking straight, I know he wasn't."

"He trusts you," Mazon said gently. "Don't let him down."

The Second swore a steady stream of curses. When he'd gotten it out of his system, he eyed the Weaver. "I still don't like the idea of hiding. Makes me feel like a rat."

"If you strike before we're ready, you'll just be handing the Land over to Taj." Mazon released a slow breath. "You saw what he could do. We're no match for him yet."

Brazet reluctantly nodded. "So what do you suggest?"

"First, we attempt to make contact with Landon."

"That would be a neat trick," Brazet sniffed.

Mazon knew the Second believed Landon was dead but he didn't know about the power the ivory dragons carried. Mazon refused to succumb to such thoughts. If he did, there would be no hope in trying to fight Taj. He continued over Brazet's remark. "Second, we send word out to the people. They must know who is in control of the Land now. If we can convince them that he really is Taj, we may gain their support."

"And third?" Brazet asked when the Weaver stopped.

"And third, let's hope we can keep Taj from finding us," Mazon said grimly. "Or this is all over."

**   **

Landon was floating. He felt as if he were on a breeze going wherever the wind decided to take him. It was nice, relaxing, soothing. He briefly wondered if he was dead and decided that if he was then there was nothing he could do about it, so he might as well enjoy this sensation of complete ease. Still, there was a sense of urgency rippling across his mind as if he had to get somewhere. Where, he didn't know. He couldn't see or hear a thing; he could only feel. Nothing was physically touching him and yet everything was somehow reaching out and grabbing hold of him. He soon discovered it wasn't his body the Land was touching but his mind. Perhaps he was dying and this was how it felt just before you took your last breath. Only he couldn't remember why he should be dying? What had happened? Where was he? But he didn't care enough to pursue that line of thought. He enjoyed the serene sensation pulsing through him and pushed away the urgent feeling that kept disrupting it.

However, that urgent feeling did not leave him; it suddenly and forcefully took on a life of its own. It began searching. Landon couldn't stop it no matter how much he concentrated and now felt like a small child being dragged along by a hurried, anxious adult. Whatever this entity inside of him was looking for, it finally found it and dragged Landon right along. He was no longer floating; he was plummeting. It was as if he were caught in a whirlpool, spiraling into somewhere dark and unknown. When he came crashing down to his destination the impact was severe. He smacked through a solid surface and plunged into a whirlwind of confusion and pain. This new environment pulled at every fiber of his being and tossed him around violently, trying to dislodge him. Landon felt like he was drowning in a deep sea unable to free himself, either on his own or with the painful help of whatever was trying to get rid of him. He was attacked brutally from all angles by some unseen presence that he couldn't fight or fend off. When he was left beaten and helpless, he waited anxiously for the final strike from the inhospitable host of this frightening place, but it paused, studying him for the first time. After a moment it withdrew, leaving Landon alone in a suddenly calm, however empty location.

Dazed and frightened, Landon attempted to stand but found he couldn't. He couldn't even feel his legs. It was then that he began trying to make contact with the rest of his body but with no luck. Perhaps he truly was dead and this was what death meant; alone in an empty place for eternity. He was about to give in to his despair when he became aware of something. He could suddenly hear.

He heard sounds, voices coming to him as if through some hazy dream state. He tried to open his eyes but couldn't, so he continued to listen and concentrate until the voices became clearer. But the more he listened, the more he knew he'd never heard these voices before. He tried to open his eyes again, using all of his strength, until he was able to push forward through a thick fog and, at last, he could see. The view before him was dim for some reason and he couldn't focus completely. Where was he? Suddenly, the memories from the castle came crashing back to him. One of his own Defenders had stabbed him with a sword. No, not his Defender; it was a skeleton that had been transformed from one of his men. He remembered that Presiding Officer with those piercing black eyes staring at him, and Mazon being with him just before the Land faded. But where was Mazon now?

He strained to see and was able to make out the shapes of a row of houses surrounded by trees. He tried to turn his head but it wouldn't respond. After a moment of trying he gave up and continued to stare straight ahead at one house directly in front of him, attempting to find something that might lend him a clue as to where he was. But if he was injured, what was he doing in front of some strange home and outdoors? This didn't look like the castle or anywhere else he'd been to for that matter. He opened his mouth to speak but nothing happened. Becoming more frustrated and angry he started to scream, when someone filled his vision and halted his outburst. A large, bony woman, with deep lines in her face from scowling, as she was doing right now, stepped into view.

She was looking down at him. Why was she taller than he was? Did he shrink? She asked in a sharp tone, "Do you enjoy stealing from honest people?"

It was more of an accusation than a question. But stealing? Him?! He was the Kazimeer; he had no reason to steal. He tried to ask whom this old hag thought she was addressing, when a voice came from him. Only he wasn't the one who spoke.

"Old wench! I's wouldn't steal from ju ifs ju paid me."

The voice sounded young and had a soft undertone even though it was obvious whoever had spoken was angry. But who spoke if it wasn't him? He knew *he* certainly didn't speak with that dialect. It sounded like Granate; the most popular speech of the common people used throughout the southern parts of the Fire and Water providences. It was full of half words and sounds but Landon had studied enough languages and was able to understand it.

Suddenly the ground was in his face and after a moment he realized he had been pushed. He heard the woman snap from behind him, "Get out of here before I have my husband deal with you, you little thief!"

He was on his feet and walking swiftly in seconds. Then he broke into a dead run once out of sight from the house. He didn't want to run, though. He wanted to find out what that woman was talking about and tried to stop but without success. He kept moving rapidly forward, dodging trees and leaping over large stones expertly until he was deep within a forest. Strange, he didn't even feel winded but heard himself breathing hard as though he was.

Landon tried desperately to concentrate and focus, but the Land before him grew dark. Then he realized his eyes were closed only he didn't close them. What was going on?

That's when the young, soft voice grumbled, "Wha' smatter wit me? Old wench mus 'ave knocked me head too 'ard."

Landon frantically tried to move anything. An arm, a leg, a toe, but nothing happened. However, he was still aware of what was going on and did somehow run through the forest. Where was he exactly? The young voice groaned again and suddenly Landon could see.

However insane it sounded to him, and although he couldn't feel his lips, he called out carefully, "*Hello?*"

There was no response, so he called again. The young voice laughed tiredly, "Great! Be's 'earin' voices now."

Panic gripped Landon and he quickly called out, "*Who's there?*"

That laugh came again along with a mumbled, "Come on. Wench dinn't hit me dat 'ard."

"*Who are you?*" Landon demanded.

"A'right!" the young voice shouted. "Who's dare! Where's ju?"

"*I wish I knew!*" Landon shouted back and saw the trees suddenly spin around before him. He wasn't moving his body so how could he turn around? And he couldn't feel his mouth, so how was he talking?

"Come out!" the young voice demanded. "Come out and fight me face to face. Stop usin' dat magic."

"*Magic?*" Landon asked, beginning to suspect what had happened to him.

"Ju mock me?" the voice snapped. "Come out!"

"*Silence!*" Landon shouted, trying to concentrate on his thoughts. Mazon? What did he do to him and why? The horrible realization of his situation was becoming clear fast. "*Listen.*"

"Nuff of dis," the voice spat.

Landon saw the trees pass by him as he began moving again. "*Stop this walking at once and attend to me, you feeble minded fool!*" He managed to grab the attention of the person he was having this odd conversation with and stopped moving. "*Where do you hear me?*" It was an absurd question for him to ask but he had to know if his suspicion was correct.

"She's dinn't hit me dat 'ard," the voice whispered.

"*Where!*" Landon demanded, using the same ice tone he used on the Counts. When there was no response he thought perhaps he was dreaming this whole bizarre situation, but then the voice answered.

"U'm losin' me mind."

"*No!*" Landon hissed. "*I have lost my body!*"

There was another pause, which gave Landon a moment to realize something else. He was sensing emotions from this person he seemed to be attached to. A deep feeling of dread came pouring into him.

The young voice spoke just as unsteadily as Landon suddenly felt. "I's 'ave never messed wit ju Weavers. I's stick to me own 'usiness. Why's turchure me?"

"*It is I who is being tortured,*" Landon assured. "*Now, for the last time, tell me where you hear me?*"

"Can't believes U'm answerin' dis," the voice growled. "Fine. I's play dis game of jurs." There was a long moment of silence, but finally the voice answered, "Me mind. Dare! Now will ju go 'way!"

Landon no longer paid attention to the voice. All his attention was focused on one thing; what did Mazon do to him! Why did he trap his consciousness inside of someone else? Was he that badly injured? And *who was this person anyway*?

"Wha' ju mean, who's I's?" the voice asked.

Landon would have started if he had a body to start, stunned that this person could somehow make out his thoughts. He formed words with his essence, discovering that was what he had been doing all along, and tried to keep himself calm and in control. He was the Kazimeer, after all.

"*What are you called?*" No immediate answer came. Light but if this person didn't think things thoroughly through before speaking. Landon was not used to such hesitant responses and grew impatient. "*Well?*"

The answer was not what he expected and certainly not at all used to hearing in such a heated tone. "Eat me bones! Dis isn't funny annimore. Where's ju?"

"*You already know where I am,*" Landon replied steadily. "*My body was badly injured. My Weaver must have placed my consciousness here, inside you, although I never knew he had such power.*"

"Jur Weaver? Who's ju?"

"*I am Kazimeer Landon.*"

The young voice snorted out a laugh, "Yeah, right. I's forgit to tell ju, U'm Jaron, Owner of da Four Seas. How's much a fool ju take me fure!"

Landon felt a small amount of satisfaction. He managed to get this person to tell him his name after all. As if feeling his triumph and not liking it, the voice, Jaron, started moving again.

Landon snapped, *"Would you stop walking when I'm trying to speak! I already take you for a fool!"*

"Well, ju talk likes da Kazimeer but U'm not stupid."

"That remains to be seen."

The person's fury rose instantly and he growled defensively, "Errione knows da Kazimeer was killed two monf ago."

Landon was momentarily stunned. Killed? Was that true? Was this death, being trapped inside some other person? He had already been proclaimed dead for two months? But he was just at the castle!

The young voice was talking again, "But I's tink ju're a Weaver out to 'ave some fun wit a poor unspectin' thief."

"You really are a thief?" Landon asked absently.

"A stupid Weaver at dat," Jaron murmured.

Landon felt himself moving faster through the trees and his anger increased. How dare this peasant, this thief, call him, the Kazimeer, stupid! He commanded the thief to stop but felt a wall pushing him back into darkness. He mentally banged on that wall, which seemed like hours, before he broke through. When he peered through the thief's eyes, it was already dark outside with the exception of a small fire in front of him. He felt exhausted even though he knew he didn't have a body to exhaust. Still, he planted himself firmly in the front of this young thief's thoughts and focused his mind to speak again. If he was to get anything accomplished he had to remain in control of his emotions. It took much effort.

"Look, little thief---"

"I's ain't little!" the thief snapped. "And I's got rid of ju!"

"You cannot get rid of me. I am entangled in your mind. Now, before you start proving what a fool you are again, just answer some simple questions."

"I's don't believes dis."

"Believe it, because I'm certainly having trouble grasping onto this whole situation myself!" How did this person make him loose his temper so quickly? He regained his control again. *"Where are we?"*

"Ifs I's answer jur questions, will ju jus leave me alone?"

"I would be happy to do just that."

"Fine. *I's* is in da Wind providence, on me ways to Aman."

"No! You must go back..." But back where? To the castle? He couldn't return there even if he was in his own body, not alone anyway. Then where else could he go? He quickly sorted out his priorities. *"...to the Morphers Training Halls."*

"Wha'?"

"You must go to the Morphers Training Halls in Nela."

"I's is goin' to Aman," Jaron replied casually, shrugging off Landon's command.

Landon was furious that this thief would disobey him and so directly. That was treason. Even the Counts, however much they disliked him, would obey his orders. *"You will go to the Morphers Training Halls in Nela or else you and I will be together for a long while."*

"Ju is a knock in da head given to me by's dat old crow."

"I am the Kazimeer!" Landon shouted. *"You are one of my subjects and will do as I say."*

"Da Kazimeer is dead and ifs he's was still alive I's is not da Kazimeer's subject." The statement infuriated Landon even more.

"The Kazimeer is not dead, thief. And when I am free from your petty mind, I will haul you before me in the High Room and show you how much of my subject you are."

"I's lost ju once today, I's do its 'gain. Makes dis easy on bof of us and leave me alone."

"You may block me out but you cannot run from me. Remember that thief. If you do not do as I command you will never lose me."

"Sleep wit da snakes," Jaron cursed, sliding down onto the ground.

The fire winked out of Landon's vision and he suddenly felt foggy. He did not sleep, although he was certain the thief did, and lingered in a hazy state until the thief awoke. Once Jaron was moving again, Landon continued to harass him throughout the day, well into the night, and into the following day.

"The Morphers Training Halls are just in Nela. That couldn't be more than four, maybe five days from here." He hated to appeal like this, but if he was to get out of this mess, he'd have to compromise his principles a little. The thief didn't respond to him. *"The Masters will know what to do. They will be able to release me from this cobweb infested hole you call a mind and then you will be free to do as you like."* Landon left out the part where he arrested this person for confessing that he was a thief and a traitor.

The thief finally spoke. "I's 'ave plans fure ju."

"I truly hope the Training Halls are in those plans, thief."

"Not zactly. Wha' I's had in me mind was more likes Banishin'."

"What do you have in mind? There is nothing in here!" Perhaps it was this odd and frightening situation or perhaps it was because this person flat out disobeyed him, but whatever it was, this thief could make his anger boil faster than any other person Landon had encountered. That included Seg, who used to be able to set him off with a sneer, but Seg was dead and he was trapped inside this thief. He needed to get out of this boy's mind or else how could he begin to gain control of the Land again. *"If you Banish me you will most likely Banish yourself."*

"I's don't tink so."

"And can you speak in a complete sentence," Landon growled. Listening to nothing but that Granate accent was pushing him toward madness.

"Wha'?"

"Exactly! 'Wha.' Enunciate!"

The thief was silent and Landon could feel him hesitating. Jaron said defensively, "I's do not!"

"*Right, you don't.*" It took Landon a moment before he figured out what the thief was hesitant over. "*You don't even know what it means, do you?*"

"Corse I's do," Jaron sniffed and continued moving.

"*Then tell me. What does 'enunciate' mean?*"

"I's don't 'ave to tell ju."

"*Right. Juze don't 'ave to tell me cause juze don't know wha' it means,*" Landon mimicked harshly. "*Jus tell me weze goin' to da Training Halls...you miserable, incompetent, feeble-minded, little* THIEF!"

"We's goin' to sees a Weaver," Jaron replied calmly, unaffected by Landon's loud outburst.

"*A Weaver would do nothing for you,*" Landon said calmly. He didn't feel so calm, though. The idea of going to a Weaver to perform a Banishing on him was most unsettling. He still wasn't exactly sure how Mazon placed him in this person's mind but if Mazon could put him in, another Weaver could take him out...permanently. "*Only the Masters will know how to undo my Weaver's spell.*"

"Why's a Weaver pick on me anniway? Why's put ju in me head?"

Landon had been wondering the same thing all this time. Mazon must have been desperate to do such a thing. "*I wish I knew. He must have had a reason. Perhaps you were the closest person at the castle.*"

"Wha' castle?"

"*My castle.*"

"I's never at da castle."

"*You weren't?*"

"I's never even 'member wantin' to be's at da castle."

Landon would've shook his head in confusion if he could and muttered to himself, "*This is so confusing.*" For a brief moment, he felt sympathy coming from the thief. Sympathy for him. His anger flared again. He didn't want sympathy; he wanted obedience. "*If you seek out another Weaver to Banish me, it will only foul things up so badly you would probably be stuck in here with me.*" The feeling of sympathy was replaced with exasperation.

"I's a'ready am," Jaron hissed under his breath.

He stopped walking and Landon saw the Land spin upwards as the thief looked into the sky. The sky. He suddenly had a rush of longing to be there again. He loved to fly. He missed it already. Two months? What if Mazon thought he truly was dead? What then?

"Deese Maders of jurs."

"*Ma...ST...ers. Yes?*"

"Dey can git ju out?"

"*Yes.*"

"Wha' ifs dey can't?"

"*They will,*" Landon assured, hoping now the thief was making the correct decision. The sky disappeared and the forest came back into view.

"I's takes ju to deese Ma...ST...ers. Ifs dey can't git ju out, I's Banish ju." He started off again.

Landon said nothing but felt a wave of relief wash over him and settled down. The Masters would know how to undo Mazon's spell. They had to know.

He lost track of time as he found he often did unless he looked through the thief's eyes to see what time of the day it was. He snapped his attention back to his surroundings when the thief stopped, apparently for the night. It wasn't the lack of movement that caught Landon's attention, though. It was what he saw, or rather, what the thief saw.

Jaron was kneeling next to a river, scooping up handfuls of water and drinking. But each time he bent over the water, Landon saw the image reflected back in his mind's eye. He had no immediate words to say as he stared through hazy eyes at the image of the person he lived in now.

He couldn't help himself and moaned, "*Oh by the Light!*"

His thought was so strong it startled Jaron, who had thought the voice in his head had gone silent for good. "Wha'!"

"*I'm inside a boy!*" Landon cried. The thief's voice sounded young but Landon had no idea on how young. He didn't even look old enough to grow whiskers yet. His eyes were soft brown, matching his tangled hair hanging to his shoulders. His face was gentle yet had a hardness to it that reminded him of Mazon. Mazon, curse him! What did he do?

"I's seventeen," Jaron snapped and pulled away from the water.

But Landon knew, as sure as he knew his own name that the boy was lying. It was so clear, almost tangible, what he was trying to hide that Landon easily shifted through his thoughts and found the truth.

"*You're fourteen,*" he stated. The boy was quiet; not even thoughts were coming from him. Keeping none of the sarcasm out of his voice he jeered, "*Oh excuse me. Juze fureteen. Now do you understand me?*"

"How's far is deese cursed Halls of jurs?" Jaron growled softly.

"*Four, maybe five days away.*"

"I's hope I's can find a Weaver 'fore den to Banish ju."

Landon would almost swear he could see the boy's smile and knew that he meant it. Still, he was just that, a boy! How much harm could he do? He growled more to himself than to Jaron, "*Great. I'm trapped inside the feeble mind of a thief boy.*"

Jaron did not answer, although Landon felt the emotion of pure hatred wash over him. Only Landon wasn't sure if it really was coming from the boy or from him, probably both. He had no idea how he was going to survive with this boy until they made to the Halls, but it didn't matter how he got there, so long as they did. The Masters must know how to pull him out of this child and return him to his body. That is, if he has a body to return to.

BETRAYALS & REVELATIONS

Jaron moved through the forest for two days before Landon realized they were not going straight to the Training Halls. He had only traveled there a few times by route of the main road but he could make out enough of the Land to know they were nowhere near the Halls. He demanded that Jaron go there immediately.

"I's need to stop at Aman," Jaron explained.

"*You don't need to stop at Aman,*" Landon insisted. "*You need to get to Nela.*"

"I's need pesses."

"*Pieces,*" Landon corrected as he did often with the boy. "*Then why don't you get a job if you need them so badly?*"

"Yeah, right," Jaron sniffed. "Likes dares lots of jobs out dare jus waitin'."

"*There's plenty of work waiting for someone who actually* wants *to work, instead of stealing off honest people.*"

Landon felt the boy pause and could tell he was thinking. Perhaps he was starting to make some sense to this thief and his pride began to swell.

"Ju's don't 'ave a clue, do ju's?"

Landon's feeling of pride dropped and he would've sneered if he could. "*I believe you have that backwards, boy.*"

"Ju's don't 'ave anni idea wha' really 'appens in da Land. Ju's jus sit on jur ass and believes dat erriting is a'right."

"*I do plenty, boy. Far more than a miserable thief like yourself would ever begin to understand.*"

"I's understand dat ju do nutin'," Jaron sniffed loudly. "Ju ain't even da Kazimeer. Jus some rich Weaver who's got nutin' better to do wit his time den to piss me off." He stopped and ran a hand down his face in annoyance. "Ifs I's don't 'ave pesses, we's not goin' anniwhere, cause I's starve fure we's do. I's doin' wha' I's 'ave to do first and burn ju ifs ju don't likes its."

Landon reined in on his anger and resisted the urge to argue further. He remained silent, shielding his thoughts from the thief as best he could. That had been another fun discovery for both of them when they found out they could pick up on the other's thoughts easily if they were strong enough.

"And don't give me dat att-IT-tude. We's git dare soon nuff."

Thoughts Landon could hide; his feelings were a different story. He withdrew into the boy's mind so he wouldn't have to talk to him anymore and only came forward to check on their progress.

When they arrived in Aman, Jaron moved through the overcrowded streets briskly not stopping for any beggars or peddlers. He kept his small pack tucked under his tunic, being a thief himself and knowing how easy it was to lift such a pack from people, and headed straight for the side streets.

Landon observed all he could through the thief boy's eyes utterly amazed at the condition of the town. He was glad he couldn't smell because he had the feeling it would make him sick. Did Nat ever know about the condition this place

41

was in, and if so, why did he let it remain this way? Making a note to clean up this awful sore on his beautiful Land once back in his body, he fixed his attention on where they were headed.

The loud sounds of the streets fell behind as Jaron moved silently and easily through the side alleys. Landon asked several times where they were going but the boy refused to answer, always moving around one corner or the next until they were standing at the mouth of a long, thin alley. Jaron took a quick breath of reassurance and began to stroll down the alley, glancing around at the broken walls and filth with indifference.

When he traveled half way down the alley, four large bald men holding spears leapt down from the walls and landed directly in front of him. Landon was startled but Jaron rolled his eyes, placed his hands on his waist, and watched them with amusement.

After a short moment, the four men smiled at him and one came forward, speaking with a thick eastern accent. "Ya be taking ya time in coming."

"Problems," Jaron answered flatly. Landon was surprised how controlled and sure the boy's voice sounded because he felt his fear clearly. "Da Mistress?"

"She have be waiting return of ya," the bald man said, gesturing with his spear for Jaron to move forward. He did and was suddenly surrounded by the four men as an escort.

They continued walking down the alley and Landon caught a glimpse of the large structure that came into view. He remained quiet and watched all he could through the thief's eyes, hoping that the boy knew what he was doing.

They stopped at the door and the same bald man said, "On ya go. Mistress be waiting."

Without looking at him, Jaron moved sure-footed into the structure and jogged up the five flights of stairs nodding to each of the armed men placed on every landing. He reached the top not even out of breath, stalked down the long, dim hallway, and came to a closed, guarded door at the end.

A sensual voice behind the door told the armed men to let him in. He strolled into a candle lit room and spotted the Mistress sitting on a pile of pillows in the corner. She seemed to rise without effort and glided over to him with a smile that could melt ice. Landon realized that if he had eyes they would be bulging right now and felt the thief boy's sudden embarrassment.

Losing his normally cool composure, Landon exclaimed, "*By the Light! Hello!*" Kazimeer or not, he was still a young man.

The thief boy's embarrassment deepened and Landon was almost certain he was flushing. The Mistress stood an arm length away from him revealing that she was most certainly revealing. She was dressed, if one could call her that, in different colored pieces of silk wrapped conveniently over certain areas. The rest of her flawless skin was half covered by gold and jeweled covered bracelets and necklaces, exposing the rest for the eye to admire.

Tossing her long, silky, black hair over one shoulder her smile deepened. "Jaron, darling, what do you have for me?" she asked like a child asking for sweets.

Jaron reached under his tunic, pulled out his sack, and emptied the sparkling contents onto one of her pillows. The Mistress mused over the small pile of jewelry and single gems, then bent down and ran her small hand over them.

Landon couldn't help himself again and blurted out, *"Blessed Kyriea! I knew there was reason for me to go through this ultimate torture."*

Jaron sent the sharp message silently. "Shut up!"

Landon closed his thoughts and watched eagerly through the boy's eyes. The Mistress finally stood, nodded in approval, and glided over to a bone box placed on top of one of her pillows. She pulled out a leather pouch and tossed it to Jaron effortlessly, giggling musically when he nearly dropped it. He tested the weight of the pouch in his hand and then glared cynically at her.

"Don't even," he announced and tossed the pouch back.

It landed on the floor before her. She stared from it and then back to him. "Jaron, darling, what is the problem?"

"How's 'bout ju actually pay me or do I's need to take me stuff back?"

They had a brief stare down and then Mistress snapped her fingers crisply. A servant appeared out of nowhere, snatched up the pouch and handed it to her. She opened it and peeked inside. She gasped, her hand flying to her throat.

"Oh my goodness! How did that happen?" She stared back at him. "I can assure you, Jaron, darling that I had nothing to do with this deception."

Jaron smiled thinly. "Corse not."

"I had your payment right in this pouch. I cannot imagine who would put these metal pieces in here like this. There must have been a mix-up."

"I's understand," Jaron continued pleasantly.

She met his gaze sincerely. "You know perfectly well I do not conduct my business affairs in this manner."

"Never," he said, still smiling thinly. "How's 'bout ju jus pay me and we's furegit da whole ting."

"Of course," the Mistress said, flashing him a dazzling smile. She returned to her bone box and then paused. She turned back to him with a look of revelation. "You know, I have the most wonderful idea."

"How's nice fure ju. Its mus be's good to 'ave one once."

She ignored his comment. "I have a job in the Wind Providence that you would be perfect for."

"I's was perfect fure da job I's jus did. How's 'bout ju keep reachin' fure dose coins."

She sighed and pulled out another small pouch and tossed it to him. This time he caught it in one hand and again tested the weight. He continued to glare. "Dis is less den we's talked 'bout."

"Hear me out," she said, gliding over to her pile of pillows and stretching out. "There is a certain piece I want you to retrieve for me in the Wind Providence. A ring; silver with markings around the band, containing a black stone in the center. One little ring and I'll make it worth your while."

Landon's lust was pushed aside for a moment as the memory of the castle came back to him. He once again saw the blonde man standing in his receiving chamber, mocking him with each passing moment. That necklace he wore. It was silver with markings around the edge, and the large black stone in the center. The necklace he wouldn't let him examine and the same black stone that turned white and sent the streak of light at his face. Panic swept over him and he demanded the thief boy to leave.

However, the boy ignored him and asked the Mistress, "How's much me while?"

"*Would you forget about that!*" Landon shouted. "*She's tricking you. Go!*"

"One thousand pieces if I receive it by the end of the month," the Mistress tempted.

"Is dat gold or copper?"

The Mistress's smile deepened. "What do you think?"

Jaron's eyes widened and he sniffed a laugh. "Da end of da month is less den two weeks 'way. Take dat long to reach da Wind providence." He paused skillfully then offered, "Five 'sousand."

"*I don't believe you,*" Landon growled. "*You're haggling! You're actually haggling! Get out of here!*" Jaron's eyes squinted slightly, trying to close out Landon's shouts and concentrated fully on the Mistress, who rose and took a step forward.

"Jaron, darling, you're the best thief I know of," she praised sweetly. "But I do have my limits. Two."

"Five."

"Three."

"Five," Jaron stated firmly, locking his eyes with hers. Landon roared, much the way he did when he was morphed and caused Jaron to wince.

The Mistress saw his brief flash of discomfort, smiled without warmth and stated, "Three. Final."

Jaron moved closer so he was in front of her and smiled. "Not in'rested, den." He bowed respectfully with a sweeping gesture of his hand and turned to leave.

Landon was just happy he was leaving but still tense, and tried to look all around but with no success. He would only see what the thief boy saw. Jaron moved around the guards at the door easily and approached the stairs. However it seemed at that moment all of the armed, bald men from the other levels had grouped together and didn't want him to leave, blocking the stairs with their spears pointed at him.

"Mistress not be finished with ya," one said, trying to force him back down the hall.

"Mistress was very finished wit me," Jaron replied calmly. He attempted to walk around them but was pushed back.

He bounced off something, turned around, and expected to see more bald men. Instead, he found himself staring into two, deep, black holes that once held eyes. The rest of the face was pasty white and a black hood covered the head. Jaron soon realized there were two more behind this one, who took advantage of his distraction by locking its bony fingers tightly around his wrist and began pulling him back toward the Mistresses' chamber.

Jaron cried out and pulled frantically until he broke free from the hold, crashing into the mass of armed men behind him. They all tumbled down one level of stairs together only being stopped by the stone wall. Jaron quickly untangled himself and got to his feet as he pulled his weapon free. Landon caught a quick glimpse of metal and thought it was a sword. Then he noticed it was only a small knife.

"That's what you intend to protect me with!" he demanded. *"One small blade!"*

Jaron forced him silent and tried to run backward down the stairs keeping everyone in front of him. Something dropped onto his shoulders from above, forcing his face to a stair and whacking his chin hard against it. He didn't have to look to know it was one of those eye-less beings and swung madly with his knife. He caught the being across the face but it seemed to have little if no affect and the eye-less creature picked him up by the front of his tunic and tossed him over the railing.

Jaron caught himself from falling by grabbing onto the wooden ledge of the railing. An ear-splitting scream from overhead filled the entire hall and nearly shook his grip loose. It came from one of those eye-less beings from above and seemed to be aimed at the eye-less that was still standing over him. The being tried to grab his wrists to hoist him up but Jaron was not about to be handled by this thing. He glanced down briefly, judging the distance to the ground. Then he swung his head around and saw more armed men racing up the stairs. He made a decision.

Landon realized what the thief was going to do a second before he did it and shouted at him to stop. Jaron closed out his voice, let go of the railing, and fell the rest of the four levels. For a brief instant, Landon felt something familiar then the ground was in his line of vision and he heard the boy grunt with pain. Within seconds, they were racing down the alley with Jaron swinging his small knife at anyone jumping in front of him, dodging spears with skill, and finally making it into the center of town again.

Panting, Jaron blended in immediately with the crowd and tried to be as invisible as possible. Landon saw a chance to do something he wanted to do since he became trapped in this frustrating situation.

"Duck inside a tavern."

"Wha'?" Jaron asked silently.

"Go inside a tavern. Get out of sight."

"Dat'll be's da first place dey look fure me."

"No. The first place they'll look for you is outside of town. If you stay with a crowd, they will be less likely to do anything if they're able to locate you at all." The boy hesitated, despite Landon's logic. Landon forced himself to shield his eagerness or else the boy might just leave to spite him. *"Just trust me on this."*

"Ifs I's go into a tavern, I's 'ave to git someting'."

"And...?"

"And dat cost pesses, dat I's don't 'ave, tanks to ju."

"I'll reimburse you the copper coin," Landon grumbled. *"What happened to that purse of coins you just risked my neck for?"*

"She's dinn't pay me."

"Then what did she do?"

Jaron pulled out the small pouch and pulled free a small, circular object but it wasn't a coin. "Iron pesses." The voice didn't answer but Jaron could almost see an unconvinced expression staring at him in his mind's eye. "I's *can* feel da difference 'tween iron and gold, ju know."

"You should be proud," Landon said dryly. *"Then why didn't you say anything like you did the first time she tried to trick you?"*

"'Cause dat's when I's knew someting was wrong. One time, fine. Twice? Yeah, she's was after someting more."

"Look, just go inside."

"Why's ju want me to?" Jaron asked suspiciously.

"To save my hide." He paused. *"And yours."*

Jaron attempted to look around casually, trying to spot either the Mistress's men or those eye-less things. He didn't want to think too long about what those beings could possibly be, but the brief memory of them made him listen to the voice. But it would only be this one time.

He ducked into the nearest tavern and ignored the voice muttering how he should find a larger one with more people. Jaron didn't know why the voice should care what tavern he went to and decided he wouldn't risk going out into the streets until after dark. Even if those things were still searching for him, he could blend into the shadows easier.

He was about to sit himself down in a corner when the voice urged him to move closer to a group chattering away near the center of the tavern. Jaron instantly acted stubborn and refused to be budged. However the voice wouldn't let up and Jaron knew it wouldn't until he did what it wanted. He was too tired to argue anymore today, so he reluctantly moved to a nearby table but kept his back to the people there. At least it kept the voice silent. Jaron was happy for a moment of quiet.

An older barmaid came over and asked what he wanted. Jaron mentally did a survey of all his possessions. He wasn't being stubborn when he told the voice he'd have to order something. He'd be thrown out otherwise. He knew he had a few, a very precious few, pieces on him and didn't want to waste them on a simple drink. Still, a beer would taste good about now, especially after the past couple of days. He ordered promptly and told himself he'd have just one, then be on his way.

After he painfully handed over a copper piece for the drink, he leaned back in the chair and nursed it, but couldn't help overhear the conversation at the table behind him.

"Dung! Pure dung!" a deep male voice snapped. "All I know is my levy has double ever since Blasdon took charge."

"You're paying for protection," another man said.

"Against what!"

"Morphers."

"Morphers, my ass!" the first man growled. "But I will tell you what has happened. Not only has my levy gone up to pay for protection, but my workers, my morpher workers, have either been killed or just got the Light out of town. So now, my work force is down, so my productivity is down, so now this levy that was supposed to be for protection has taken food out of my children's mouths!"

The heated tone the man used sent warning bells off in Jaron's head. He didn't dare turn around to look. In fact, he wanted to get out of there and started to quickly finish the rest of his beer.

"No. Don't."

Jaron froze mid-gulp. "Don't wha'?"

"Don't leave yet. I want to hear this."

"Why's?"

"Because I need to hear what's going on with the Land and I very well can't rely on you to provide me with that type of information. I bet you don't even know who they're discussing, do you?"

A thought slowly dawned on Jaron. "Dis is why's ju wanted me to come in 'ere. So ju could listen to dis stuff."

"You just figured that out? Yes, thief boy, that's why I wanted you to come in here."

"Den why's dinn't ju jus ask me?" Jaron was getting angry.

"Because I knew you wouldn't. Now hold your tongue, boy."

"No I's won't!" He was really angry now. "Why's!"

"Because you're incognizant and there's no reason why I should have to suffer with your unenlightened ways. Be silent!"

Jaron was so stunned he couldn't react. He felt his face glowing with anger. He didn't know what 'incognizant' meant, but the way the voice said it, it had to be an insult. He wondered why he didn't get up and walk out. Why should he stay, just because the voice wanted him to? He realized that a part of him wanted to listen as well. Perhaps it was the part that the voice now occupied, but he was also curious to hear what these people were talking about.

"…just wonderful." The second man was saying. "Things couldn't be better. I can't remember the last time I could walk down a street in the middle of the night and not fear for my life."

"That's because you're being watched," the first man sneered. "Watched constantly. Oh, don't dare speak against lord Blasdon or you'll find your head handed to you."

"That's a bunch of spiteful nonsense. Lord Blasdon is a kind man. A man of the future. Do you know what he did? He opened a school for the children. A place where they can learn."

"Yes," the first man sniffed. "Learn his way."

"When did the Kazimeer *ever* care about our children and their future? If they didn't learn a trade by apprenticeship or were born into a business, they could forget about a decent life."

"And how much levy do you pay for that school?"

"I'm happy to pay it."

"Happy to pay to have your children's thoughts twisted to his way of thinking? He's not opening their minds, he's stealing them."

"What you two are forgetting is the most important thing." A third voice spoke up, one Jaron hadn't heard yet. "No one person should be in control of our lives. Neither the Kazimeer nor this Blasdon should be telling us what we can and can't do, have and have not. The people should decide it. How can any person living so isolated from everyone have the slightest idea what's best for them?"

"Did you hear what happened to the rest of the Kazimeer's forces?" It was a younger woman that spoke. "I hear they were removed...for good."

"They put up quite a fight," the second man said. "I'm surprised the castle's still standing."

"You know," the woman said in a confidential tone. "I heard lord Blasdon's got'um all under his control now. Or had them killed."

"Child," the second man said wearily, "you really shouldn't listen so much to such street talk. It's all nonsense."

"I think she's poxing right," the first man said.

"Don't use such language in front of a young girl!" the second man warned.

"Or you, I suppose," the first man jeered. "Your virgin ears hurt?"

"Could we knock off the petty insults?" the third man snapped. "Why should we be under the thumb of anyone? I say the Kazimeer's death is a sign. A sign that it's time for the people to rule for themselves."

"That's what lord Blasdon is trying to do," the second man said.

"Why do we need anyone to do that? We know what we need, we know what we can do, let's just do it."

"You're speaking of rebellion, sir," the second man said slowly.

"I'm talking about standing up and taking control of our lives for ourselves."

"You probably all don't remember this." The voice belonged to an older woman. It shook slightly when she spoke. "But when I was a young girl, half the Land suffered from a famine. The ground had been overworked, the crops sold for the highest coin, and after enough of that, the food was all gone. The rich folk sold off what was left to the highest paying customers. Us common folk just couldn't afford to pay." She paused for a breath and not a person uttered a sound.

"But," she continued, "Kazimeer Nada knew what to do. She made those rich folk give up their pieces, made them distribute the food properly. She got down on her hands and knees and worked the ground with us, side by side, until we could grow crops again. I saw her, she did." She stopped again briefly. "We *needed* someone to take charge, someone impartial. We needed someone who understood the Land. The Kazimeer's have always understood the Land like no one else."

After a pause, the second man spoke up. "That's what I'm saying. Lord Blasdon is very much like Kazimeer Nada was."

"Now you're being nasty," the first man spat.

"I'm serious," the second man insisted. "He's already done so much for the people and will continue to do more, so long as folks like you don't stand in the way of improvement."

Hosting the Kazimeer

"What improvement!" the first man yelled. "Last time I looked, my fields were still dying from this damn plague. If the Kazimeer was the cause of the plague, why are my fields no better now that he's dead? In fact, they're worse!"

"It takes time to repair such damage," the second man said.

"Why can't we repair our own damage?" the third man asked. "Why must we rely on someone else to do it for us? Are we sheep?"

"But what if we can't?" the young woman asked timidly.

"If people were given time to work on the problem, we'd be able to fix it. Instead, we're off doing the tasks assigned to us by others, while the Land rots."

"Do not worry, child," the second man said, ignoring the third's opinion. "Lord Blasdon will find a solution. I swear, he was sent by the Kyriea."

The first man snorted. "That's because the Kyriea didn't want him anymore."

The chair scraped across the floor again and was followed by another. "I'm sick of your closed mind!" the second man shouted.

"And I'm sick of your voice," the first man growled. The sound of a punch immediately followed.

Jaron knew better than to stick around when a fight was breaking out. He quickly got up and headed straight for the door. He looked back briefly to see the two men swinging at each other madly, the third man attempting to break them up, while the young girl moved the older woman out of the way. Jaron hurried out into the street again and quickly left town, heading into the forest.

Landon was busy trying to understand all that he had heard. It left his mind feeling numb. It appeared that most people were glad he was dead. Maybe he shouldn't bother trying to find a way out of the thief's head. Why should he? By the time he'd managed to pull back Blasdon's…Taj's…grip off the Land, he'd be in time to witness a Bloodshed amongst his people. Unless that's what Blasdon wanted? Maybe he wanted a Bloodshed across the Land, let the people kill themselves over a matter of opinion, and then when they were exhausted and weak, take control.

Landon's anger boiled. He couldn't let that man take *his* Land. If he was actually doing something good for the people, Landon could almost find it in himself to swallow his pride and let him rule. But he wasn't. He was destroying the Land; the Land his entire family-line had worked so hard to keep safe and at peace. And how *dare* that feeble fool compare *his* mother to that demon! His fury tripled. He could barely contain it. He wanted to scream, to kick something, anything physical to release it, but he couldn't. He suddenly realized that he wasn't the only one who was angry. So was the thief boy.

"*What?*" he snapped. "*Are you still wounded because I didn't tell you why I wanted to go into the tavern?*"

"No," Jaron answered shortly. He stopped his brisk pace through the forest. "I's not wounded by's dat. But dat is one more point fure ju."

"*What do you mean?*"

"I's mean dat ifs ju's da Kazimeer, likes ju say, den it's only natural dat ju lie."

"*The Kazimeer doesn't lie.*"

"Really?" Jaron chuckled and sat down with his back against a tree. "Wha' ju know; a lie to cover up nather lie."

"*The Kazimeer doesn't lie.*"

"Ju jus did its 'gain," Jaron snorted. "Light, I's startin' to believes ju is da Kazimeer."

"*You are still angry about the tavern, aren't you?*"

"No. I's not," Jaron admitted. "I's really not angry at all." He thought something over for a moment. "I's tink it's ju."

"*Me?*"

"Yeah. I's tink it's ju bein' pissed 'bout wha' dose people said. Who's Blasdon anniway?"

"*I knew it,*" Landon grumbled softly. "*You don't even know who's in charge of the Land at the present time.*"

"I's know," Jaron said with a nod. "No one is."

"*No. A twisted Weaver, who had enough power to take over my castle and run the Land into dust is.*"

"But he's not da Kazimeer."

Landon was stunned silent for a moment. What was the boy saying? "*Do you believe me when I say I'm the Kazimeer?*"

"Nope."

Landon had to chuckle. "*So you still think I'm some Weaver out to have fun with you.*"

"Yup."

"*Won't you be surprised?*"

"I's tink ju will be's."

Landon was stunned again. "*What does that mean?*"

"Its means," Jaron said, stifling a yawn. The beer had made him sleepy. "I's tired." He stretched out and put his hands behind his head.

Landon would've shaken his head in confusion if he could. Instead, he directed the topic toward one he needed to address. "*Now are you going to go to the Halls?*"

"Nope," Jaron answered after a long pause. "Not 'till I's know wha' is goin' on."

"*About what?*"

"Likes, wha' dose tings were back at da Mistresses'."

"*I don't know,*" Landon said. He suddenly felt his anger rise again when he remembered what happened. "*Fool boy! Why didn't you leave when I told you to?*"

"Ju's don't know nutin' of survival."

"*Survival! I was the one who said we should go.*"

"Ifs I's dinn't argue da price she would 'ave become doubtin'. One 'sousand indeed. Too little fure so much. I's was hopin' to confuse her long nuff fure me to git out of dare. I's told ju dat I's knew someting was wrong." He stretched and rolled his tired muscles so they wouldn't stiffen. "Not good fure her, though. Ju don't pay people fure jobs word gits 'round. Soon ju don't 'ave annione doin' jobs fure ju, no matter how's good ju looks." He examined his skinned palms for the first time and his other bruises carefully. "But why's did she want me to look fure dat ring? Why's is its impantant? So impantant dat she would deal wit such nasty tings?"

"*Blasdon must want it,*" Landon answered trying to think of why.

"I's seen him," Jaron said, bringing Landon out of his puzzle. "Dat's da twisted Weaver, eh? Ju's 'member him lots. Why's?"

"*He tried to kill me.*"

"Well, I's know why's I's want to do its, but why's did he's?"

"*Because I'm the Kazimeer.*"

"So."

"*So? Boy, do you even know why the Land has a Kazimeer?*"

"To be's a big pain in da ass."

"*I am an ivory dragon morpher,*" Landon stated proudly, ignoring the boy's comment. "*The Kazimeer is there to protect the Land.*"

"And a fine job ju's doin' too," Jaron jeered.

"*Don't mock me, thief boy. It was not my decision to be trapped in your feeble mind. That is why we must hurry to the Training Halls now that you've proven, once again, what a complete fool you are.*"

However, the boy didn't respond the way Landon thought he would from his remark. He didn't seem to be angry or upset, in fact, he seemed... pleased? But what did he have to be pleased about? Not only were they nearly killed by some strange creatures but also he had failed miserably at his task of getting pieces. So why... He suddenly knew. Either the boy was concentrating hard or they were starting to know each other better. As if he heard Landon's thoughts, Jaron reached under his tunic and pulled out the same jewels and stones he had left on the Mistresses' pillow and held them up in front of his face so Landon could see.

"*How did you do that?*"

"Easy."

"*But how? She was right there.*"

"Me hand moves faster dan anni eye can sees," Jaron said proudly. "When I's bowed I's snatched dem up. I's knew she's dinn't pay me as soon as I's felt da bag da second time. Dat's when I's started wonderin' wha' was goin' on. And den when I's told her no to her second offer, I's knew she's wasn't goin' to pay me period. So, I's took back me stuff. I's find someone else who's will pay fure dem." Satisfied, Jaron carefully tucked the jewels into his pouch, then stretched out again.

"*What are you doing?*"

"I's tryin' to sleep."

"*You can't sleep out here. You must keep moving. The longer you take to get to the Halls, the longer I'm stuck in here.*"

"And da longer I's keep 'avin' to listen to jur big mouf," Jaron muttered as he began to doze off.

Landon was about to argue but then decided why bother. The boy was already falling asleep. Instead of fuming over the boy's disobedient attitude, he directed his energy to work on a plan. He had to be ready to move the instant the

Masters figured out how to remove him from the thief's mind so he could remove that parasite from his castle. He wasn't about to give up on the Land. He couldn't.

Hosting the Kazimeer

WEBBEN

Taj strolled through the castle halls, appearing at ease to all who saw him while his mind chattered away with his daily problems. Still, it didn't bother him. Being in control of the Land again gave him energy he never knew he had. He felt great.

He stopped by the kitchen, as he always did each day, where a freshly baked tray of sweet cakes awaited him. The servants bowed when he entered but he ignored them, his eyes wide and delighted as a child's as he looked over the tray, deciding which one to take. He wasn't a person who enjoyed food. In fact, he felt that eating was a chore, but sweet cakes were his one weakness. He chose the biggest one and bit down with relish. He moaned with pleasure and closed his eyes. He was not worried about poisoning since he could counter any poison with a thought. Besides, most of the servants were witness to his take over of the castle and knew what would happen if he caught them doing any such thing. They remained loyal out of fear, which worked fine for him.

He left the kitchen without a word and headed toward the lower level of the castle. When he first saw the dungeon after so many centuries, he'd been disappointed. What had once been his beautiful, elaborate torture cell, turned into rust and dust. It took a good portion of the Kazimeer's treasury to bring it back to its original splendor.

He didn't acknowledge the two sentries bowing their heads to him as he entered the dungeon and took his seat in the place of honor he'd set up for himself at the rear of the chamber. While he waited for his sentries to bring the prisoners before him, he let his mind wander.

He did dispatch most of that mutant's army, but not all. There were still a few faces he never saw being brought before him. One was the Weaver the creature introduced to him. Mazon, he believed he was called. That old man, who actually had the nerve to throw a spell at him. What annoyed Taj was that he had been unprepared for it. Granted, such a spell would've thrown a normal person over the balcony and it merely pushed him back a few steps. Still, it *did* push him back. And that had been enough distraction for the old Weaver to snatch the mutant and take off with him. Taj was certain that mutant was dead. After all, his power joined with that of his necklace struck the beast directly where he aimed and he saw that pale, limp body bleeding like a river's flow. What had him confused, though, was that the old Weaver carried him off. Why take a corpse? Did the old man believe it was his responsibility to give that thing a proper burning? No one was distraught over the Kazimeer's death, and those who were never voiced their grief. Taj didn't even allow the Death Bells to be rung; there would be no mourning for that creature.

What disturbed Taj the most was the old Weaver and the mutant's body were nowhere to be found. There was no possible way the Weaver could've left the castle, not with his troops crawling all over and the hundreds of people who were outside that day. He would've been spotted. And Taj felt no residue of magic, so that meant no Transfer spell had been cast. So where did he go with a corpse? It bothered him enough for him to forcibly put it out of his mind. If he didn't think about it, he'd eventually come up with an answer.

However, thinking of the mutation brought his thoughts to Abbnar. It was Abbnar who was responsible for the ivory dragon's existence. Wasn't he the least bit concerned that his creation was finally destroyed? Taj knew the old man must know, by now, what had taken place. Abbnar wasn't *that* isolated. Why hadn't he shown himself yet? What was he waiting for, what was he planning? Taj almost wished he would attack, at least then he could counter it. This unbearable waiting left him slightly jumpy.

Not that he was sitting idly, just waiting for Abbnar to come for his head. He'd already positioned his troops in every town, every village, in an effort to seek him out before he had a chance to attack. But Abbnar was cunning and slippery. He wouldn't be found before *he* wanted to be. Taj actually found it ironic. For so many years he had been the one in hiding, now it was Abbnar's turn. Taj's advantage was that he knew the man too well. Abbnar was not nearly as patient as he and would not wait two decades before showing himself. There was already evidence that Abbnar was aware of his presence. The fact that the Land was still suffering was one.

Once he had taken control, he discontinued his spells on the Land. However, they didn't dissipate. They'd gotten worse. Taj knew the old man was trying to use the same tactic *he* used on the beast Kazimeer. Only Taj was a far better dust kicker than the ivory thing was. He knew how to placate the people long enough for him to figure out how to undo Abbnar's spell.

Taj blew out a sharp breath through his teeth. Thinking of Abbnar always made him cranky. He wasn't in the mood to feel cranky today. He instead directed his attention to the struggling man who was being dragged before him. The man wore the dirty, torn uniform of the Kazimeer and had been caught sneaking around the castle. Directly behind him, was the sentry Taj decided to blame for this breech also in chains. Catching this ex-Defender sparked up his alarm. If there was one, there were more, and if there were more, where were they? Taj had his sentries search every nook of the castle but they found no one else or any possible internal entrance the Defender could have used. Taj originally thought that he must have come in from outside, which meant the few forces left behind by the Kazimeer were nearby. But after extensive searching of all the homes, shops, and forest there were no secret bases, no cowering group of Defenders, nothing. It bothered Taj, more than he liked to admit. He wanted answers and was determined to receive them from this man.

He smiled and leaned forward in his chair. "How are you today?"

The ex-Defender hadn't been beaten or tortured in anyway but he was a mess from hiding beneath whatever rock he found to crawl under. He sneered openly with cracked lips but said nothing.

"Well I'm fine, thank you," Taj said pleasantly. "I'm just curious to know where you came from."

The ex-Defender sniffed with contempt. "So. The great Taj doesn't know everything?"

Taj kept his expression neutral but his heartbeat quickened. Very few people knew his true name. Even most of his own sentries knew him as Blasdon. Knowing how his true name was synonymous with an array of unpleasantness, he chose to keep it a secret from the Land. The only other people, outside the loyal few, that he chose to enlighten were all dead. At least, he knew five of the six were dead. The only one he was starting to have doubts about was that brat creature. And now this mysterious Defender, who appeared out of nowhere, just called him by his true name. Coincidence?

"I'm flattered that you call me by the name of such a benevolent man, however I believe you are mistaken. My name is Blasdon."

"Your name is filth!" the ex-Defender spat.

Taj shook his head with a patient smile and waved his hand at his sentries. "Chain these two up so they do not run away, then leave us. I wish to speak to them privately."

His sentries wordlessly chained the ex-Defender and the accused sentry to the wall and quickly left the dungeon. Taj rose only after they were gone. The instant he approached the prisoners, the sentry began to sob openly.

"Please, my lord! I do not know how he got in. I was at my post! I was alert and at my post. No one got by me! Please, I beg you."

Taj stood directly before the whimpering sentry and held up his hand. "Just…shut up," he said smoothly and referred to the ex-Defender. "He is not blubbering and he knows what is to befall him. Don't you?" The man sneered but said nothing. Taj turned back to the sentry. "See, he knows and still he does not beg me for life. I wish I had a hundred more like him, but he does not believe in my cause, and therefore would be useless to me." He cupped the man's face gently and spoke slowly. "The reason you are here is because you are a pathetic, cowardly, feeble piece of spit and therefore you are also useless to me." The sentry started to sob again, a few tears landing on Taj's hand. Taj wiped his hand off on the front of the man's tunic in disgust but continued to speak softly. "Now, I will have you watch this brave man meet his fate before I take my time with your rehabilitation." The man sobbed harder and Taj patted him on the head affectionately.

Taj turned back to the ex-Defender. "It would really help if you told me where you came from."

The ex-Defender grinned tightly, "The Kyriea's pouch."

Taj sniffed a laugh. "I've seen the Kyriea and there's not a single pouch on him, so try again." The ex-Defender was silent. "It would make things easier on you if you just told me. Otherwise, I'll have to search for it in your mind." The ex-Defender continued to glare at him but still held his tongue. Taj stared deeply into the man's face. "Such nobility, such bravery…such stupidity." He spread his hands. "As you want."

Taj returned to his seat and summoned his power. He felt it rush into him but held it in, letting it build in strength. When he was satisfied that it was enough, he aimed it for the ex-Defender's mind. He watched the man's body arch as his power struck him and started to rip through his mind, searching for information. However, he was also preparing the man to be a loyal, perfect servant, something he did with the others that were captured from the ivory thing's army. Flashes of a hundred memories came to Taj but it was useless information and nothing he needed to study further. He let his power burn through them, leaving emptiness behind.

The ex-Defender's body violently shook and jerked, pulling on the chains that held him still. The sobbing sentry cringed and looked ready to wet his trousers, while he watched with wide eyes at the man next to him. Taj ignored the physical reaction to his power; he was only interested in digging out this information.

More memories from the man came to him, but none that said where he'd been hiding or whom he was with. Taj dug deeper, letting his power burrow fiercely into the man's mind. His power smacked into a mental wall, a barrier prohibiting him from going further. Someone had put a ward on this man. Someone who knew he might be captured and didn't want anyone to know where he came from. Taj became excited and slammed his power into the barrier, shattering it instantly. The moment the barrier was broken through, the information it was protecting vanished, as if the man could no longer remember it without the barrier. Taj's anger exploded out of him as he tried to retrieve the information before it disappeared. It was pointless but he still tried, tearing at the portion of the man's mind with such fury that blood poured from every orifice on the ex-Defender's body.

Taj let out an enraged roar then slumped back in his chair, while his power hovered in the man's now blank, empty mind. How could he have been so foolish! It took a moment before the answer would come to him. He never had expected such a powerful ward to be present. He underestimated it, thinking it was only a block when it was actually much more. Whoever this man had been with knew how to cast such an influential spell. Taj's first thought was that it was Abbnar but he quickly rejected that idea. Abbnar would never be so careless as to send someone into his territory who would get himself caught. If it had been Abbnar, the man would've either disappeared the moment he was discovered or would meet with some merciful, quiet death. Abbnar would never have allowed it to go this far without doing something. His second thought was of the old Weaver. Now that made sense. Send an ex-Defender that was stupid enough to be loyal to a dead mutant, with a spell that killed him if he was questioned. But the man called him Taj. He never spoke his true name in front of the Weaver. Could that thing still be alive? It wasn't possible and yet seemed to be the only answer he could come up with.

If that mutant was alive, though, he couldn't be in good shape. He'd taken quite a beating before disappearing with the Weaver. Could that beast be ruling from a deathbed? But Taj didn't want him ruling at all. He wanted him destroyed, gone, off the face of the Land permanently. He growled softly when his attention was caught by the ex-Defender's face, bloody and slack, waiting for him to complete what he started.

"Oh," Taj mumbled absently. He waved his hand, allowing his power to open up the man's mind to receive its new host.

This was a trick he learned a long time ago from a Death Conjurer. It was beautiful, actually. All he had to do was wipe a person's mind clean and open up a narrow gateway to the spirit realm, allowing a greedy spirit, still hungry for life, to enter into the empty mind. The entity would be happy enough to have a living body and therefore completely grateful to the one who gave it life. Taj then had a loyal servant to do things a regular person would never agree to do or have enough power to do it with. He watched excitedly as the transformation took place. When the spirit entered the ex-Defender's mind, his body was changed to accommodate it. When death wrestles with the living, death always wins. The man's skin turned white, his eyes sunk in and seemed to disappear.

The change only took a few moments and when it was finished, Taj had a perfectly good Mytock, a name he called them from his original tongue meaning 'blind one'. They weren't blind but looked as though they were and besides, he liked the way the name rolled off his tongue.

Taj looked over his new creation. "An oath of loyalty, now!" A spirit's oath was better than that of the Kyriea's. He also made sure to bind them to their words as they spoke, so there would be no chance of betrayal.

"Master," the voice was breathy and rasp. "I owe my existence to you and pledge my unconditional loyalty to you and no other for as long as I survive."

"Good enough," Taj said. He gestured absently to the chains holding the Mytock and they fell to the floor. The Mytock stepped forward and bowed. Taj nodded impatiently. "Yes, yes. I want you to get out of that uniform before I vomit on it. But before you go..." He stared at the terrified sentry and smiled. "Have something to eat first." A freshly, reborn spirit was always hungry and just adored feasting, especially when the victim was an arm length away.

The Mytock turned its head toward the trembling sentry. Its face remained blank but Taj could tell it was delighted. Taj sank deeper into his chair to watch the fun as the Mytock approached the sentry, who had already begun to let out curdling wails. Despite the noise, Taj heard the rapid knocking on the door and held up a hand for the Mytock to wait.

"What!" he shouted.

A sentry entered, briefly glanced over to the Mytock and its prey, and kept his eyes pinned to the floor. He bowed deeply. "My lord. We've found another intruder."

"Really?" Taj asked. "Where?"

"He was found hiding in one of the studies during a routine check."

Taj growled loudly. "Why is it I have sentries to guard my home?"

The sentry hesitated for a moment then answered uncertainly, "To protect you, my lord?"

"Is that before or after intruders come into the castle?"

"Before, my lord."

"Ah, I see." Taj nodded slowly. Without warning, he slammed his fist down on the arm of the chair, making the sentry flinch. "Then why is it not being done?" The sentry said nothing and remained standing with his head bowed. Taj didn't expect an answer and in his current mood, any answer would have been the wrong one. He was pleased this man realized that and held his tongue. He breathed deeply to soothe himself. "Where is Second Dapp?"

"I do not know, my lord."

"Find him. Tell him I want to see him, now!" The sentry nodded but remained, obviously apprehensive about speaking again. Taj sighed, "What?"

"The intruder, my lord?"

Taj considered it briefly. "Bring him to me."

"Yes, my lord." The sentry nodded again and quickly left.

Taj settled back into his seat and gestured for the Mytock to continue. He thought it would be fitting, this intruder seeing what his own fate would be, one way or the other. The Mytock had just begun to sink its nails into the screaming sentry's forehead when Taj heard the high-pitched cry from outside the closed door.

"Whoa, whoa, whoa!" he said quickly. "Stop." The Mytock froze, but its hand remained positioned on top of the sentry's skull. Taj strained to hear over the sentry's whimpering as the cry came again.

"Let me go, you big fool head!"

Taj sprang up from his chair and lunged for the door. He flung it open just as one of his sentries was about to open it. Taj looked at the stunned sentry's face then down to the prisoner he held. The young boy stared up at him with wide-eyes and a trembling bottom lip. Taj ran a hand over his mouth in an attempt to hide a smile and looked back to the sentry.

"He didn't give you too much trouble, I hope."

The sentry was unsure how to take his remark. "No, my lord."

"Well that's good. Young boys have been known to over take big fool heads, such as yourself." The sentry didn't answer but Taj could see the humility in his face. The boy, however, gave a small smile. "Let the child go," he ordered. The sentry did so and the boy wrapped his thin arms around himself. "Now, run along and attend to your duties. Perhaps you'll be able to snare one of those dangerous, castle stomping rats."

The sentry bowed, gave a quick, "Yes, my lord," and hurried down the hall.

Taj stared down at the boy with a broad smile. "What's your name?"

The boy looked up at him and then around at the walls of the hallway. "I've never been down here before. It's scary."

Taj looked around too, as if he never considered it before, and nodded. "I guess it can be a bit scary."

"The Kazimeer never used this place."

"I only use it for storage myself."

"For what kind of stuff?"

"For stuff that I don't have a use for right now." Taj smiled. "Would you like to go back upstairs?" The boy nodded vigorously. "All right. Just give me one minute to finish putting some stuff away." Taj reentered, closing the door quickly behind him so the boy wouldn't have a chance to steal a peek, and talked softly to the Mytock, who was still waiting with its hand positioned on the sentry's head. "Tear out his throat," Taj told the Mytock. "I don't want to hear him screaming."

Before Taj could say another word, the Mytock plunged its other hand into the sentry's neck, tearing at the muscle and flesh. The sentry's body jerked and his eyes and mouth were opened wide but only soft choking sounds came from him. Taj blinked slowly at the speed the Mytock moved and shook his head slightly. "When you're finished here, report to me."

Taj turned on his heels and left the Mytock to finish its meal, already hearing the sound of flesh ripping as it pulled the sentry's scalp back. He opened and shut the door behind him in a flash and smiled at the boy. "How about some milk and sweet cakes? You look starved."

The boy nodded and Taj walked with him back up to the kitchen. The child seemed to be sure of where he was going, which peaked Taj's curiosity. When they entered the kitchen, Taj shooed all the servants out and got the boy a cup of milk. The sweet cakes were still on the table and Taj offered one to the boy, who took it carefully. Once the boy took a bite, he inhaled the rest. Taj figured he was comfortable enough to be asked some questions.

"What's your name?"

"Webben," the boy said around a mouthful.

Taj leaned on the counter with his face propped up by his hands. "What are you doing here, Webben?"

The boy stared at him with big eyes and swallowed hard. "I used to work here."

"Oh? What did you do?"

"I was the Kazimeer's personal servant," Webben said proudly. His shoulders slumped and his face fell. "When there was a Kazimeer."

"And where have you been since? Hiding in the castle?" Taj was hopeful. Perhaps this child would reveal the location of the others.

"No. When the fighting started, I ran away."

Taj nodded. He could see that, a young boy ducking around his preoccupied sentries, since he was small enough to get by them without being seen. He gestured for the boy to go on.

"But...I had nowhere to go," Webben said softly.

"Don't you have a family?"

"No."

"So where have you been staying?"

"In the woods. But it was real cold last night. I didn't know where else to go, so I sneaked in."

"How?"

"The study's window." The boy smiled shyly. "The lock's old and if you jiggle it enough, it'll come loose." His smile vanished and he stared at Taj fearfully. "But I won't do it again. This was the only time, I swear! I'll leave now."

"Nonsense," Taj said, stopping the boy gently. "You used to work here, so you will again."

Webben chewed on his bottom lip. "But some people say you had the Kazimeer killed."

Taj sighed sadly and squatted down so the boy wouldn't have to crane his neck. "Webben, have you ever thought that someone was doing something good, but they really weren't."

"I don't know."

"What about the Kazimeer? Did you like him?" The boy shrugged. "Do you think he liked you?"

"Well...he was always kind-of yelling at me."

"What about everyone else? Was he nice to them?"

"He was always kind-of yelling at them too," the boy admitted.

"Does that sound like a nice person?"

"I guess not."

"Now, if someone's always yelling at people who are close to him, what do you think he was doing to the Land?"

"I don't know." Webben scratched his head. "Yelling at them too?"

"Probably." Taj nodded. "But he was probably doing worse. He was doing things that really hurt the Land."

"He was always saying how he wanted to help the Land. Why would he do that?"

"Why did he yell at you?"

Webben thought about it for a moment. "I don't know."

"It's hard to say why some people do things, bad things." He held the boy gently by his narrow shoulders. "You see, Webben, I didn't want to hurt the Kazimeer. All I wanted to do was remove him, stop him from doing all these bad things to the Land. I didn't kill him, Webben. His own creations turned on him. Did you see that?" The boy shook his head. "Well, I saw it." Taj leaned closer and spoke confidentially, "And if you thought that place downstairs was scary, you should've seen what I saw." Webben stared at him curiously and Taj nodded. "I still have bad dreams."

"*You* do?" Webben asked.

"Oh yes. Everyone has bad dreams once and awhile. Don't you?"

"Lots of them."

"I can imagine. Things are pretty strange right now, aren't they?" Webben nodded. "I know. What I'm trying to do is make it so they're not so strange and scary. Do you want to help me?"

"How?" the boy asked carefully.

"Well, you could work here again if you want."

"I could?"

"Sure." Taj smiled and rose to his feet. "I could use someone like you to help me. Someone who already knows what's happening here, the routine, who's who. I really need someone like you, Webben."

"I don't know," Webben said and chewed on his bottom lip again.

"How about this," Taj offered, "try it for a few days. If you like it, you can stay. If you don't, we'll see about finding a place where you will be happy. How does that sound?"

Webben considered it and finally nodded. "All right. I'll try it."

Hosting the Kazimeer

Taj smiled and walked the boy out of the kitchen. "Let's see about finding you a bed chamber. There are only hundreds of them."

"My bed chamber was in the servant's quarters."

Taj acted outraged. "I will not have *my* assistant sleeping on some straw mat on the floor. No, you will have your own chamber."

Webben smiled a real smile and Taj couldn't help but grin back. This was going to work out just fine. When they arrived at an unoccupied chamber down the hall from Taj's own, he held open the door for the boy to enter.

Webben hesitated and glanced up at him. "Are you really Taj?"

He laughed hard and soon the boy joined him. They went into the chamber and got Webben settled.

Taj never answered his question.

JYNX

Jaron started off in the direction of the Training Halls the next day, much to Landon's relief, but he took his time getting there, purposely staying within the forest and avoiding the main road. Landon asked why the boy didn't think he needed to follow the main road and Jaron grumbled that they would be harder to find among the trees. Landon soon discovered that was true, since the boy couldn't seem to find *himself* among the trees. He kept getting lost and ignored Landon's recommendations until days later when they found themselves nowhere near the Training Halls. Landon kept his comments to himself but Jaron felt his strong emotions taunting him.

"Dis is not me fault," he grumbled one evening. His stomach gnawed away at him and he was exhausted from the days of traveling.

"Oh no, of course not," the voice in his head replied with flat sarcasm. *"How could I possibly blame you, even if you don't listen to my directions."*

"Jur directions is from da main road," Jaron pointed out sharply.

"If you would just listen to me, we would have been there by now."

"Listen to ju, bah! Ju're nutin' but a pain in me head."

"And I will continue to be until you listen to me. I know this Land better than you, thief, so perhaps you would follow my directions from now on so we can get to the Halls before we both grow old together." Jaron was crawling around on the ground and Landon asked sharply, *"What are you doing now?"*

"I's got to eat," Jaron mumbled and continued to crawl, turning over rocks and pushing aside branches.

"Do you think your prey is just going to be waiting for you to find it?"

"Yup," Jaron replied as he turned over a large rock.

Landon's first reaction was mild disgust when he saw the hundreds of grubs, bugs, and worms slithering around in the dirt. His disgust increased when he realized what Jaron was going to do. *"You can't."*

"Corse I's can," Jaron sniffed at him. "Its tide me over 'till I's can find someting bigger to eat." Jaron scooped up a handful of his squiggling supper and brought it to his mouth.

"Wait!" Landon cried. *"Wouldn't it be better to starve?"*

Jaron rolled his eyes, although he knew the voice in his head couldn't see it, and tossed the handful into his mouth. Landon was aware he couldn't taste or physically experience anything the boy did, but his imagination got the better of him. He could suddenly feel the bugs crawling around in his non-existent mouth, feel the worms and grubs slide down his non-existent throat, and felt his non-existent stomach roll over several times.

Jaron growled irritably at him, "Go 'way! I's done dis all me life and now I's 'ave problem cause of ju. Go 'way!"

Landon obliged immediately, ducking back into the boy's mind and waited. Every so often he would come forward just enough to see if the thief boy was finished and each time he quickly withdrew because he wasn't. A large, satisfied belch from the boy told him it was safe to come fully forward again.

"*That was the most---*"

"Not a word!" Jaron snapped, cutting him off. "Not all of us 'ave our meals prepared and brought to us by's slaves."

"*Slaves? Boy, what are you talking about now?*"

"If's ju's really da Kazimeer, which I's still don't believes, but ifs ju is, den ju're actually a slave-mader."

"*It's ma...ST...er and I am no such thing.*"

"Do people works fure ju?"

"*Well of course,*" Landon stated as if it was the most obvious thing.

"Do ju pay dem?"

"*Yes.*"

"How's much?"

"*Enough.*"

"'Nuff? Wha's dat mean?"

"*It means enough,*" Landon snapped defensively but he started to think. How much did he pay his servants? How much did he pay Webben? *Did* he pay Webben? It was something that never occurred to him before.

"'Nuff to leave ju and go somewhere else?"

Landon was becoming flustered by the questions, especially when he didn't know the answers. "*How should I know what people do with their earnings?*" He regained his mental footing. "*And my servants would not want to leave me.*"

"And why's is dat?"

"*I give them a home, clothes, food; they want for nothing.*"

"'Cept dare freedom," Jaron answered, in a tone which implied the conversation was over.

Landon was not about to let the thief take the lead on this. "*They are not slaves! They are there by their own free will. They can leave whenever they want.*"

"Cept dey can't. Ju provide dem wit erriting and dey is so dependent on ju dat dey *can't* leave. Where would dey live if's dey 'ave no home? I's really doubt ju pay dem 'nuff to save up for a home somewhere else. Ifs dey left dey'd be's starvin' in a week, 'less dey somehow managed to find apprenticeship. But I's bet dat most of jur servants are too old to begin bein' an apprentice. Jus 'cause ju don't see chains, doesn't mean dey aren't dare and jus as oppressin'."

Landon was stunned by the boy's sharp tone and words, when another thought struck him. Did the thief just say oppressing? As if he heard him, Jaron suddenly started again.

"And I's want ju's out of me head!"

"*Then perhaps you should go to the Training Halls instead of wandering all over the Land, boy. The sooner you get there, the sooner I will be gone from you. And if the Masters don't know what to do, I'm sure they'll know who we can go to.*"

Jaron was silent, which caught Landon off guard for a moment. He expected the boy to say something and he couldn't feel any emotion coming from him. When Jaron did speak it made Landon more unsettled than the silence.

"Wha' do ju mean, *if's* da Maders don't know wha' to do?" The boy's voice was stiff and had dropped a tone, so it sounded like it was coming from his gut. It actually made Landon nervous.

"I'm sure the Masters will know what to do. I was just saying if *they didn't---"*

"Ju said," Jaron interrupted firmly, enunciating each word clearly, "da Maders would know wha' to do. Dat is why's we's goin' to deese Trainin' Halls in da first place. Now ju're not sure?"

Landon felt a tight grip around his neck and then remembered that he didn't have a neck, but the sensation was still the same. Soon the tightness traveled to the rest of his fictitious body. He was being squeezed, crushed; he was being killed. The logical side of him said that was impossible since he had no body to die but his other side, his dragon side, immediately struck out in defense. He pushed hard against the weight crushing him, so hard he could almost feel his muscles straining. As quickly as it came, the vice he was in shattered, leaving him free but wary.

Jaron said nothing, but Landon could hear his labored breaths and would bet that his heart was pounding. He could suddenly feel the boy's emotions, which had been absent only an instant before. He was frightened, just as Landon was, and both were wondering the same thing; what had happened? Although Landon was completely bewildered about it, he felt that Jaron had a slight advantage over him. It was a brief, distant thought, one Landon wasn't sure if the boy knew he was thinking about, but Landon picked up on it just the same; *not again.*

It was gone before it formed completely but Landon was certain it was what Jaron was thinking. Not again, what? Did this boy have people taking up residence in his mind often? He kept his thoughts closed off to the thief and stayed quiet.

Jaron finally broke the silence by speaking softly. "I's take ju's to da Halls. Ifs deese Maders can't git ju out, I's take ju somewhere else but jus leave me alone 'till den."

Landon agreed and withdrew into the thief's mind. He would say nothing.

He held to his promise quite well. For three days they traveled, the thief getting lost constantly, but Landon held his tongue and suppressed his feelings. It was not out of fear that he remained silent, although he still wondered what happened the other night, but he didn't utter a sound because he was proving a point. The boy asked him to leave him alone until they reached the Halls, and he was doing just that. So what if the thief boy got lost every other minute, so what if they wouldn't get to the Halls by the time Landon died of old age, he was leaving the boy alone, just as he promised. He didn't have a problem traveling around in someone else's mind. His feet didn't hurt by the end of the day. He didn't need to chew on roots and...Light help him...bugs. He still had no idea how the boy ate those things and tried not to think about it when he did. So, as far as he was concerned, he had it easy and wouldn't upset the balance, since the thief told him his advice was not needed.

On the third evening, Jaron started a small fire and collapsed in front of it, but was certainly debating something. Landon felt the boy finally make up his mind.

"Where's do I's go?" Jaron grumbled. Landon didn't answer. After a long pause, Jaron asked again, "Where is dis place?" No response. "I's knows ju're still dare. I's feel jur nose in da air att-IT-tude so jus answer me."

Landon let his consciousness release a long weary yawn as a response but said nothing. He wanted the thief to say it; say that he needed him. He tried to give off a feeling of indifference but it was difficult. The fact was that for the past three days it had been pushing him toward madness not to hurry the boy along. Light knew how his Land was doing. They stayed within the forest most of the time so he hadn't even seen, with the exception of Aman, how the rest of the people were fairing. He had to get out of this boy's mind but no reason to let *him* know of his urgency.

"Where's do we's go!" Jaron snapped.

Landon slowly came forward and pushed a feeling of confusion into the boy. "*Oh? Are we at the Halls,* already?" He paused. "*Oh. We're not. I'll just go back to leaving you alone until we get there.*" He started to withdraw.

"Looks," Jaron growled sharply. "Jus tell me where deese Halls are."

"*Nela.*"

"I's don't know where Nela is. I's never been dare and I's never had a reason or desire to be's dare 'till now. So jus tell me." He took a deep breath and grumbled under it, "Please."

Landon played with the idea of making the boy grovel more, but decided not to and immediately came fully forward and looked around. Trees, trees and more trees. Oh, and a rock here and there. That was it. He would never be able to tell where they were just by looking at the forest.

"*You're going to have to get to the main road. Then I'll be able to point you in the correct direction.*"

"If's ju 'aven't noticed, dose tings 'aven't come lookin' fure me lately. Don't ju tink dat maybes it's 'cause I's 'aven't been on da main road?"

"*Do you want to get to Nela or not? You can duck back into the forest as soon as I get my bearings. Although, you'll probably just get lost again.*"

"Fine!" Jaron snapped. "I's go to da cursed, bloody main road. 'Appy?"

"*I would be happier if you came to this decision three days ago.*"

"I's be's 'appier if's ju's jus went 'way."

"*So would I.*"

"Are the two of you married?"

Jaron leapt to his feet and pulled his knife out in one swift movement. He scanned the dark forest looking for who spoke but saw no one. That made him even uneasier. He turned around slowly with his knife poised to jab into anything that came near him and squinted to see against the darkness.

"*There,*" Landon called out to him.

Jaron would have snapped that 'There' meant nothing to him, especially when he didn't know what 'There' the voice meant, but then he saw it too. A small shadow, sitting on one of the rocks about a foot away from his camp. He kicked himself for being so caught up in his argument with the voice that he didn't notice someone sitting so close to him. He still glanced around, knowing how one person usually had friends hiding in the darkness, but mainly kept his eyes toward the shadow.

"*Ask who it is,*" Landon said, but Jaron didn't repeat the question.

He knew how to play this game too well. If he opened his mouth it would give the person a better idea of his position. If he remained silent and motionless, he could be taken for a shadow himself. So he waited and ignored the voice telling him to ask questions. The figure on the rock giggled and shifted its position.

Now Jaron could make out just a few more details about who he faced. The small giggle told him it was a girl and a young one at that. She was sitting with her legs crossed and balanced herself on the rock with ease. His first reaction was to relax, knowing full well that he could take on a small girl. But he didn't, remembering how he had been used as such a decoy before. No one ever suspected a small child to be mixed up in something foul and those who did were the ones who were easiest to rob.

"I'm no decoy," the girl said playfully. Jaron, who was already standing perfectly still, froze even more. How did she know what he was thinking?

"*She's just a girl,*" Landon told him. "*Just yell at her or give her a smack and she'll go away.*" Obviously, Landon didn't understand what had just happened to him.

"Tell your friend," the girl said in a biting tone, "that he should watch what he says."

That caught Landon's attention. "*She heard me?*"

"He's not me friend," Jaron answered, making his voice sound more sure and strong than he felt.

"Of course he's not," the girl laughed. "And you are not his. But Taj would give his left eye to know where the two of you are."

"*Taj!*" Landon cried the same moment Jaron did.

Jaron got a hold of himself quickly and sniffed, "Taj is jus a child's tale." He waited for the voice in his head to agree but when no answer came, he found himself swallowing hard. "Right?"

Landon's thoughts began pouring over the scene at the castle again. Granted the man called himself by the Dark Master's name, but hearing someone else name him so bluntly gave him pause. Could that really have been Taj? *The* Taj? But how was that possible?

"Right!" Jaron repeated firmly, wanting desperately to be supported in this, even if it was by the voice.

"*Perhaps not, thief boy,*" Landon reluctantly admitted.

Suddenly, Jaron saw the blonde man with black eyes that Landon thought about so often. *That* was Taj? "Dis is a fine time to tell me such tings," Jaron told him silently.

The girl continued. "Oh, don't worry about me." Jaron could tell she was smiling, though he still couldn't see her face. "I don't like Taj so I won't be helping him. I might help you two though."

"*Great,*" Landon moaned. "*Another child. What kind of army am I raising?*" Jaron ignored his remark, however, the girl didn't.

She sighed irritably and screamed into Landon's mental ear, "I can hear you!" Both he and Jaron winced from the loud volume she used and Landon still heard her words ringing in his mind long after she had fallen quiet. She spoke aloud again in her sweet, childlike voice. "I would think you would be thankful for any help you could receive, Kazimeer. But since you don't, I won't bother. I have more important things to do than worry about your feeble self." She rose and stood on top of the rock, staring at Jaron for a moment.

"*Ask who she is!*" Landon demanded of Jaron.

The girl sighed again and raised her head to the sky. "Why are boys so unbelievably stupid?" She looked back toward Jaron. Her voice was almost a whisper and laced with mockery. "I can hear you, fool Kazimeer, and it's a wonder I even bothered offering my help to you when obviously Taj is the better choice. At least *he* knows my value, where you do not." With that she vanished.

Jaron blinked several times trying to find her shadow but couldn't. She just disappeared. He remained in his attack stance for long minutes until he was fairly sure no one else would be dropping by this evening. Only then did he relax.

"Wha' 'ave ju gotten me into?" he moaned.

"*I don't know,*" Landon replied sincerely.

They both experienced a restless and sleepless night.

**   **

Jynx settled down among the branches of a tree, closed her eyes, and concentrated. She directed her aura at one person, knowing she'd grab his attention. He may appear to be patient and unflustered, but she knew he was curious too. He'd be too curious not to investigate. She could nearly feel it; that shift in the air, smell of that certain magic only he used, and could almost see the race to find her in her mind's eye. She giggled softly to herself; this was always the best part. She loved games of the mind, loved to haggle, and loved to see the look on people's faces when she demonstrated her talents. She was casting spells before she could talk and had mastered the advanced spells only known to the Teaching Masters by the time she was six. Yes, her body was young, but her mind and her spirit were old. Very old, she was certain, and she would not waste what the Kyriea had given her.

The wind became stronger and she opened her eyes to scan the treetops. Ah, there it was. The disorientation of the air and again, that certain smell of magic only linked to him. She kept her eyes pinned to the spot and made her face hold a small smirk as the figure of a man appeared and hovered over the branches only a few feet away from her. He took one look at her with those pitch black eyes and sniffed.

"How did I know?"

Jynx shook her head. "I don't know what you're talking about."

"Piss and manure, little one," he responded. "You've been broadcasting smugness across the entire Land." He paused and his expression became harsh. "What do you want?"

"Me?" Jynx asked innocently, pointing to herself. "Not a thing." She smiled. "What do you want?"

"I want to not play games tonight," he said coldly. "You aimed your aura at me so strongly it nearly knocked me over. You wanted my attention, you got it. What do you want?"

"I wanted to know your thoughts on the current situation of the Land."

His pitch black eyes narrowed with suspicion. "Why?"

"Because there seems to be a lot going on that's out of your control." She smiled thinly. "I thought you might want some help."

"Not yours."

"Pity. I could help you a lot."

He sighed irritably. "I have no time for this."

She saw his power start to churn around him. He was going to Transfer. She quickly said, "Why haven't you found the Kazimeer yet?"

The power stopped churning and he stared levelly at her, but he didn't offer anything.

Her smile returned. "Are you about to tell me he's dead?"

"I wasn't about to tell you anything," he said smoothly.

She could just about make it out. That little flick of power from him. He was good at covering up his casting but she could see the slight shift in magic. Her smile widened. "You're searching for him right now, aren't you? Bet you can't find him."

He put his head to one side. "Oh and let me guess. You know where he is."

"I might."

"You might or you might just be trying to find a way to betray me again." Her expression darkened but she didn't say anything. "Yes, that sounds more accurate."

"What sounds even more accurate," she began in a sharp tone, "is that for once you and your great power can't actually find someone."

"If he were out there, I would find him."

Her grin started to return. "You really can't sense him, can you?"

He was silent and continued to stare hard at her. She forced herself not to shift around under his gaze and held his stare. Out of nowhere a sudden rush of power flowed over her. He was trying to pull the information out of her mind. Did he think she was so foolish as to not have a spell in place for just such a threat? But she quickly discovered he wasn't trying to pull the information from her; he was trying to re-trace her path. He was trying to see where she had been lately. She made sure he came to a dead end.

A smile started to spread on his face but it was quite creepy. "So you supposedly know where the Kazimeer is, but you won't let me find him. You just wanted to share this information with me for...what? Fun?"

"I was just curious why you can't find him yourself."

"I would find him if he was there to find."

Her eyes widened with genuine surprise and she beamed. "Oh wow! This is just too weird."

He continued to study her. He wasn't sure, she could see it in his carefully blank expression. Finally he tossed his hands into the air. "If he is still alive then he mind-traveled. And he didn't come to me, so where could he have gone?"

Jynx shrugged. "Just some thief."

"Oh that sounds believable," he muttered. "And you know this because...?"

"I met him. I wanted to be sure myself." She wrinkled her brow. "He seemed a little aggravated."

"Oh I'm sure after meeting you he is no longer just a *little* aggravated." He glared at her. "How are you so sure?"

"I heard him. I heard the Kazimeer. He's in that thief's mind."

The man sniffed. "If he mind-traveled you wouldn't have heard him at all."

"I would if I were granted certain abilities."

"I know how far your magic can go and no matter how powerful you think you are, there is no way you would be able to hear an ivory dragon who has mind-traveled."

Jynx merely grinned and shrugged. "If you say."

"I do say. And I believe you are wasting my time with foolish games." He raised his hands and paused, studying her. "If the Kazimeer really has mind-traveled, and you want to help, then I suggest you find a way to bring him to me and quickly. Otherwise, don't bother me again."

With that, there was a surge of power and he vanished from sight. Jynx let out a breath she had been holding and allowed herself to relax. Well, wasn't that interesting. Why could he not sense the Kazimeer? Could the thief be blocking his magic somehow? So many questions but she was talented in discovering answers. She did so like challenges.

**   **

The following morning Jaron made his way quickly to the main road. Landon had the suspicion the boy was hurrying now because of last night's encounter with that girl. He didn't care what got the thief motivated, so long as he got to the Halls this season. The boy did not speak with him once since last night, which gave Landon some time to piece together what he had learned over the past few days.

He still found it hard to believe that Taj ever existed, especially in his own lifetime, but if it were true it would explain many things. All the plagues on the Land, the way his Defenders were transformed into skeletons, and that odd necklace. If that person really was Taj he was in trouble, and so was this thief if he didn't get to the Halls. How could he do anything while he was trapped in this boy who fought and argued with him at every turn?

Jaron arrived at the main road and came to a dead stop.

"A'right," he said, speaking for the first time since last night. "Where's we's?"

Landon peered through the boy's eyes and growled sharply, "*Do you think you can walk a little further so I can tell what towns are nearby?*"

"Ju's said to gits to da main road. 'Ere I's is. Where's we's?"

"*On the main road,*" Landon replied flatly. "*Dat's where weeze is.*" Landon felt the boy's anger rise at his remark. Good. Maybe now he'd be reasonable. "*Just walk, thief boy.*"

"I's don't likes dis," Jaron grumbled.

"*I didn't ask if you liked it. Just do it!*"

Jaron reluctantly moved and soon picked up his speed to a fast pace down the wide, dirt road. Anyone they passed barely gave the boy a second look but Jaron felt as if all eyes were on him watching everything he did. When they had gone about two miles, they stood across from the entrance to a town called Tirsak.

Landon quickly calculated their position and made his voice as sarcastic as he could. "*Congratulations boy! We're absolutely nowhere near the Halls. In fact, we're in the opposite direction! Maybe if you start going in the right direction today, we can be there in...oh say...another week or two!*" Jaron clicked his tongue a few times, turned on his heels, and entered the surrounding forest again without a word or thought to him. "*North, boy. Go north.*"

Jaron didn't respond and continued moving until the main road and Tirsak were long left behind. Only when they were deep within the forest did Jaron stop and scream at the top of his lungs.

"*Are you hungry?*" Landon asked. "*Perhaps there's a milk bottle for you back in Tirsak. And a fresh diaper. When was the last time you were changed?*"

"I's really wants to gits ju out of me head and backs into jur own body, so I's can beat da livin' snot out of ju!"

"*Oh little boy, when I get my body back you will have that opportunity.*" The thief did not know that he was no ordinary Kazimeer. He had been a Second for far longer and learned to fight both in hand-to-hand combat and with a variety of weapons. He wasn't great, but he was certain he could tie this boy into a knot and bounce him a few times before he tossed him into his dungeon. It was that thought that made him really want to get to the Halls soon.

"Eat me bones!" Jaron hissed.

"*You wouldn't want me to do that, thief boy.*"

Jaron plopped down and forced himself to relax. There was no point in having a shouting bout with this voice if he was too furious to think of quick replies. When he felt his muscles loosen up and his anger slip away, he waited.

He didn't know how much time passed while he sat there but it wasn't long before the voice asked irritably, "*What are you doing now?*"

Jaron smiled broadly. He knew that person in his mind wouldn't be able to keep his thoughts closed for very long. He kept his voice level and light as he responded, "I's tinkin'."

"*No you weren't. Believe me, you haven't had a single thought since I've been in here.*"

Jaron ignored the remark and continued. "I's tinkin' 'bout wha' ju is. Really is."

"*The Kazimeer. Or have you been unable to retain such a simple thought as that?*"

"Dat's right," Jaron said with false surprise, slapping his thigh. "Ju're an ivory dragon merfer. I's forgot."

"*Morpher. How hard it is to pronounce that? Mor-Pher. See how simple it is!*"

"I's bet ju's really a maggot." Landon ignored the boy's attempt to stir up his anger. "Or maybe a cave bat. No, dat's not its. Wait. Lemme sees. I's know! A thronge worm!" Landon did not respond and tried to hold his anger steady. He knew the boy was just trying to provoke him and he wouldn't give the thief such satisfaction. Jaron chanted happily, "Ju is a thronge worm. Ju is a thronge worm." Why was Landon letting this boy get the best of his anger? He knew he should ignore him but still felt his temper rise steadily. "I's eat thronge worms fure me meals. I's tinks I's eat one now!"

Landon knew the boy was perfectly aware of how much it sickened him to be present when he ate those things. He started to withdraw deeper into the boy's mind but found that he couldn't. He tried again but still he couldn't retreat.

A sudden flash of surprise then satisfaction came from the boy and Landon knew he was doing this on purpose somehow. He was forcing him to stay in the front of his mind so he could disgust him as much as possible. On cue, Jaron started quickly crawling around looking under rocks and branches. Landon's anger mounted. How dare this thief hold him prisoner like this! How dare this little, insignificant boy think he could force him, the Kazimeer, to stay where he didn't wish to be! Furious, he banged on the mental wall that Jaron put up when he didn't want him coming forward, only this time it was keeping him from going back.

Jaron snickered quietly and continued to crawl around in the dirt, looking specifically for a thronge worm. They were fat, slow, lazy, and stupid. He didn't know why the voice didn't just retreat like he always did but Jaron was happy that he was sticking around for this. It gave him some satisfaction about this whole situation when he could goad this person. Now where was a thronge worm when you wanted one? He was hungry anyway so he might as well find a big, fat, juicy one and eat it slow. Oh yes! Nice and slow. Maybe that would push this person out of his mind once and for all.

Landon suddenly felt a flash of pain. Only it wasn't coming from the boy, it was his. Actually his. But how? He'd been beating on that solid barrier when the pain struck. He was suddenly aware of something; he could feel his left arm. It was an odd sensation, as if he was still pressed up against the barrier but his left arm had somehow broken through and was on the other side. Then he discovered it wasn't his arm at all. It was Jaron's and he had control over it. With his anger still fuming and his one arm free, he went into action.

Jaron didn't find a thronge worm but found the next best thing. A bunch of long thin worms just waiting to be gulped down. He snickered loudly, hoping the voice in his head could hear and was still watching. He reached out with his hand to scoop them up, only his hand didn't respond. It stayed planted firmly on the ground as if someone was restraining it. He looked down at it curiously but saw no binds. Why wasn't it moving? Out of nowhere his left hand snaked up and smacked him awkwardly in the face.

"*Try to hold me prisoner, will you!*" the voice in his head snapped. His left hand came back to punch his face.

Jaron tried to figure out what was happening. It didn't take long. His left arm and hand were no longer under his control and were attacking him. He screamed and tried to pry off his own hand that had become attached to his face and was pushing its fingers into his eyes and cheeks. However, since he had opened his mouth, the hand reached in, grabbed his tongue, dug its nails into it, and pulled.

"*Maybe now you'll speak clearly!*"

Still screaming, Jaron yanked the hand off of his tongue and pinned it to the ground by holding it at the wrist and watched in terror as it squirmed and struggled to get loose. He leaned his body weight into his hold; he'd break his own arm if he had to, but he didn't have to. As quickly as it started, his hand stopped fighting him and relaxed. He didn't let it up though, and continued to watch it with wide eyes, as if it would spring into action at any second.

Landon stopped for two reasons. One, he didn't feel it was right to use the boy's own body to attack himself, no matter how much pleasure it gave him. The other reason was he could no longer hold onto his control; he felt exhausted and sore as if he had been fighting for days. Maybe he had or maybe it was the boy's own weariness rubbing off on him. During the few moments when he was recovering from his small retort against the thief, he realized what he had just done. He actually had control over the boy's arm. Solid and complete control even if it was for only a few moments. It frightened him, but again he wasn't certain if it was just him or the boy's emotions mixed in with his own. Whatever it was, he was terrified. What was happening to him?

Landon thought he was shaking until he remembered he didn't have a body to shake, and discovered it was Jaron who was doing enough for the two of them.

Suddenly, with a fury Landon didn't think the boy had in him, he shouted, "Out!"

Landon quickly got back under his calm control and asked, "*How do you propose I do that?*"

"Out!" Jaron shouted again, leapt to his feet, and shook his head vigorously back and forth, as if he could jostle him loose from his mind. "Go! Leave!"

"*We went through this before,*" Landon answered, still trying to figure out what he had done and how.

"I's gits ju out," Jaron grumbled. He snatched up his pack and took off into the forest.

Landon noticed they were heading back to the main road. He knew what the boy was going to do. "*Take me to the Halls and this will be over.*"

"I's won't wait annimore. I's not goin' to wait 'tills ju's do someting likes dat 'gain! I's jus a thief. A simpel, 'appy thief. I's was 'appy once. I's had nice jobs. Simpel jobs. No eye-less tings attacked me. Me own hand never tried to pull out me own tongue. A Weaver. Yes, a Weaver will Banish ju. But I's want ju in a tangible shape first so I's can beat ju!"

"*What does tangible mean?*" Landon asked quickly. This was the second time he noticed the boy using a word too large for his vocabulary…but not for Landon's.

"I's don't know and I's don't care! I's want ju out!" He stopped walking and thought about the question again. "Ju're tryin' to take over me mind too. Ju give me words I's don't know. Ju put thoughts in me head I's don't want. No Halls fure ju. A Weaver!"

"*Look, thief…Jaron, you can't do this. I have no control over what words you do or don't speak.*"

"Dat's jus great," Jaron mumbled. "Den if's ju's don't 'ave anni control, who's does? I's don't! And if's ju don't den we's bof screwed, ain't we's. But I's not screwed, thronge worm. I's git ju out."

"*If you do this and it works, which I doubt, then you will be responsible for the murder of the Kazimeer and the last ivory dragon. Do you want such a crime on your head?*"

"Who's will know?" Jaron countered. "Who's know where ju is?"

"*My Weaver. The one we need to find. The only way we will accomplish that is if you put aside this foolish idea about Banishing and just go to the Halls.*" The boy ignored him. Landon tried desperately to gain some control over his movements, but it seemed that every time he nearly grabbed hold his mental fingers would slip. Panic and fear gripped him. What would happen if a Weaver Banished him? He didn't want to consider it and continued to speak calmly to the boy.

"*Would you just stop for a moment and listen to me.*"

"I's should 'ave done dis from da start. Lis'nen to ju is wha' got me in dis mess in da first place. And if's I's kill ju…good!"

Landon tried to think of something to say to prevent him from going anywhere except to the Halls when he suddenly felt uneasy. Something was wrong. He peered out through Jaron's eyes but saw nothing out of order. Still, something felt wrong.

He called out urgently, "*Jaron!*"

"Shut up."

"*Jaron stop! Now!*"

"Eat me bo…" He trailed off and slowed down his pace, looking all around at the surrounding forest and wondered, as Landon did, what was different. Then it occurred to Jaron. It was quiet; no birds, no wind, nothing. Landon connected to the boy's thought and also noticed the eerie silence. Jaron continued to stare around at the trees, licking his lips uncertainly.

Landon said firmly, "*Go!*" The boy nodded to himself and began to move again. "*Faster. Move!*"

Jaron broke into a sprint, but it didn't last long when he collided into a wall. He landed flat on his back and quickly lifted his head up, however nothing was there.

"*Go!*" Landon cried again.

Jaron tried only more tentatively this time. There was something blocking him. He turned back the way he had come, went no more than three steps, and ran into another invisible barrier. Soon, he discovered, he was surrounded.

Landon was beginning to panic and tried to calm his thoughts enough to think clearly. If he had his body, he could morph and fly out…how high were these walls?

"Try to climb them," he called frantically to Jaron, who already had the same idea.

Jaron leapt up and tried to grab hold of an edge, but he only fell back to the ground. Then he noticed they had another problem; the invisible wall he had tried to climb was pushing against his foot with mild strength. Jaron was on his feet again and placed his hands carefully on the wall, feeling it move him backwards across the ground.

"We's bein' squeezed," he said in almost a singsong way. Landon heard the desperate fear in the boy's tone and wondered if his emotions had anything to do with that. Still, he had to remain composed.

"Go under," Landon suggested, cursing the fact that all he could do was advise.

Jaron tried to dig but the wall kept pushing him away. He walked away from the wall coming toward him and bumped into the one that was behind. He reached out to either side of him and his fingertips brushed against more unseen barriers. Landon heard the boy's breath coming out in short, sharp gasps, and felt his panic rise to new levels.

Screaming a curse, Jaron drew his knife and tried to fight what he couldn't see. The wall shattered the blade, leaving him holding the wooden hilt. The space was becoming much smaller when Landon felt something through the boy; actually it was what he sensed.

"Look up!" he demanded. Jaron did helplessly and saw what Landon had sensed. Their ideas connected again. *"Do it!"*

Using all of his strength, Jaron sprang upward.

DARK WORKINGS

Most of the streets were empty and dark. It rained earlier that day, not only washing away the stink in the streets but also a dozen more acres of crops. The wet stones made the moon shimmer off of them so that it was actually nice to watch your feet walk instead of looking where you were going.

Unfortunately for the young couple, they hadn't been watching. Had they, they might not have ventured down the dark street, where a group of four men waited in an alley for people such as them. They were grabbed before they could cry out. The young husband fought against three of the group, while the young wife was pushed up against the alley wall by the fourth, who slapped her every time she called out for her husband. The husband was beaten to the ground and kicked repeatedly in the side until he could do no more than lie there and grunt with each blow. The fourth man tore at the wife's dress, while keeping both her wrists held in his grip. She cried and pleaded but only received another slap to keep her silent.

"Hey!" he called out over his shoulder, while trying to undo his trousers. "Haul him up. I want him to see this."

Two of the men grabbed the husband under the arms and pulled him to his feet. One yanked the man's limp head back by his hair, while the other slapped him to make his eyes open.

"Now you watch!" one hissed in the husband's ear. "Watch while we do her. Maybe we'll do you too."

The young husband found a burst of energy fed by rage and struggled against the hold on him. He was punched in the stomach by the third man, which made him double over, and had his head pulled up again by his hair. The fourth man was still trying to undo his trousers while the wife fought him. He grabbed her hair and slammed her head against the stone wall, making her body sag.

It was then that the four men heard the faint whistling coming from the street. The fourth man hissed at the others to be quiet and slammed his hand over the wife's mouth, while watching the end of the alley. The whistling became louder until a silhouette stood directly at the mouth of the alley. The group kept their victims silent and remained motionless, hoping the figure would continue on its way. When it didn't and continued to do nothing but whistle, the fourth man became agitated.

"Hey!" he called out. "Whistlin' man!"

The figure stopped whistling and turned its head toward them, pointing to itself as if to say, "Who? Me?"

"Best get lost before you find some trouble," the fourth one warned. The figure turned down the alley and walked slowly toward them. "Ah pox me!" He looked over at the third man and jerked his head toward the figure. "Take care of it."

The third man drew a dagger and advanced on the figure quickly. He pointed the dagger at the tall man who came into view and growled, "If you don't want this in your throat, you best turn around right now and keep walking."

The stranger looked down at the dagger and pushed it aside casually, while glancing over the third man's shoulder at the scene. He shook his head.

"I'm glad to see such savagery still running wild but even this is a bit too crude for me." He looked directly at the fourth man and grinned. "Can't get excited without forcing yourself on a woman? At least try to hold onto some dignity. Woo her away from her gentle sir, get her drunk, something…but this?" He looked over to the young husband still being held up by the two group members. "And you. You should know better than to bring such a delicate creature into the night streets. Bet you won't do that again, will you?" The husband barely managed to shake his head.

The fourth man stared at the stranger in complete amazement. He snapped at the third man, "Shut him up!"

The third man moved to strike the stranger with his knife, but the man grabbed his wrist and twisted the dagger from his hand. The wife made a muffled scream when she saw the attack and the fourth man slapped her silent again. The stranger held onto the third man's wrist tightly but leveled a hard stare at the fourth member.

"Even *I* do not strike women. I'll kill them, but I'll never strike them." He glanced down at the man he was holding onto and pushed him back against the wall. He clapped his hands rapidly. "All right, boys. Fun's over. Let'um go."

The four men laughed quietly and exchanged knowing glances. The stranger smiled. "I made a jest and I didn't even know it. How delightful."

The fourth man grinned. "Why the pox should we listen to you?"

The stranger winced. "Such language in front of a lady. Not that she hasn't heard it before but show some degree of respect." He approached the fourth man slowly. "Let her go."

"Burn you!" the man spat.

The stranger shook his head wearily. Without warning, the fourth man was thrown down the alley by some unseen force. The wife flinched from being released so suddenly and then again when the stranger stood next to her and cupped her already swollen face gently.

"I wish I could take those bruises away but you need to remember this."

He turned his head toward the two men holding up her husband. They were also thrown back by invisible hands, letting the young husband fall to the ground. The stranger offered his hand to him and pulled him to his feet. He joined the couple's hands together and spoke to the husband.

"Now take her home and care for her. And remember how you almost lost her because you didn't think." He touched the husband's forehead gently with his finger. The husband stared at him dumfounded but managed to nod. The stranger stepped back and waved them on. "Now go on. Go home."

The couple stumbled quickly out of the alley, holding onto each other tightly. The stranger waited until they were gone and rubbed his hands together while looking at each of the men. "Well, it's just the five of us now."

The four men moved closer but it was obvious that they were wary. The forth man took the initiative and stepped close enough so he and the stranger were face to face.

Hosting the Kazimeer

"Just who do you think you are!" he hissed.

The stranger smiled, admiring the boy's spark. "I think I'm Taj."

The four men exchanged glances then cackled so hard that all of them had tears rolling down their cheeks. And Taj joined them, laughing just as hard and saying in between roars, "Isn't that a hoot!"

The second man finished his laughter first, waved his arms up and down, while he wiggled his fingers, and mimicked sounds of the dead. This prompted the others to laugh harder and Taj joined them for a little while longer. When he had enough, his laughter came to an abrupt stop and he fixed his eyes on the boy who made fun of him.

"No," he chuckled. "It's not like that. It's like this." The second man exploded on the spot while the echo of his laugh still bounced off the alley walls and his blood and insides splattered on the others.

Taj protected himself from the backlash and watched calmly as the other men stood in shock and stared at what had once been their companion. Actually, there wasn't much left to stare at.

"Wasn't that a ride!" Taj grinned.

The three men slowly looked at him in utter silence. The fourth man, obviously the leader of this small group, lunged himself at Taj silently and swiftly, with a long knife already drawn. Taj slammed him up against the wall of the alley without ever raising a finger. He watched in amusement as the young man struggled against the power that held him there.

Taj glanced over to the first man and sneered, "Want to see it again?" The young man ran down the alley, leaving behind the other two. Taj's face twisted with disgust. That had been a bad choice for the boy to make. If Taj hated nothing else it was cowardice.

The black stone glowed white and a streak of power followed the young man down the alley and around the corner. The young man made it no more than four steps into the street before he was melted down to where there was nothing left but his smoldering boots. When Taj turned back to the other two, the third man who had been sent to 'take care of him' and 'shut him up' was trying to get the leader down from the wall but was having no luck against Taj's power.

"Now, now," Taj said and released the leader from his hold.

The man fell straight to the ground, barely caught himself from smashing his face into the stones, and then lunged again for Taj, much to the distress of the third man, who was encouraging him to leave. Taj froze the leader in the middle of his run and walked around him slowly.

"You still wish to attack an enemy no matter what the odds are against you." He stopped in front of him and smiled. "I like that. But I'll get to you in a minute." He fixed his gaze on the other man who appeared to be debating if he should run or stay. Since he was staying, Taj knew he was worth something. He wiggled his index finger at him. "You. Come here." The young man stayed rooted to his spot and the color drained from his face. Taj growled impatiently and enunciated slowly, "You...come...here...now."

With a twist from his mind, Taj pulled the man to him, stopping him just a step away from where he stood. The young man opened his mouth to speak and

Taj waited curiously. Would he plead for life or whip out an insulting quip? Instead, the young man's mouth closed and he said nothing. With lightning speed Taj grabbed the back of the boy's head.

"Now, let's see what you got in there." The boy would have struggled if he could, but Taj's mind grip prevented him from breathing, let alone moving.

He found what he wanted to know. The boy was not a leader but an excellent follower. Loyal, trustworthy, obedient and his connections with the higher, criminal leaders were few at best and not at all solid. Still, he had the perfect makings for the host of his Mytock creations. He released the young man, who staggered back breathing heavily, then froze him, and turned his attention back to the leader. He released him from the Holding spell and immediately the leader started to attack again. Then he thought better of it and remained still with a defiant expression that Taj found delightful.

"So tell me all that you know," Taj grinned. When the leader refused he used mild force. When he still refused Taj used greater force. But even as the young man lay on the ground sobbing about who he knew and what they did, Taj still felt him thinking and planning how he would backstab him. Taj could hardly wait for it to come.

Once the immediate business was taken care of, Taj took both of his new serfs back to the castle and put them with the others he gathered that evening. He always enjoyed scouting the Land for new information and talent. Most of the people he gathered tonight would be used for Mytocks, but a few, such as the young leader, would be useful in other areas. He couldn't help but feel a warm glow inside of him knowing that he made the streets just a little safer than they had been. He did so care about the Land.

He had left his new servants in the care of a few Mytocks and was heading for his personal chamber when he heard,

"My lord."

Taj glanced over his shoulder, looked surprised, and turned around with his arms out-stretched to embrace Commander Grec. "Tell me it's good news." He gave her a quick hug and took a step away from the stunning woman.

"Do I ever have anything else to report?" Grec grinned wickedly.

"Your modesty is one of your best qualities." Taj smiled and gestured for her to follow. "Come. Let us talk in more pleasant surroundings." They didn't speak again until they entered an elaborate sitting chamber. He offered her a chair, walked to a small table with a fresh pitcher of wine on it, poured two glasses, then sat across from her, as he handed her one. "So, tell me. What brings you all the way from the Soil providence?"

"An update," Grec stated, took a sip of wine, then continued. "And to have your approval, of course, before I proceed any further." Taj leaned slightly forward and waited while Grec took another sip, licked her lips, then smiled. "Did you know the morphers are gathering and hiding?"

"I suspected." Taj shook his head slightly, then a smile slowly spread across his face. "Why? Have you found?"

"I have found," Grec stated triumphantly.

Taj scooted forward in his seat. "Where?"

"Archway," Grec answered sweetly as she swirled her cup around.

"Archway!" Taj jumped to his feet with a smile splitting his face. "That is so perfect!"

"Mmm, I know. One of my scouts reported they are gathered in the inner city."

"All of them?"

"From what I understand, a large portion. They're keeping a low profile. In fact my scout admitted he found out by accident. He happened into an alehouse and noticed how slow business was, but the owner was just restocking. So he watched for business to pick up and when it didn't, came to the conclusion that the owner was housing more than just rats. But if you ask me, it sounds like they're planning an attack."

"There couldn't be *that* many of them," Taj muttered. "Besides, Archway is huge. There's no way they could overcome my forces there."

"Should I dispatch your army to finish off the nest?" Taj didn't answer right away and Grec did not ask again knowing how dangerous that could be. Taj finally shook his head slowly.

"No. Not yet. They're not planning an attack. They're gathering. Archway *is* huge, so what better place to round up all the morphers, then move them elsewhere." He turned toward her. "How is the mood of the people there?" Grec teetered her hand back and forth, and Taj grinned. "The Soil Count resides there, doesn't he?" She nodded slowly. "Here's what you do and if you do this right, Archway will be firmly set in place. There must be figure-heads, other than the Count."

"Indeed. Quite a few, actually."

"Assassinate some. Not all, just enough so it's noticed." He thought about it some more. "Take a few children too but make sure it's evenly distributed among the commoners as well as the nobles."

"Children, my lord?" Grec asked looking a bit confused.

Taj raised half his lip into a playful sneer. "Morphers eat children, you know."

Grec suddenly understood and rose to her feet. "And tie it all to the Soil Count."

"Loosely at first, then tighter, but never outright. Let the people make up their own rumors and soon they will be screaming for his blood. Then we destroy the nest of foul, child-eating morphers who are the Soil Count's vulgar army for the ex-Kazimeer."

"And the people will cheer your name."

Taj gave her a half-cocked smile. "As they should."

"It will be done immediately, my lord."

"Let me know when Archway is secure," Taj said, gave her a quick kiss on the cheek and then an even look that clearly meant dismissal. Once he was alone, he sat back in his chair, swirling the wine around in his cup.

What was Abbnar up to? This sudden horde of morphers didn't just decide to do this on their own. Perhaps Abbnar was building an army but Taj was about to slice it apart. Satisfied, he finished his wine in a single gulp and left the sitting chamber. No sooner did he make it down four halls when the familiar call came to his ears.

"My lord?"

Taj groaned inwardly. He turned to see the servant cowering slightly, with his head bowed, and his hands wringing his smock.

"What?" he asked irritably.

"My lord, Second Dapp thought you would be interested to know that your…" He swallowed. "…Mytocks have returned."

"Very well. Tell Second Dapp I'll be with him shortly." He stalked off, not bothering to wait as the servant bowed at the waist and mumbled his answer.

Within what Taj thought was a short amount of time, he entered what had once been called the High Room but now was called the Justice Hall. He sat down in the uncomfortable white throne and reminded himself again that he must have it removed. He'd just been so busy that such small details escaped him. He waited until Dapp was at his side before he allowed his sentries to admit the three Mytocks.

The head Mytock moved soundlessly toward him. These were by far the best batch he had ever made. They were silent, quick, and deadly. They remembered everything they saw with such clarity and gave those memories freely to him. Yes, it was good to have reliable creatures working for him again. He was proud. The Mytock gave its cloak a sweeping motion and knelt before him with its head bowed.

"I bring news to you Master," it said in a breathy whisper. Taj saw Dapp shift nervously when the Mytock spoke, a common reaction. He waited for the Mytock to continue. "Several contacts have been made throughout the Land to locate your ring. They search now for it."

"Any progress?"

"Not yet, Master, but it cannot be long."

"What else?" The Mytock hesitated, which surprised Taj. "Well?"

"We believe we found the one you seek."

Taj leaned forward in the throne. "Which one? I seek many."

"The one with the great power. The one you wanted us to search for during our travels."

Attempting to hide his anxiousness, Taj commanded, "Show me."

Instantly the image came to his mind. Taj studied the face that flashed before him and shook his head. "That's not him."

"Forgive me, Master, but we felt his power. It was quite strong."

"That's not him. Too young." Taj slumped back in the throne. "But if you cross paths with that one again, bring him to me. I might be able to use him."

"Yes, Master." The Mytock bowed deeply and left with the others.

When the Mytock said they found the one with the power, Taj knew it was too good to be true. He'd been searching for him ever since he was lost twenty years ago. At the time, he'd only been a small child, barely four or five years, but his power was so intense, so raw Taj knew he had to have it, had to harness it. It was actually a stroke of luck since he'd just returned from the Pit and was beginning to build up his strength. It so happened that his camp was near the same place where a mother walked daily with her small son. At first, he didn't know what the surge of power was around the same time each morning and began to fear that it was Abbnar. But when no attack came, he went to investigate and stumbled onto the greatest find ever.

After watching for a few days, he decided to take him. He killed the woman; no sense in having some distraught mother making a fuss over her lost son and ruining his plans, and took the boy in. He moved his camp and began to slowly teach the child about his gifts. Light, but he was strong, even then. By now he must be so powerful he may even rival him. Then one morning he awoke and found the boy was gone. He searched but never found him. Now he spread the word wherever he went about the boy, hoping he could locate him once more. It would be a great advantage to him if he could harness that power. But no doubt the boy was probably dead.

He studied the image again that the Mytock sent him, hoping he'd find some trace in that face of the one he wanted. But it couldn't be. The boy he had must be twenty-five or so by now. This one had the face of an infant. Too young, far too young.

Disappointed, Taj glanced up to Dapp, who was still standing at his side.

"My lord, you wanted to see me?"

"Yes." Taj nodded. "I want to discuss Archway." He rose from the throne and walked across the hall. Dapp followed obediently. "We'll be cleaning out some morphers there soon."

DISCOVERIES

Jaron caught the branch hanging ten feet overhead and dangled from it while his fingers tried to claw into the wood. He risked a look down, but still was unable to see anything other than the folds of dirt being pushed closer together. He swung his legs up to grip the branch, hung upside down, and wondered if he was clear of the barrier. Those walls seemed awful high when he tried to climb them. The next branch was only a little further away and if he just stretched his fingers he could probably grab it, but he was too terrified to do anything other than cling to where he was. Landon urged him to move higher but Jaron suddenly didn't have the strength to move. Then he started to lose his grip.

Actually something was pulling him down. Jaron looked at the ground again and both he and Landon were caught between conflicting feelings of confusion and dread. A large, empty hole appeared within the confines of the invisible walls and unseen hands were trying to pry Jaron loose and make him fall into the hole. Jaron let out a panicked cry and Landon felt the boy's thoughts whirl around in his mind in a desperate attempt to formulate a plan; so was he. Landon frantically searched for a solution, while Jaron fiercely tried to maintain his hold. Landon heard the boy cry out again and peered through his eyes, only to stare into a pair of beady, black ones.

Landon's first reaction was panic, remembering that Blasdon had those same eyes. Then he noticed these eyes belonged to a phoenix. He had only seen one or two of them before but there was no mistaking those rich brown feathers and the sheer size of it. They were larger than falcons and hawks by nearly doubling, sometimes tripling their size. The reason Jaron screamed was because the phoenix had dug its talons into his forearms, but not as an attack. It was trying to hold him up against whatever was yanking him down into that hole. Jaron winced as another phoenix sunk talons into each of his legs and hung onto him. Landon never saw a phoenix come near people before. They just didn't.

The tugging between the phoenixes and the invisible being went on for several long moments before it gave up and released Jaron. A deep sound came from the ground, as if the Land was moaning about its defeat, and then the hole closed over. The sounds of the forest returned. Once that happened, the two phoenixes released Jaron and flew away as if they suddenly had other things to do. Jaron automatically fell to the ground and landed on his chest with a hard thud.

He sucked in gulps of air, trying to recover from the breath he had just lost, and kept his face in the dirt. He didn't want to move or see anything. He especially didn't want to remember there was someone inside of his mind. He just wanted to lie there and forget about demons without eyes, invisible walls, and large holes that tried to drag him into them. He wanted to sleep and almost did until he heard the shuffle of footsteps moving toward him.

He bolted upright but remained on his knees and blinked several times at the person who stood before him. Why did she look familiar? When she spoke, though, he and Landon remembered.

"All right. You're worthy."

This was the same girl from last night. The one who vanished into nothing and could hear Landon. Jaron got to his feet so she wouldn't be looking down at him and now had to look down at her. She barely came up to his shoulder, which meant she was really tiny, since Jaron barely came up to most other men's shoulders.

"Werdee? Of wha'?"

"My protection," the girl answered in a matter of fact tone.

"Did ju do dat?" Jaron asked carefully and jerked his head toward where the barrier had been.

"Well I had to be sure. I don't go around protecting just anyone. They have to prove to me that they can take care of themselves." She smiled wickedly and batted her eyes at him. Jaron, however, was furious. So was Landon.

"You twisted, sick, little whore."

The girl clicked her tongue and shook her head sadly. "I can hear you, Kazimeer."

"I know you can, sweetheart," Landon sneered in return.

Her eyes went wide. "Ooo! You called me sweetheart! No one's ever called me that before."

"Small wonder. You probably kill them before they can open their mouths."

"Now don't try to flatter me anymore, Kazimeer, or I may just snatch you up for a husband."

Landon growled sharply and said to Jaron, *"Let's go. Banishing would be better than listening to this child any longer."*

For once, Jaron didn't argue and moved briskly around the girl. However, she was immediately at his side, walking with her hands clasped behind her back.

"Banishing?" she asked in her sweet voice. "That would not be the smartest thing you could do, Jaron."

Jaron nearly tripped over his feet and rounded on her. "How's do ju know me name?"

"Well of course I know your name," she stated wearily, as if Jaron was the dumbest person alive. "And a fine one you've picked for yourself too. Do you know what it means?" Jaron didn't answer and moved quickly through the forest trying to get away from this girl. She remained at his side.

"What does she mean, 'picked for yourself'?" Landon asked curiously. Jaron ignored him too.

"He's had plenty of names," the girl answered for him. "He just liked Jaron the most and kept it after he finally freed himself."

"From where?"

"Slavery."

"Slavery?" Landon snorted loudly. *"Nonsense. There hasn't been a slave-trade in over three hundred years."*

"That's how much you know Kazimeer."

"Yes, I do know. There hasn't been a slave-trade in three hundred years," Landon insisted.

"Looks!" Jaron shouted and came to a halt. "Would da two of ju's shut up." He pointed a finger at the girl. "Ju go 'way and leave me alone. And ju," he directed the remark at Landon, "jus shut up."

"I will not shut up until you take me to the Halls."

"That's a sound piece of advice," the girl said with a short nod.

"Wha' do ju's know 'bout its?" Jaron hissed.

"I know that if you Banish him, you'll be dead within five minutes. He is your only source of protection right now and if he goes, you go. The Training Halls would be the safest place for both of you. I could help you get there."

"Why's ifs he's goes, I's go?"

"Because *he* will want you alive because you contain the Kazimeer and *he* wants to finish him properly. But if the Kazimeer is killed by some clumsy spell, and *he* finds out you did it, then *he* will not only be plenty pissed but may just kill you out of spite."

"Who's 'he'?" Landon asked, already knowing the answer.

"Taj, of course," the girl stated.

"So," Jaron said slowly, "ifs I's Banish dis voice in me head and...Taj finds out 'bout its, ju're sayin' he's be's pissed?"

"I would think so."

Jaron leaned closer and grinned. "Or he's may jus pat me on da back fure doin' his work fure him."

"What!"

The girl blinked at him. "You can't seriously be thinking of working with Taj?"

"Why's not? Ju seem to know a good deal of facts fure someone wit jus a passin' in'rest." He ignored the girl's stunned expression. "Looks, tell dis Taj person I's sell da voice to da highest bidder."

"You'll sell me!? You can't do that!"

Jaron clicked his tongue and smiled. "Guess it'll change jur mind 'bout dare bein' a slave-trade, won't its?"

Landon was too outraged to reply.

The girl sniffed a laugh, "You think *I'm* working for Taj?"

"How's else would ju know so much, likes how's dis Weaver is in me head?"

"He's not a Weaver, he's a morpher."

"Weaver, merfer, he's a pain!"

"True, but so are you. That doesn't mean someone should Banish you, does it?"

"So how's did ju know he's in me head?" Jaron asked suspiciously.

The girl sighed irritably, "Look, I was asked to watch out for your ass." She paused and deliberately stared at Jaron's backside. "And what a cute ass it is." Jaron growled under his breath and began walking again. The girl scurried to catch up with him. "I'm just trying to help."

"Help!" Jaron cried. "Wha' help I's need from a girl who's tried to kill me!"

"It was a test. Simply a test and you passed. Let's hope you don't pass any of Taj's tests or else he'll really become interested in you. Honestly, I think he already has. With my help, he'll never find you."

"I's fine," Jaron grumbled.

The girl spread her hands. "You have my help anyway." She turned on her heels and began walking away. Then she turned back, wearing a sweet smile. "Just so there are no hard feelings, I will give you my name. It's Jynx."

Landon barked out a laugh, "*It figures.*"

"Dat's da perfect name fure ju," Jaron said with a tight grin.

"As Jaron is the perfect name for you. However, 'Beautiful Light' does not seem to fit this filthy, smelly thief I see before me." Jaron was about to snap a curse at her but she threw her head back, giggled, and disappeared.

Jaron blinked slowly several times then mumbled, "I's dinn't imagine dat, den."

"*No,*" Landon stated and asked, "*Ju never saw a Weaver Transfer?*"

Jaron growled, "Stop makin' fun of me."

He started back to the main road. Landon was startled. Making fun of him? He didn't make fun of him. The boy was certainly touchy. For that matter, so was he.

"*Where are we going?*" he asked sharply. "*To find the highest bidder?*"

"To dat village. Wha' ju call its? Trisot?"

"*Tirsek. And why? Is there a Kazimeer sale going on there?*"

"Light, but ju don't likes its when someone threatens ju. Maybes ju stop and tink next time 'fore ju threaten someone."

Landon momentarily held his tongue. He couldn't think of a retort to that statement, so instead he asked, "*Then why are we going there?*"

"I's want to sleep in a bed, I's want to eats real food, and I's need pesses. So, da sooner ju lemme do wha' I's need to do, da sooner we's be's goin' to jur Halls."

"*This delay can cost us more than just losing traveling time. Didn't you hear what that girl said?*"

"Ju believes her?"

"*She's obviously a strong Weaver, she can hear me in your mind, and she seems to know about things that no one could possibly know. So yes, I believe her when she says that…that person may already be looking for me…you…us, and I think it would be wise if we's did what she said.*"

"Stop its!" Jaron snapped sharply.

"*Wha'?*"

"Ju're doin' its 'gain! Leave me speech alone!"

"*I wasn't picking on jur…*" He trailed off in utter shock. Oh Light! He was talking with that Granate accent. The same way the boy picked up on his words he was now picking up on the boy's. No, no, no! He wouldn't. He was the Kazimeer and the Kazimeer didn't speak with such an accent. He would have to watch what he said. "*I wasn't doing it on purpose.*"

"Ju don't seem to do lots of tings on poypose. Ju don't want to be's in me mind, ju don't want to take over me hand. Ju jus don't 'ave lots of control over jurself, do ju's?"

"Let's just get to Tirsek, get your business out of the way, and get to the Training Halls. Agreed?"

"Fine." Jaron shut him out again and returned to the main road.

**   **

"Ma'lord?"

Taj turned around and had to glance down to see who spoke to him. He smiled warmly. "Yes, Webben?"

The boy smiled in return and held out a piece of parchment. "This just came for you. I was also told to tell you that there's a present for you in the High Roo...Justice Hall."

Taj took the note but didn't read it yet. Instead, he bent down on one knee so he could stare the boy in the eye. "You know, Webben, you have been here for a while. What do you think?"

"I don't know. It's all right, I suppose."

"Am I as bad as you thought?"

Webben's eyes grew wide with horror. "I never said you were bad, lord Blasdon. I swear, I never did!"

"I know," Taj reassured. "What I meant was, do you like it here? Will you stay?"

Webben shifted from one foot to the other. "I...I'm not sure."

Taj's eyes widened slightly. "Not sure?"

"I feel like I'm betraying the Kazimeer if I do."

"I see." Taj nodded sincerely. "Webben, I'm going to tell you something and I want you to remember it always. Understand?" The boy nodded wordlessly. Taj placed his hands gently on the boy's shoulders. "Whoever is in charge of the Land, whether it is the Kazimeer or I, remember your duty is to help the Land. The Land needs boys like you; energetic, smart boys who will grow up to be energetic, smart men. I'm trying to help the Land and need someone like you to help me do so. I don't want you to stay because you feel you have nowhere else to go. If that's the case, we'll solve that problem, but don't feel guilty about staying because you think you're betraying anyone. The only thing you would be betraying if you left, would be the Land."

Webben chewed on his bottom lip. "I want to help the Land, but..." He trailed off.

Taj smiled and ruffled the boy's hair. "Why don't we give it a little more time, all right?" The boy nodded and Taj rose to his feet. "Well now, I suppose you should be getting back to your work."

"Yes, ma'lord." The boy's shoulders slumped and he began to leave.

"Webben," Taj called out and waited for him to turn around. "I understand the Feshare' are in town to raise the people's mood a little. Would you like to go with me to see them perform tonight?"

Webben's eyes widened with excitement. "Would I!"

Taj smiled. "Well then finish up what you're doing so we can go."

"I will!" Webben nodded eagerly and charged out of the chamber.

Taj held his smile after the boy left. How perfect this would be. The people seeing him out in town entertaining a servant boy; it would do wonders for his image. Besides, he liked Webben. He liked the potential he had, the potential to be a dutiful, loyal servant to him. He always liked children for that reason. They were so easy to mold when they were young, having no real ambitions or ideas of their own. And if they did, he could usually change their minds. He always pictured himself as being a good father but never had the opportunity to find out, despite several attempts before and after the Pit. He supposed he was just never meant to have children of his own and must settle for the spawn of others.

He remembered the note he was holding and tore it open.

My lord,

Archway has been taken. Also, enjoy the gift I've had my men bring you. I'm sure you'll find it acceptable. Perhaps even worth reward for such excellent service, as always.

Your best Commander,

Grec

It couldn't have been clearer or more enjoyable to read. In fact, Taj read it over and over as he walked to the Justice Hall. He couldn't wait to hear the gruesome details from Grec when he saw her again. No doubt she would relish every moment of it. He wondered just how many morphers were killed? No matter, if Grec said Archway was his, then they were all wiped clean from the town. He tossed the note into the air casually and raised his hand, having a small flame erupt from it, burning the note completely before it ever touched the ground.

Upon entering the Justice Hall, he saw the four Mytocks and then his eyes fell on who they flanked. His heart leapt into his throat with joy but then crashed disappointedly when he took a good long stare. It was not who he thought it was; it was not Abbnar, but the prisoner was definitely related.

It only occurred to him then that he hadn't actually *seen* Abbnar since he returned two decades before. He wasn't surprised he could remember what he looked like, though. He burned that man's face into his memory the entire time he'd been in the Pit, so he wouldn't forget. Now standing there in his presence must be one of Abbnar's own. He approached slowly and studied the man surrounded by Mytocks. His hair was mostly white with just a hint of black and those cold blue eyes stared back defiantly at him. But his face, that face was what caught Taj off guard, however briefly. Although there were wrinkles and sags, the resemblance was close…very close.

"Well," he said as if greeting an old friend and grinned, standing before the prisoner. "What is this?"

Although he asked the question to the prisoner, a Mytock answered. "This is the being you have been searching for, Master."

Taj glanced toward the Mytock stiffly and normally would have just destroyed it for speaking without permission, but he was in too good a mood right now. "No, he isn't. Close, though, and that's good enough." He stepped closer to the prisoner and whispered, "I would much rather have had your father." He was taking a stab at the relationship but assumed it must be correct. The resemblance was too close to be anything else.

The man took a breath as if to sigh wearily then suddenly spat into Taj's face. The Mytocks reacted immediately, holding the man tight and sending quick surges of pain through him that made his body arch.

Taj held up his hand. "Enough." The man's body went slack and his head hung for a moment but then stared up at Taj hatefully again. "I'm glad to see that unpredictable temper still runs strong in your blood." He wiped the spittle off on the man's tunic, waved his hands, and the Mytocks released him. The man was a morpher but had no real power, so Taj was perfectly in control. He walked around the prisoner slowly and spoke softly, as the man continued to stare straight ahead. "Does it not bother you that you will be the one destroyed and not your father? Are you not the least bit miffed that your body grows old, while his remains young? That you are nothing but a puppet he can dangle wherever he wants? You know, all you have to do is tell me where he is and I'll exchange you for him." He stood before the man again.

The man's sharp eyes rose to meet his but he still said nothing. Taj waited as the silence stretched. He finally laughed and shook his head.

"I would have been surprised if you did agree. I also would have had a lot more respect for Abbnar if he had taught his children how to be so underhanded. But he has not and you stand there like a statue, thinking that if you say nothing you are being loyal." He leaned an inch away from the man's face. "You are being foolish. I take what I want, surely your father has told you that. I will find out where he is whether you tell me or not."

"I doubt it."

Taj jerked back when that low voice finally spoke. He chuckled, "Light! You have a tongue!"

"Oh, I have a lot more than that," the man sneered. However, he was also silently calling out, *"Father? Father do it!"*

"I can Transfer you now. I have the connection," came the urgent response.

"Father, you can't. He'll find you and the encampment. He'll trace your power there. You must do the only thing left for you to do."

"I won't! I'm getting you out of there."

"And risk everyone's life just to save mine? That's foolish and you know it. Do it now, father."

"No!"

"What are you doing?" Taj asked curiously, feeling the strange sensation coming from the man.

"Father, now! There's no more time. By your hand, not his!"

"NO!"

"I'm dead anyway. Do it!" Taj's eyes grew wide as he suddenly realized what the man was doing. *"Papa, PLEASE!"*

Taj reached out with his power to shield the man's mind but another rush of energy made it there a split second before his did. It streaked through the man's head like fire, consuming everything. Within seconds, the man's mind was ash and his body crumpled to the floor in a heap.

Taj screamed a curse to the ceiling and irritably walked away from the dead man's body. Abbnar would kill his own son before he'd let him have him. He underestimated Abbnar; he never thought the old man would do something so worthy of him. He glanced toward the body and debated butchering it before leaving it for Abbnar to find. Instead, he would have to settle for what was convenient.

He looked over to the Mytocks. "Have two sentries take the body to the center of Sevatzer and display it. Have them tell the people he was an assassin left over from the boy Kazimeer and had been sent to poison the Land. Tell them I never touched him, but the power of the Kyriea struck down this evil that continues to linger in our Land."

Taj, you know that's not true. Since when did you start to lie? You were always such an honest child, even if that honesty is misplaced. Why do you say things that are not true?

No, it wasn't completely true. Damn but if his conscience didn't decide to speak up at the most inconvenient times. He shoved it aside and continued with his orders. "Be certain they know his body is only being displayed to warn those who are still loyal to the boy Kazimeer's darkness. Make sure the message is spread throughout the entire Land. Go!"

Two Mytocks jumped to his command and began to scoop up the body. Perhaps it was the way the light touched the dead man's face or perhaps it was the look of peace he now wore, but something in Taj's mind clicked.

"Wait!" he shouted. The Mytocks remained still, holding the man's body up by his limp arms. Taj stalked toward the body and grabbed the face, staring into it intently. After a moment, he released it. "Take him."

The Mytocks dragged the body out of the hall, while Taj let his mind slowly and carefully piece together this puzzle. If he changed the hair and eye color and smoothed the wrinkles in the skin…it could be. And if *that* was the case, then the boy could certainly have the same power. And if *that* were true, then he may be the same boy he'd been searching for all these years. Taj laughed out loud and stared up at the ceiling. Could his luck have been so good so long ago and he not even know it?

Leave him alone.

Taj growled in frustration. What was with him? Since when did he have second thoughts about anything he set his mind to? When did he develop a sense of guilt?

Taj, I will not let you corrupt him. He's all I have left. For my sake, leave him alone.

Taj shook his head to clear it. The words sounded so clear in his mind, he began to wonder if perhaps Abbnar was playing some type of trick on him. But he didn't feel the old man's presence anywhere. It must be a part of his tired, old mind that decided he should not take advantage of what laid in his path. He would stamp out that part of him as quickly as possible. There was no room for morals when one is trying to gain leverage. He laughed again. Could the boy in the Mytocks vision actually be the *same* one he lost all those years before? Taj's laughing abruptly stopped.

And the one he recently let slip through his fingers?

"Dapp!" he roared and charged out of the Justice Hall. The age. The boy's age was what had thrown him. "*Dapp!*" If he was who Taj thought he was, then he would age differently. He would appear around the age of...Oh dear Light! "*DAPP!*"

A group of servants came pouring out of every crevice, responding to his shouts. One approached him tentatively. "My lord. Second Dapp is not---"

Taj grabbed the servant by the front of her dress and raised her off the floor. "Then find him!" he hissed as he shook the woman. "Find him now!" He threw the woman down, sending her sliding across the polished floor. She quickly scrambled to her feet, half bowed to him, and scurried down the hall, telling the other servants to help her look.

Taj stopped in the middle of the hall and forced himself to calm down. In his moment of panic and anger, he'd forgotten himself. He didn't need the help of petty servants to find Dapp. He closed his eyes and pulled on his bond with his Second. It took only moments for him to intrude into the man's mind.

"*Dapp.*"

He'd obviously caught Dapp off guard. "My lord?"

"*Who else would it be! Come see me.*"

"Yes, my lord."

"*No, right now! Stop whatever you're doing and run to me, this moment. Not in a minute, not in a second...NOW!*"

"Yes, my lord," came Dapp's winced response.

Taj knew he'd caused pain in his Second's mind but didn't care. He wanted to hurt someone. He was furious with himself for making such a foolish mistake. The servant he'd sent running off came hurrying back down.

"My lord," she said quickly, "Second Dapp is---"

Taj didn't wait to hear anymore. He roared in rage and shot out his arm. His necklace glowed white and a ray of light exploded from his hand, and struck the woman in her middle. The light quickly spread throughout her entire body, like a web of fire. Taj enjoyed her screams and watched in delight as the light ate away at her slowly. When there was nothing left but dust, he looked down the hall where a small group of servants were standing, staring from him to the pile of dust with wide, disbelieving eyes.

For a moment he didn't care if they saw what he did, but servants talked and soon that talk would be out in the streets. Then he'd have to worry about regaining the people's trust. It would be far too much ground to lose over one servant. He released his power into each of their minds quickly and carefully, twisting the brief memory until it snapped and faded. When he released them, they blinked sleepily and stared at each other in slight confusion. None of them would remember what happened to this woman; they would only notice that she was no longer around.

Taj sneered at them and pointed to the pile on the floor. "Can't I get anyone to clean this place properly?"

Instantly, the five servants descended upon the pile of dust and began scooping up handfuls of it. Taj returned to the Justice Hall and waited for Dapp, who arrived promptly and out of breath.

He calmly explained to his Second that he wanted as much information about the boy as possible. His name, his age, where he came from, *everything* and he wanted it now. After Dapp left to make the necessary preparations, Taj went to a balcony where he could overlook Sevatzer and spied two sentries dragging the body toward town. It was quite appropriate that he used Abbnar's son as a symbol of his justice. He may not have found any information about where Abbnar was, but he did put together a puzzle that would cause Abbnar even more pain. That made him smile.

"Ma'lord?"

Taj turned around and saw Webben standing uneasily behind him. Taj slapped his hand to his forehead. "You know, I almost forgot."

"We don't have to go if you're busy, ma'lord."

"Nonsense," Taj said with a smile. "I think we owe this to ourselves." He extended his hand and the boy took it carefully. Taj gave it a light squeeze. "You know, I'll bet there's all sorts of foods down there that are bad for us. What do you say to stuffing ourselves silly?"

Webben nodded with a wide grin. Taj led him out of the castle and walked with him to town. He was not going to take a horse, despite the distance, and wanted everyone to see that he didn't. He would not let anyone think he flaunted his wealth. By the time he arrived, he was pleased to see Abbnar's son placed just as he'd specified with a sign around his neck that said simply 'Land Killer'. Thankfully the Feshare' were performing in the inner city, not the outer, so the stench wouldn't mess up his evening.

Less than an hour later, because he was nowhere near the body, he didn't witness that it suddenly burst into flames and burned quickly, leaving behind nothing but ashes that scattered in the dry wind.

DARRELL

Jaron arrived at Tirsek by suppertime and the smells coming out into the streets made him aware of his stomach and how empty it was. But he had no pieces so first he had to sell the jewels he took back from the Mistress. The easiest and fastest way he could do that was to find a gambling room. If he couldn't sell them or bet them, at least he could pick up some neglected sacks hanging around on the patron's belts. However, if he could avoid doing that tonight, he would. No sense in drawing more attention to himself than necessary.

He dipped into the hushed conversations of people and the one place mentioned the most was called The Fat Dragon. He smiled inwardly at the name only because it bothered the thronge worm so much, and set about finding the place. When he asked where it was, he either received no response or the person sent him wandering all over the town. Several times he heard the thronge worm sigh loudly but he ignored him and continued looking. It must be tucked away somewhere because he should have found it by now.

"Turn around," Landon said.

Jaron casually did so and silently asked, "And?"

"Well, what does the sign say?"

Jaron looked up at the sign hanging over the door directly in front of him. Then he glanced into the window and saw several people laughing, drinking, and gambling. "Da Fat Dragon," he replied full of confidence.

"No. You can't read, can you?" Jaron was furious and stalked off down the street. *"It's the other way, thief boy. Two streets down on your left. You've walked by it about five times now."*

"Why's dinn't ju tell me!"

"You didn't ask."

Jaron headed back down to the deserted street and stopped at a string of shops. There were still several lights lit inside most of them and since he didn't want to be seen peering into windows and looking shady, he reluctantly asked, "Which is its?"

"It's the green sign, over to your right. See it?" Jaron did and approached carefully. He studied the sign and saw the small, fat, green dragon on the corner of it. It looked kind-of cute actually. Landon didn't think so. Dragons weren't supposed to be cute; they were supposed to be ferocious. *"Just get this over with, boy."*

Jaron ducked inside and immediately smelled the food coming from the kitchen. His stomach grumbled, urging him to hurry up, but he had to be cautious. He had lots of expensive jewelry hidden in his jerkin and anyone of these men could easily beat him and take it if they chose to. He had done this far too many times before and knew not to underestimate anyone.

He searched the room and found a table that looked promising. He nonchalantly made his way over toward it, stopping now and then at the other tables so it would look as if he were choosing a game he preferred. When he reached the table surrounded by older, wealthy looking men and women, he casually wedged his way through the small crowd of people near the table and watched. The game was dice. He was good at dice and apparently, so was Landon as he came fully forward and gazed at everything like a child eyeing presents.

"Ooo! This is a big table."

Jaron paid him no attention and concentrated on the game. He must watch for who was the heaviest bidder, make sure he got involved in a game and lost one or two. Then he would up the stakes and bring it all to him in the end. He stood there looking as if he had nothing better to do this night and watched with amusement. Sooner or later someone would notice his smug expression and offer him a roll, asking if he could do better.

"No! Fool! Bank it off of the sides, not the back!" Landon shouted at the roller whose roll cost him fifty silver. *"Stupid fool. Never off the back."*

"How's ju know 'bout dice ifs ju da Kazimeer?" Jaron asked silently.

"I was a Second before I was the Kazimeer."

"A second wha'?"

Landon growled. *"Never mind, thief boy, just do what you're going to do so we can move on."*

"I's will ifs ju would shut up!" Jaron snapped.

The thronge worm was interrupting his concentration. He needed to watch everything or he could lose all he had hidden in his jerkin. He didn't want to go begging for work from Mit or Phila again and Light knew he could never go back to the Mistress. The thronge worm had ruined his chances of working for her ever again.

"All three! Roll all three!" Landon shouted excitedly. He was getting more caught up in the game than Jaron was but Jaron wasn't here for the excitement. *"No! Bloody fool! Not two. Take all three and roll. Ah, stupid, ass...I knew it. I just knew it. He lost everything."*

"Shut up!"

"Would you stop telling me to shut up. No one can hear me."

"But me."

"Yes, but you," Landon snapped impatiently. *"I'm minding my own business now, so hush."* He immediately was focused on the game again. *"Roll you ass! Roll!"*

"Do not tells me to hush, thronge worm. Jus shut up!"

"Who are you tellin' to shut up, Scant!"

Jaron slowly turned his head where his eyes met a large, muscular chest. He followed the body up until he saw the hard, scarred face glaring down at him.

"Sorry. I's talkin' to me."

The large man grunted and turned his attention back to the game.

"You shouldn't talk to me out loud, you know," Landon offered.

"I's don't want to talk to ju at all. Don't say anniting."

"How can you let him call you a Scant?"

"He's be's twice me size. He's can call me wha'ever he's wants."

Landon didn't respond and turned back to the game. He became completely absorbed in it again until he heard Jaron grumble and the table was out of his sight. Landon saw through the boy's eyes that the big toad, who called Jaron a Scant, pushed him out of the way.

"Don't let him get away with that!"

"I's find 'nather place," Jaron told him silently.

Landon felt his temper rise quickly; *no one* pushed *him* out of the way. Seg used to push him around all the time and he hated it because he could never do anything about it. He suddenly felt himself more connected to the boy than he had ever been. It was the same odd feeling he had when he momentarily gained control of Jaron's arm. Perhaps it had something to do with his anger. Whatever it was, he knew his words would now be heard and not just by Jaron.

"I suppose big lard asses need more room to spread out."

The toad turned around slowly and fixed his eyes on Jaron, who actually had been the one who spoke the words. Jaron felt sick. He could feel his mouth, knew he had control over it, and yet the voice in his head also had control. And it was getting him in trouble.

"I's sorry," he said quickly and gave the man his boyish grin. That usually disarmed people. However the large toad continued to glare at him. "Talkin' to me 'gain."

"You seem to do that a lot Scant," the toad growled stepping away from the table toward him.

"Yes," Jaron said, bobbing his head up and down. "Yes I's do…because there are no other intelligent minds to speak to otherwise. Yours especially."

"Wha' are ju doin' to me!" Jaron cried to Landon.

"I'm sorry, but I can't stand it when---"

"---stupid, ugly, masses of flesh believe they actually hold some type of brain in their fat heads and can do more than grunt and squeal." Jaron nearly slammed his hand over his mouth to keep the voice from saying more, but he was picked up by the front of his tunic and was staring the large toad in the eye.

"You have an awful big mouth, Scant."

Without his control, Jaron's left hand came up and pointed at the man and his mouth started moving again. "Better to have a big mouth, you pathetic toad, than to have little to no mind whatsoever. And at least what comes out of my mouth doesn't smell so foul."

The sounds of the Fat Dragon were falling quiet as everyone turned to watch what was going on. Luckily for Jaron, his size usually saved him in situations like this and the toad knew it. It would seem unfair and cruel to beat such a small boy when he was such a big man. The toad shook him hard by his tunic a few times then brought him close to his face again.

"One more word out of you, Scant, and I'll shut you up myself."

"And do not call me a Scant, you piss-filled, rotten son of a whore." That finger was pointed in the toad's face again. "I am the Kazimeer."

The toad studied Jaron, who looked like he was going to be sick at any time, then bellowed out a laugh and flung him to the floor. The rest of the Fat Dragon crowd who heard what Jaron's mouth had said also roared with mocking laughter.

94   Hosting the Kazimeer

"The Scant's mad!" the toad called out to the crowd, making sure everyone heard him. He looked down at Jaron still laughing. "Oh Kazimeer, your coach is waiting outside. Why don't you go get in it!" The crowd roared again and Jaron was not so gently escorted out of the Fat Dragon by two of the tavern's Keepers.

He landed face first on the dirt road and made sure he spun around quickly to glare wickedly at the Keepers before they disappeared back into the tavern. He'd been thrown out of taverns before but never because of something like this. He was furious; so furious he wanted to cry and actually found himself swallowing a lump or two in his throat. That's what this voice in his head did to him. It made him cry, made him humiliated, made it so he couldn't get pieces or a bed or food. Within the next hour every tavern and alehouse would know of the boy who claimed to be the Kazimeer and he would be shown the door as soon as he walked in. He got to his feet and dusted himself off before he stalked down the dark street.

"*I'm sorry,*" Landon said gently. He felt the overwhelming flow of shame and hurt in the boy and wanted to ease it. "*It was my fault. I didn't mean to embarrass you. I just wanted to put that big ass in his place.*"

Jaron did not answer until he found a quiet alley that no one else had decided to use as his or her sleeping quarters tonight. He went all the way to the rear and slid down the wall, trembling with rage.

"Ju dinn't want to put annione in dare place. Ju jus wanted to tell errione who's ju is."

"*No, that's not true. I didn't like him calling you a Scant and pushing you around like that.*"

"Liar!" Jaron hissed forcefully. "No, ju dinn't likes him calling *ju* a Scant and pushin' *ju* 'round. Not me. Ju weren't tinkin' 'bout me. Ju don't care 'bout annione but ju."

"*That's not true.*"

"Corse it's true," Jaron grumbled. "Ju jus want errione to know dat ju is da Kazimeer and ju 'ave power. Well, ju ain't da Kazimeer right now. Dey don't sees ju, dey jus sees me. And I's don't 'ave anniting. Do ju hear me, ju…thronge worm! I's 'ave nutin' 'cause of ju!"

"*I'm sorry.*"

"Burn ju, sorry! Now, I's gits to sleep in a bloody alley, and I's gits to go 'ungry, and I's… I's…" Landon heard his voice choking. He never meant for the boy to be so upset. He never meant any harm by this. "I's 'ave nutin' 'cause ju 'ave to let errione know dat ju's da Kazimeer. Well errione knows now at me expense. Tanks *so* much!"

"*I'm sorry,*" Landon repeated. "*Tell me how I can make it up to you.*"

Jaron laughed without humor and shook his head. "Go 'way. Shut up and go 'way." Jaron wiped his nose with the back of his hand, pulled his knees up to his chest, and rested his head on them.

Landon withdrew into the back of Jaron's mind, feeling like the biggest piece of dung in the Land. It was true he never meant any harm to come of this, but everything Jaron said was also true. Ashamed and disgusted, he closed himself away in Jaron's mind and didn't say another word.

Jaron felt him retreat and wanted him to come back just so he could yell at him some more. This was better, though. He could die a happy person if he never heard the word 'Kazimeer' again and if he never heard that voice in his head anymore. He still didn't believe this person was the Kazimeer. The Kazimeer was dead. However, he saw images from the thronge worm of a wealthy home with high walls, embroidered tapestries, gold statues and servants. That added more hatred to his already growing loathing of this person. This person had more than he ever would and still took away what little he could get.

He'd come so close to destroying this person before. How had he done it? He didn't remember and also couldn't remember what had stopped him in the first place. He could feel that person's neck in his hands as he squeezed, but then his grip was broken and he didn't try to get it back. What a fool he was for not killing this being when he had the chance. He would have to take him to those Halls to get rid of him. Or to the one called Taj...he shook his head. Despite what this accursed pain in his head did to him, he couldn't see himself making a deal with someone who called himself by that name. The name Taj was used to scare children into staying in their beds at night or finishing their supper. He knew the legends, everyone did, but he found the idea of someone calling himself Taj to be a bit frightening. No, he'd have to go to those Training Halls to be finished with the thronge worm. Then he could return to his normal life without having someone watching his every move. Filled with hatred, he somehow managed to doze with his head on his knees.

He was jolted awake by a sharp cry. He listened and remained frozen, although his body already ached from the hard ground and demanded that he stretch. Another choked cry came again from the mouth of the alley. Drawing his spare knife out of his sack and remaining crouched, he inched along the alley until he made out the figures of five people. The victim was being held up against the wall by two men, another had a hand in the victim's hair and was pulling the head back, and the last man held a knife to the victim's throat, slowly peeling away the skin.

Without thinking, Jaron leaped onto the back of the person with the knife and jabbed his own into the person's chest. A loud scream escaped from the man he had jumped on and he staggered backwards, pushing Jaron hard against the alley wall. Jaron released his grip and ducked around the bleeding man to attack the one who'd been holding back the victim's head and was now racing toward him. Jaron spun around quickly and let his leg fly upwards into the man's face as he charged for him, knocking him to the ground. Jaron noticed the victim, who was a tall man, had his arm tightening around the neck of one attacker, while his boot found the groin of the man Jaron knocked over and stamped on it hard.

Jaron heard the shuffled steps from behind him and swung his leg around again, landing his foot across the man's face he stabbed earlier, which flung the man around before he fell onto his stomach. Someone's hand was on his shoulder and Jaron quickly turned and sunk his knife into the flesh before he saw it was the victim. He quickly pulled out the knife and the man immediately thrust his bleeding wound into his mouth.

"Sorry," Jaron whispered, but the man shook his head and released his wound.

"Let's get out of here," he offered.

Jaron noticed the last two men were sprawled out on the ground and agreed completely. His pack was still tucked away under his tunic and he was glad he didn't take it off before he went to sleep. They hurried out of the alley at a fast trot and made several twists and turns down the streets before the victim slowed to a walk. They were both breathing hard and the victim was limping and sucking his hand again.

"Sorry," Jaron said.

The victim turned his eyes toward him and chuckled. "You're sorry? You just saved my neck. I mean that." Jaron saw for the first time just how much damage those people did to this man's neck. It was bleeding a lot and Jaron was ready to take his tunic off, when the man took off his own and pressed it against the wound.

"Ju should go to a Healer," Jaron offered.

The man chuckled again. "Good thing my brother's one." He saw Jaron's concerned expression and smiled reassuringly. "It's not as bad as it looks. It's just a gusher but no real harm done." He clapped Jaron on the back. "I can't thank you enough. Why did you help me like that?"

"Why's were dey attackin' ju?"

The man sniffed. "'Cause I'm a morpher. Damn lunatics are everywhere now, saying how all the problems with the Land are the morpher's fault. What a bunch of dung." He studied Jaron as they continued to walk slowly down the street. "Are you one?"

"Me? No."

"Then why did you help me?"

"Four 'gainst one is no fair." Jaron shrugged. "'Sides, dey were keepin' me awake."

"Ah, a street sleeper, are you?" the man asked with a friendly smile. Jaron shrugged again. "Well, let me at least repay you, although Light knows it isn't enough. But let me offer you a roof over your head tonight."

"It's a'right. I's fine. No big deal."

"No big deal!" the man gasped and chuckled again. "Please! I've never seen one so young kick so hard."

"Practice."

"I guess. My name is Darrell." The man offered a hand and Jaron shook it once.

"Marty." It was a force of habit to give a false name but it always seemed a good practice to keep. He could never be too careful.

"Well, Marty, at least let me offer you something," Darrell said.

Jaron refused again with a smile and walked with Darrell until they came to a string of small houses behind a row of shops. In the doorway of one was the silhouette of a person and as they headed for that house, the person left the doorway and rushed to meet them. It was another man and Jaron assumed this was Darrell's brother the Healer. He immediately took the blood soaked cloth away from Darrell and growled sharply.

"Again?"

Darrell tried to nod then winced. "It's not so bad."

"It looks like it almost was," Darrell's brother warned.

"Thanks to this young man, it wasn't," Darrell said and gestured to Jaron. "He saved my life." Darrell's brother looked over Jaron cautiously. "And he's not a morpher," Darrell added, to which his brother nodded.

"A good thing that not everyone's gone mad. Thank you…a…"

"Marty," Jaron said. "I's did nutin', really."

"He refuses to take anything either," Darrell said softly to his brother.

"Please, let us offer you something," Darrell's brother said, almost pleaded. "A meal, something. We don't have much but---"

"It's a'right," Jaron stated as he casually moved away from them. That was also a force of habit. Never accept anything from anyone on the first meeting and even though his stomach demanded that he accept their offer, he politely refused.

Both of them looked disappointed and before Jaron could duck out of their sight, Darrell called out to him, "I will repay you."

Jaron nodded but said nothing and moved back into the streets, looking for another place to finish out the night.

He was aware that the thronge worm watched everything going on and, although he said nothing, Jaron could tell he was pleased that he did not take the two brothers up on their offer. But it wasn't because of *him* that he turned down a bed and food; it was his own distrustful nature. In fact, he was almost tempted to turn around and do it just to spite the thronge worm but changed his mind. His habits were too strong and he couldn't break them, and wouldn't break them just to spite some voice in his head. He would finish out the night as he originally planned before he decided to play rescuer. It would be his decision, his choice, and not the voice's. From now on he'd make sure he was the one to make the decisions no matter what the thronge worm wanted. With that thought firmly in place he found another alley, tucked himself down at the end of it, and dozed off until morning.

When morning came, Landon was still silent.

GENTLE THIEVERY

Jaron tried a few taverns and alehouses, just to see how fast word spread around this town, however his original suspicions were correct. He didn't even make it in the door at most places before the Keepers asked him, as politely as they would a piece of filth, to leave. A mad boy hanging around was bad for business. The entire time the voice in his mind remained mute, which made Jaron feel relieved. Had the voice said one thing to him this entire morning, he probably would have shouted aloud and then really would've looked mad to everyone. When the sixth tavern denied him entry, and the jeers and taunts from the townsfolk made him even more noticeable, he admitted to himself that there was only one other way he could get pieces and possibly a meal. He left the town and started down a small path he was certain would lead to a farm.

He observed several farms that morning but was searching for something specific. He finally found what he was looking for on a wheat farm several miles away from the town. He remained out of sight, as he had done with the other farms, and watched the daily activities of the people living there. This particular farm had the conditions he needed. The man he saw moving about the fields was an older man with a large belly hanging over his trousers and a hard, withered face. He cursed a lot to himself and then shouted those same curses over his shoulder to his wife. She was as tired looking as he was, although not as plump and answered his curses in a tight voice with as few words as possible. Jaron remained hidden and watched them, knowing what would happen once the sun reached its high point. He witnessed it too many times before to not know what was coming.

On cue when the sun reached its peak and the heat was at its strongest, the man left the fields and started for the small house. His wife met him with a cup of water in her hands that he snatched greedily and drank in one gulp. Now Jaron couldn't hear a word but all the same knew what they were saying. The husband was saying he was going into town to pick up some supplies. The wife knew he wasn't and asked if he could at least come home sober. The husband snapped that he always did and stomped into the house. After a few moments he came out and the wife asked if he left any pieces for real supplies. He backhanded her and walked to the barn without looking back. The wife didn't cry out from his slap, which meant he'd done it so often it no longer affected her. A few minutes later the husband was on horseback, galloping down the small path and heading toward town.

Jaron ducked down further and watched him ride by, then shifted his gaze toward the house. The wife went back inside, looking defeated and even more tired than she had earlier. Now he would wait. He waited at least an hour before he removed his pack from under his jerkin, flung it over his shoulder, then got on the small path and headed for the house. He felt the voice in his mind watching everything he did with curiosity but it never asked what he was doing and Jaron didn't offer any explanations. It was the voice's fault he was forced to do this in the first place.

When he was still far enough away from the house he called out asking if anyone was home. The wife came out after a few minutes and eyed him suspiciously but when he came closer she seemed to relax. He knew what she was thinking, just a boy. This was one of those few moments when he didn't mind being thought of as just a boy. In fact he even enhanced his expression to appear more boyish and harmless. Yes, he was simply a young boy, on his way to an apprenticeship, and was making a living during his travels by doing some work in exchange for a meal. He offered his services and after a moment of hesitation, she agreed there were some things he could do.

In fact, there were plenty. It seemed the husband tended to the wheat only and did the other chores just when he needed to. Otherwise, Jaron was certain, the wife did everything else. He started in the barn, which had two more horses, a milking cow and didn't look like it'd been cleaned in years. The hay hadn't been changed in some time and the smell was horrific. The animals were unsure of this stranger and made no guesswork about the fact that they didn't want him coming anywhere near them. One horse nearly kicked his face off; the other whinnied and reared up on its hind legs, trying to stamp him into the ground. The milking cow was much kinder. It only pissed on him when he tried to move it out of the way, then strategically placed a pile of manure so Jaron couldn't help but slip on it and come crashing down, becoming covered in the cow's filth. Landon snickered quietly and Jaron grumbled a string of curses that no one so young should know so fluently. It was then that Landon felt something surge through the boy. He didn't know what it was. It wasn't an emotion, not exactly. It was...he really didn't know and had no way to describe it, but it was nearly tangible. Whatever it was, it seemed to pulse through Jaron as he rounded on the trio of animals.

He glared at each of them and stated clearly, "Eee-nuff!"

His single word hit each animal like a blast. They blinked and backed away from him. Then they looked...Landon had no other word for it...they looked guilty, like a bunch of students who got caught throwing spitballs behind a teacher's back and had been scolded for it. After that, they behaved. Landon couldn't believe the boy got that to work. Or maybe the animals sensed his mood and knew better than to push their luck.

When Jaron left the barn, he saw the wife sitting on a short stool with a washtub in front of her, scrubbing clothes vigorously. She looked up as he stumbled his way across the yard and smiled sympathetically. She told him there was a brook just in the back of the house and gave him a large tub so he could scoop the water out and wash himself. He took it gratefully, picked up his sack, and slipped quietly behind the house. Now that he had convinced the woman of his so-called reason for being there, it was time to get down to his real business. He felt puzzlement coming from the person inside of him but ignored it and filled the tub with cold water, stripped off his disgusting clothes, and scrubbed his skin until it burned.

However, every movement he made was careful. Every gesture, every time he bent down or stood up, it was fluid and deliberate. He wasn't sure if she was watching but the fact was he wanted her to watch; that was the whole point of

Hosting the Kazimeer

this little side trip. And if he caught her watching him, he could blush faster than any girl. It was a trick he had learned from Ham, his mentor. Ham told him there were times when a thief just had to resort to any and all possibilities and the more prepared he was the better. Ham told him all the ways to get into a woman's bed and then took him to Misty, who showed him what to do when he got there. It was Ham who taught him how to blush quickly; how to raise his own body heat and make it come into his face. Ham always said women loved it when a man showed such emotions and told him that if a young lad like himself did it, it would melt hearts and provide pieces. And it did. He learned all of this by the time he was twelve and since then slept with over a dozen women and made some fine pieces doing it.

Landon's mouth would have been gaping if he had a mouth. All of the boy's memories of his intimate lessons came flowing into his mind and Landon could do nothing but watch with disgust. This thief...this boy had a fuller sex life than he did. Well, that was to say that anyone had a fuller sex life than he did but still...he was just a boy! The more vivid the memories became the more Landon wanted to squirm away from this boy's thoughts. What had him confused, though, was when the boy had been so uncomfortable when he made remarks about the Mistress. Why! Obviously, he had enough experience. The answer came to him quietly.

"I's embarrassed fure ju, not me. A so-called Kazimeer lustin' over someone likes da Mistress, as ifs she's was a pess of meat or someting. At least I's make women feel good 'bout demselves. All ju do is leer at dem and make dem feel cheap."

Landon found that he could be more stunned than he already was. Still, he didn't respond. The boy asked him to stay silent so he did. He ducked further back into his mind, which he could tell made the boy glad. He didn't want to witness any of this.

Jaron finished washing then dressed in his only other clothes. He dumped the dirty water onto the grass, carefully picked up his old clothes, careful not to touch them more than necessary, and brought the tub back to the front yard. The woman was no longer outside but he saw a glimpse of her moving about within the house. Not yet, too soon. He took his dirty clothes and washed them quickly in the tub of soapy water the woman had been using, then squeezed them out tightly and whipped them around until they were only damp. He stuffed them back into his pack and waited until the woman came out again.

She nodded at him in approval and smiled. Jaron could tell she'd once been pretty but all these years of living with that husband and on this farm took away her soft looks. Still, he could imagine how she once looked and held that image in his mind whenever he stared at her. She approached him with a cup of water and offered it to him. He smiled shyly and took it with a quiet thank you, being sure he poured on the Granate accent. Women not from the south, he discovered, loved it when he spoke, even if certain voices in his head didn't. He drank slowly and watched her as she walked around to the back of the house. Within the next few moments he heard the splitting of wood and quickly went to join her. He saw her with an ax in her hand and the small log placed on the block that was only halfway chopped.

Jaron asked softly, "Wha' ju doin'?"

The woman turned around and smiled at him. "Need fire wood if I'm to give you a hot meal."

Jaron shook his head and moved next to her. "Zactly. I's do. Dat's wha' ju feedin' me fure." He took the ax from her, being sure his fingers brushed lightly against hers and handed her back the cup. "Tank ju's," he smiled and nodded at the cup. He turned to the block, repositioned the wood, and went to work again. She stood there watching him for a few moments then headed back inside the house. After a few chops, he looked down at his clean tunic, acted as if he only just thought that it would get dirty so soon, and removed it. He placed it on the ground behind him and continued chopping. After a few more logs had been split, he heard a sound, then realized it was the voice in his head making loud gagging noises. No, *he* would not ruin this last chance for him, and forcefully blocked the voice out.

He felt eyes on him. Good, that was what he wanted. He wanted her to see his young chest without any hair, see the scars on his back, and see his small but tight muscles flexing with the work. He pulled the ax free from the wood, pushed his hair away from his face, and turned ever so casually, toward the rear window. There she was, staring at him. He met her eyes briefly, flushed, and quickly turned back to splitting logs.

Landon choked loudly again. "*You're a whore!*"

Jaron didn't respond and kept focused on what he was doing. The voice said no more but Jaron felt the disgust and shock coming from it and for a moment hesitated about what he was doing. Then he was furious and forcefully shoved the voice to the back of his mind and continued until every log was split in two, each time thinking it was the thronge worm's head.

When he finished, he gathered up an armful of logs and walked around to the front of the house. He waited at the door until the woman saw him and had him place the logs by the hearth. She told him that was enough to bring inside for now, so he stacked the remaining logs outside, threw on his tunic, and went back inside the house. Whatever she was cooking smelled wonderful and tasted better. He quietly commented about what a fantastic cook she was. It made her smile; it made Landon gag.

During supper, he decided it was time for some talking. Just a little so he could figure her out better. He asked if she worked the farm by herself. She said no. When he asked if she had a husband she said no again. Ah, a clear invitation. Although he wasn't positive if that old, pudgy man he saw was in fact her husband, he didn't believe a brother or father and definitely not a friend would have slapped her the way that man did. No, she was lying because sitting in front of her was a young man whose body and face were still soft and without age, who worked hard, who stared at her as if she were still desirable and who didn't let her chop wood and complemented her cooking. So even though she may not have sex in mind yet, she didn't want the possibility to be shattered because she mentioned that she was bonded to another man.

This was the tentative part. There had been times when Jaron worked hard, just as he promised he would, got his meal then was shown the door. There were other times when he didn't need to go through with it because the woman would either trust him so much or was simply absent minded and would leave long enough for him to roam the house freely, picking up whatever he could find that wouldn't be immediately missed. He usually did have to go to this extreme to get pieces, because most people kept their valuables in their bedchambers. And that was far too private a chamber to be allowed into without some type of physical reason. Oh, he could have tried to force his way in but that usually meant someone would be on his trail sooner than he liked and besides, he wasn't a violent person, he just knew how to defend himself. He also could have pretended to be ill, and had done so in the past, but discovered that never worked very well because the woman wouldn't leave him alone and usually called for a Healer. So sex was usually the easiest way into someone's pieces chest. Still, he didn't mind it *that* much.

They quietly talked about the farm, where he was going to apprentice, where his "family" lived, what her name was, Allaendra, and so on. All the time he met her eyes, casually brushed her hand with his, and listened intently when she spoke as if it was the most interesting thing he had ever heard. He helped her clean up the supper dishes and they sat and talked some more. When the light outside became soft and purple, he reluctantly hinted that he should be leaving. This was the moment where she would either let him go or give him another reason to stay. She chose the second option and gave him work to do in her bedchamber; the work he had initially set out to do.

He lay on his back with Allaendra snuggled against his chest and rubbed her back gently. This was the part women also liked and appreciated, attention afterwards. Apparently, it was something their husbands didn't do, so he always made sure to hold them, kiss them softly, rub their backs or smooth their hair. He also made sure he acted as if he fell asleep at some point because that was something else women thought men did after sex and almost expected it. He did it for another reason, though; to get them out of the bedchamber so he could rummage through it. Woman usually found a burst of energy after sex and rarely lay with him.

After he stared at the ceiling for a while, he made his hand slowly come to a stop on her back and breathed deeply. He felt her move away from him and kiss him softly on the cheek, to which he made his mouth twitch slightly as if he was smiling in his sleep. He heard Allaendra let out a happy breath, felt the weight shift on the bedding as she rose, and heard the door close quietly.

He remained still and waited, just in case she decided to return right away, but the instant the door was closed, the voice in his head started, as if Allaendra could have heard him before.

"*So how many children have you fathered?*" he asked in disgust.

Jaron silently responded, "None."

"*How do you know? Do you go back and check?*"

"Nope."

"*Then how do you know?*"

"I's 'spose I's don't den."

"*You twisted...*" Landon stopped himself from swearing a string of curses because it would do no good. Instead he spat, "*And you say I only care about me. What about you? How many bastards do you have wandering the Land? How many of these women have been ruined because of what you did to them?*"

"Wha' did I's do?" Jaron chuckled softly. "I's made dem feel good fure a change. I's made dem 'member wha' its likes to be's a woman 'stead of a pess of meat dat gits slapped 'cause her 'usband feels likes its."

"*And what makes you think their husbands don't find out about you?*"

"Dey wouldn't tell."

"*How do you know! How do you know you just didn't make things worse for this poor woman?*"

"She dinn't 'zactly protess, ju know. I's dinn't hear her say, 'Stop', once, did ju's? Why's I's talkin' to ju's anniways? I's 'ave work to do." He opened one eye slowly and searched the bedchamber. Allaendra was still gone so he sprang out of the bed and began to look through the drawers, careful not to disturb anything. The drawers held nothing so he studied the floor, looking for a loose board, while Landon continued.

"*What happens when they find out that you stole from them? How do they explain that to their husbands, whore!*"

"Oh, is dat me new name?" Jaron asked and dropped to his knees to look under the bed. "I's never takes erriting. 'Sides, dare 'usbands never find out 'bout me 'cause dey will never tell dem. I's safe."

"*As if I actually cared about your well-being. No, their husbands will just beat them more thinking their wives stole from them! How come you can't kill a hare to feed yourself, but you can destroy these women's lives?*"

"I's dinn't hear her say no. I's don't tink I's da first tra-VEL-er she's taken to her bed. Damn!" He was having no luck in finding the stash. He thought quickly about where he would hide pieces in this chamber and moved to the corners.

"*That doesn't make it right!*" Landon roared.

Jaron ignored him and found what he was looking for. In the far right corner of the chamber there was a small floorboard loose. He pried it up and underneath it in a small wooden box he found over four hundred pieces, some documents he couldn't read, and a few pieces of jewelry. He took a hundred of the pieces and left the rest. As he was replacing the floorboard, he heard a loud noise coming from down the hall and froze.

"*I hope it's her husband and I hope he castrates you.*"

Jaron quickly shifted his gaze to the window. Yes, it was night but it wasn't that far into the night. Usually, husbands such as Allaendra's would stay out until very late and come home so drunk they couldn't find their feet, let alone him. When the noise faded, he leapt over to where his boots were, placed the pieces in them, and hopped back into bed, pretending to be asleep.

Now he definitely heard footsteps coming toward the door and it opened slowly. He remained still and kept his breathing heavy as the footsteps came to his side of the bed. A hand ruffled his hair gently and Jaron made the first movements of waking up.

The hand gripped his hair hard and hauled him up by it so fast he hardly had time to register what was happening. His eyes flew open in time to see the wooden floor coming up to meet his face.

BONDING

Jaron tried to turn his head but the more he tried, the tighter the grip in his hair became. He was flipped over onto his back and his head was banged against the floor before he felt a foot on his neck and one on his groin. He was in trouble. He focused his eyes, struggling to breathe as the foot on his neck stepped down, but didn't dare move because of where the other one was placed. He finally saw his attacker and was surprised when it wasn't Allaendra's husband. It was a man with small, narrow eyes and a sharp face. He reminded Jaron of a hawk but Jaron never saw him before. He always tried to keep some type of mental record of who he'd stolen or cheated in the past, just so he would know who his attacker was. In this case, he was lost.

The hawk-faced man stared at him for a moment but in that time Jaron could see they were not alone. He saw four other faces staring down at him, all wearing the same mask of amusement. One of them he did recognize, much to his horror. It was one of the people he saw last night at The Fat Dragon. He never said anything to this man but remembered seeing him at the dice table. He was the one who the thronge worm kept shouting at when he lost. Obviously, it was Jaron who was in the loser's position at the moment. He stopped struggling for air and remained still, since that's what attackers usually wanted from their victims, complete surrender. He would give it to them until he could figure out what was going on.

It worked. The pressure from both ends eased up and the hawk-faced man said to the others, "Dress him and bring him."

With that, Jaron was hauled up and roughly stuffed into his clothes and boots, but not before they removed the pieces from them. Then he had both of his arms yanked up high behind his back and was marched out of the bedchamber and into the sitting chamber. It was dark and he tried not to stumble since the man pushing him from behind had longer legs than he did, but he couldn't match the pace. He tripped but when he fell forward the man holding onto him did not loosen his hold and a surge of pain raced up his arms. He didn't cry out; that was a lesson he learned a long time ago, never cry or it will just get worse. He landed on his knees and wondered if they were smashed from the force of his fall.

He still couldn't see and was breathing in short, quiet gasps, trying not to provoke these people any more than they already were. But who were they and what did they want with him? His mind was racing. No wait, not his mind. It was the thronge worm's mind. Jaron was too terrified and in too much pain to think clearly, but the thronge worm was calculating, planning, thinking of things that Jaron couldn't begin to understand. That was fine since, without warning, a light was in his face, forcing him to squint against the brightness. When his eyes adjusted, he saw what he had tripped over and almost screamed; Landon did.

Allaendra's body was sprawled out in the middle of the floor or rather it was Allaendra's mutilated body. From the top of her head down to her neck, she'd been split in two, just like the logs outside. But he didn't scream. He wanted to, but out of habit kept it locked inside his throat and stared at the corpse with blood and brains flowing from the split head all over the floor.

"Look what you did," the hawk-faced man accused. Jaron couldn't pull his eyes away from the body that had been Allaendra a few moments ago. The same warm body he'd made love to was now a cold, stiff corpse. He barely felt something being smeared onto his hands but then came back to himself, remembering what the hawk-faced man just said. He looked up at him and the hawk-faced man shook his head. "Just look at what you did."

Jaron felt a handle being forced into his trapped hands and his fingers were made to grip the handle. He knew what he was being forced to hold and now knew what had been smeared on his hands. One of the attackers handed the hawk-faced man the ax with Allaendra's blood still dripping from the blade and Jaron's soot finger marks all over the handle.

Jaron didn't know these people, so why were they trying to frame him? He didn't understand, however, Landon seemed to be fitting everything into place neatly and quickly.

"He's not trying to set you up. He's giving you an alternative. He's trying to make it impossible for you to refuse."

Jaron was still confused. Alternative? What alternative? This man hadn't said...

"When her husband finds her like this, and you conveniently next to her, I'm sure he'll wonder why you would do such a thing to a beautiful creature. He will probably thank the Guardian for what you have done but still will have to show his remorse and revenge. I believe hanging is popular here. Burning also." The hawk-faced man glanced to the others who all nodded in agreement. He turned back to Jaron. "Yes, probably burning for you, after they've castrated you of course." He grinned at him, but Jaron kept his expression unreadable and his eyes pinned to the man's face. He couldn't bear to look at the body lying on the floor.

The hawk-faced man leaned closer and spoke softly, "Or you can come easily, quietly, and willingly with us, and these good people will never know it was you who so violently butchered a poor woman."

Now Jaron knew it was time for him to speak. He was surprised his voice sounded as level as it did when all he really wanted to do was retch. "How's could I's possibly turn down such an offer?"

"You are wise not to," the hawk-faced man said with an unpleasant grin and tossed the ax next to Allaendra. His finger markings were still on the handle, which Jaron figured was in case he changed his mind. Without further words the large man holding his arms behind his back dragged him to his feet and forced him outside.

Jaron was at least glad to be outdoors where he could inhale without smelling Allaendra's blood or insides. When he was marched half way across the farm, he was pulled to an abrupt halt and felt a rope being tied around his arms and hands while they were still awkwardly up against his back. It hurt but he didn't make a sound and immediately began to undo the knots as soon as they were tied. The person tying the knots would never notice so long as he only moved when the person yanked up on the rope to make it tighter. He also kept his shoulders loose while he tensed up his arm muscles, so the bonds would be a little slacker when he relaxed.

He had no intention of staying with these people and every intention of getting away from them as soon as he was able. The voice was quiet but still calculating. This was *his* fault too!

"*I had nothing to do with this,*" Landon replied calmly to the boy's harsh thought.

"I's know dis has someting to do wit ju's," Jaron answered silently. "Too many strange tings 'ave 'appened to me since ju came. I's know dis is jur fault!"

"Stupid fool. Didn't even defend himself." The voice came from behind Jaron but didn't sound like the hawk-faced man. However, it was the hawk-faced man who answered.

"Not stupid. Smart. Very smart, for he knows there is no other path to take but ours, so why bother arguing." The hawk-faced man walked in front of him as the large man finished tightening his bonds. He grabbed Jaron's chin and forced him to look him in the eye. "He knows he would have just come with us anyway, but in more pain if he argued. Isn't that right?" Jaron didn't answer and met his stare levelly. The hawk-faced man laughed. "See. He still knows when not to answer. Something you should have learned a long time ago, Patai. It would have saved you a few beatings." Jaron heard the man called Patai grumble something, then saw him walk by them toward the path leading to town. The hawk-faced man's eyes narrowed slightly and he said softly, "But since I know what games you are playing, boy…"

Without warning, he slapped Jaron with all of his strength. Jaron didn't make a sound as his head flung to the left more than it should have, but again it was another trick. He learned to move his face in the direction of a slap or punch that way there wasn't any resistance from his face and the pain wasn't as extreme. Plus the way his head jerked so helplessly made his attacker always feel better and the slapping or punching usually stopped sooner. Still he felt the sting of it and the hawk-faced man grabbed his chin again.

"No wonder my lord wants you so badly." He pushed Jaron's face away with another slap and followed Patai's lead. Jaron was shoved roughly forward to follow.

The thronge worm's fury was worse than his own was. Jaron could feel him stomping around inside his mind and also felt his helplessness about not being able to do anything. Jaron actually appreciated the gesture but he couldn't do anything either. He simply continued to work on his knots carefully until they were loose enough for him to free himself at a moment's notice. He felt the thronge worm come forward and peer through his eyes. To accommodate, Jaron shifted his eyes slowly around so the voice could see everything and perhaps pick up on something he had missed. At this moment, he wouldn't mind a bit of help even if it was from the thronge worm.

Landon saw something and told the boy to stare at it. He did without arguing and for the first time since these people appeared, Landon felt a small amount of hope. Jaron saw what the thronge worm was looking at and immediately protested.

"I's don't know how to use one."

"Yes, but I do."

"Well dat doesn't help me now, does its?" Jaron felt Landon calculating again. That made him nervous.

"If you allow me the use of your left arm---" He never got to finish.

"No!"

"Listen. That puny knife of yours isn't going to do much against these people. Not to mention, I don't think you have it on you, right?" Jaron agreed reluctantly. *"But if you get loose from the ropes and go for that sword, I can use it and maybe we can get out of this mess."* The sword Landon was referring to was on Patai's hip.

"Dare is five of dem and one of me."

"I saw what you did last night."

Last night? Oh right, the attackers in the alley. That was last night? It felt like a hundred years ago to him now. He was shoved roughly from behind because his pace had slowed and he nearly tripped over his feet. He steadied himself quickly and moved on, keeping up with the others so he wouldn't need to be reminded again. The path was so dark, how could he possibly see to snatch that sword? Worse yet would be to let that voice have control of his arm; the same arm that attacked him. What was to prevent this voice from stabbing him the instant they got away from these people?

"Do you think I want to die?" Landon asked, hearing the boy's thoughts and feeling his fear clearly. *"I want to live as much as you, in my own body. But you must let me do this or else Kyriea knows where we'll end up."* He felt Jaron's fear briefly turn into contempt at the mention of the Kyriea's name but what hadn't changed was his hesitation. *"I want to help you."*

"Ju want to help ju."

"Maybe so but if it benefits you in the process, what do you care?"

Well, that was true. Besides, it would only be his one arm the thronge worm had use of and Jaron would make sure it was for a short amount of time. Just until they got out of this situation. He was still wary and reluctant, though.

"Fine. Then be a helpless slave the rest of your life."

Jaron was instantly furious. "I's not---"

"You will be. By the Guardian, thief! Show a little courage and a little trust."

Still furious, Jaron dropped his mental guard and gave Landon the opportunity to move in. Landon knew the boy was doing it only because he was so angry and to show him that he was wrong. He didn't care how the boy came to the decision, just so long as he let him try. Honestly, he wasn't even sure if he could gain control as he did the other day but he carefully maneuvered forward, trying to link himself to the boy's arm. It was easier than it had been the first time since Jaron was willingly allowing him to do it. It felt as if he was slipping his own non-existent arm into a glove that quickly became his own flesh. He twitched it just to be sure he had control.

"Don't move!"

Jaron's command was loud and firm in Landon's mind so he did as Jaron directed and held the arm still. It was odd though, considering he was pressed up against the barrier with only his arm and eyes able to do anything. The rest of him was still trapped.

Jaron could feel his arm but when he tried to move it, it didn't respond. It was more frightening than the situation he was in now but if the thronge worm could do as he boasted, perhaps it would be worth it. The hawk-faced man and Patai were in the lead and the others were behind, with the large man walking directly alongside of him. How was he going to break free from the last binds of the rope, lunge forward, and have the thronge worm grab that sword before the large man reached out and snapped his head off?

"Well, you are going to have to help just a little bit."

"I's know!" he growled and thought quickly. He was never one to plan things out before he did them; he just did them. The more he thought about a plan, the worse it turned out so he decided to just move. "When I's say go, ju grab dat sword and ju better know how to use its."

"I'll need to see," Landon reminded him. *"I can't get it if you're looking the other way."*

The boy's frustration was strong. "Oh, I's 'sposed to be's blind too! 'Member, I's 'ave to gits ju dare. Dat arm ju got don't 'ave feet."

The visual the boy thought of when he said that made Landon chuckle, although he was probably more nervous than Jaron. It was hard enough to fight when he did have the use of his whole body. Now he only had an arm. How would the boy know when to dodge or to thrust the rest of his body to follow through with a particular style? Landon was starting to think this wasn't such a good idea. He felt a wave of irritation from the boy, who clearly picked up on his uncertainty and then heard him silently shout, "Go!"

Landon yanked his arm and immediately felt the ropes slide away. The arm ached from being twisted for so long and it took a moment for the blood to rush back into it before it started to respond to him. Then he was moving, or rather Jaron was, right up behind Patai. As Jaron feared, the large man behind him attached his hands onto his shoulders and pulled him backwards. By now the hawk-faced man and Patai turned around, noticing that something was going on behind them. When they saw that Jaron had broken loose, they both advanced to restrain him again.

Jaron struggled against the grip holding him as his left arm hung at his side. He silently screamed for the thronge worm to do something but Landon ignored him and tried to keep that sword in his range of vision as best as he could. However, with Jaron flinging himself back and forth, it was difficult. Patai was coming closer and Landon waited. Almost…Patai was almost close enough for him to grab it. He was about to snap at the boy to stop moving around so much when he felt the sensation.

At first he wasn't sure what was happening, then discovered the boy didn't know either since he felt the same sensation too. They both shared an extreme moment of sheer panic as their minds collided together. Jaron thought

Hosting the Kazimeer

Landon was trying to possess him and Landon thought Jaron was trying to destroy him. Soon the panic passed and they both realized it was neither.

They were linked. They'd been linked before only now the connection was stronger. Landon knew he was still trapped in the boy's mind but now he was aware, *very* aware, of the rest of the boy's body and thoughts. He had no control over them but knew exactly what the boy was thinking and how his body was moving. The same went for Jaron as he felt this person's feelings, saw his thoughts in his mind's eye and knew what he knew, even if he didn't understand it. He felt that if he turned his head quickly enough he could actually catch a glimpse of this person inside of his mind.

Patai was close enough now and they both knew how to move to accommodate the other. Jaron leaned back into the large man's hold and shot his feet out into Patai's face. As Patai stumbled backwards, Jaron leaned forward, ripping his arms loose. His left hand snaked out and snatched the hilt of the sword. Jaron tumbled over and rolled out of the way as the large man reached down to grab him again. He tripped and fell on his face when Jaron rolled forcefully into him. Now Jaron and Landon saw the other two who Jaron had only seen briefly back at the farm. They each had a sword in hand and were advancing quickly. Jaron leapt to his feet and his left arm moved the sword slowly, almost hypnotically, in front of him. His right arm was still all his, though, and it was without a weapon. The large man was on his feet again, lunging for Jaron and Patai was closing in from behind. Jaron also briefly noticed the hawk-faced man had stepped out of the way of the fight and watched with amusement.

All Jaron heard from him was, "Don't kill him!" Well, that was a good thing because Jaron had no problem whatsoever about killing all of these people. Neither did Landon and he thrust the sword at the large man who jumped away from the blade. Patai sprang onto Jaron's back and tried to force the sword out of his hand. Jaron locked his right elbow and hurled it around, catching Patai in the side of his face but it didn't knock him off.

Landon also tightened up on *his* elbow and thrust it back, hoping to jab it into Patai's stomach. He made contact with something and it wasn't until he heard Patai's labored moan that he figured out where. Apparently, after Jaron had landed his blow, Patai moved up a little on Jaron's back so he wouldn't be able to catch him in the face again. However, he raised himself just enough to put his groin where his stomach had been a moment before. Patai rolled off Jaron and lay on the ground unmoving.

Landon would have finished him completely but the two men with swords were swinging them at Jaron, who was ducking and dodging well. Landon made each of his attacks wider, so he could counter two blades instead of one, but still it was awkward and difficult. He also became aware that Jaron's reach was way shorter than his own, so many of his attacks missed because he was too far away.

Jaron picked up on this and after he ducked to avoid a blade whizzing over his head, he came up with a small jump and stood so close to one of the men, he could be standing on his toes. Then Landon realized he was.

The jump had been directly on the man's feet. He winced and tried to make a stab at Jaron but he was so close he couldn't bring his blade around to do it. Jaron then saw what he needed and plucked the dagger away from the man's belt. He sidestepped in time to see the other attacker, who had been trying to lunge his sword into Jaron's back, but instead implanted it into the man's gut.

The man screamed and blood spat out from his mouth and again Jaron heard the hawk-faced man shout, "Don't kill him!" But he still was out of the way and not joining the battle.

There was a moment of delay because the attacker was yanking his sword free from his partner's gut. Jaron made use of the moment to knock the attacker's feet out from under him and cause the lodged blade to rip further up the man's abdomen.

Landon raised the sword to bring it down on the attacker's throat but it was blocked by the large man, who grabbed the blade. Landon quickly pulled it away, taking part of the large man's hand with it, and Jaron managed to stab him in the shoulder before scrambling out of the way. The large man staggered briefly and the attacker had his sword free from the dead man's body and was on his feet.

Jaron backed away slowly, making swipes with his dagger, while Landon did the same with his weapon. The attacker ran forward, while the large man circled around, trying to get behind Jaron. Jaron tried to keep both in front of him but the attacker leapt into the air and immediately engaged him in battle. Actually, it was Landon the attacker was fighting, as Jaron watched his left arm do things with a sword he would never have been able to do. The attacker's sudden advance, however, gave the large man time enough to move almost half way around Jaron. He was now in between both of them, dividing his attention up as equally as he could. He'd make a stab at the large man, cutting him or throwing him off balance, then looked back to the attacker and let Landon have his turn. One thing was certain, he was getting tired and dizzy.

Landon kept seeing his opponent come in and out of view. So while Jaron was trying to keep the large man at bay, he would swing the blade wildly hoping to ward off any blows coming from the attacker until he could see him again. This was not the way he learned how to fight but it was better than doing nothing. One of the times when Landon was blind, he felt the attacker's blade slice across his arm. No, not his arm, Jaron's, but he felt it too. Jaron spun around with a kick to the attacker and then turned back to the large man, catching him hard in the gut. He immediately turned back to the attacker so Landon could have his few seconds. Either they looked like the most skilled fighter or a complete mad boy swinging two blades in every direction.

Landon's turn was almost over, so he swung upwards quickly, trying to catch the attacker in the neck, but his aim was awkward and he slammed his sword into the side of the attacker's face instead. The attacker screamed and was out of his view as Jaron turned back to the large man. Suddenly someone was on his back and Jaron knew it was Patai again. Having enough of his sides being kicked, he ignored the oncoming large man's attack and whipped his dagger over his shoulder into Patai's ear. Now there were two men screaming. Jaron forced Patai off of his back but he was too late to fight off the large man, who drew back his fist and used all of his strength to punch Jaron in the jaw. The punch sent Jaron flying through the air and then he landed hard on his back.

Jaron couldn't breathe and struggled for air, but the large man crossed the distance between them in two strides and lifted him up by his tunic. Jaron was flying backward again and landed with such incredible force that it knocked out the few gulps of air he managed to take. He also noticed both of his hands were empty and saw the weapons lying half way across from where he was. The initial punch from the large man must have knocked them out of his hands. He was being pulled to his feet from behind, but he hardly noticed since the first breath of air managed to make its way to his lungs and he breathed desperately.

The hawk-faced man had his arms pulled behind his back and whispered in his ear, "Have you gotten the fight all out of you yet?" Jaron couldn't answer, only coughed violently when his lungs started to work again. "I don't think he has," the hawk-faced man said to the large one. "Why don't you help him use up all of his fight."

Jaron raised his eyes long enough to see the large man stalking toward him and feebly tried to release his arms from the hawk-faced man's grip. He turned his head away not wanting to see which part of his body got beaten first and saw the shadow moving silently toward him. He would have been afraid if he had time to register what he was seeing, but the shadow moved so quickly that he couldn't make the connection fast enough.

Suddenly the shadow was next to him and then had its mouth half way down the hawk-faced man's head. The hawk-faced man released Jaron, who rolled out of the way, and was making a howling sound as the creature sunk its fangs deep into his eyes and cheekbones. The hawk-faced man beat at the creature with his fists but that only angered the beast more and it sunk its fangs completely into his head and tore half of it away, leaving everything from the nose down still intact. The rest of his head was spat out by the creature and landed a few feet away in the grass.

Jaron and the large man both were frozen, staring at the body as it twitched and released its last gurgled scream. The creature made a noise that sounded like a growl and a screech blended together, and stepped closer toward them. Too afraid to run or fight, Jaron studied the beast. It looked like a cross between a leer-cat and a bat. It had the paws of a leer-cat and half of it was covered in brown, coarse looking fur but it had big, black, skin-covered wings rising up from its back and no tail. The eyes were a leer-cat's, alert and cunning, but the snout and mouth were an odd mixture of the leer-cat's powerful jaws and a bat's fangs. Jaron knew he'd never seen such a thing before but suddenly he knew what it was.

"A grafton," both he and Landon said silently together. However, the grafton paid him no attention and bounded for the large man who'd just come out of his daze. Jaron saw the first spurts of blood fly from the large man's neck and turned away still unable to move. Landon told him to run but even his command was weak. He was also too tired and afraid to do anything but sit there inside of Jaron. He even released the arm back to the boy now knowing neither of them had a use for his sword skills. They both heard the final gurgles of life from the large man, then Patai, and finally the attacker with half of his face missing. The grafton took the other half.

That growl-screech sound came from behind him and Jaron slowly turned his head to stare eye to eye with the grafton. He no longer felt fear; he was angry. Angry about this whole situation he was in, angry that these people had killed Allaendra, and angry that he was going to have his head bitten off by this thing. His eyes narrowed and Landon felt an unbelievable surge of strength come from him as he lunged for the grafton. However, the beast backed away from him so Jaron landed face first in the dirt. When he raised his head and spat out the dirt in his mouth, he froze once again. The grafton changed slowly; its paws became hands and feet, the fur seemed to withdraw into the skin, the wings folded and melted into the back, and the snout shrunk to form a mouth.

The naked man spat the blood from his mouth several times before raising his head toward Jaron and smiling.

DARRELL REVEALED

"Darrell," Jaron whispered in amazement.

The naked man spat out more blood and glanced over to the dead, bleeding bodies. "Stupid, arrogant fools," he whispered. He ran his eyes over them a moment longer then quickly got up. He walked past Jaron and pulled him to his feet. "We should be going now."

Jaron didn't argue and found his pack lying a few feet away on the path. Apparently one of the fighters dropped it before they moved in to attack him. He scooped it up and followed Darrell, who also stopped long enough to throw his clothes back on and pick up his own pack. Without words, they moved swiftly through the trees and away from the town. The only sound aside, from the night creatures, was Darrell spitting now and then.

Even though Darrell did risk his own neck to save his life, Jaron was still wary of him. He couldn't shake the image of the grafton ripping off the top of the hawk-faced man's head. He made sure he kept a step behind him and off to the side, just so he had a clear path to run if need be. Landon remained quiet but watched as much as he could. He wasn't too certain about this man either.

When they traveled well into the forest, they stopped by a river and Darrell pulled out two lighting rocks while Jaron found leaves and twigs for a fire. Once it was lit, they each had a better view of the other and Jaron could tell that Darrell was well packed.

"Goin' somewhere?" he asked, nodding toward the pack.

Darrell glanced down at it, then back to Jaron. "Thought it would be a good idea to leave after last night." Suddenly his eyes narrowed with concern and he reached out toward Jaron's face. Jaron instinctively jerked his head away. Darrell smiled weakly, then pointed. "Your ear's bleeding."

Jaron reached up and felt the sticky moisture around his ear. He pulled his hand away and saw the blood but only shook his head. "Was bleedin'. It's not annimore."

"Yeah, but still, when you got a wound like that you should make sure it's treated. I have some herbs and leaves. My brother made sure I was well stocked before I left."

"I's fine." Jaron got to his feet to prove it, but wavered from the blood rushing to his head. Darrell caught him from falling into the fire.

"No, you're not fine," he insisted, then asked as a test of memory, "What's your name?"

Jaron opened his mouth to tell him, but Landon screamed, "*Marty! Remember you're Marty!*"

"Marty," Jaron answered and Darrell nodded with satisfaction. "Tanks," he told Landon silently. Landon only sagged with relief and couldn't believe he was helping this boy lie to the man who just saved both their hides. Still, they couldn't be too careful.

"I think a nice refreshing wash up would make us both feel better, eh?" Darrell glanced toward the river and Jaron agreed with a nod while pulling himself gently away from Darrell's hold. He was hesitant about stripping in front of some man he'd only met once before today but Darrell had no reservations as he peeled off his clothing and sloshed into the water.

Jaron saw images flash before his mind's eye of young men and women taking off their clothes just as casually as Darrell had done and stood with each other talking and laughing, and never once having their eyes stray. Jaron realized he was seeing other morphers but from when? He'd never really been around morphers, until…

"They're my memories," Landon grumbled. *"My days at the Halls."*

Jaron felt his annoyance and backed away from the images that were not his. Also, it unnerved him a bit to see such clear memories that belonged to someone else. He pushed them aside, carefully took off his clothes, and waded into the cold water. The cuts on his skin burned from the cold but soon it felt good against his sweaty, dirty skin, and he floated around until he almost started to fall asleep. It was Darrell's call that brought him out of his trance. He was already out of the water, dressed, and had something cooking on the fire. Jaron finished washing. When he was done he considered dressing in the same clothes, but decided against it and put on the clean ones in his pack. After he was finished washing out his dirty clothes and stuffed them away, he sat across from Darrell and enjoyed the warmth of the fire.

He noticed there were two small pots simmering. One had what looked and smelled like stew in it but the other one held some green mixture that smelled like old feet. He wrinkled his nose and Darrell chuckled.

"I know. But it's great for sealing up cuts and healing bruises and from the look of you, I see you have plenty." Jaron started to protest but Darrell raised his brow. "I'm still repaying you for last night."

"Repayin' me!" Jaron cried. "I's should be's takin' care of jur wounds."

Darrell showed him his arms and face, then smiled broadly. "I don't have any. Now." He carefully picked up the bowl with the green, foot smelling mixture and sat next to Jaron. "Let me see your ear first."

Jaron recoiled and shook his head. "I's fine," he stated.

Darrell sat back and plopped the spoon in the mixture absently. He nodded indifferently. "I'm sure you're right. It's not that bad. I'm sure the little sprites won't even bother with you."

Jaron studied him closely. "Wha' little sprites?"

"Oh, the little sprites that enter wounds and make them worse. You see they're attracted to blood."

"I's never 'eard of dat," Jaron stated.

Landon never heard of that either but figured out what Darrell was trying to do. Even though he couldn't see Jaron's wounds, he felt the boy's pain, and pride, and if this man was trying to frighten the boy into receiving the cure, the wounds must look bad. Landon decided to help Darrell in his task.

"He's right, you know. Those little sprites end up in the most inconvenient places."

"Besides," Darrell said, "if they are attracted to your blood, it's only your ear." He looked Jaron up and down. "Oh, and your arm, and your forehead, and your…well, anyway I'm sure they won't do any more than just make your ear fall off."

"*You still have your other one.*"

"Dey can't do dat," Jaron protested nervously.

"Sure they can," Darrell said with a nod. "You see, what they do is enter the wound and suck up the blood. Then they replace it with their magic. Didn't you ever see a wound all green and puffy?" Jaron nodded slowly. "That's their magic at work. My brothers a Healer and I know all about this stuff."

"*And once they're finished with your ear, they'll move on to the rest of your head,*" Landon offered. Jaron didn't answer but Landon felt the boy's deep dread and confusion. "*Everything on your head is connected. Didn't you ever have an illness in your nose that made your whole head feel like it was going to pop?*"

Jaron answered him silently. "Yeah." Then he became more confident. "But dat went 'way."

"*Well sure. It's only an illness, there's no blood to attract the sprites. But if you're bleeding, that's like ringing a dinner bell. And once they're attached, they'll spread to the rest of your head, feeding as they go.*"

"I've seen some nasty wounds," Darrell said, shaking his head slowly. "I've seen people come to my brother long after the sprites have done their magic, but by then it's always too late."

"A'ways?" Jaron asked meekly.

"Always," Darrell said gravely and nodded firmly.

"*I suggest you hurry up and get to the Halls before you decay.*"

"A'right!" Jaron shouted. "I's put its on." He reached out for the mixture but Darrell shook his head. "I's can do its meself."

"Yes, I'm sure," Darrell said and began applying the mixture to Jaron's ear. Jaron jerked, not only from the pain but also from Darrell being so close to him. If Darrell noticed, though, he didn't mention it and continued. "But you'd probably not put enough of this stuff on for it to heal you. I know it reeks, but it does work. By morning you'll never even know you were in such a fight." He worked silently for a moment, while Jaron sat there stiffly, then asked offhandedly, "Any particular reason five men would want to kill you?"

"None dat I's can tink of. I's tink dey thought I's was someone else." Darrell sniffed a laugh but said nothing. "Wha' were ju doin' dare?"

"I told you, I'm leaving." Jaron flinched slightly as Darrell pulled out his arm but he didn't seem to notice Jaron's reaction and started applying the mixture to a large cut. "I didn't believe it would be a wise thing to walk through the center of town, inviting last chance attacks, so I stuck to the forest. Then I heard all the commotion and metal banging and went to take a look. I can't tell you how surprised I was to find you at the center of the trouble." Jaron wasn't sure if he was being sarcastic or not so he held his tongue. "I decided to pay you back, since you wouldn't accept my offer last night."

"Why's is ju leavin'?"

"After those asses tried to remove my throat, Tirell and I thought it would be better if I went elsewhere."

"Tirell?"

"My brother, the Healer. See." He showed Jaron his neck, which had been torn apart last night, but now looked fine. He held up the bowl. "It works, I'm telling you. Now where else did they get you?" Without waiting for an answer, he moved his hand to apply the mixture to Jaron's face, but Jaron pulled back slightly. Darrell waited for a moment and then slowly tried again. Jaron let him but tensed up and kept expecting to see those hands turn into claws. Darrell continued by commenting, "I'll say this, though. From what I saw, you were even more impressive than you were last night."

"So were ju," Jaron muttered under his breath.

Darrell stopped what he was doing, sat back on his heels, and stared at him confused. "I told you I was a morpher."

"I's know," Jaron said as if it didn't matter whether or not this man tore off people's heads with his mouth.

"You just didn't think I was a grafton. That's what I was, you know."

Jaron gave a silent "Oh" and nodded. He didn't even know how he knew what that creature was. Perhaps it had to do with Landon and he didn't think it was wise to bring up Landon just yet to this man. Landon, feeling his reservations, was half-relieved and half-insulted.

Darrell continued. "You thought I was a puppy or a fish or something else harmless, didn't you?"

"I's dinn't know," Jaron answered quietly.

"Oh please don't get all tense around me now. I'm not going to suddenly morph out of control and do anything to you, you know."

"I's know," Jaron said, squirming a little. "Its jus I's wasn't 'spectin' to sees ju at dat moment." He paused, realized what a fool he was being, then added, "I's wasn't 'spectin' to piss in me trousers at dat moment, eeder."

Darrell stared at him blankly for a moment then threw his head back and laughed. He had one of those contagious laughs, Jaron noticed, and soon he joined him. Darrell smeared a glob of the mixture down Jaron's nose, washed his hands, and dished out supper.

Jaron ate as if he hadn't eaten in days, which surprised him since he gorged himself back at Allaendra's. The instant he thought of her name, the image of her lying on the floor came back to him. He pushed it away or else he wouldn't be able to keep anything down. Both of them cleaned out the pot so that it needed very little washing when they were finished.

"Tomorrow night you cook," Darrell said. He leaned back on the ground with his hands clasped behind his head.

"Who's says I's goin' to be's 'round ju tomorrow night?" Jaron challenged playfully, but Darrell looked disappointed.

"I was just hoping for the company, is all. I'm sure you were going your own way when you were attacked by those five fools."

Jaron felt like a fool himself when he heard how disappointed Darrell sounded. Here the man just saved his life, tended to his wounds and shared his supper, and Jaron couldn't find the time to spend another day with him?

"I's could use da company too," he said softly. "It's not always easy travelin' alone."

"*Hey!*" Landon cried.

"Ju're not company," Jaron told him silently. "Ju're annoyin'."

"*Just make sure you stay on the right path, thief. You've delayed too long as it is.*"

"Where's ju's headed?" Jaron asked Darrell.

Darrell shifted his eyes toward him. "Archway."

Jaron suddenly saw a map in his mind and knew Archway was past Nela. It was further north, so he could be on his way to the Halls and have some decent companionship for a few days. But how did he know where Archway was? Landon growled loudly. Oh, that's how. Still, he played dumb.

"Where's dat?"

"North. Far north where they don't mind morphers so much, I think. From what I've heard, that's where a lot of the morphers have fled, since it's no longer safe for us around these parts. People are just too insane lately." He looked back up into the night sky. "Ever since the Kazimeer died, the Land hasn't been the same." Jaron felt an overwhelming amount of pride flow from the thronge worm and it took most of his restraint not to choke aloud. "I mean, there are many things that are better since he's died."

"*What!*"

"Likes?" Jaron asked, almost wanting to snicker aloud at the thronge worm's fury.

"Oh, please Marty. You can't see the change?" Darrell pulled himself up on one elbow and stared curiously at him. "I mean…all right, here's an example. Tirell is a Healer but he never apprenticed anywhere, mainly 'cause we needed pieces and couldn't afford to let him go off. He's good at what he does, though, and would never try to heal anyone he wasn't sure he could handle. But because he never apprenticed, by the old laws, he couldn't practice and if he was caught practicing healing, he could be arrested and subjected to punishment. But now, he's free to practice all he wants, with the understanding that if he messes up he is solely responsible, but at least he's given a chance. Anyone has a chance now. It's not just left up to the nobles or the ones with all the pieces, like it was when the Kazimeer was alive. A poor man, like my brother, has a chance to make a name for himself and provide for his future, and to do what he's not only good at, but loves."

"*And let some poor person get healed wrongfully because the Healer doesn't have enough experience.*" Landon shouted in return. "*Those laws were made to protect the people against swindlers!*"

Darrell continued, not hearing his outraged cry. "But you see, now that everyone is becoming equal, morphers no longer have the protection they once did under the Kazimeer, since he was a morpher himself. Before, no one would even think of hurting a morpher, let alone killing one the way they've been." He smiled weakly. "I suppose there's good and bad in every situation. No one can please everyone, but it seemed to me that the Kazimeer was just trying to please those important people with power or pieces, and the rest of the Land could go to the wind. Still, now the morphers are without protection." He sniffed and glanced at Jaron. "At least he was good for one thing, eh?"

Jaron opened his mouth to agree just to irk the thronge worm but Landon snapped, *"You do and I'll find a way to make your life miserable."*

"More den ju 'ave?" Jaron jeered to him then answered Darrell. "I's really wouldn't know."

"I suppose you wouldn't. Just hope you never have to rely on one person's position to save your own ass." Darrell leaned forward and said in a hushed tone, "Did you know the new Kazimeer killed the old one and his heir just to get the throne? What kind of guide is that for the Land to follow, eh?"

Landon was seething, which Jaron felt strongly and changed the subject just to calm the thronge worm down. He stretched out and said casually, "Well now, I's guess I's could go north. I's 'aven't been up dat way in a while." He glanced over to Darrell to see his reaction.

Darrell smiled. "Good. Then you can cook tomorrow after all."

With that he rolled over and Jaron soon heard him breathing deeply. He would have loved to do the same, however, the thronge worm wouldn't stop babbling about how the Guardian could give such stupid people such wondrous gifts. And how dare this peon speak of the Kazimeer as if he meant nothing to the Land, *and* accusing him of murder. Jaron finally gave up trying to silence him and dozed on and off through the night. However, each time he awoke, there was the thronge worm ranting some more to him, as if he actually cared. He was also not surprised when in the morning Landon told him that he didn't trust this person.

"'Corse ju don't," Jaron told him. "'Cause he's doesn't tink ju're anniting special. Needer do I's."

"That has nothing to do with it," Landon half lied. *"But don't you find it a bit convenient that he happened to be right there when you needed him?"*

"When I's needed him was back on da farm 'fore Allaendra got killed. Jus be's tankful to da Guardian or da Kyriea or a rat's ass dat we's bof still 'ere. And shut up!"

Landon felt the boy's sudden anger and held his thoughts to himself. No reason to get the thief all worked up over this. He'd be talking about Banishing again. So long as he made it to the Halls, Landon would keep quiet.

After Jaron washed off the remaining healing mixture, he did have to admit it worked as well as Darrell boasted, they traveled north, talking about idle things, although Darrell did most of the talking. Jaron could see why he wanted someone along with him; he needed someone to listen to him. However, Jaron enjoyed his company just as much. He always spent most of his time alone, except when he was in the slave-trade and before Ham disappeared on him, and it was nice to have someone else to make the day's go by faster. He liked Darrell. He was funny, smart, and seemed to have a supply of boundless energy. Jaron discovered this when they stopped for the night and Landon mentioned how far they had traveled that day. At this pace, they would be at the Halls in another few days.

In a way, Jaron would be disappointed when he reached the Halls and had to make some excuse to leave Darrell's company. But he figured he could catch up to him once these Masters plucked the thronge worm from his mind.

Since he agreed to cook supper this night, he set out into the surrounding forest with a string he had tucked away in his sack. When he saw the string, Darrell commented about how he would have air-stew for his evening meal, but Jaron simply asked him to get the firewood and he would bring back supper. He felt the thronge worm peeking through his eyes and almost shoved him away, but didn't want to bother right now, so he let him watch. When he had gone deep into the forest, he tied half of the string into a loop, placed it on a small patch of clover, and then held the other end while sitting only a foot away from the trap.

"That's it?" Jaron didn't respond. *"Darrell's right. You will be having air-stew tonight. No wonder you eat bugs."*

Jaron said nothing and got comfortable. Sometimes he could sit there for hours before anything wandered into his trap and other times a horde of animals would come to him, almost fighting against each other to see who would be killed first. Tonight it was neither, simply one hare.

The hare hopped slowly toward the loop, stopping along the way to munch on a patch of grass but never for long. It made a direct path toward the trap. Landon wouldn't have believed it if he didn't witness it for himself. The hare was practically moving straight for Jaron's trap, as if it knew what Jaron was waiting for. When it reached it, the hare began chewing its last meal of clover and didn't move from the spot. Then it ducked its head under the loop in one quick movement, so that the string hung loosely around its neck, and then continued chewing.

"I don't believe this."

Jaron blocked out the thronge worm's bafflement and surprise, and hesitated. He hated doing this and didn't even know how he did, but they always came to him eventually. No matter if it was minutes, like tonight, or hours, the animals would come to him and await their deaths by his hands. He slowly wrapped the excess string around his hand, trying not to disturb or frighten away the hare, although he knew he could jump up and down right now and the hare would never run away from him. It would be quick. He always made sure it was quick and hoped the pain was minimal. He gritted his teeth, apologized silently to the hare, then yanked the string tightly. Both Jaron and Landon heard the snap as the hard jolt broke the hare's neck.

Jaron opened his eyes, not remembering closing them but he always did when the moment came, and went over to the hare's limp body. The kill was clean. The hare still had clover hanging out of its mouth and probably didn't know what was happening until it was done. Jaron hated doing this but he had to feed another person tonight so he put his own self-loathing aside for now, untangled the string from the hare's neck, and carried it back to the camp.

Darrell was still collecting firewood when Jaron returned carrying their supper in his hands. He just stared from the hare's body to Jaron's face.

"That was fast," he finally said.

Jaron shrugged, pulled out his knife, and began cleaning the hare's body. Once he was finished he sliced up the meat, and added it to the pot that Darrell had filled with mushrooms and herbs he had found while gathering the firewood. They ate in silence, mostly because Jaron didn't feel like talking or listening. He just wanted to brood.

"Oh I see. Killing the Kazimeer is fine but killing a hare leaves you feeling devastated?"

He pushed the thronge worm back and forced himself to start a conversation. "So wha' will ju do once ju git's to Archway?"

"Probably what I've always done," Darrell replied in between mouthfuls. "Tavern work."

"Oh?"

"Not much, is it? But it pays well, usually." Darrell tilted his head to one side and he set his bowl down. "And what is it you do, Marty?"

"Jus odd jobs, 'ere and dare."

"Oh yes, odd jobs. Stealing purses here, seducing someone's wife there. Yes, you're very talented."

"Do ju 'ave anni place lined up yet?" Jaron asked louder than he intended, trying to drown out the thronge worm's voice.

Darrell only blinked at him confused, then said, "None yet, but I hear there are plenty of opportunities. Morphers are drinking for two." Jaron only chuckled because Darrell did, but he didn't get the joke.

"Morphers change from one shape to another. Two shapes. Drinking for two. Get it now, boy?" Jaron ignored him.

"Why do you ask?" Darrell asked him. "Are you looking for tavern work too?"

"Maybes." Jaron considered it. "But first I's 'ave to tie up a few loose ends titly."

"Tightly," Landon corrected with a moan.

"Well if you decide to wander past Archway, find me. Who knows, you may find it to your liking there."

"Maybes." Jaron nodded. They passed the remainder of the evening with more idle talk but Landon had pulled back into the boy's mind and watched, keeping his comments to himself.

He didn't like this Darrell and it wasn't only because of the things he said about the Kazimeer either. He still found it too convenient that Darrell showed up just when they needed him the most. Although, like Jaron said, there were plenty of bad times before that when he could have arrived. He didn't trust him. Jaron did, though, which bothered him more than he liked to admit. And it wasn't just because he thought the boy was in danger either. It was more of what he felt. Not betrayed, that was too strong a word. More like…left out.

He'd been left out plenty of times before this and it never bothered him as it did now. Seg always left him out and got others to do the same, since Seg was going to be the Kazimeer one day. The morphers at the Halls followed Seg's lead, but even when Seg wasn't around, they still excluded him. He always thought it was because they were nervous around him since he was the Second to the

Kazimeer, but now he was starting to think it wasn't that at all. Maybe it was just him. Maybe he *was* the annoying, thronge worm who had no right to be Kazimeer. Ah, but he was just feeling sorry for himself. It was being trapped inside this boy's mind for so long, that's what it was. Once they reached the Halls and the Masters pulled him out, then he'd feel better.

He noticed the boy had fallen silent and so had Darrell. He didn't come forward, though, and still couldn't shake the self-woes he was feeling no matter what he thought of. Suddenly, he was being poked only it wasn't a physical sensation. But he did feel someone poking at him mildly as if they were checking to see if he was still there.

"*Yes?*" he asked, wondering why the boy was checking on him. The boy's feelings changed from anxiety to relief. Relief? "*What?*"

"Ju were quiet."

"*I'm often quiet.*"

"Ju weren't peekin' eeder. Ifs ju're not talkin' ju're lookin', so I's wondered ifs ju were still dare."

"*Here I am. Same place I've been for weeks.*"

The boy's mood change rapidly again, now from relief to annoyance. Without another word to him, Jaron forced himself to go to sleep. Landon felt him drift off and cursed himself again. How did he always do that? Make people angry when all he was doing was stating the obvious. Perhaps it was his tone. Mazon was always telling him that he sounded like he was constantly pissed-off, but how was he to control his tone? That's how he sounded. His self-pity mounted and he stayed in the back of the boy's mind and brooded.

A sharp cry brought Landon forward and snapped Jaron awake. A few glowing sticks were all that remained of the fire but Jaron soon saw that Darrell was gone. He was on his feet, knife in hand, and searched the area. He strained to hear any sound and tried to filter out the night creatures. A muffled groan answered him. He darted off, barely touching the ground as he ran toward the sound. It was growing louder and he knew it was Darrell.

A hard blow knocked him onto his back. He had time to blink his vision clear before he was being hoisted up by the front of his tunic and pulled nose to nose with a face that looked like it was chopped out of stone. He was pushed away into the grip of someone behind him as the stone faced man advanced. Jaron kicked out with his feet, sending the attacker stumbling back, then leaned forward and flipped the person holding onto him over his shoulder. He struck out with his knife when the attacker moved toward him again and caught him across the chest. The delay was long enough for him to race by them toward the sound of Darrell's cries.

Landon's uneasy feeling became stronger when he thought of something the boy didn't. "*He's a morpher. He can just morph to protect himself.*"

Jaron didn't hear him and he nearly tripped to a halt and came to a small clearing at the ledge of a cliff. Darrell was just barely able to keep his grip as he hung over the side and kept scrambling to get a better hold. Jaron heard the grunts and shrieks from below the cliff and remembered the sound. It came from those eye-less creatures. And they were trying to take Darrell.

Darrell saw him as he entered the clearing and cried, "Help me!"

Jaron raced toward him but was hurled backward. When he raised his head, a bit dizzy from the impact, he didn't see anything in his way. He leapt to his feet and moved forward while Darrell screamed for him to help. Again he was thrown back, only this time when he looked up he did see someone.

"Don't go near him," Jynx said calmly. She pulled him to his feet and gave him a push in the opposite direction. "Run."

"Ju're mad," Jaron hissed and tried to push by her. Jynx waved her hand and sent Jaron flying across the clearing, landing him back into the forest. Landon shouted at Jaron as he got to his feet and advanced toward her.

"Why would those creatures take him and not you? I don't trust this. Listen to her and run!"

"Please! Help me!" Darrell shrieked, as his hands started to slip.

Jaron was ready to run over Jynx if need be, but he didn't have to as the two men who attacked him in the forest leaped out and Jynx had to turn her attention on them or be squashed beneath them. Jaron raced toward Darrell, who had one hand stretched out for him to grab, and Jaron reached for it. That's when Landon saw it. The sparkle twinkling out of Darrell's collar. It was the sparkle of a chain, a chain he remembered seeing once before. A necklace.

"Don't!" Landon shouted but Jaron continued to move forward.

Overwhelmed with fear, Landon reached for their connection and solidified it further. For a brief second he could feel legs, then the sensation was gone. Jaron lost his balance for that moment and came crashing down face first into the dirt, only a few inches from Darrell's outstretched hand. Jaron looked up and reached for it, suddenly finding he was having a difficult time controlling his body as Landon made every attempt to stop him.

"Help me, Jaron!" Darrell shouted. "Please!"

Jaron froze, mid crawl with his hand still outstretched.

He never told Darrell his real name.

As if Darrell also realized his mistake, he hoisted himself up over the ledge and snaked his hand out to grab Jaron's. Jaron was thrown away by the unseen force, only this time he didn't mind it. When he stopped rolling, he scrambled to his feet and saw that Jynx not only disposed of the two attackers but now had herself in between him and Darrell.

Jaron studied the man's face and tried to pick out what was different about it now. It had changed ever so slightly. The jawbone was sharper, the cheeks were more drawn, the hair was now blonde instead of brown, but the look of hatred did more to change the person he'd just spent the past two days with than anything physical. This person before him was frightening and held so much anger in his eyes Jaron found he couldn't look from them. He wanted to shout, or whimper even, but he couldn't do anything but stand there and stare. Darrell shifted his head from him to Jynx, but Jaron found he still couldn't move because someone had suddenly seized him from behind, wrapping strong arms around his body and pinning his own arms to his sides.

He vainly fought against the grip, but the more he did, the tighter it got until he felt the air being pushed from his lungs. He forced himself to relax, in the

Hosting the Kazimeer

hopes that the grip would loosen; it didn't but it didn't get any tighter either. And there was no way for him to stick his knife, which he remembered he had locked in his grip, into this person. A voice spoke calmly in his ear.

"Just relax."

Jaron felt his fury rise quickly. He hated being trapped. He hated being told what to do. And he really hated being lied to. He kicked wildly at the person behind him and twisted back and forth but the grip never loosened. He was squeezed so hard he couldn't breathe and made a soft groan sound in his throat.

Darrell glanced over to them and spoke softly to the person behind him. "You break anything on him, I'll break you." Immediately the grip loosened, though Jaron was having a hard time just trying to find air again, let alone fight his way out of the hold. The person who had been Darrell smiled at him and the mere sight of that gaze held Jaron completely still. "I told you that first night that I'd repay you. Just let me take care of this wench first." He held Jaron's eyes for a moment then looked away, allowing Jaron to breathe again.

Landon, throughout all of this, was trying to watch the man called Darrell. He noticed one change Jaron missed. His eyes changed color. They'd gone from blue to pure black and Landon had only seen one other person with such eyes. Blasdon, or rather, Taj.

Taj looked Jynx up and down, and growled at her, "You whore."

Jynx didn't so much as blink and held her ground. Her face was completely composed and she spoke in a level voice. "I didn't know you held me in the same regard as your mother. How kind of you."

Taj laughed in his throat and suddenly Jynx's body jolted as if she had been struck by lightning. She made no sound but there was one coming from the ground as the ledge of the cliff dropped away, nearly taking Taj with it. Jynx's body stopped jolting and her eyes held Taj's levelly as he steadied himself from his near fall.

"Aren't you the little pest," Taj hissed.

"Can't concentrate on two things at once?" Jynx mused. "You're weaker than I thought."

"*She's provoking him,*" Landon said. "*Why?*"

Jaron didn't answer and remained limp but felt every move the person behind him made. He was waiting for the right moment and was almost ready when Jynx did cry out. He saw her being raised off the ground and flung against one of the trees. Within an instant from her crash landing, she was on her feet again and hurled a fireball at Taj, who blocked it easily.

"*His grip is loose, Jaron. Now!*"

Jaron snapped back to himself and also felt what the thronge worm had noticed. He spun around, still within the confines of the person's arms and plunged his knife into the man's gut. The man didn't make a sound but Jaron was free and bolted into the forest. He heard a shout that shook the air around him and chilled his blood, but that only made him move faster.

At first he didn't think anyone was following and only heard his own heavy breathing and his heartbeat pounding in his ears. Soon, though, he heard the pursuit. It was quiet, almost sounding like a wind rustling across the trees, but

Jaron knew what a thief's advance sounded like, and this was nearly the same. He increased his speed, not caring what direction he went in and neither did Landon who could only encourage him to move faster.

The first pursuer dropped down from the trees and landed in front of him. Jaron collided into the large eye-less creature and would have fallen onto his back, but the eye-less grabbed the front of his tunic in one hand and placed the other on top of his head.

Jaron had known pain in the past. He had been through four different owners and over ten different slave-Masters. He could take a punch or a whipping without wincing once. But what he felt now was beyond any level of pain he had ever experienced. It ripped across his mind like a fire, tearing at him in places he never knew existed until now. Landon felt it too and he joined Jaron in his screams.

The agony stopped. Jaron wasn't sure it had until he opened his eyes and himself staring at the ground. It subsided slowly, lingering in different parts of his mind, making his muscles twitch, and then finally it was gone. Jaron felt the thronge worm recovering just as slowly but he was still there, and soon he felt him peeking through his eyes again. Jaron raised his head to find out why the eye-lesses stopped torturing him. He wasn't sure what he was looking at; neither was Landon.

Sitting on one of the eye-lesses shoulders was a boy, maybe a year or two younger than Jaron, who was beating the eye-lesses head like a drum and shouting some nonsense words at the top of his voice. Attached to each of the eye-lesses arms and legs was another child, either biting or hitting the eye-less, making it howl. The children laughed or whooped, making the eye-less even angrier. Jaron looked behind him to see another three eye-lesses in the same predicament as the one in front of him. For each eye-less there were about five children. The shouts of both the children and the eye-lesses drowned out his heartbeat and nearly blocked out Landon's voice, which sounded like it was coming from down a tunnel.

"*Run!*" he shouted.

Jaron tried to comply, but his legs wouldn't push him up and his stomach wanted to retch. He turned his head and tried to stand again, but only succeeded in falling on his face. He lifted his head and met a pair of sharp, brown eyes. Jaron pulled himself up further, but even sitting on his knees, he still had to look down at the small boy standing before him.

"Hello," the boy said with a soft smile.

Jaron couldn't answer, feeling his stomach lurching every which way. The shouts of the eye-lesses and the laughs from the children still boomed around him but he heard the boy quite clearly. Perhaps it was because he was so close to him. The boy extended his small hand and Jaron took it without thinking, and got to his feet easier than he expected to. The boy trotted around the shrieking eye-lesses and led Jaron into the forest. Jaron didn't question where they were going. He was just glad to get away from where ever they just were, and found it a bit odd that this small child had more presence of mind than he did at the moment.

Hosting the Kazimeer

When they finally stopped the sounds of the eye-lesses and the children were far behind them. The boy led him to a pile of rocks and sat down, forcing Jaron to sit down as well. The boy smiled at him again.

"You can stay here. You'll be safe." The boy's voice was soft and sweet sounding. Jaron liked listening to it and found it had a quieting effect on his racing heart. "They will not find you until you're ready. Until they're ready. Until I say you're both ready." He leaned closer to Jaron and dropped his voice to a confidential tone. "I usually don't interfere like this."

Jaron nodded once, to give the impression that he understood, when he actually had no idea what this boy was talking about. His head was dizzy and he felt exhausted. The boy nodded once in response to him, then got to his feet. He smiled gently at Jaron, who felt like he should thank him or offer the boy something, but his mouth wouldn't cooperate with his mind. The boy's smiled deepened as if he had, and then he winked out of sight.

Jaron dropped his head to his knees once the boy was gone. He didn't understand what was going on and hated it. He knew he was not bright and normally didn't understand half of what was said. But he really felt his ignorance when things happened to him and there was nothing he could do to prevent them from happening or even understand why they were.

"*...let me through!*" Landon's voice was so loud Jaron winced from the pain that streaked across his head.

"Wha'!"

"*Why did you block me out?*" Landon demanded.

"I's dinn't."

"*You did! I've been beating on a barrier as thick as a dragon's tooth.*"

"I's dinn't mean to den."

"*Where are we?*" Landon asked, noticing their different surroundings.

"I's don't know. I's jus ran."

"*We shouldn't stay here too long.*"

"We's be's safe 'ere."

"*I doubt that.*"

"No, I's tink we's will."

"*Why?*"

"I's don't know. We's far 'way from dem now. We's be's safe 'ere." But why he knew that, he wasn't sure. In fact, he wasn't even sure how he had gotten here in the first place. He didn't remember running, like he wanted to. But he must have or else how could they have gotten this far into the forest. He figured he was tired and whatever that eye-less thing did to his mind was enough to scramble his brain for a while. He just needed to sleep and then he'd be all right.

"*That's not a good idea,*" Landon warned as he felt the boy's sudden weariness. But even as he said it, Jaron was drifting off to sleep.

Darrell Revealed

ABBNAR

Taj rounded on the boy the instant he realized he was free from Dapp's hold. He shot out his hand and hurled a bolt of cold straight for the boy to freeze him in his tracks. The boy ran too quickly, though, and his power struck a tree, turning it to ice. Taj growled and flicked his wrist. Three Mytocks materialized out of the air and instantly charged after the boy. The girl smiled smugly at him and flicked her own hand before he could release his power to stop her. No matter, whatever sprites she had working for her would not prevail over his Mytocks. This girl would be nothing now.

He growled softly, trying to keep himself composed. "I warned you when you left my services not to interfere with my tasks. If I remember correctly my exact words were, 'Do not even *sneeze* in my direction'."

Jynx blinked innocently. "Ah-Choo."

Taj smiled. "Was that a challenge or a pitiful attempt at humor?"

"Take it however you wish, foul one."

Taj's answer was a ray of fire that shot from his palm toward her. Jynx's hands fluttered instantly and mists of smoke rose before her wielding a shield that conducted the flames away from her and directly at Dapp. Taj stopped his flow immediately, not wanting to incinerate his Second. The flames winked out of sight a moment before Dapp was consumed by them, but no doubt he was a bit singed around the edges.

Taj stared steadily at the girl, trying to keep his rage in check. He wanted to make her pay for his mistake but somehow it wouldn't be enough just to destroy her. She was always so smug, so sure of her feeble power and intellect. What if she knew just *how* he was able to locate the boy? Would she remain so smug? Taj didn't think so and began to work with his idea.

He kept his tone level when he spoke "I don't need this aggravation."

"Sure you do. It keeps that old mind of yours active."

Taj's mouth crooked a smile. "Old, eh? Well, I suppose it is. But age does have its advantages."

"Yes. Death will come for you sooner."

"Are you sure about that? In your position, I would not make such a statement."

"You will not kill me," Jynx chuckled. "You do not have the nerve."

"I'll admit," Taj said and nodded slowly, "you do make it difficult." He stared at her smug smile and prepared to wipe it off permanently. "Considering the way you continue to assist me."

Jynx's triumphant smile slowly faded with suspicion. "I have not assisted you, foul one."

"Oh, but you have," Taj insisted. "When all my informants failed, when even my own powers were…blocked mysteriously, it was you, my former student, who found the one I've been searching for." Jynx said nothing and continued to stare at him with doubt. Taj raised a brow. "Surely you know I've been looking for him. Why else would you have visited him before now? I did notice that

128

small exchange between you two. You obviously met with him already, no doubt frightening him with tales of my power. Why else would you do that, unless it was to assist me?"

Taj studied her expression carefully. It was as he expected, confused, suspicious, and uncertain. He broadened his smile. "And how crafty of you to let me track you, without ever showing sign of it."

Jynx's face tightened. "I did not---"

"Because, surely," Taj said loudly over her, "a Weaver of your skill would know when another Weaver is tracking her line of power. I know *I* taught you that and I ...why Jynx? You look pale, dear. Is something wrong?"

Jynx's fists were clenched at her side, her jaw was locked, and her eyes blazed with fury. "I did not help you," she spat coldly.

"Of course you did." Taj smiled. "No need to be modest. Playing your pranks on the boy was just a front; I see that now. You knew I would feel your magic and follow it, curious to see what could make you expend so much energy so quickly. No mere prank would be worth the amount of power you were radiating. Naturally, it must have been so I would take notice of you."

The look of horror on Jynx's face almost made up for his loss...almost. If she'd stayed out of his way he would never have lost his concentration and Jaron would've been bonded to him at this very moment. It would've been a strong bond too. At that crucial moment, Jaron had been willing to risk his own life for him. The boy's feelings were of protection, friendship, maybe even love, and those feelings would have made the bond solid and unbreakable. Even if Taj chose to slit the boy's throat a moment later, he still would be unable to fight him and would press the blade to his own throat at Taj's command. It would've been perfect.

But no, this girl saw fit to undo twenty years of searching by making him lose control of his senses for that one brief, important moment. All the hours of planning, all the reliable fighters and scouts he sacrificed just to make his image of Darrell more believable to the boy, all of it had been for nothing.

The thought made his anger boil again but he held it in, and forced himself to keep talking calmly. She would crack first, not him.

"And I would never have been able to find my special jewelry without your help."

"You tricked me about that," Jynx hissed.

A slow smile spread across Taj's face. "Perhaps. But I did not trick you about this. In fact, I didn't even mention it to you. I've been too busy to keep up with our...unusual...relationship. You did it all on your own. Without you, I would never have been able to find him either." He could tell by her expression that she was furious with him and herself. About now she was kicking herself for being so foolish and unwary, and realizing the magnitude of what she had done. He stared at her and said the one thing that would push his point home. "Thank you, Jynx, for your help once again."

Jynx screamed in hatred and launched her power at him. Taj expected it though, and not only blocked her energy but held onto her streams like they were the reins of a horse. Jynx twisted her power madly trying to break them free from his hold but Taj was not going to be shaken. She tried to add more force attempting to rip Taj's grip loose but all he did was gather up the additional power, tearing it away from her control. Finally, she stopped struggling and glared at him.

"Well," she hissed. "Shall we dance now or what?"

Taj shook his head and smiled a little. "That temper of yours will be the death of you." He wrapped her power around his hands tightly, forcing her to be pulled toward him. "And, no, we will not be dancing, although I am a wonderful dancer."

Jynx smiled. "I've seen you dance, Taj."

Taj just smiled back and encircled Jynx with her own power, now under his control. Jynx concentrated, trying to tap into her energy once more. The energy itself resisted Taj's command, like a loyal dog being told to turn on its owner, it was not so easily manipulated. Taj's will and concentration were stronger than Jynx's and the circle began to close in around her. She began to suffocate from her own power and frantically she searched for a weakness in Taj's hold. She found one; no larger than a pinpoint, but it was enough for her to pour her power into it. Her energy, recognizing the command from its original owner, responded eagerly and absorbed the new flow instantly. With most of her power back under her control, she pushed against the shell giving herself a moment to catch her breath. Taj, now having to resort to using his own power, applied more pressure, forcing the energy around her. Jynx pushed it back, forcing Taj to use more power. The pushing back and forth made the energy expand and compress until it finally shattered.

Jynx brushed off her hands as if she had just finished gardening and forced herself to smile, although she could feel her body trembling from exertion and terror.

"Well, well, well, well, well. Looks like you really do have…nothing." Before Taj could react, she swung a mental fist the size of a boulder at him. It broke apart a second before it made contact.

"Please don't tell me that's the extent of your powers," Taj sighed wearily. "I was really hoping for a challenge."

He raised her off the ground without waiting for her response. She fought frantically against the hold but her power was still recovering from breaking loose the first time and had no influence on Taj. He held her in the air for a moment and waited to see what she would try next. He was satisfied when he could feel her using all of her strength just to break out of his grip. Then he burrowed his power inside of her and began to force her body to split apart. Jynx now concentrated all her energy on keeping herself in one piece, but Taj's hold tightened and the tearing inside of her intensified. Despite her pride, she screamed through clenched teeth. For an instant, she tried smashing her magic against Taj himself, hoping to disrupt his hold on her long enough for her to get free, but Taj had a shield so thick her magic simply bounced off of it. She was in trouble. She hated to admit such a thing but she was no match for such power. She purposely sent that hopeless message through her mind over and over, hoping Taj heard it.

He did. Such weakness in one he thought was so strong. It actually made him angry to find that he misjudged her. But playtime was over. He reached into her mind ready to crush it like a shell, when he came across a strange sensation. At first he couldn't place why her mind should be feeling different, as if someone else was inside her mind and yet the sensation was so familiar. An instant later he figured out what the girl had been doing all along.

The second he figured her out, he pulled away from her mind but found he was entangled in a complex net of energy. The girl had more strength than he gave her credit for and she knew it, when another smug smile spread across her face. He pulled forcefully at the binds that were holding onto his power when the lightning bolt struck only a few yards away from him.

Taj would like to have said it was his complete control over the situation that finally freed him from the trap the girl had placed for him, but actually it was his overwhelming fear. He ripped his power away from Jynx, who collapsed and panted heavily. Taj realized that must have taken a lot out of her, and thought of finishing off the little wench right there. However, another burst of energy landed in between him and Jynx, and he caught the first glimpses of the figure appearing out of the corner of his eye.

"Well, well, well, well, well."

The voice he heard was not Jynx's. Light, he was not prepared for this! He reached out with his power, releasing a surge of raw energy at the spot where the figure appeared, but something grabbed hold of his magic and twisted it into knots. He was trapped again and this time the power holding him was just as strong, if not stronger, than his. He couldn't break loose.

That soft voice filled his ears again. "Look who crawled out of his little prison."

"Yes, remember that," Taj said as calmly as he could. "I did get out."

"You want me to finish what I started then, yes?"

"It took you long enough to even track me down, old man."

"Yes, but patience..." The figure stepped out where Taj could see him clearly. Taj stared mutely at his old rival who stood only a few yards away from him. He couldn't believe how very little changed after a millennium and yet how so much changed. The old man looked a bit more haggard, tired, and the heated passion that always used to burst out of him seemed to be gone. He appeared relaxed, almost weary, as if he couldn't care less about this encounter. Abbnar continued speaking in his smooth tone, "Patience...you silly, silly boy...is a gift you seem to lack."

"Oh, do I?" Taj sneered and fiercely tore at the binds holding his mind captive. He must think his way out of this while the old man was still gloating over his victory.

"You see, if you did have any patience, you would've known of my arrival but you were too busy picking on little girls to be aware of anything else. You're not focused, Taj." The last part dripped with sarcasm and Taj felt an invisible finger poke his forehead. "If you had enough smarts, you would've known that not just you could follow a Weaver's line of power to its source. You should be careful when you're casting."

Taj was a bit terrified but he was more furious. He tried to buy some time as he worked on the mental knots encasing his power. "Tell me, old man, how is that wonderful family of yours? Your children?" The last sentence jolted him just as Taj wanted, but not enough for him to break free. "Kill any lately?"

Abbnar's voice was instantly filled with loathing. "You have."

"I did nothing. If I remember correctly, it was your power that killed him, not mine."

"Better than to let you have him."

"You admit it then," Taj taunted. "Such a cold response from a father."

"Thankfully, the Land and you will never know what it is like to be one, since you will never spew your spawn."

"I happen to know of one young man who is in dire need of a home." He grinned. "Maybe you know him. I think he was lost. Perhaps I will adopt him."

"Not while *I* live."

"But I've already done it, while *you* lived." Taj could've been mistaken but the old man seen genuinely surprised to hear that. Then his surprise turned to fury.

"Impossible!" Abbnar snarled.

"No, not impossible. *FACT!*"

His taunts were working but they were not enough. Taj would never be able to stand up against him, especially since the old man seemed twice as furious now and not after he'd spent so much of his power on that little wench. He glanced toward the girl and an idea worked its way into his mind.

Using the last of his strength, he pounded through just enough knots of power and stretched out his energy, not toward Abbnar, but toward Jynx. Let's see if he could stir the old man's passion again.

Taj guessed right. The instant he threw his wave of energy toward Jynx, a wall went up between it and the girl. But the hold on his mind slipped enough for him to break through it completely. He immediately cast Transfer on himself, Dapp who had been bleeding all over the ground the entire time, and his Mytocks. He wanted nothing left behind for Abbnar to take.

Taj Transferred all of them back to the castle, making sure to leave a path so tangled and mangled, not even Abbnar should be able to follow him, at least not without some advance warning. He landed them all into the Justice Hall, and after a quick head count, allowed himself to breathe.

**   **

The moment Taj vanished, Abbnar threw his head back, shot out his arms to either side of him, and screamed. The crackle of lightning and rumble of thunder answered him. When he looked back down he saw the image of a being he knew far too well and instantly stalked toward it.

"You lied to me!"

"I never lied," the image answered calmly. "I withheld."

"Why did you never tell me that he ended up with---"

"Because I knew you'd react like this."

"I'm not supposed to be upset? I'm supposed to be happy to---"

Hosting the Kazimeer

The image interrupted softly. "I would expect you to remember exactly *why* we are going through all of this in the first place."

Abbnar took a deep breath but his anger wouldn't dissipate. He looked around toward the forest. "Was he here? He was, wasn't he?!" He began to move forward.

The image deliberately blocked him. "Abbnar, no."

"Let me by," he warned.

"No. Not yet."

Abbnar's anger exploded out of him again. "Let me by! Or I swear to the cursed Light I'll---"

"You'll what?" the image asked calmly. "Beat me, kill me? Go ahead if it makes you feel better but you're still not getting by me."

Abbnar thought about testing the being's word then decided against it. He backed away but was so furious his whole body shook. The being's face saddened and it reached out for him. "Look at you. Do you want him to see you for the first time like this?"

Abbnar jerked away from the being's touch and his eyes narrowed. "First time? What do you mean first time?"

"Abbnar," the being said patiently, ignoring his question. "You don't know what I'm trying to do. There's more at stake here than you know."

"You're not going to let me find him, aren't you?" Abbnar accused. The being shook its head slowly. Abbnar turned away. "I'll never forgive you for this."

"I know," the being said sadly. "I knew when I made the decision. But I always hoped that you would come to understand." The being tried to peer into his face but Abbnar moved away. "I still have that hope, Abbnar."

Without another word, Abbnar vanished into the darkness.

Jynx, who remained on the ground during the entire confrontation, allowed herself to sit up. "Wow!" She looked over to the being. "I've never seen him that pissed, not even at me, and I can always piss him off."

"He'll calm down," the being answered. It stared back at her and smiled. "I still need your help."

"Oh no!" Jynx got to her feet quickly, despite the remnants of pain still coursing through her body. "I've had enough, thanks." The being said nothing, just continued to look at her with its pleasant smile. "I've done what you asked."

"Yes I know but...he still needs you."

"He's the Kazimeer! Why should he need me?"

The being cocked its head to one side. "Jynx."

"Oh come on!" she cried and threw her hands into the air. "I hate getting in between those two."

"I know. No one says you have to get in between them, though."

"But you know I will." The being continued to look at her and Jynx narrowed her eyes, staring suspiciously at it. "What's the big deal anyway?"

The being smiled. "Oh, now Jynx. If I told you, the whole Land would know in under an hour." She scowled but the being continued evenly, "He's about two miles northwest of here."

"Who, the thief?" The being nodded. "How'd he move so quickly?"

"I helped. Be gentle when you wake him."

"What makes you think I'm even going to help you again?" she challenged. The being smiled warmly at her and vanished. Jynx crossed her arms over her chest and stared up into the sky. "I'm not going to do it!" She waited but there was no response. "I said, I'm not going to do it!" Again, no one answered her.

She stood for a few moments, tapping her foot impatiently and waiting for the being to return. When nothing happened, she hissed under her breath, "Who am I kidding?" She trotted off into the forest, heading northwest.

Hosting the Kazimeer

TANTRUM

Taj closed his eyes for a moment and told himself to stop shaking. When he felt sure of himself again he opened his eyes and stared over to Dapp who was still on his knees bleeding from his gut all over the floor. Taj had to admire the way the man never made a whimper or a plea, just pressed his hand against the wound to stop as much of the bleeding as he could, while Taj did what was important first. The Mytocks he'd sent after the boy stood a few feet away from him. They glanced around the Hall and at each other in confusion, then noticed him and immediately bowed, waiting for him to command them. They didn't have the boy with them, so naturally he wanted to know why.

He screamed to himself for being so foolish. How could he have made so many mistakes in one evening? He never made such gross errors. He never lost an entire opportunity over a simple slip of the tongue. And never in his wildest plans did he ever conceive of Abbnar and that cursed girl in league together, especially after the way he had her betray the old man. As far as he knew, Abbnar would kill the girl on sight. When did they form an alliance against him?

A quick throat clear from across the Hall made Taj realize he was not alone with just his group. His commander, Alexen, was also there along with several more of his fighters, assassins, and messengers, obviously awaiting his return. He held up his hand and Alexen stopped in his tracks and waited. Taj approached the kneeling Mytocks and stood before the head one.

"Well?" he asked sharply.

The Mytock replied in its breathy voice, "Master, I will show---"

"No!" Taj roared. "You will tell me." He didn't want to admit, even to himself, that his power was taxed at the moment. Keeping up an illusion spell for a solid day took a lot out of any Weaver. To view a Mytock's memory would be too much for him right now. "Where is he?"

"Master, there were spirits protecting him."

"Child spirits, no doubt," Taj sneered. "Why did I create you if you can be stopped by something as feeble as a bodiless spirit?"

"Master, we were outnumbered. Our defenses had no effect on them."

Taj made a mental note to improve his next batch of Mytocks so they would be able to fend off spirits, at least a little. Dealing with Jynx's sprites was not something he'd counted on when he made this group. Still, his fury grew and he grabbed the Mytock by the front of its robe and pulled it eye to socket with him. "You were told to bring me that boy. You did not. I am distressed over this. Very distressed."

"Master, the creature you seek," the Mytock offered quickly to appease its Master. "The ivory dragon."

Taj released the Mytock and stared questionably at it. "Yes?"

"It is within the boy's mind."

"What?" Taj hissed. The Mytock repeated its answer.

Taj wanted someone to wake him out of this nightmare, because that's what it was. He ran his hands over his face slowly and stared at the Mytock levelly. "You're telling me," he began softly, "that the beast I seek is inside that boy's mind?"

"Yes, Master."

"The same boy I sent you to return to me."

"Yes, Master."

"The same boy you did *not* return to me."

"Master, as it was explained, he was protected---"

Taj waved at the Mytock impatiently. "I've already heard your excuses for failing me. *Why* didn't you contact me immediately?"

The Mytock stared at him as curiously as it could. "Master, you did not feel the additional presence?"

"We are not discussing me!" Taj roared. "We are discussing you and your failure. Why did you not contact me?!"

Taj was not about to admit that for the two days he spent in the boy's company he didn't notice the presence of the ivory dragon. However, despite his attempt to ignore that fact, the simple answer was he didn't notice it because he didn't search Jaron's mind. And for the life of him he couldn't understand why he didn't. He never made such gruesome mistakes! Why didn't he take a moment to peer into the boy's thoughts! This was a nightmare! That ivory beast just slipped through his fingers, as well as the boy's power. His mind worked quickly to console him or else he'd crack for sure.

Desperately, he arrived at a reason. It was because of the boy's power, that's why he didn't risk looking into his mind. With such unpredictable power, Jaron may have been able to sense his true identity before he wanted him to. He couldn't risk having Jaron discover who he was before the bonding, which, he was forced to remind himself, never took place also because of his error.

Taj growled loudly to quiet his thoughts and waited for the Mytock to answer him.

"Master," the Mytock began carefully. "You only stated you were seeking such a creature; you did not state you wanted it retrieved."

Taj's eyes widened and a sharp cackle escaped from him. "Oh, I see. So, just because I didn't specifically state I wanted you to bring that thing back, you didn't. Is that what you're saying?"

"Yes, Master."

"Ah!" Taj nodded and fixed a hard glare at the Mytock. "Then where's the boy? I did tell you to retrieve him, didn't I?"

"Master, it was explained---"

"Oh again with this!" Taj threw his hands into the air and turned away from the Mytock. "Yes, yes, I heard it before. The fact that both the person I wanted retrieved and the thing I've sought are within the same body gave no sign of importance to you. No reason whatsoever to alert me that you were having a problem carrying out your orders."

"Master is never pleased when he is disturbed."

Taj grabbed the Mytock by its robe and lifted it off the ground so its feet dangled. "Don't you think this might have been one of those times I would've made an exception!" He threw the Mytock to the floor and walked away, looking down. His eyes fell on Dapp and he forced a smile onto his face. "Don't you think I'm taking this really well?"

Dapp nodded slowly and croaked softly, "Yes, my lord."

"I thought I was." Taj nodded to Dapp then spun around to face the group waiting for him. He turned so quickly, the small group sucked back, eyeing each other with concern. Taj pointed at Alexen. "What do you want?"

"Noth…nothing, my lord."

"Horse dung!" Taj stated. "You've been waiting here for some reason."

"It's…" Alexen swallowed hard. "It's nothing to concern yourself with, my lord. It can wait."

"I'm already pissed off. I doubt whatever you have to say can make it much worse." Alexen hesitated and Taj's eyes narrowed. "Speak or I'll tear it from your tongue."

"My lord," Alexen began immediately. "There have been several reports that your Land is still dying." Taj stood there, his expression unreadable, and stared directly at the commander. Alexan continued timidly, "The people are becoming nervous, my lord. There is talk of them gathering with plans to overthrow you." Taj slowly blinked once but did not respond. Alexan stuttered over his next words. "Also, my lord, I fear Jubian has distressing news."

Taj shifted his gaze toward the assassin he'd sent to kill the Water Count. She came forward and knelt next to Alexan. "My lord. I fear I have failed you. The Water Count has disappeared. No one knows where he has gone and I have searched half the Land looking for him. I haven't found him."

Taj inhaled deeply, looked away, and stared off at nothing, while his mind churned on the events which had all taken place in under half an hour. Without looking at his Second, he spoke levelly, "Dapp."

The Second's response came unsteadily. "Yes, my lord?"

"You know how much I value you, Dapp."

"Yes, my lord. Thank you, my lord."

Taj glanced over to him. "How long have we known each other? A little over twenty years?"

"I believe so, my lord."

"You were just a boy back then," Taj said and smiled. "Remember how it used to be? Just the two of us. We could practically read each other's thoughts."

Dapp sniffed a laughed and coughed violently as a result. He wiped his mouth with the back of his hand. "I know you could, my lord."

Taj's smile broadened. "Yes, but you were pretty good at guessing mine. We worked so well together. We still do. And that is how it should be again, since…" He spread his hands. "I can't seem to find reliable help these days." He rounded on the small group and his eyes shifted from them to the Mytocks. He raised his voice so all who stood there would hear his words. "Tell me, Dapp, if you can believe this. I see before me one assassin who has the audacity to admit failure at such a simple task. A task that should be second nature to her by now, and yet she acts as if a plump, old Count has the right to outwit and outmaneuver her. What do you think of that, Dapp?"

Dapp spoke softly, "Terrible, my lord."

"I also see a pitiful excuse for a commander, telling me how the Land is still dying and peons are threatening to overthrow me. Should I be bothered with such problems? Isn't that why I have hired and paid good pieces to such people as this round slob, so they could handle such situations? So they could do what is necessary without precious time being wasted?"

"You have, my lord," Dapp agreed.

"And my creations," Taj sneered, glaring at the Mytocks. "Who take things quite literally, as I've just discovered, which makes me wonder why I even bothered to place them in these bodies at all. If I wanted mindless, unthinking slaves, don't you think I would simply have saved myself the effort and time, and wiped clean the minds of those they inhabit?"

"You would've, my lord," Dapp said.

"Did I not take my power, my life's blood, to create such beings, so they could actually use what little brains they possess?"

"You did, my lord."

"And what is my reward for such effort? What is my satisfaction? The two people they knew were extremely important to me slipped through their fingers, and therefore slipped through mine, because they could not fight off measly sprites and didn't think with those feeble minds of theirs to ask for my assistance. They just...*guessed!*"

Dapp held in a cough, knowing it would hurt if he released it, and struggled with his words. "It is disheartening, my lord."

"It is, isn't it," Taj said, running his eyes across the tense people in his Hall. "You know what else is disheartening. The fact that that little pain in the ass, Jynx...you remember her, don't you?" Dapp nodded in response. "That she and *him* have teamed up against me." Taj chuckled coldly and shook his head. "They have teamed up against *me*. Well, you were there. You saw."

"I did, my lord."

"And did I fight them off?" he asked loudly.

Dapp answered clearly so all could hear. "You did, my lord."

"Did they stand in my way?"

"No, my lord."

Taj stared at his servants, neglecting to voice a couple of points that were still racing around in his mind. Such as how terrified he was of facing Abbnar again and going back to the Pit. That he didn't notice the ivory thing in Jaron's mind when his Mytocks did. And Jaron, the one who would've made all the other problems trivial, if he didn't make such a stupid slip of the tongue.

The echo of pounding feet reached his ears and a few seconds later a young messenger came racing into the Justice Hall. The young man dropped to his knees when he saw Taj and spoke quickly through gasps of breath. "My lord. I just received a report that your scouts have found the one you've been searching for. The thief. They're bringing him to the castle as we speak."

Taj rolled his eyes. "First off, they did not find him, I did. Second, I know where they were because I sent them there to keep watch on the thief. And third, they're dead because I killed them. Anything else you'd like to add to that redundant report?"

The young man shifted nervously from Taj's sharp tone and spoke reluctantly. "Actually, my lord, they did mention news that may interest you. The thief claims to be the Kazimeer."

Taj's shoulders began to shake and after a stifled snort or two escaped from his nose, he began to laugh openly. Even his scouts knew about that accursed thing in the boy's mind and he didn't! He laughed long and hard, which slowly prompted everyone else in the Hall, with the exception of the Mytocks and Dapp, to laugh with him uneasily. Taj looked to each of them as he continued his laughing fit, nodding to Alexan, then the failed assassin, then finally his eyes landed on the young man still kneeling on the floor.

Taj felt his mind snap.

A fiery blue ball of rage replaced the weakness he'd felt upon returning to the castle. The ball rapidly filled with his frustration and hatred until it nearly consumed his mind.

Without warning, his laughter turned into a shriek so loud it shook the walls. He tapped into the power of his necklace, combining it with his own, and released a blue streak of fire across the entire Hall. The fire was suddenly everywhere, eating away at the floor, the walls, the tapestries, the throne, even the high domed ceiling. The light cast a reflection down on him from above that came from the stained glass window set in the center of the ceiling. Taj stared down at the reflection and felt his rage bloom again when he realized what it was. He snapped his head upward and stared at the picture the stained glass made of an ivory dragon. Oh, something else he never noticed! He just couldn't seem to spot that ivory thing, could he!

Taj screamed again and threw his hands above his head. Streaks of red light exploded from both his palms and shattered the glass picture above him. The colored glass shards rained down into the Hall, forcing everyone to cover their heads, except for him.

Taj looked around the Hall at his handy work. The fire was still destroying everything; however, it did not take the people. He just wanted to shock them first. The young messenger was his first target and he hurled a ball of ice at him. It froze him the instant it hit, then Taj followed up with another that scattered the frozen body into several tiny pieces. Alexan and the failed assassin he slowly melted until the remaining flesh bubbled with heat. The Mytocks he twisted together to form one vulgar being, which he then allowed the flames to consume because he no longer wanted to look at it. Anyone else who was foolish enough to remain in the Hall, he simply imploded and let the fire take away the mess.

The only one he left alone was Dapp, although in his rage he almost destroyed him as well. But then common sense told him not to destroy the only real, loyal person he had. The flames stopped as quickly as he started them. The Hall smelled like burnt wood, cloth, and flesh. Taj spun around to see the white throne melted, but still intact. Another wave of fury washed over him. He roared and the necklace glowed once again. White light ruptured from the black stone and exploded the throne into a shower of small fragments that rained down around him and on Dapp.

He wanted to destroy more but quickly got control of himself. He breathed deeply until he felt his rage settle. Only then did he turn to Dapp, who still was kneeling and also breathing deeply and erratically. He approached his Second and pulled him to his feet.

"We have made a mistake," Taj said softly.

"Yes, my lord," Dapp agreed, his voice sounding raspy.

"We cannot let such a mistake happen again," Taj said smoothly.

"No, my lord."

"Here's what you will do. I want you to handle his acquisition. You personally and no one else." Dapp looked at him and Taj saw the hesitant twinkle waiting to come out. Taj smiled. "Yes you can use force, but only if need be and not anywhere near his head or face. He holds a very special guest who I do not want to run away on me again. Understand?"

"Yes, my lord."

"Also, have commander Grec find these so-called people who are gathering against me and either have them persuaded or destroyed. Either way I don't care, so long as they cause no trouble. Assign new assassins to handle the death of all the Counts. I don't want any problems from them later down the road." He began to walk away then turned back and added as an afterthought, "Oh. And take care of that wound."

Dapp nodded gratefully that his lord had allowed him to be healed before he went to carry out his orders. But he was anxious to get moving and hoped the Healer wouldn't take too long. He couldn't wait to meet up with that boy again and repay him for this.

BIRTH OF THE STONES

Taj waited for Dapp to stumble out of the Hall before he also left, after giving orders to his servants to have the Justice Hall repaired by the following day. He headed for his chamber and once the door was closed, flopped onto the bed and covered his eyes with his arm. He was tired; too tired. He used too much power too quickly but a few hours of sleep would cure that. He could have used his magic to rid himself of his fatigue but didn't want to waste what power he had left, just in case he found a true need for it. It wasn't long before there was a rapid knock on his door.

Taj bolted upright, his anger still not completely cooled. Couldn't these fools do anything for themselves! He stalked to the door, threw it open, and glared at the messenger so hard he was surprised the young man didn't burst into flames. The messenger did look as if he wanted to pass out, though, but didn't dare and with shaking hands gave Taj the note he carried. Taj tore open the note, nearly ripping it in two, and read it quickly.

Then he read it again slowly. And again, even more slowly. He screamed, not in anger but in pure joy. The messenger actually ducked when Taj screamed but remained where he was for the reply. Taj beamed at the young man for a moment then retreated into his chamber and seeped into Nigel's mind. He definitely caught the commander off guard.

"My lord?" Nigel blurted out.

"*Excellent work,*" Taj told him. "*Does anyone else know?*"

"No, my lord."

"*Keep it that way. Do you have it in your possession?*"

Nigel hesitated briefly. "No, my lord."

"*Why not!*"

"My lord," Nigel began slowly, "I have taken a brief look at the object. It is safe where it stands, but I was not going to touch it."

The fear and awe in Nigel's tone was clear and made Taj laugh. Many of his own people feared the necklace's power, no doubt the ring would be held with the same reverence. It was something unknown, something powerful, something he had control of and they didn't. It was just as well that Nigel didn't touch his ring. He wanted to be the only one to lay hands on it.

"*Very well. The standing order is to guard that tunnel at all seconds of the day and no one is to enter before I arrive. I do not want the piece retrieved or touched. I will arrive tomorrow morning.*"

"Understood, my lord," Nigel agreed with relief.

Taj withdrew from the commander's mind and returned to the messenger. "Back you go. Run along now." He waved his hand, shooing the young man down the hall.

"Is there any reply, my lord?" the messenger asked uncertainly.

"Commander Nigel has his orders and you have yours. Go!"

The messenger scurried down the hall and Taj waited until he was out of sight, then closed the door behind him, and screamed again. He bounced on the

141

bed, like a child whose parents weren't home, then finally lay on his back, grinning up at the ceiling. He would have gone tonight, but his power was so exhausted he didn't think he would be able to withstand the simple act of putting on the ring.

The ring! It was found! It was his! After so long with neither piece in his possession and then just the necklace, he wondered what it would be like to have their combined power added to his once more. The creation of both stones had been risky but worth it. Taj held up the necklace before his eyes and stared at it with a smile. It was the setting of the stones that had been the key to their imprisonment. The fine silver casing with prongs all around, digging into the entire border, while two silver clasps crosscut over the stone, holding it firmly in place. Such a simple yet wicked design. One Reece and Jeralyn never knew he added to their original specifications.

Ah! Reece and Jeralyn; two powerful *Trislarns*. More powerful than he was at the time. They had the advantage of age and experience, but it was their age that was their downfall. He stared at the stone dangling before his eyes and remembered that all he originally wanted to do was remove them from power without killing them. He never believed it would actually lead to one of the more crucial moves of his life.

An image formed in his mind of a Taj who was far younger than he was now, dressed in full armor, sweaty and tired from battle, walking into the Main Hall. His step used to have more spring, even with the additional weight of his armor. A helmet was tucked under his arm, displaying his blonde hair plastered to his head by sweat and grime, and despite his tired muscles and joints, he managed to kneel before Reece and Jeralyn.

"My lord, my lady, it is done."

Reece shifted in his throne and grunted. However, Jeralyn was far better at extending praise. She leaned forward and gave him one of her melting smiles. "The *entire* northern region?"

"All in your hands," Taj assured. "Every village, every town, every person, loyal to your authority."

Jeralyn leaned back. "And it only took you five months."

"What took so long?" Reece demanded of him.

Taj stared at him at a lost for an immediate answer. "Well, my lord…ah, you see…there were twenty towns and dozens of villages scattered throughout the region. Every town and village had to be overcome with force. Our enemy was expecting the takeover. It was not easy but it has been accomplished."

"And let me guess," Reece growled, "it was all accomplished because of you, right?"

"Not to sound conceited, my lord, but yes, it was."

Reece and Taj locked eyes for a moment. Suddenly Reece exploded with a booming laugh and nudged Jeralyn. "He's a sharp one, he is."

"Yes, dear," Jeralyn sighed and nodded patiently. "I know."

Reece slapped his hands to his thighs and rose. "Well, my lad. It's good to have you back but go get yourself washed because you're stinking up my home."

"Whose home, my love?" Jeralyn asked with a mocking smile.

Reece glanced at her then turned back to Taj. "You're stinking up *her* home. When you no longer smell like a morpher, come join us in our sitting chamber. There is much to discuss."

"Reece," Jeralyn scolded. "The poor boy has just returned. I'm sure he's half starved and exhausted. Surely what we have to say can wait."

Reece stared at Taj waiting for his answer. Taj always hated when they put him in the middle of their discussions. He would have to side with one of them and that usually meant the other would be annoyed with him. But by the look on Reece's face, he knew the old man was determined to have his way about this. Besides, Taj was curious. They so rarely wanted to discuss anything with him that he would jump at the chance to be involved. His empty stomach and tired body could wait.

"I am fine, my lady," he said to Jeralyn. "Allow me to make myself presentable and I will join you."

Taj never bathed so quickly in his life after returning home from a battle. Usually he liked to soak for hours but this time his mind raced with a dozen possibilities of what they would discuss with him. He couldn't wait to find out. By the time he rapped on their sitting room door, he still had no reasonable answer and would have to curb his anxiousness. Reece ordered the servants abruptly out of the chamber and Taj waited until the three of them were alone before addressing them.

"My lord, my lady."

Jeralyn eyed him coldly. "Why do you always address him first?"

Taj smiled at her. They were alone now and he could allow himself to take on a more comfortable attitude with them. "I always address age before beauty, my lady. It gives me great pleasure to have your name last on my lips, so that I will feel it sitting there longer and hear its sound echo in my mind and heart."

Jeralyn cackled openly while Reece shook his head and poured wine for the three of them. "How many women have you bedded with such lies?" she asked.

"Enough," Taj said and sat down across from her.

"And do they swoon in your arms when you tell them they are the only one for you?" she asked playfully while taking her cup from Reece.

Taj also took the cup offered to him and began to answer her question with an insulting quip when Reece stared into his face.

"Careful, boy. You tread on thin ground here."

Taj snapped his mouth closed, knowing how jealous Reece could be with Jeralyn. Even though the man knew Jeralyn was completely devoted to him, he would never find any amusement with any man, including him, flirting casually with her. Taj nodded respectfully and turned his eyes toward Jeralyn. "I will refrain from answering that question, knowing that the answer could possibly result in having my head handed to me."

"A wise boy." Reece nodded in approval and sat next to Jeralyn. He raised his cup toward Taj. "First a drink to your recent victory. We are both pleased with your efforts and dedication. We know you will always do your best to do what is right by us and by the Land."

Taj could drink to that and did, feeling pleased that they took the time to praise him so strongly and yet his stomach could not uncurl, feeling as if a sword was about to come down on his throat. An awkward silence followed with Reece and Jeralyn eyeing each other, wordlessly asking the other to begin. Finally, it was Reece who leaned forward, rested his arms on his knees, his cup dangling between his hands, and stared directly at Taj.

"And now I'd like to raise my cup to another victory." He lifted his cup and Taj followed his example. Jeralyn hesitated for a moment then slowly joined them. "To the end of a very long Bloodshed."

Taj smiled. "Abbnar's army is almost completely crushed. You'll have his head on a platter soon."

"No, Taj," Reece answered softly. "We won't."

"Ah!" Taj nodded knowingly. "So you will leave nothing behind. That's better. No reason to make him a martyr." Taj raised his cup high. "May his death be painful and pave the way for your perpetual rule." He took a large drink to salute his own toast.

"We are calling a truce," Reece stated plainly.

The sweet wine in Taj's mouth instantly turned sour. It took much of his self-control not to spit it out and he painfully swallowed. He stared from one to the other, his eyes wide and uncertain. "This is a jest, yes?"

Reece and Jeralyn exchanged glances again and then Reece stared back to Taj. He shook his head. "No jest."

Taj ran his hand over his mouth absently and stared at them in shock. After a moment he chuckled lightly and clicked his tongue. "I'm sorry. I must have had my ears boxed too many times over the last five months, crawling through filth and risking my life and power to claim the Land in your names, that I don't believe I heard you correctly. I thought I heard you say you were calling a truce."

"You heard correctly," Reece answered stiffly. "And there is no reason for your tongue to be so sharp."

Taj cupped one hand to his ear and leaned forward. "Eh? I'm sorry, boxed ears again. No reason, did you say?"

"Taj," Jeralyn asked curiously, "are you upset?"

"But allow me to explain why." Taj emptied his cup in one gulp to wet his suddenly dry mouth and looked from one to the other. "For the past century I've been putting my ass on the line for you two and now I'm being told…not asked like an equal but told like a slave…that it was all for nothing. My beliefs, my life has been for nothing?!"

Jeralyn stared at him skeptically. "I thought your life was for the Land."

"So did I," Taj answered sharply. "Until you two decided to fold."

Reece slammed his cup down on the table that separated them and glared at Taj. "We are not folding," he stated firmly.

Jeralyn saw her lover's temper flare and added quickly, "The Land has been healed and you have made that possible. The excess of morphers have been eliminated from draining the Land's energy. Abbnar and his misguided ideas stand alone now. If he continues to fight us he will be finished, he knows that. It is pointless for him to do so."

"And," Reece added, his anger slightly calmed, "it is pointless for us to waste our power fighting him. Why beat a dead servant?"

"Because sometimes," Taj stated stiffly, "it is better to make sure the servant is dead than to risk the threat of him recovering and slipping a knife into your heart. Abbnar will find a way to rise against you the moment you let your guard down. He will not abide by any truce."

"He would have no choice," Jeralyn said smoothly.

Taj laughed openly. "And you believe he would allow a Bonding to be placed on him? Even if the three of us held him, he would find a way to break it."

"You sound as if you have respect for the man," Reece said.

"I have distrust of the man and I know him. I have stared at him from across battlefields, I know how he thinks and I know what he's capable of. He's shrewd, unpredictable, and slipperier than a wet toad. If he actually *does* agree to any truce, I would watch for the dagger hidden under his sleeve when he shakes hands with you."

"Now it sounds as if you have fear of the man," Jeralyn commented.

Taj stared at her levelly. "I have no fear of him, my lady, but I do consider him to be a threat. And in my opinion, threats should be eliminated before they can do real harm."

"We know Abbnar as well," Reece said. "We know him far better than you. It does not give us pleasure to fight our own, as I'm sure it does not give Abbnar pleasure."

Taj sniffed and murmured under his breath, "You didn't see him laugh his ass off when he took out your eastern headquarters."

Reece ignored the remark and continued. "The power of the Land is balanced between us four now. If he were to die, his power would be split between the three of us, upsetting the balance until the Land could become adjusted. The Land has suffered too much as it is. It's time to end this."

Taj stared at them and knew why they were so determined to call a truce. They were old and could no longer take the pressure of the Bloodshed. They wanted to rest, to reap the pleasures he had given them. Without him they wouldn't have stood a chance against the traitor Trislarns. He fought their battles, while they remained here, locked away from the reality of just what they were fighting for. True, the morpher population had decreased but did they know that Abbnar was encouraging the breeding of more? Did they know that Abbnar was tampering with forces he knew nothing about to create new morphers? Did they know Abbnar was teaching the sacred lessons of the Trislarns to common farm boys, just because they showed a spark of the gift? He'd seen firsthand the threat Abbnar represented, while they remained hidden and dictated to him what would be done. And up until now he never questioned them once. But he was not about to let Abbnar have the Land just because they were feeble and weary.

He was suddenly determined to stop them from making a mistake he was not prepared to pay for.

Jeralyn leaned forward. "Taj, understand that there comes a time when old ways must end and new ways begin. This is one of those times."

Taj rubbed his eyes with his thumb and forefinger. "What I don't understand is how you can give up when you have his head directly under your heel?" He looked up at them in confusion. "Why are you willing to take the chance of allowing him to roam free after all you've gained? After all you've fought for, why risk losing it all to him?"

"We are risking nothing," Reece assured. "A truce does not mean we are admitting defeat but that we have the advantage. We will decree what will be acceptable and what will not. If he does not abide by it, he will die."

Taj smiled cynically. "Then his child will take over where he left off."

Jeralyn and Reece stared at each other in puzzlement then turned to Taj. Jeralyn spoke first. "Abbnar has no children."

"Not yet." Taj grinned. "But in six months that will change."

"When did he get married?" Reece asked in amazement.

"About a year ago." Taj was enjoying flaunting information about the enemy in their faces. Information they should know but didn't. And they didn't know because they came to rely solely on him for information about the happenings of the Bloodshed. It was their fault entirely; they'd become lazy and comfortable when what they should've been doing was keeping an eye on things for themselves. Taj was in the position to twist the information anyway he wished in order to make things happen the way he wanted.

He continued, "And when that child is born, don't think for a second that he won't fill its head with lies about you and the condition of the Land. The child will be brought up hating and fighting you because Abbnar does. Not to mention the power that will most likely be within the child from the beginning will be crafted by Abbnar to withstand you."

Taj shook his head and spread his hands. "You can't win this one. If you kill Abbnar, the child will grow up crying for vengeance against you; if you allow Abbnar to live, the child will grow up wanting to taste your blood because of what Abbnar will tell it. The only way around this problem is to never let the child suck in its first breath of air, but then you'll have to contend with a most distressed father-to-be for killing his first born."

Taj let his words sink in, letting them arrive at the only alternative left to them. "The only way to avoid this," Reece said softly, "is to destroy both the father and child."

"Exactly," Taj answered with a slow nod.

Jeralyn seemed to be pleading silently with Reece. He spread his hands. "We never counted on him having offspring."

"I know but..." She searched for words and Taj could tell what she was thinking. She didn't want to destroy Abbnar. For whatever reason, she wanted him to remain alive. It disgusted Taj to see such compassion for the enemy and he looked away. She threw her hands up in exasperation. "How can we even defeat him? He knows when we're near, just as we know when he is. Sneaking up on him doesn't work; he'll just go into hiding. He can battle any of us one on one, but if we try to overpower him by attacking together our power gets crossed and

Hosting the Kazimeer

we end up attacking each other." She looked from one to the other. "We've tried this before and it doesn't work."

Taj had already come up with the solution before she presented the problem, but still pretended as if he was thinking long and hard on the subject. When he finally spoke it was hesitant and unsure. "What…what if we were able to somehow…combine all of our power as one?"

"That only works with short bursts of power," Jeralyn stated. "It would never be enough to overpower him."

"Actually, there is a way," Reece said. He stared off at nothing as he spoke. "If one person was the conductor, the other two could relay their power through that person, thereby combining the force to act as one. It would be under the conductor's control and all the others would have to do is willingly release their power into that person." He looked from Taj to Jeralyn. "But the conductor would have to physically be in contact with the others in order for it to work."

"Abbnar would notice the three of us standing together in a group," Jeralyn said. "If that wouldn't be enough to make him suspicious, nothing would."

"What if Abbnar couldn't see the other two?" Taj suggested. "What if they were out of sight?"

"Then the whole idea is worthless," Reece said impatiently. "I just told you there would have to be physical contact. What would we do? Jump out at the last moment to form a connection? It would only take Abbnar a second to realize what we were up to and Transfer."

Taj chewed on his bottom lip uncertainly and then his face brightened. "What if the other two appeared as something harmless? Something Abbnar wouldn't recognize right away. Something small like a…a mouse or a…stone. Something small enough that Abbnar wouldn't detect it, yet able to make contact with the conductor. The size and shape of the two shouldn't have any effect on their power, should it?"

"No, it wouldn't." Reece nodded slowly, his face clearly showing that he was entertaining Taj's idea.

"But you can't cast while morphed, you know that," Jeralyn stated.

"They wouldn't have to cast," Reece said. "Just channel their power. The conductor would do all the casting." He pointed a finger at Taj. "A stone, I like that. Not many multi-morphers around anymore who can pull that off. It wouldn't be suspicious. The conductor could keep them in a pouch until the last moment then hold onto them."

"Or," Taj suggested innocently, "the stones could look like pieces of jewelry. That way they would already be in direct contact with the conductor. There wouldn't be any risk if they fell out or were taken away at the last crucial moment."

Reece nodded again. "I like that."

"Why are we even discussing this?" Jeralyn asked testily of Reece. "We had already decided on a truce."

"Taj is correct, my love," Reece answered gently. "If Abbnar has children, he will raise them to believe in what he believes. They will join him in his fight."

Jeralyn shook her head in frustration. "What difference does it make if he has offspring or not? Why does that suddenly change everything we discussed earlier? Were we going to forbid him to procreate in that truce? No, we were all going to end this Bloodshed and get on with our lives, working together for the Land." She leaned back and stared hard at Reece. "At least, that's what I thought was going to happen."

"My love," Reece began levelly. "You remember Abbnar as your student. As that young, bright boy who would dazzle you with new, daring spells. I was fond of him too, but that changed the moment he decided to remain blind to the needs of the Land. Taj has had more recent contact with him." He stared at Taj briefly. "If he says Abbnar will not abide by this truce, I believe him." Jeralyn sniffed in contempt and looked away from both of them. Reece, obviously pained by her cold attitude, reached out and took her hand. "Can we afford *not* to finish what has begun? Will it be safe for *our* children if he and his live? This Bloodshed could continue throughout generations and I do not wish to leave behind such a legacy. We were here when it began, we should finish it before we move on."

Jeralyn remained silent for some time, keeping her face turned away from Reece but her hand still stayed in his. Finally she clicked her tongue and stared at Reece. "So we're back to killing him again, I see. Then I will agree to participate under one condition. If we fail, if this ridiculous stunt does not work, there are no second chances, no further attempts, we simply offer our truce and end it. Agreed?"

Reece kissed her hand tenderly. "Yes, my love. I agree."

For the first time since the argument between them began, Taj spoke up. "Do not fear, my lady. This will not fail."

Jeralyn fixed a cold stare at him. "How are you so sure? Do you have the power of prediction suddenly?"

Taj laughed softly as if she'd made a joke. "No, my lady, but his army is severely crippled. The capture of the northern region has practically done him in. There is little chance that what is left of his forces will rise up once he and his spawn are gone. And Abbnar will never be expecting such an attack, especially when only one of us will arrive to discuss the truce."

"Oh I see," Jeralyn spat. "So when this pitiful attempt fails and we actually do wish to discuss peace, he will be even more distrustful than he is now. Then there will be no hope of a truce between us."

Taj's brow narrowed as if he hadn't considered this possibility before. He had and already devised the perfect solution, but he had to make it appear as if her words caught him off guard. After long moments passed with him appearing to be in deep thought, he breathed heavily, sat up straight, and stared directly at them. "Then let me be the conductor."

"What?" Jeralyn asked in surprise.

"Let me be the conductor. I will be the only one Abbnar will ever actually see. He will have no knowledge of your involvement, particularly if you appear to him as jewelry. If it fails, you can say I acted alone and that you had no knowledge of my intent."

Reece spoke slowly. "If it fails, and we claim such a thing, he will demand your head as an act of our good faith. If the truce is to take place, we would have to agree."

"I understand that," Taj said humbly. "And I'm prepared to make such a sacrifice if it will benefit the Land."

Reece and Jeralyn considered his words, while Taj sat there meekly. He had no intention of ever having his head placed on the chopping block for Abbnar's benefit. In fact, if all went well, he wouldn't have to obey these two ever again.

As he suspected, they agreed to his plan. They even insisted on making their own settings for the stones they would become and sent Taj off to have them made once their designs were complete. Taj added a few minor adjustments, which would not be detected until the stones were actually placed in the settings. Jeralyn became the ring and Reece the necklace. After they had morphed and were placed in the settings, both spoke to him about their discomfort with the prongs digging into them. They became quite alarmed when Taj clamped down the silver strips that crosscut over them. But Taj assured them it was necessary, not only to keep them secure but to make them appear as much like harmless jewelry as possible.

He and Abbnar met in one of the last remaining neutral towns and sat in a nearly deserted tavern, tensely discussing the preliminaries of the truce. Abbnar didn't seem that surprised not to see Reece or Jeralyn about, since Taj usually did all their dirty work anyway. If he felt their presence, he wasn't able to locate them. However, he was genuinely surprised when Taj congratulated him on the upcoming birth of his first child.

Actually the meeting had gone quite well and by the end of it he and Abbnar were even doing a bit of reminiscing. Once they were outside, Reece and Jeralyn told Taj that too much time had passed and now was the moment for the attack. They released their power into him, melding it with his own. Abbnar had no warning or time to react when Taj struck him square in the chest with such a force that it threw him back several feet. The morphers and Weavers Abbnar brought with him for protection were destroyed instantly by a wave of flames that erupted from Taj's hands.

It was in that brief moment when Abbnar was lying stunned on the ground and the bodies of the morphers and Weavers were burning before him that Taj realized just what he had at his fingertips. He looked down at his hands, unable to believe the power that just came from him and what it did. Reece and Jeralyn were shouting at him to finish off Abbnar while he was still disorientated but Taj was not about to let him off that easily. Not when he could play with him all he wanted.

What he wanted to do was lift Abbnar off the ground and bounce him around a few times before he forced his power into the man's mind to squeeze it like a grape. What actually happened was he released his power to grip Abbnar but it escaped from him too quickly and struck a shop just beyond him. The shop caved in on either side as if a giant's fist just squeezed shut. The power then continued to another shop and then another, crushing each one as it went along.

By then Abbnar was unsteadily trying to get to his feet, obviously shocked by what was happening around him. Taj redirected the flow of power toward him but it found another target before it found Abbnar. A woman, who had come running out into the street to see what was happening, imploded instantly as the power brushed against her skin.

Reece and Jeralyn tried to pull their energy away from him, but Taj was in control now. He felt exhilarated, reborn. His whole body tingled with the added power coursing through his blood. His mind never felt more complete or sure in his life. He wasn't about to give up such pleasant sensations.

He attempted to redirect his flow again and for the briefest of seconds caught Abbnar's eye. The struggle in the man was evident; he wanted to stay and fight him but knew he wouldn't survive it. Outrage, passion, and fear poured from his expression. Taj could see his own death in Abbnar's eyes but knew it would never happen. Not when he had this triple power at his control. Abbnar would never be able to destroy him.

Taj's confidence was unparalleled at that moment but it cost him. He heaved the stream of power directly at Abbnar just as the man was attempting to Transfer. If he'd moved just a second sooner he would have destroyed him. But instead his power met with Abbnar's protection and for an instant the sound of sizzling filled the air. A moment later, the stream ripped through Abbnar's shield as he began to vanish. Blood shot out of every orifice in the man's head. His eyes, nose, and ears all had thick flows of blood pouring from them, while his chest heaved and a stream of red exploded from his mouth. Then he disappeared but Taj would never forget that image. Although he didn't know it at the time, he would recall Abbnar's bleeding face when he needed to be cheered up the most. It always worked.

However, the moment Abbnar vanished, Taj's rage rapidly increased and he had the means at his disposal to express his unhappiness with vigor. He exploded buildings, melted the people, and burned anything he laid his eyes on. He never actually wanted it to go as far as it did but he was unable to get this new power under his control. It seemed to take on a life of its own and fought him with each spell released. By the time he was able to calm and restrain his power, the entire town was nothing but a smoldering waste of burning wood and flesh.

Taj dropped to his knees with a scream of pain and delight. Never did he imagine it would be like that. It was almost like discovering that a plain, quiet girl was actually a wild, unstoppable lover, and it gave him the same sensation of satisfaction and made him hunger for more. He was finally brought back to himself by the cries of anger and outrage from Reece and Jeralyn. They called his actions abominable and horrific and demanded that he release them immediately.

Taj laughed until his sides hurt and spoke aloud. "Or you'll do what?"

Both of them had several unpleasant alternatives if Taj didn't do as they commanded but they also knew they were in no position to carry out their demands. Attempts at trying to unmorph only met with pain. Taj's careful adaptations to their setting designs paid off. The prongs would only dig in deeper if they enlarged and the silver crosscuts threatened to crush them before they ever made it to their full size. They were trapped. They couldn't return to their regular shape without killing themselves and they were too bent on revenge to simply die without repaying Taj for his deception.

And they remained trapped after all these centuries. It helped that inevitably they lost their minds to the shape they held, so Taj had an easier time controlling them eventually. But never did the feeling of loathing and revenge dissipate from them.

Taj chuckled to himself and swung the necklace back and forth gently. They could despise him all they wanted, there wasn't a single thing they could do about it. He told Reece tauntingly that he would not be alone for long. The essence of Reece didn't respond. He was so insane by now he only responded to direct pain, which Taj was only too happy to provide.

Both pieces were taken from him just before he was sent to the Pit. By the time he escaped, Abbnar placed both of them under his accursed watchful eye, which didn't make it easy for him to take them back. The spell protecting the necklace and ring was difficult to undo. The enchantment would send the protected item into the Land if it was tripped and even the original caster would not know where the piece ended up.

He sent a Weaver to infiltrate Abbnar's camp to regain both pieces a few years back. The Weaver was able to retrieve the necklace without setting off the spell but panicked at the last moment and tripped the trap for the ring, sending it off into the Land. When the Weaver returned with just the one piece, he made the young Weaver hand over the necklace then he nearly destroyed her for making the mistake of losing the ring. Unfortunately, the stupid, young Weaver escaped from punishment and only now seemed to be coming back for revenge.

That didn't matter now, though. The ring was finally found in a small town called Botin, in a coal mine for Light's sake! Clever, Abbnar, but not good enough. Taj knew the ring must have been buried deep within the Land after the Weaver tripped the protective spell but knew it couldn't remain hidden forever. By tomorrow he would have both powers combined with his own once more. The necklace's was strong even on its own. When combined with Taj's inner power it gave him enough strength to perform many levels of magic at once and still not be drained. With the ring's power added to that and eventually the boy's…he would truly be unstoppable.

He kicked his feet happily and then forced himself to relax, so he could sleep and regain some of his strength. He would need it simply to absorb the additional power of the ring. He could barely sleep, knowing that tomorrow the ring would be extracted, and the magic would be his again.

As he began to drift off, his thoughts turned toward the boy and that beast. But Dapp would locate and retrieve him soon enough. There was still hope that Taj could use the boy as he wanted, if he could just gain his trust again. Then he'd be able to destroy the ivory dragon with ease. He just needed his luck to hold out.

HISTORY LESSON

Jaron awoke when he felt someone tapping his shoulder. He bolted up and his hands grabbed hold of someone before his eyes were even open. When he did open them, they were staring at Jynx, who wore a flat expression of tolerance. He immediately released her, leapt to his feet, and backed away, not wanting to have anything to do with her or anyone else for that matter.

"*Easy. Take it easy,*" Landon told him calmly, feeling the boy's sudden jolt of fear. "*She saved both of us when she didn't have to. I doubt she'd come back just to do us harm now.*"

"The Kazimeer speaks wisely...for once." Jynx tossed Jaron's pack down in front of him. "I was concerned when my friends told me you took off. I didn't know if something happened to you."

"Nutin' 'appened," Jaron snapped. "I's left."

"You could have stumbled into Taj's hands. My friends would have taken care of you."

"I's don't need to be's taken care of," Jaron hissed. "Not by's a bunch of children anniways. 'Sides, how's was I's to know dey was jur people?"

"You should have guessed." Jynx said. "Who else but me would have the spirits of dead children on her side? How did you get here?"

"I's..." For an instant Jaron wasn't sure. He shook his head. "I's ran I's guess. I's wanted to git 'way from dose eye-less tings." Something else occurred to him. Something he hadn't really considered before now. "Wait! Ju tellin' me *dat* was Taj?! Da real Taj?!"

"Yes," Jynx answered slowly with a hint of mockery in her tone. "Who did you think it was?"

"Jus some guy!"

"Well, Taj is just some guy too."

"But..." Jaron began dumbfounded. "He's looked different."

"Of course, he was using an illusion."

"But he's merfed into dat...ting. Dat grafton ting. Dat was no illusion."

"I'm sure it wasn't. Taj is a morpher too."

Both of them gasped at the same time, "He is?!" Even Landon was surprised to hear that.

"Yes, he is. Trust me there aren't many people around anymore who can morph and cast."

"But..." Jaron started again, still unable to believe it. "He's was nice!"

"*What*?!" Landon cried.

Jaron shrugged. "Well, he's was."

"That's because he wanted something from you," Jynx said and looked cynical for a moment. "Taj can be nice right up until he's not." She got to her feet. "You should get to the Training Halls. It would be safer for both of you."

"*How did you know it was him?*" Landon asked her.

"I should ask you the same question, Kazimeer."

"I saw that necklace and remembered it from when he came to the castle," Landon answered. *"But he never wore it during these past few days."*

"Of course he didn't," Jynx stated impatiently.

"Then why did he have it on tonight?"

"Because, Kazimeer, that necklace he wears is half of his power."

"You mean he's powerless without it?" Landon asked excitedly. If that was the case, and he could find a way to remove the necklace, then he---

"No," Jynx said, interrupting his thoughts. "I said it was half of his power. Taj can do quite well on his own without either the necklace or ring."

"Did ju say ring?" Jaron asked.

Jynx fixed a flat stare at him. "Yes, little thief, I did. I believe it's the same ring you were asked to locate."

"How's did ju know dat?" Jaron asked suspiciously.

"One hears things."

"That ring is lying around somewhere in the Land, where he *can snatch it up?"*

"Pretty much," Jynx said with a nod.

"Do you know where it is?"

"I wish I did."

Landon didn't believe her, but if she were lying he wouldn't find out by bluntly asking her. For now he must work with what he had. He shifted the conversation back to his original questioning. *"But why would he put the necklace on at the last moment?"*

"Because he wanted all of his available power ready at his command," Jynx replied.

"To do wha'?" Jaron asked. He really didn't want to hear the answer.

"You don't know?" Jynx half smiled and put her hands on her hips.

"No," Jaron snapped. "Why's should I's?"

"Kazimeer, do you know?"

"Now how would I know what that foul demon's up to?"

"Because I thought you might be smart," Jynx stated firmly. "Obviously, you are not."

"How's did ju find us, by's da way?" Jaron asked suddenly, mostly to cut off the sharp string of swears that Landon was ready to use on the girl. "I's find its a bit too useful dat ju were dare when we's actually needed ju."

"Good point," Landon growled softly.

Jynx shifted her weight from one foot to the other lazily and rolled her eyes as if she were about to explain the most elementary concept to an idiot. "Taj used his power at the last moment and I tracked him. The same way he found you two in the first place."

"I's don't understand," Jaron mumbled, feeling stupid.

"Taj cannot track you but he can track me."

"Why can't he track us?" Landon asked.

"For one, I'm shielding you."

"And the other?"

"But Taj could find me," Jynx continued as if Landon hadn't asked the question. "The last time I was with you, he traced my power which led him straight to you. It was my fault completely, I was careless."

"*And now?*" Landon asked sharply.

"Now, I know better. He won't catch me off guard again, I promise. Anyway, I think that once Taj found you, he made sure not to use his power. But for some reason he did, I think *he* got careless and I was able to find him. Lucky for you two that I did." She met Jaron's eyes. "He would have bonded you and then you would have had no choice but to go with him. That's what he wanted the extra power of the necklace for; he wanted to make sure the bond would be complete with you."

"Wha's dat?" Jaron asked.

Jynx squinted at him curiously. "What's what?"

"Bondin'? Isn't dat wha," he swallowed hard, "married people do?"

Jynx thought about it. "Yes. I guess some do, anyway."

Half of Jaron's upper lip curled into a disgusted sneer. "I's don't want to marry...*him*."

Jynx blinked at him thoughtfully, then fell to the ground, rolled on her back, and cackled loudly. When she finally got a hold of herself, she rolled onto her stomach, kicked her feet up behind her, and held her face in her hands. "Oh, you poor dear! No, that's not what you would have to do and that's not what it means."

"Den wha' does its mean?"

"Kazimeer, you're awfully quiet." Jynx smiled. "Do you know what it means?"

"*Yes,*" Landon answered softly.

"And that makes you uncomfortable?" Jynx asked.

"*Of course.*"

"Why?"

"*Because it's not right.*" He continued before she could ask. "*It's not right to force someone to bond against their will.*"

"Ah...but he wasn't trying to force Jaron to bond. He was simply going to do it when Jaron's essence was most open, most impressionable."

"I's still don't understand wha' ju two are talkin' 'bout."

Jynx smiled warmly at him. "Then I will tell you, but sit down, for Kyriea's sake. You're making my neck cramp." Jaron sank to the ground slowly, but still kept his distance from the girl. Jynx swung her legs back and forth in a rhythmic motion as she talked.

"A Master's explanation of bonding is: Any two or more cores that join together to form one presence." Jaron's expression was blank. "What that means is any two or more people can have their essences joined so they are more closely...aware of each other. So they know what the other is feeling or even thinking sometimes. It's an intimate joining of minds."

"But," she continued, "even though normally it is done with consent, it does not always need to be that way. A bonding can be forced on someone if their will is weak and their mind is easily manipulated."

"Why's would someone want to do dat?"

"So that person can be controlled," Jynx said, but Jaron shook his head, not understanding. "You see, normally a bonding is consented to by both people involved, so no one person can take over the other's will. That doesn't mean that they can't, though. If one person's will is weaker than the others, the dominant person can literally control the other." She sat up and stared levelly at Jaron. "All he had to do was touch you at that moment and it would have been all over."

"Da person has to touch ju?"

"Yes. How else can the spell be transmitted?"

"Well, ju dinn't say dat," Jaron grumbled. "Dare's magic involved?"

Jynx slapped her palm to her forehead. "Sorry, I get ahead of myself sometimes. Yes, there is magic involved." She smiled at him. "What, did you think you could just walk up to someone and say, 'Hi! Let's get bonded.'?"

"Dat was me estimation," Jaron answered with a tight smile of his own, but Jynx was studying him curiously now.

"Your what?" she asked.

Landon quickly changed the subject. "*So...he could have bonded with Jaron at that moment, because Jaron's mind was so open that it would have accepted the bonding before realizing what had taken place.*"

"Correct," Jynx answered. "And once it happens, there's no way you can break such a strong bond, unless the person who did it decides to remove it. I don't think Taj would have obliged you there."

"But why's would he's want to do dat to me?"

"I don't know." Jynx shrugged. "But I can guess. Let me see...oh... maybe he wanted...let's say...an ivory dragon." She grinned at Jaron, rocking back and forth on her bottom. "I dare say that Taj is quite aware of the Kazimeer's presence in you...especially now."

"*You're saying he may not have noticed before?*"

"I think he was suspicious," Jynx said casually, "which was probably why he made the extra effort to observe Jaron himself."

"*But how would he even guess that I was here? The last time he saw me...I mean Light, the whole Land thinks I'm dead. Why would he think differently?*"

"Well perhaps if some thief didn't walk around taverns saying he was the Kazimeer, I don't think he would've caught on."

Landon felt a sensation ripple through him, which was the equivalent of someone jabbing their elbow into his ribs. He moaned, "*Didn't I already apologize for that?*"

"No," Jaron growled. "Ju said ju were sorry fure gittin' me thrown out. Ju dinn't say snot 'bout bein' sorry fure avin' Taj come lookin' fure me."

"*How was I to know?!*"

"If's ju were really da Kazimeer ju would 'ave."

"*I AM the Kazimeer!*"

"I wouldn't worry too much," Jynx said to Jaron. "I mean Taj is twisted, cruel, heartless, and insane...but he's not stupid. The last creature he wants to piss off is the ivory dragon. I think he's really afraid of facing one again. All I've ever heard was how the last one locked him in that void he calls 'the Pit'. Can you imagine what this one will do to him?" She nodded toward Jaron, but he got the idea that she was referring to Landon. However, she seemed to be waiting for some kind of answer from him.

He answered innocently, "Piss on his head?"

Jynx exploded with laughter, mainly from the seriousness in which Jaron had answered. Landon didn't find the comment as amusing.

"Great strategy, boy. I'll remember that."

"Well, how's do I's know wha' ju 'sposed to do!" Jaron snapped, feeling stupid again. "Light! Why's can't a Weaver jus finish him off?"

"No," Jynx choked, shaking her head. "A Weaver's magic would have little effect on him."

"Why's not? Jur's did."

Jynx immediately stopped her giggling and stared sincerely at him. "Aw! You're sweet," she said as if he was an infant. "No, my magic's good, but not that good. I'm just a great dust-kicker." She leaned closer to him. "Didn't you see me getting thrown all over the place? No, I can play games with him, but to set out and destroy him? Taj is far too powerful, especially with that necklace. Even if a dozen Weavers got together, it just wouldn't have that much an effect."

"Why's?" Jaron asked.

"Because he's very powerful on his own and, as we just established, he's also a morpher."

"So," he sniffed.

"A morpher's magic and a Weaver's magic are different," Landon answered. *"The best way to describe it is, a Weaver's magic deals with the elements, a morpher's magic deals with the body."*

"What about a Death Conjurer?" Jynx asked with a smirk.

"There are still some practicing? I didn't think anyone taught that dark art anymore?"

"Well there are only a few around," Jynx admitted.

"Wha's a Death Co'jureer?"

"Someone who only works with the dead. You know, command demons, bring skeletons to life, and such." She wrinkled her nose in distaste. "Nasty stuff if you ask me, although I know a bit of the art myself. Most Weavers do, but some totally immerse themselves in it."

Jaron shuddered at the thought of someone actually wanting to use magic on the dead. "Dare aren't anni 'round 'ere, are dare?"

"No! They're few and far between. Trust me, you'd know if one were around. They smell like death after working with it for so long." She stared off for a moment and muttered, "Except for this really cute one I know." Jaron's eyes bulged and he felt Landon's shock. She didn't notice their reaction and turned back to Jaron. "Well, anyway, Taj has the power of both a Weaver and a morpher. Probably knows a bit about Death Conjurer's spells too."

"So shouldn't a merfer or Weaver be's able to destroy him?"

"If you could get around his protection, I'm sure a hundred or so Weavers and morphers might make a dent in Taj," Jynx explained. Then she grinned. "Good luck getting around his protection. It's practically impossible."

Jaron concentrated on his thoughts and spoke them slowly. "So Taj has da magic of a Weaver and a merfer, so dare's too much magic fure annione to git 'round."

"That's basically it," Jynx praised and nodded.

Jaron thought about something for a moment, then asked flatly of Landon, "Den why's is ju so im'pantant?"

"*What?*"

"Ju is jus a merfer. Why's is ju im'pantant if's jur magic won't 'ave anni effect on Taj?"

"*Because I'm different.*"

"Why's?"

"*I'm an ivory dragon.*"

"So? How's will ju be's able to fight Taj?"

"*Because that's what all the records show from the last battle,*" Landon snapped irritably. "*An ivory dragon defeated Taj.*"

"But Taj is back now," Jaron taunted.

"*All right, fine. The last ivory dragon Banished Taj.*"

"Wha' if da records were lyin'?"

"Oh, now there's something I never thought of," Jynx said. "I just always took it for granted. So did everyone."

"*The records are not lying,*" Landon answered heatedly.

"How's ju know?" Jaron insisted. "How's do ju know ju won't be's as useless as errione else?"

Landon thought about it quickly and came up with the obvious reason. It was almost as if he were snapping his fingers in the boy's face. "*Then why else is he trying to destroy me?*"

"Ah! That's a good point," Jynx added.

Landon continued more confidently now. "*If I wasn't a threat to him, he wouldn't have bothered trying to bond to you so he could destroy me.*"

"That's a real good point," Jynx said. "He wouldn't have bothered killing the other two either if you weren't all a threat to him."

However, Landon was momentarily stunned. "*Killed the other two?*"

Jynx shook her head confused. "Surely, you knew that? It was Taj's hand behind the death of the Kazimeer and his heir. He meant to get you too, but obviously that didn't happen." She narrowed her eyes. "You didn't know that?"

"*I suspected, I guess, but I never actually…*" Landon breathed heavily, "*…knew for certain. How did he do it?*"

"Taj is quite the herbalist," Jynx said softly. "A mixture of certain herbs and roots, with just a bit of magic, can have quite an effect."

"How's do ju know so much 'bout dis Taj?" Jaron asked suspiciously.

"I have my sources." Jynx got to her feet. "Now you should be getting to those Halls. The sooner the Kazimeer gets there, the better."

Jaron's brow wrinkled. "Why's do ju keeps callin' him da Kazimeer?"

"Because I am, thief."

Jynx opened her mouth to answer, then instead just grinned and winked out of sight. Jaron jumped back when she did, shocked by how quickly it happened.

"Let's get out of here," Landon offered, suddenly feeling as if his skin were crawling, if he had skin.

Jaron picked up his pack and headed in the direction Landon told him to. Landon was momentarily lost in his own thoughts. That man…Taj…had actually killed Nat and Seg. It was him who gave them that horrible illness. So horrible that he had not been allowed to see or go anywhere near them once they had taken ill. He couldn't even carry out the rite of passage from the former Kazimeer; it had to be done by Mazon and Brazet instead. What bothered him the most was he didn't feel as bad as he thought he should.

That's when he noticed the boy, or rather, noticed the emotions pouring from him. Landon could feel his shame and fury at being taken in so completely by Taj. Landon would have told him not to feel that way, since he hadn't suspected that Darrell was Taj either. But he thought the boy would only resent him more for saying so, and held his thoughts to himself, making sure they went the right way this time. He just wished he could make the boy feel better somehow.

THE PIT

Taj was surprised that even though he slept little, he was exceedingly alert. He walked through the halls, checking on last minute situations before he headed to Botin to claim his ring. Dapp left during the night; the plans to pacify the people were taking place; the Justice Hall already had dozens of workers bustling about repairing the chamber. He felt good and actually happy.

His good mood left him when he Transferred to Botin and found it under attack. It seemed to be the last leg of the battle, with his army prevailing, but Taj felt his insides knot and twist. Morphers were fighting against his army and morphers equaled Abbnar. He searched quickly for Nigel's mind but only found emptiness. Nigel was dead. So what became of his ring?

He stalked through the small village, ignoring the final fights taking place around him and headed straight for the mine, which was at the bottom of a small hill, leading away from the village. Standing guard at the mine's large, dark opening were two of his Mytocks. Scattered around the entrance were a dozen or so mangled bodies of those who came too close. Taj noticed a few corpses were part of his own army; Nigel must have instructed the Mytocks well.

Taj's logical mind told him everything was all right but his gut was screaming that all was wrong. He approached the Mytocks and addressed them sharply.

"Has anyone entered?" He knew it was a foolish question but it still came out of his mouth.

"No, Master," one of the Mytocks answered.

The knot in Taj's stomach tightened and he pushed the Mytocks out of his way and headed into the mine.

It took a moment for his eyes to adjust to the darkness and he dared not cast a spell before he knew exactly where his ring was. He walked cautiously down the narrow, dark tunnel, straining to hear more than his own footfalls. After he counted fifty steps, he saw a glint of light flickering at the end of the tunnel. He proceeded even more cautiously, keeping his back up against the wall of the passage, and looking over his shoulder every few steps. He thought he would be more excited than he was, but couldn't shake the gnawing at his gut that something was terribly wrong. He couldn't wait to take his ring and leave this place.

He reached the end of the tunnel and stepped through a small opening. The opening revealed a wider area where the ceiling was higher, allowing Taj to straighten to his full height. The glint of light he'd seen before was now a brilliant glow coming from all over the room. He squinted against the brightness and focused in at what lay directly ahead of him, his ring. A second later, after his eyes had adjusted to the light, he saw what else was placed here.

Hundreds upon thousands of images of his ring. All of them placed in small, crystal boxes and each sitting on its own white pedestal. They stood so closely together that a child could barely squeeze between any two of them. They

159

lined the floor of an immense cavern, stretching almost to the limit of his vision like an uneven carpet of glittering, glass blocks.

Taj knew what the crystal boxes meant. They were protective spells, much like the first one Abbnar used on the ring, only now they were protecting even the illusions. If he failed to deactivate the spell surrounding any particular crystal case, it would trip the magic and transfer its contents off into the Land…somewhere. That held true whether the case held an illusion or his true ring. He'd have to exercise maddening concentration that was, if he could even begin to tell which was the real ring.

In the few seconds he stood there and summed up the situation, his breathing became hard and raspy, and his fists were clenched so tightly that his nails dug into his palms, drawing blood. Taj threw his head back and roared a curse at Abbnar so loudly he heard the crystal cases jingle. He quickly reined in his hatred and anger, and focused back on the many images of his ring. He would break through this small game of Abbnar's, retrieve what was his, then pummel Abbnar into the Land so hard, that he may just pop through on the other side.

While Taj scanned the images, his eyes looked beyond the rows of crystal boxes and his breath caught. At first all he could do was gape, but soon his confusion and shock were gone, and his fury filled him again.

Abbnar stood on the opposite side of the many images and was smiling broadly and wickedly. Taj breathed out sharp hisses through his teeth but forced himself not to strike. If he did, he may disrupt whatever other protective spells Abbnar placed in the area. He was not expecting to see the old man so soon again. Instead, Taj just returned the smile and waited.

Abbnar spoke softly. "Is there something wrong?"

"Nothing to concern yourself with, old man," Taj stated smoothly.

"Oh?" Abbnar cocked his head. "You sounded upset for a moment."

"No such thing." Taj grinned tightly. "I often scream curses at you."

"Do you?" Abbnar chuckled and beamed happily at the images. He stared at them briefly and then looked back to Taj. "Beautiful this way, aren't they?" Taj didn't answer. "The way they all shimmer against the light. It's a shame, really, that something so beautiful could be just as foul as you."

"Beauty is all decided by who views it," Taj said levelly. His anger was mounting. He was furious, not only because of his ring, but because Abbnar was only a stone's throw away from him and he couldn't risk an attack. And the old man knew it.

Abbnar smiled wickedly again. "Well, it's your judgment, I suppose. Go ahead. Take one."

"I will when I'm ready."

Why wasn't Abbnar attacking him? Perhaps he also didn't wish to risk upsetting some spell. But then again, why was Abbnar here in the first place? He obviously went through all the trouble to set this illusion in place, why didn't he just take the ring? Or was it because Abbnar wanted to be smug and tease him before snatching his prize away? That sounded exactly like Abbnar and by the look on the old man's face, it was precisely that.

Taj attempted to rattle him in the hopes of getting his power to dissipate a little. "You waste your time and life, old man."

"Indeed?"

"Such a feeble spell could not keep me from my own."

"Indeed?" Abbnar repeated in the same smug tone. "Then please, find your own."

"Do you have so much time on your hands that you can play these kinds of games with me?"

"I made time especially for you, Taj." Abbnar grinned. "And you are stalling. You always did. Remember?"

It took Taj a moment before he did remember what the old man was referring to. He felt a smile play on his lips. "You still find that funny?"

Abbnar's shoulders shook from silent laughter and he mimicked Taj's voice, "'I sprained my eyes, Master Kan. I cannot possibly take the examination with sprained eyes.'"

Taj chuckled, "He bought it."

"No he didn't," Abbnar snorted. "You still had to take the exam and if I remember correctly, you did quite poorly."

Taj grinned. "That was because of my sprained eyes."

Abbnar shook his head, sniffing a laugh. "Master Kan saw straight through you...just as I do now."

Taj's smile fell faster than a stone. "Why must you take a happy moment and turn it sour?"

"I'm just doing what you always do, Taj."

Staring at the old man's condescending, confident expression, Taj was suddenly reminded of their first encounter. Granted, it was a long time ago, longer than either he or Abbnar would admit, but he still remembered it clearly. It was during his first year in training. He was five and not very controlled with his power yet, if at all. One day a group of older boys began teasing him. Not so sure of himself, he ignored them but the boys grabbed him and held him down. Each time they touched him, shocks raced through his body, making him spasm. He remembered the way they laughed, especially when he begged them to stop. But they didn't, even after he wet himself, unable to keep his body from losing control. They continued shocking him until he could cry out no more.

That's when Abbnar showed up. Being only ten at the time, he was older than the boys attacking him were and larger too. He pulled the two off by the backs of their tunics and asked them if they wanted to pick on someone their own size. To the boys, who were around seven years old, a ten-year-old was a threat; to Taj he was practically an adult. After giving them a few shakes for good measure, Abbnar let them go. Taj remembered how they took off as if their heads were on fire but then recalled the way Abbnar looked down at him.

There was pity in his face and Taj wanted none of it, even at his young age. He had said to him, "I didn't need your help!"

Abbnar had shrugged indifferently. "Then I won't help you again."

After that, Taj worked constantly with controlling his magic and weaving spells. The next time those boys caught him alone again *he* wasn't the one to wet his trousers. But Taj always resented Abbnar for stepping in. It was *his* fight and even though he was losing, it was still his to handle. He always thought Abbnar was too confident when dealing with him after that. As if by breaking up some boyhood fight, Abbnar thought he was stronger than him. Taj was about to wipe that confident look off the old man's face for good.

Defiantly, he drew his cloak up around him and rose into the air slowly; he didn't want to risk walking into the images and setting off a trap. Abbnar nodded once in understanding and amusement, and also rose to the same level. Taj hovered in a cautious circle around the outer limits of the cavern while Abbnar mirrored his movements on the opposite side. When Taj had surveyed the entire floor, he raised his eyes to stare at Abbnar, seeing if he would give away some clue.

Abbnar merely smiled at him and that smile offered nothing but arrogance.

Taj tried to unhinge him. "We never got a chance to catch up the last time we met." Abbnar continued to smile. "I believe I was asking about your family and how I wished to adopt. Were you not going to give me advice on the matter?"

"You see, Taj," Abbnar said, "you don't learn. You try old tricks several times and never realize they will not have the same effect twice. Now, either make your choice or admit failure." He grinned cynically. "Or do you wish to ask me for help?"

That tone! That condescending tone was what shivered up Taj's spine, filling his body with rage. Still, he kept his voice level. "You may find yourself asking for the assistance, old man."

"Indeed?"

"Why do you use the Weaver girl as your guide to find me? I believe your power is not what you make it out to be."

"Perhaps you would like to find out," Abbnar challenged.

"I am not a fool, old man."

"Ah, but you are," Abbnar said pleasantly, as if he were complimenting him. "You are the biggest fool the Land has ever seen. If you were not, perhaps I wouldn't have taken *your own* and hidden them so well from you." Abbnar paused and his smile twisted into half a sneer. "And you *still* haven't been able to find them."

Taj refused to let his words affect him. "Are you blind, old man, or do you not see what I possess." He gestured casually to the necklace. "It is not I who is the fool. The fool is one who allows himself to be taken in… enchanted if you will…by his own enemy."

Abbnar stared at him blankly for a long moment and Taj could feel his triumph mounting. A loud crash forced Taj to whip his head around to see that one of the crystal boxes had exploded. He turned back to Abbnar and glared at him.

"You should hurry," Abbnar said, meeting Taj's stare levelly.

Taj ignored the remark while he strained to hear the cry of the ring, the same cry the necklace often made. Also, because of the necklace, he should be able to narrow down the location, since the two pieces were so intimately joined.

He nearly lost himself in the search when he was jolted out of it by Abbnar's jeering tone.

"Come now, you foul thing. I did make time for you but only for so long."

"You may leave whenever you wish, old man," Taj responded stiffly.

"And miss the look on your face when you lose that accursed piece again? I don't think so."

Taj stared at Abbnar coldly. "When I retrieve that 'accursed piece' you will be sorry you played such games with me." He tilted his head slightly. "And why are you risking giving me the opportunity?"

"I told you. I would not miss your expression."

Taj saw Abbnar bite down on his bottom lip as if holding in a laugh…or perhaps he was preventing himself from saying more than he wanted. He knew Abbnar was trying to unnerve him, trying to get him to make a mistake. In the back of his mind, though, he wondered exactly what else the old man had done.

The mine suddenly shook and several rocks fell from the ceiling, shattering more boxes.

"Soon they'll be all gone," Abbnar crooned.

Taj pushed Abbnar's taunts aside and now drifted carefully over the pedestals toward the center of the illusions. He could feel the ring. That certain hum it had, especially when he was so near. It was the hum of fear. He stopped over one of the pedestals and clearly heard the cry of the black stone. He smiled toward Abbnar, but the old man's face was unreadable. Taj carefully began undoing the protective spell; a feat made all the more difficult by having to remain suspended over it.

A box directly next to the one he was working on shattered, spraying shards of crystals over Taj, nearly making him lose his hold on the spell. His body jerked and all he risked was turning his head in Abbnar's direction.

"Do you mind," Taj asked flatly. Was Abbnar just going to let him take the ring or would he continue with these childish attempts at distracting him?

"Pardon me, foul thing, but as you know I am an 'old man' and cannot control myself sometimes."

Taj barely heard him and paused a moment in his work. Abbnar was not going to let him take the ring, of that he was certain. He was merely making him jump through hoops, playing his little game, and when Taj did break through the protective spell, Abbnar would snatch the ring away from his grip. Taj had to outthink him. He had to gain an advantage, since this entire situation was currently in Abbnar's control.

His mind spun with possibilities but each involved either attacking Abbnar outright or playing along until he found a weakness in Abbnar's plan. But there must be something more he could do; something that Abbnar would not expect which could tip everything in his favor. He forced his wild thoughts still and started over again.

He knew more about the pieces than Abbnar, since Abbnar was too afraid to use them. The pieces were powerful; they feared him; they were connected to him. And right now one of them was caught in Abbnar's little trap! Taj forced himself to hold in his anger and not let it control his decisions. He backtracked through his thoughts when he suddenly had an idea.

The pieces *were* connected to him and Abbnar may not know that. If he could lock onto the ring and hold it tightly, he would be able to follow it. He would be able to go with it even if the spell was activated, and that would send both the ring and him into the Land…and Abbnar would not know where.

Taj forced himself not to look happy about this and kept his expression neutral. More rocks and debris from the ceiling fell onto more boxes but Taj only smiled inwardly. Abbnar could play all the games he wanted. In fact, Taj would oblige him completely and even trip the spell himself; then he and his prize would be out of this place and deep in the Land before Abbnar knew what happened.

Slowly, Taj latched onto the ring's essence. He felt the ring cry out at his mental touch and it took much of his will power not to smile at that. He wrapped a mental hand around the ring and squeezed tightly, so that he would not lose his grip when the protective spell was broken. Then he proceeded in undoing the spell, just to give Abbnar the performance he wanted.

He stole a glance at the old man but couldn't read anything in his expression. It was steady and serious. Taj was suddenly reminded that Abbnar only looked so serious when he was raising power. But why would he be raising his power? To attack him? Did Abbnar figure out that he had the ring in his grasp? A rumble from over Taj's head made him glance up. A small rock was falling straight down, aimed for the crystal box Taj's true ring was trapped in. In that moment, Taj was able to connect all his loose ideas together.

Abbnar jostled the rock loose to fall on the box and activate the protective spell. Which meant, Abbnar wanted to trip the spell on purpose. And why? Because he *knew* Taj was holding tightly onto the ring. And that meant the ring was *not* going to go into the Land!

Half a second before the rock struck the crystal box Taj started to yank his mental hand away from the case with the ring still in his grip. The rock hit the box and out of nowhere a violent wind whipped through the mine and just beyond the box a small vortex appeared, growing larger by the second. Taj immediately recognized what the vortex was; the Pit. And the ring was being sucked into it.

In the few seconds this took place, Taj's mental hand only had time to withdraw a few inches away from the vortex. Without warning, a strong, iron grip was attached to his mental hand, pulling it back toward the Pit. Taj snapped his head toward Abbnar but the man's face was expressionless. Panic spread through Taj like a fire and was consuming all logical thought. He shouted to himself that if he panicked he would make a mistake, but that didn't stop the overwhelming fear pulsing through him at the sight and sensation of being so close to the Pit again.

As he tried to pull his mental hand away from Abbnar, he spoke as steadily as he could. "Come now, old man. There's no reason for this." Abbnar said nothing and his face showed no emotion whatsoever. Taj fought the urge to swallow and tried again. "We can discuss this like civilized beings, you know." The grip only pulled harder, forcing Taj to focus every last bit of his concentration on pulling back.

"Abbnar, you're making a mistake!" Taj shouted. His voice shook, but he couldn't help it. His heart was beating so hard he kept expecting to see it explode out of his chest. Abbnar said nothing and relentlessly pulled Taj closer to the Pit. Taj felt a fury well up within him and screamed madly, "I got out before! I'll do it again!"

His shouts had no influence on Abbnar and in fact, Taj felt another iron grip slap down on him and both were pulling him straight to the vortex. Taj was beyond panic now and like a snared animal, frantically twisted and yanked his body trying to pull himself free. He could already feel the essence of the Pit reaching out toward him. He could feel its emptiness just brushing against him, trying to get a hold.

"Abbnar!" Taj screamed no longer caring how afraid he sounded. "What do you want!" Abbnar's face showed nothing. "Do you want me to beg? I'll beg!" Abbnar said nothing and continued to drag him forward. Taj pulled and fought insanely and he shouted at the top of his voice, "Abbnar, please! I beg you to stop! I'll do whatever you want!" His cries had no effect on the grip at all. Taj felt tears rolling down his face and made no attempt to stop them. He had never been more afraid in his life, not even the first time he was placed in the Pit.

Taj didn't even notice he had fallen to the ground until he heard the shattering coming from all around him as he wildly struggled and crashed into the other pedestals. Abbnar did not ease up and even when Taj looked deeply into the man's eyes he saw nothing there. No emotion, no regret, not even triumph. His eyes were cold and empty. That made Taj fear him even more.

Taj tried feebly to attack Abbnar, but it only shook Abbnar's body slightly and made him lose his own strength. He quickly gave up on that method and concentrated completely on yanking himself free. He mentally begged the Kyriea to stop this and soon heard his own voice making choked moans and sobs as those requests were spoken aloud.

"*Abbnar please! Oh Light! STOP THIS!*" Nothing; no response or flicker of emotion responded to his wailing.

A small thought danced through his mind; let go of the ring. It was so simple and he was so afraid and panicked that he didn't even think of it. Still making sobbing noises and his own physical and mental structure shaking violently, he focused every ounce of his strength in making his mental hand release the ring. It was difficult since Abbnar tried closing his fist over it, but the Pit was starting to get a hold on him. He was frantic, desperate, and terrified.

A surge of wild, raw strength pulsed through Taj as he forced his mental hand to open at the same instant he yanked it away. A horrible, animal-like sound exploded from his throat as he pulled with everything he had. He landed flat on his back and watched numbly as the ring shot into the Pit and the vortex vanished.

Raspy breathing filled the mine as Taj remained on his back, exhausted and shaking. He slowly turned his head to look at Abbnar, whose face now showed emotion. Shock, confusion, and yes...regret. Absolute and complete regret was quite clear in the old man's features. Before Taj was able to sit up, he shrieked with pure rage and aimed a crackling bolt of energy straight at Abbnar.

In a wink Abbnar vanished and the raw power zipped through the spot where he'd been a second before and collided into the mine wall.

The entire mine shook but Taj barely noticed. He was still screaming wildly and incoherently at Abbnar as he staggered to his feet and released his power at anything in his view. He raced out of the room just as the ceiling caved in from the force of his energy. The tunnel of the mine also collapsed behind him as soon as he passed through it.

Billowing waves of black dust came pouring out of the mine and into the bright sunlight as Taj exploded from the entrance with the force and fury of a thousand thunderstorms. Before the guarding Mytocks had a chance to look at him they were turned into fine streaks of paste.

Taj stalked up the small hill back to Botin and sent out ribbons of power to encircle the small village. Anything the ribbons touched exploded or burned. Taj didn't care if they were his army, the villagers, morphers, or even parts of the Land. Every living creature met with the same force of raw energy and was destroyed on the spot, while Taj continued to rant hysterically.

After a few moments of screaming panic and wild bursts of power, the village of Botin became silent. Taj stood in the middle of it, breathing hard and finally getting his mental control back. His mood changed from hot, red rage, to an eerie, white calmness.

He looked down at himself, noticing the black dirt covering his entire body and felt the stickiness of the dried tears still on his face. Slowly he ran his hands over his face, smoothed back his hair and was instantly cleaned. He brushed his hands against each other and raised his face to the bright sun, letting its warmth wash over him and cleansing his mind.

He glanced around the destroyed village and smacked his lips together absently. He was hungry and not just for food. But for now food would have to suffice because if he allowed himself to think of Abbnar, he would go off on another rampage. Instead he gathered all of his memories of the past few moments and tucked them deeply into his mind, letting his hate feed quietly on them. One thing made him content, however, and it was the knowledge that Abbnar knew he had made an inexcusable mistake. He smiled at the thought and raised his face to the sky again.

"He should have killed me," he said aloud to no one. His smile widened and with a final survey of his destruction, he Transferred himself back to the castle, almost giddy with quiet revenge.

THE HALLS

The old man stood at the edge of the field with his eyes closed and his mind open. Lying next to him in the tall grass was a green dragon, who had its large head on one of its claws and was sleeping lightly, letting out a soft snore sound every so often. They'd been coming out here every day for weeks but if there was ever any sign of him it was feint and distant. The old man told himself not to worry, but when he heard the screams from his lost students coming down from the Halls that had been overrun by those creatures and fighters, he couldn't help but worry.

Something passed across his mind, barely touching it. The old man sniffed the air deeply, and then tentatively reached out further with his mind. He was sure he felt it this time and quickly sucked in a breath that startled the dragon out of its sleep. The dragon was now sitting up next to him and watching him carefully.

"Master Orren?" it mind-spoke to him.

The old man didn't turn to face him but allowed a small smile to pass his lips. "He is coming."

**   **

Jaron remained on the main road for days but protested continuously that it was not safe. Landon told him that he could not find his way through the trees and if they were to ever make it to the Halls this season, Jaron would have to follow the only way Landon knew. Jaron grumbled under his breath a lot during those days but did as Landon said. He traveled well into the night and then only stopped for a few hours before he was on the road again. Landon had the feeling the boy was trying to get to the Halls as soon as he could just to get rid of him.

When the terrain became rockier, with blankets of snow scattered across the ground, and sharp cold winds ripped through Jaron's bones like a knife, Landon knew they were close. He began peering out of the boy's eyes all the time now and remained forward even when the boy slept. When the Halls finally came into view, Landon felt his tension draining away, only to be replaced by anticipation. Jaron, frozen by the icy winds, managed to pick up his pace when he saw the Halls too. They appeared small, naturally from such a distance, however the closer he came the more massive they looked, seeming to grow larger with each step he took.

To get to the front entrance, Landon instructed Jaron to follow the path that veered off of the main road down a small hill. The Halls were a series of nine stone towers set in a circle, with a fifteen-foot high stone wall surrounding all but the rear entrance, which was left open for easy access to the fields and to receive supplies. The iron gate set in between two colossal pillars at the front of the Halls swung back and forth on rusty hinges, unlocked and unmanned.

Jaron stopped just before the gate and hesitated, glancing over his shoulder at the path leading back up to the main road.

"*Keep going,*" Landon encouraged.

"Dare's someting wrong 'ere," Jaron swallowed, looking back toward the Halls.

"That's doubtful," Landon lied, fully aware that there should be at least one student present at the gate. *"But we won't know for sure unless we see."*

Reluctantly, Jaron pushed the gate open inch by inch, trying to see beyond the ignored grounds overrun with tall grass, weeds, and unclipped branches. Taking a deep breath of reassurance and pulling his cloak tightly around himself, he shuffled forward down a cobble stone walkway.

"If you continue to follow this path, it will take you straight to the front door."

Jaron slowly proceeded with his knife drawn and made sure to check behind him every few steps. Something about this place unnerved him greatly. Perhaps it was just the Hall's sheer massive size or the fact that behind the doors were Masters who knew magic and would use it on him to take Landon out of his mind. He waved his hand in front of his face to brush away a fly that was bothering him and continued to move forward carefully.

"How's much furder?" he asked tensely.

"It shouldn't be too much longer." Landon was trying to see as much as he could through the boy's eyes but with Jaron jerking his head in every direction, it was difficult to make out exactly where they were.

A sharp cry made Jaron flinch and spin around until he realized it was just a crow. He couldn't take much more of this. Forcing himself to move on, he parted the branches of some over hung trees and breathed with relief at the sight of the door at the end of the path. It would take him about fifty, at the most sixty more steps and he would be there. Encouraged to move forward, but still uneasy, he shuffled on, until he heard the rustling from behind.

Jaron turned around suddenly, his knife poised to strike, but saw nothing. Absently, he smacked his cheek trying to persuade another fly to leave. How could there be so many flies when it was so cold? Many crow cries were filling the air now, but Jaron was certain that was not what he had heard an instant before. He took a few steps backwards, his knife still ready to strike, in case anyone, or anything, came out at him.

He nearly lost his footing from the tangles of weeds and grass, and danced around to regain his balance. In the process, he banged into something and turned around in time to see a hand drop from above and dangle in front of his face. He banged into a thick pole and slowly looked up to see what was on top of it. His initial thought was he must be hallucinating but Landon's sudden sharp scream echoing through his skull made him realize he wasn't.

On top of the pole was a creature pierced through its middle and hanging awkwardly on its back. Jaron swallowed bile that came to the top of his throat and quickly backed away from the thing. He banged into another pole on the opposite side of the walkway and saw another beast was hanging in the same fashion. Then he looked down the length of the walkway and saw it was lined on both sides with these gruesome creatures, each hanging on their backs, with many flies and crows nibbling and picking on the remains.

Hosting the Kazimeer

"They're students," Landon said hoarsely. *"They're half-morphed students."*

Jaron could almost make out the features on a twisted figure's face that perhaps could belong to a person. But it was difficult for him to believe that all these creatures, resembling both person and animal, frozen in grotesque, unnatural positions, with the point of the stake popping up through their middles, could ever have been a student.

The sight sickened him and he looked quickly down to the ground, breathing deeply to control his leaping stomach. However, what unnerved him more than anything was the fact that Landon remained silent ever since his first outburst. Jaron would almost swear he could hear him breathing in his ear, slow and raspy. Out of nowhere Landon roared. The sound shook Jaron's head and was so loud he dropped to his knees with his numb hands pressed to his head trying to block out the deafening noise. When Landon did stop, he could feel Landon's uncontrollable rage as if it were his own. He remembered some of these people; remembered them during classes, remembered them sneaking out at night to practice their morphing on their own without the Masters instructions, he remembered them… But he told himself these were not his memories. These were the thoughts of the person in his mind. Then why did he feel the pain of the loss as if he had known them?

Landon felt his fury overwhelm his thoughts and had the strong urge to destroy anything or anyone. He only realized how furious and wild he was becoming when the boy yelped in pain. Landon immediately tried to calm down. The boy did not need to experience any of this and he was wrong to take his anger out on him, even if he wasn't fully aware he was doing so. Landon tried to speak calmly, but when he did it came out more like a shaky hiss.

"Let's go."

"Where?" Jaron asked softly.

Landon felt the boy's sudden fear that they may be trapped together for a long while, since the Masters had probably met with the same fate as his fellow students.

"Away. Let's just get away from here."

Jaron slowly got to his feet and walked backward down the walkway.

An arrow whizzed by his ear, causing him to jerk away and fall to the ground. He raised his head in time to see several archers entering through the iron-gate and heading directly for him. Their bows were knocked and they did not fire again but Jaron had the feeling they would if he moved. Suddenly pouring out from the tangle of trees and grass alongside of the walkway were more men with swords drawn, creeping steadily toward him.

Jaron leapt to his feet as Landon shouted at him to run toward the entrance. The idea of having to run by those half-morphed corpses was unsettling but not as unsettling as having an arrow or blade pass through his body. He bolted down the walkway, trying not to trip on stray branches and had a moment to realize the archers and fighters were not attacking, simply closing off his escape back to the main road. And they were calmly marching forward toward him.

"You'll have to go around the Halls. There's a field on the other side which leads into the forest."

Jaron skidded to a halt.

"What's wrong with you?" Landon shouted. *"Move!"*

What had stopped Jaron finally came into Landon's view and he was just as stunned as the boy was.

An eye-less riding a horse was charging down the walkway straight for them. Its cloak was flying behind it and the speed at which the horse ran let both of them know it was going to bare down on them in seconds. Landon's tactical mind snapped back to him.

"Get near one of the poles." The Land whizzed before his view as Jaron looked over his shoulder at the oncoming troop. If the boy thought he could push through them he was seriously mistaken. Landon used his Kazimeer tone. *"Do it! Now!"*

Jaron jerked at Landon's cold, harsh voice and skidded across the walkway to one of the poles. The eye-less was still galloping toward him and once again Jaron looked over his shoulder.

"Ignore them!" Landon commanded. *"Look at the eye-less."* Jaron did as he was told, though he hated staring at that white face with those two black sockets. *"Get ready to push the pole when I say. Throw your knife away."*

Jaron, defiant to the end, shoved his knife into his belt.

"Now get ready and when I say to, push that pole. You do it!"

Jaron saw in his mind what the thronge worm was planning. "Its won't work!" he cried.

Landon had no time to argue. The eye-less was nearly on top of them. *"Push it!"* Jaron hesitated. *"PUSH IT!"*

Jaron leaned on the pole with all of his weight just as the eye-less was directly in front of him. The pole with the impaled student came forward with its sharp, spear like tip aimed straight at the eye-less' chest. The eye-less was too close and moving too quickly to rear up the horse. A horrible ripping sound filled the air as the spear tip broke through the eye-lesses skin and muscle. The horse fell with the sudden dismounting but soon was on its hooves and galloped back down the path and around the Hall.

The weight of both the eye-less and the student made the pole snap and fall to the ground. Jaron was sprayed with the dark blood spurting from the eye-less and frantically wiped it off of his face with revulsion. Another frightful sound filled the air as the hideous thing released its ear-piercing scream.

Jaron took a moment to realize the oncoming troop stopped their advancement and were covering their ears to block out the chilling noise, just as he did a second later. He barely heard Landon shouting fiercely,

"RUN!"

He staggered down the walkway toward the entrance, still keeping his ears covered. The scream suddenly stopped as if turned off and Jaron had to pause to shake his head clear. However the troop was not doing the same and immediately raced after him. Jaron bolted down the rest of the walkway, looking over his shoulder trying desperately to see how close the oncoming troop was to him.

"Look where you're going!"

Jaron whipped his head forward and stumbled to a halt as he nearly collided into the front door of the Halls. Landon sagged briefly with relief. He remembered the Halls enough to know that the boy was approaching the front door and with the speed he was moving, he would have knocked himself out cold.

"Go right," Landon commanded. Jaron panicked and started left. *"No! Right!"*

Jaron seemed to run in place for a moment but finally got his feet to move and dashed alongside of the Halls. Arrows began to rain down around him and the pounding of feet told him the fighters were right behind. Ducking and dodging, he ran with Landon bellowing out directions.

When he reached the corner of the Halls, he threw himself around it, lost his balance for a moment, and then took off again. Landon only hoped the following troop had the same problem of turning the corner so quickly but didn't dare ask the boy to look. Instead he instructed as quickly as he could.

"There will be a large field when you turn left around the next corner. Run straight into it. We may lose them in there."

Jaron rounded the next corner easier than the first and saw the large stretch of field lying behind the Halls. Without a second thought he plunged into it, no longer able to feel his feet or legs and puffing out cold breaths of air, which made his throat burn. His running slowed down to almost a walk when he began to get smacked in the face by long, frozen stalks of wheat. He fought his way through them, trying to stay a few steps ahead of the troop, who seemed to be unaffected by them and remained tight on his trail. Jaron soon became entangled in a heavy patch of wheat, which slowed him down long enough for a few of the troop members to catch up. Jaron cried out when he felt their hands grab him, pulling him out of his wheat imprisonment. He vaguely heard Landon saying something to him as he struggled madly, kicking and flinging his arms until he broke free. He only made it about two steps before he tripped over a green root sticking out of the frozen ground.

He rolled over quickly but had no time to think about how anything could survive in this dead field, as the troop members reached down through the wheat to grab him. Jaron couldn't roll out of the way in time, so he kicked wildly at the hands reaching for him. Within a blink, the green root swatted the members, flinging them away from Jaron.

Jaron slowly looked up to see a large, green, scaly head with bright yellow eyes rising up out of the wheat. Jaron couldn't make a sound and knew he was gaping as he lay at the foot of this creature, however, the creature hadn't even noticed him. It was staring at the troop.

Jaron crawled away slowly, the troop forgotten for the moment, never taking his eyes off of the massive head. He knew what he was looking at, but had never actually seen one so up close before. He also knew that the creature…

"Dragon," Landon corrected

…was only alive in morphers, since the beast itself had died out centuries ago. How he knew this, he wasn't sure, but his instinct told him to run no matter what the voice in his head assured him of. But he couldn't move since he was paralyzed with terror. He watched as the dragon narrowed its yellow eyes, pulled its head back slightly then thrust it forward, almost in a snake-like manner, and sent an orange stream of flame at the entire troop, covering all of them with one sweep. Jaron heard their screams as they caught fire and found that he could move again and did so, backing carefully away.

The dragon then whipped its head around toward him, coming within inches of his trembling body. It regarded him curiously, tilting its head slightly, as if trying to figure out what he was.

"*Arsan!*" Landon shouted happily. "*I'd know that crooked nose anywhere! Call him by his name.*"

Jaron opened his mouth but all that came out was a pitiful squeak.

"*Call him,*" Landon shouted, not sounding happy this time, and Jaron tried again.

Only what came out now was a fearful scream, causing Arsan to jerk his head back, standing upright again. Jaron was reminded that he had feet and used them to run across the field, still screaming while looking over his shoulder at Arsan, who watched him with flat confusion.

"*You fool!*" Landon snapped. "*He's a morpher! He'll know where the Masters are. Stop!*"

Jaron closed him out and continued to frantically scramble through the field, looking over his shoulder the entire time, until he crashed into someone that had been standing there but was hidden by the thick stalks. Both of them fell to the ground and Jaron landed on top of someone who grunted loudly from his impact. Jaron opened his eyes and saw the wrinkled face staring back at him. He grabbed the old man by the front of his robes and hauled him to his feet, while he pointed to the dragon.

"Dare! Dare!" Jaron shouted, then hid behind the old man.

"*I don't believe you,*" Landon moaned.

"Dare! Sees!" Jaron panted, staying behind the old man and ignoring the thronge worm.

The old man nodded to the dragon, then turned his head to look back at Jaron. "Who are you, boy?" he asked kindly in a soft voice.

"*His name is Master Orren,*" Landon told him reassuringly, when he felt the boy's hesitation. "*It's all right. He's one of the Masters.*"

"Me name's Jaron," he finally answered, licking his dry lips. The old man nodded, gesturing for him to go on. "I's brought Landon."

The old man's face brightened and he nodded to himself as if to say that he knew, but then he turned around and searched the field. For that matter, so did the dragon. Jaron watched as the old man closed his eyes, breathed deeply, then turned around slowly as if he were being led by his nose. When the old man opened his eyes and found he was staring at Jaron, he smiled politely then repeated the ritual. When again he saw his nose led him to Jaron, he stared at him in confusion.

"Where is Landon?" he asked, looking over Jaron's shoulder as if Landon might be hiding behind him.

"He's...he's in me mind." Master Orren chuckled as if Jaron had just made a cute joke and repeated his question, while he walked around Jaron looking for his old student. Jaron watched the old man circle him and also repeated his answer and added, "Do ju's tink I's 'ave him in me pack?"

"*Jaron, respect!*"

Jaron answered him aloud, "He's doesn't deserve me respect ifs he's tinks U'm lyin'."

"*Well do you expect him to believe you just because you say it's true? Tell him I passed the fifth test. I was the only one.*" Jaron growled sharply, then repeated what Landon had said. Master Orren stared closely at him but he still didn't look convinced. "*Tell him...*" Landon paused briefly because he didn't want to reveal something so private to the boy, but then figured the boy probably knew already so he continued. "*Tell him that I begged him to let me stay. I pleaded with him. I got on my knees and kissed his robe and begged him to overrule my brother. Tell him I tried to bribe him and I threatened to close down the Halls if he let me go back. And how he told me that I had to fulfill my role and that the Halls were no longer responsible for me. Tell him.*"

Landon felt hurt and angry as he relived the memory. He didn't bother to say how after Master Orren dismissed him from his head-station, he found Seg waiting for him outside the door. Seg, who saw his tear streaked face and smiled at him, as if to say that he would never get what he wanted and would do as he was told. Jaron, however, had also seen that memory and seemed to be waiting for Landon to finish it so he could find out what happened. The only thing that did happen was Landon walked away from the grinning face of his nephew and left the Halls the following morning. Landon felt Jaron's disappointment and outrage.

"Dats its?" he asked him. "Ju let dat little puke 'ave da last word 'bout dat!" Landon was surprised at how furious the boy sounded. He was also surprised that the boy referred to Seg as 'little puke', as Landon so often did.

What surprised both of them was when Master Orren asked softly, "Is what it, boy?"

Jaron was startled that he had spoken to the thronge worm aloud. But he also could feel how painful it was for Landon to leave the Halls, how much he hated to go back to the castle, and how much he despised Seg. All of the feelings and memories were still fresh in Landon's mind and he couldn't help but spill some of them over into Jaron.

Jaron met Master Orren's eyes, though he had to crane his neck up to do so, and said in a heated tone, "Landon wanted me to remind ju dat he's begged ju to let him stay. He's cried to ju, kissed jur robe. He's tried to bribe ju, tried to threaten ju, but ju wouldn't let him stay 'cause ju're a---"

"*Jaron! No!*" Landon shouted to cut him off. He could see the image in the boy's mind of the body part he was about to call Master Orren and knew he had to silence him. "*Did I mention he is the Head Master of the Halls? We need his help.*"

"He's should 'ave let ju stay," Jaron hissed to him.

Landon was stunned that the boy was taking his side over something that happened years before they ever knew the other existed, when he couldn't even agree with him about which direction to take. In an odd way, he found it was comforting but there was no reason to insult Master Orren now. He mentally kicked himself for allowing his feelings to be so strong that the boy felt them as if they were his own.

"He couldn't let me stay," Landon told him calmly. *"He couldn't overrule the Kazimeer's wishes."*

"Dat's 'cause he's weak and a coward," Jaron stated firmly.

Landon cringed and nearly pleaded with the boy to hold his tongue. He was certain Jaron had spoken the insult aloud and he wasn't all that surprised when Jaron echoed his very same thoughts the day he was forced to leave the Halls. But Master Orren didn't seem to hear Jaron. His mouth dropped slightly and his eyes grew wide in shock.

"Oh Light," Master Orren whispered as he stared into Jaron's face. "Landon?"

Jaron didn't pay attention to the Master when his ears picked up on the loud flapping sound coming directly above him. He slowly peered into the sky and saw the green dragon hovering overhead, craning its neck around as if it were looking for more bodies to fry. When it appeared its survey was complete, the dragon glided down and landed gently next to Master Orren. It gazed steadily down at Jaron, who felt all the blood drain from his face and his bottom lip quivered.

"I am sorry, Jaron," Master Orren asked. "What did you say?"

Landon heard the boy's pitiful whimpering and growled to himself before snapping at him, *"He's a student."*

Jaron heard and understood what Landon said, but it did him no good and his wide eyes remained locked on that massive green head with those yellow eyes staring at him as if he were a tasty morsel. He also couldn't seem to stop the pathetic whining coming from his mouth. Without warning, he felt sick to his stomach, felt very hot, and saw the Land start to waver in front of him. He closed his eyes and tried to regain his balance.

He also heard Landon's sharp voice saying, *"Don't you dare! Don't even think of passing out!"*

Jaron nodded and then mumbled, "Can I's goes to sleep, den?"

Without waiting for approval, he closed his eyes and heard Landon curse him violently, but blocked his voice out. Then he felt the cold ground smack against his face just before he dropped into unconsciousness.

THE MASTERS

Jaron awoke feeling warm and opened his eyes carefully. The chamber was poorly lit, with only one candle on a small table next to the bed...bed?! He realized happily that he was in a bed, with soft furs covering him from head to toe. He was also clean and his wounds were dressed. He snuggled down, wiggled his toes, shut his eyes, and started to drift off again when he had a thought. His eyes flew open but he didn't say anything, kept his mind blank, and listened. Several long silent moments passed. He started to smile and closed his eyes again, ready to sleep until he could sleep no more.

"I'm still here."

Slamming his fist down on the bed, Jaron sat upright and gnashed his teeth hard so he wouldn't spit out a curse. The thronge worm tricked him into thinking he was gone and remained silent just long enough to bring him hope.

"Why's?" he demanded.

"You passed out," Landon growled irritably. *"How are they to do anything if you don't tell them what happened?"*

"I's don't even know wha' 'appened! How's can I's tell dem?"

There was a rapid knock on the door making him jump, and the muffled voice asked, "Are you all right?"

"You must stop speaking to me aloud," Landon sighed.

Jaron thanked whoever was out there for their concern and reluctantly got out of bed. He found fresh water and clothes waiting for him. He washed, dressed quickly, and only then opened the door.

A young man, looking about his age, was standing there obviously waiting for him. It took Jaron a moment before he recognized the yellow eyes regarding him with amusement. This was the dragon? But he wasn't that much taller than he was and didn't appear to be more fit.

He noticed Jaron's uncertainty and said, "You certainly run fast."

Jaron felt himself flush and was suddenly interested in what the floor was doing. He also heard Landon remarking about morphers being deceivers; they didn't always match their other appearance.

Arsan led him down the hall and asked if he was hungry. Actually, Jaron was starving but declined, saying he wanted to see the Masters immediately. Landon agreed just as eagerly and couldn't help but notice that this place was not part of the regular Training Halls.

Jaron picked up on his thoughts and asked, "Where is dis place?"

"This is Skill Hall. It's where the Masters take those students with highly developed skills so they won't be slowed down by the other students."

"I wasn't taken here," Landon mumbled disappointedly.

"Ha-ha!" Jaron taunted silently. "Ju ain't special!"

"Be silent, boy!" Landon hissed. So much for the Masters telling him that he was the most talented morpher they'd seen in centuries. They probably just said it to appease him and Nat so he could leave sooner. He was aggravated but kept it under control as best he could, so it wouldn't flow into the boy.

175

"Oh, don't worry," Arsan assured, seeing Jaron's tight face and misunderstanding the expression. "It is far from the Main Halls. We're way up in the mountains now." Jaron nodded, though the location meant nothing to him, and followed Arsan without further conversation.

He was led into a large chamber with a long, rectangular table in the center. Master Orren was at the head and four other Masters were seated around the sides. Arsan escorted him to a high-backed chair at the opposite end of the table, bowed to the Masters, and soundlessly left the chamber. A lump in the back of Jaron's throat was threatening to come out, but Landon snapped at him in a tone that was the vocal equivalent of being slapped across the face.

"Now listen. Don't let them intimidate you. Just answer their questions with the answers I give you and we will both be out of this soon enough. Master Orren is at the head of the table. He's kind, fatherly, and will rip you to shreds if you push him too far. On his right is Master Shale. He distrusts everyone but he is wise. Just answer him confidently and he won't give you a difficult time. To Master Orren's left is Master Levana. She's quick and sees things behind your eyes. No, don't ask me how; just trust me on this. Do not lie to her, because she will know. To her left is Master Merrick. He's probably the only one you'll like and---

Because he loves to contradict people, that's why.

It means to be disagreeable. Now, are you listening? Mind me boy, because this is importa---

Just hold your tongue.

Your mind, whatever, and listen closely. To Master Shale's right is Master Bragn. She will rip your ear off if you give her any of your wise mouth. In fact, they all will, so just---

Yes, even Master Merrick. Just be polite and watch your language.

Oh yes, that was very funny. Ha-Ha, my sides, they're splitting. Pay attention!"

Jaron focused his attention back to the five pairs of eyes picking him apart. He opened his mouth to break the tension but Landon shouted at him to be silent until Master Orren spoke, so he did. It was a long wait. Finally Master Orren asked smoothly, "How did Landon come to be inside your mind?"

"Here we go," Landon said with as much relief as Jaron felt. *"Tell him I believe Mazon placed me in your mind because I was badly injured."* Jaron repeated the answer.

"Yes, we know about the attack on Landon," Master Shale answered. "However, we have not heard from Mazon."

"What?" Landon asked softly.

"So we cannot confirm if what you say is true," Master Shale said.

Master Orren waved him silent as if shooing away a fly. "Of course we know he speaks the truth," he said wearily. "I am sure all of us here can feel Landon's presence?" All the Masters nodded, some more slowly than others.

"Strange how's dey can only feel ju when Jynx can also hear ju," Jaron commented to him.

Landon thought about it. *"Either she's a better swindler than you, thief, or she's a powerful Weaver."*

"I's bettin' on da latter."

"*Me too,*" Landon agreed casually, but then realized what Jaron just said. *"Boy, how can you understand a word like 'latter', but not know what 'contradict' means?"*

"I's don't know," Jaron sighed inwardly and, although he didn't realize it, outwardly as well.

"Are we boring you, boy?" Master Shale asked cuttingly.

"*Just tell him no and apologize.*" Then he remembered whom he was speaking to and added quickly, "*Respectfully!*"

Jaron, though, shifted his eyes toward Master Shale and had a short stare down with him before he took Landon's advice. He never dropped his eyes, though, as Master Shale seemed to expect him to do.

"Master Shale, please," Master Orren said. "The boy has had a difficult time arriving here, when he did not need to come here at all." He looked at Jaron and smiled warmly. "We are grateful that you have done such a noble and unselfish act. And now we intend to help you and the Kazimeer."

"Ju *really* is da Kazimeer?" he asked Landon slowly.

"*Yes, boy. I've told you countless times.*"

Jaron was quiet briefly before he asked carefully, "Ju don't hold grudges or anniting likes dat, do ju? Da Kazimeer is 'sposed to be's kind, right?"

Landon realized the boy was seriously nervous about this. He thought Jaron was just being a nuisance when he refused to acknowledge him as the Kazimeer. But the truth was the boy never believed him at all and now thought he would actually do something to him. The thought of putting this poor thief, who couldn't find his way out of a barn, into his dungeon just because he called him a thronge worm and had to argue with him at every turn, was laughable. In fact, he did laugh. He roared and felt the boy relax immediately. He stopped laughing quickly, though, when he realized that only a few weeks ago he *had* been ready to put this boy into his dungeon. Had being trapped inside this boy's mind make him change? Or was he losing control of himself?

"We have not heard from Mazon," Master Orren was saying, which snapped Landon back to the conversation at hand. "It is likely that he is dead."

Landon wanted to shout at him and tell him he was wrong, but then faced the horrible fact that Master Orren may be right. But Mazon dead? If that was the case, then how was he to get---

"Den how's is Landon 'sposed to git out of me mind?" Jaron asked.

Master Levana answered, "Weaver Mazon was an excellent Weaver, but he had nothing to do with the Kazimeer's presence in your mind."

"*Then who---*"

"Den who's did?" Jaron asked.

Landon was becoming uneasy that the boy was picking up on his thoughts so easily that he could voice them before Landon had a chance to finish them himself. But he put his uneasiness aside for now and listened.

"The Kazimeer," Master Levana answered in a matter of fact tone.

"*What!*"

"Wha'!"

"If Landon's body was injured prematurely, the ivory dragon's instinct would have taken over to find a temporary host until a more suitable one could be found. You are that temporary host."

"But why's me?" Jaron asked meekly.

"You were probably just the most convenient morpher in the area," Master Levana answered plainly.

"'Cuse me?" Jaron whispered, but he was not heard since Master Bragn spoke up immediately.

"The ivory dragon would never pick out of convenience. The host would have to be of a dominant shape and stamina, or else the ivory dragon would never survive."

"It is a survival instinct that allows the ivory dragon to mind-travel," Master Levana stated. "It would have to have been the nearest morpher."

"*Mind-travel?*" Landon asked, feeling just as lost as Jaron did, although, Jaron seemed to be more in a state of shock.

"It has nothing to do with convenience or strength," Master Shale interrupted. "In fact it has nothing to do with the ivory dragons will at all. It is the Guardian's choosing. He decides who is fit or unfit to be a morpher."

"It is the host's strength," Master Bragn said in a clear voice. "We should test him and find out what shape he holds."

"We should do that anyway," Master Levana agreed. "A morpher wandering around loose, without proper training, is a danger."

"Would all of you close your yaps for a moment," Master Merrick snapped loudly. "Can't you see that the boy is obviously shaken?" He turned to Jaron, who was gripping the arms of the chair so tightly his knuckles turned white and he looked paler than Landon normally did. "I take it you did not know about this?" Jaron shook his head slowly.

"See," Master Levana said triumphantly. "How can he be of a strong shape if he was not even aware of it until this moment?"

"Enough," Master Orren finally whispered but everyone settled down as if he shouted. "How or why this boy was chosen to be the host for the ivory dragon is irrelevant. What is important now is that we separate the two."

"*Yes! Finally!*" Landon cried, but Jaron didn't share his enthusiasm.

The boy was still in shock and Landon could feel his fear running through his mind like wild horses. Suddenly he remembered something. When the boy had dropped down all those stairs and when he had leapt up into the tree to hold onto the branch. *That's* what felt so familiar. Landon had been feeling the beginnings of morphing in the boy. What shape did he take?

"I's take no shape," Jaron hissed at him silently. "I's not a merfer."

"*There's nothing wrong with being one,*" Landon comforted.

"I's not a merfer!" He shouted it aloud. All of the Masters, who had been discussing the process of the separation, turned slowly toward him and stared. Jaron stared back defiantly and said in a more composed tone, "I's not."

Master Orren cleared his throat and said calmly, "Jaron, you are. You must be, otherwise the ivory dragon would have overlooked you. The ivory dragon is the only morpher who can mind-travel, which means placing its consciousness into another morpher's mind, thereby sharing the same physical state until an empty host can be found."

Jaron stared blankly at him and Landon translated. *"He means that apparently, I can move my mind without even knowing I could do so, into another morpher's mind so I don't die. Now, whatever this empty host thing he's talking about is, I'm not sure."*

"What we must do," Master Orren continued, "is separate the ivory dragon presence from your mind and place it within a new host so it can grow. We must do this quickly before the ivory dragon's instinct assimilates itself to the host's purpose, thereby becoming the new self and reversing the roles."

Jaron waited for Landon to translate, but all he received was a feeling of dread. "Wha'!"

"He..." Landon hesitated briefly but then forced himself to continue, *"He said that if they don't get me out of your mind, I'll come completely forward and you would be where I am."*

"No!" Jaron shouted to him.

"I don't want your body, boy," Landon hissed, not liking this anymore than the thief did. He thought quickly. *"Ask him about putting me back into my own body."*

Jaron asked and Master Orren answered solemnly, "I am afraid that is impossible, considering Landon was pronounced dead well over two months ago. We concluded that Landon's body had already decayed, but assumed the ivory dragon's instinct would mind-travel to a temporary host and bring Landon to us. This is why we were becoming worried when you did not arrive immediately. Then when the Halls were attacked and we were forced to move, we certainly feared that Landon would not make it in time to be transplanted into a new host."

"Wha' is dis new host ting?" Jaron asked.

Master Levana answered, "If the ivory dragon was to assume your shape, all of the dragon's powers would be reduced if not completely lost. The ivory dragon is the strongest of all morphers and will be the only one to defeat the evil that consumes the Land."

"As it was done in the beginning," Master Shale whispered, inclining his head slightly. All the Masters inclined their heads and murmured, "Praise be the Kyriea. Praise be the Guardian."

Jaron leaned further back in his chair, trying to put as much distance as he could between him and these people.

Landon chuckled softly, *"You'll get used to it."*

"I's doubt dat," Jaron replied under his breath.

Master Levana continued, not hearing Jaron's comment. "Because the ivory dragon's power is the strongest of any morpher, it cannot be lost, for there are no other ivory dragon's in the Land. Landon is the last."

"I's 'spose it's a good ting I's dinn't Banish ju, den," Jaron said silently.

"Yes, thief. It was."

"So ju're goin' to kick dis Taj's ass from one side of da Land to da other?" Jaron was surprised when Landon began to emit a wave of fear and uncertainty. He tried to lighten his mood and joked, "Hey, ju don't 'ave to be's so fancy. Ju can jus smack him 'round, ju know. Or piss on his head."

Landon was still quiet and his fear grew. "*Let's just find out how I get out of your head, thief,*" he snapped.

"Since the Land needs the ivory dragon's power to be at its fullest," Master Levana continued, "we need to place the ivory dragon into a new host, so it can completely fill its roll and take ownership of the host, yet still have the power of the ivory dragon."

"We need to separate the Kazimeer's mind from yours and place it into this new host," Master Shale said. "The separation is performed by a series of spells which force the ivory dragon's presence to leave yours, since it is probably entangled too deeply to leave on its own, and enter the new host. It's called a Shift. We were afraid you would not arrive in time for the separation to take place."

"Wha' do ju means, 'in time'?" Jaron asked.

Master Shale stared at him blankly for a long moment then said as if it was the most obvious thing, "For the new host, of course. It will arrive within the next few days."

"*Who is it?*" Landon barked, not liking this one bit. Jaron repeated the question. Again, he received a blank stare from all of the Masters, except Master Merrick who was staring down at the table.

Master Orren answered, "It will become Landon."

"Yes, but Landon would likes to know who's else he's kickin' out of dare mind." The Masters chuckled quietly.

Master Orren answered him again. "You misunderstand. Landon will not be 'kicking' anyone out. It will be him. The mind is blank and will receive the ivory dragon's presence without any resistance, as your mind is doing now."

Landon suddenly found a new thing to panic about. He voiced, quite hysterically, to Jaron what he feared the Masters were saying. Jaron, however, thought that the thronge worm was finally losing himself.

"'Cuse me," he said with a wide smile. "But Landon seems to tink dat ju's want to put his mind into a...a baby." All the Masters nodded.

"Correct," Master Orren confirmed.

"*Unacceptable!*" Landon roared. "*Tell them they can take that idea, fold it into lots of pointy corners, and shove it up their wide back-sides! I won't do it.*"

Jaron could already feel him getting a tighter grip on his mind, entangling himself more. Jaron didn't want him to take over his body, though this alternative didn't seem fair either. But if it came down between his body and the thronge worm having a second life, he would push him out as hard as he could. Since he was still speaking for the Kazimeer, he forced himself to relax and spoke calmly. "Landon says, 'Nope'."

"*That's not what I said!*"

"There is no other way," Master Levana said simply. "The ivory dragon must survive. The foul power of Taj is loose all over the Land. This is the only way the ivory dragon can live and defeat him."

"How's can a baby fight Taj?" Jaron asked.

"*Yeah!*" Landon yelled in agreement, surprised he didn't think of it first.

"That problem will be solved once we are certain the new host has been accepted," Master Orren said. "We can magically speed up the aging process, and since Landon has already had all of the experiences of infancy, childhood, and adolescence, the process will take place much faster this time. In approximately two and a half years' time, Landon should reach his current age and power, and be ready to enter the Land again."

"*Two and a half years!*" Landon shouted. "*Two and a half cursed years! They want me to stick around for all that time, learning everything I know now, while Taj does whatever with the Land!*"

"Isn't dat a wee bit too long to wait?" Jaron asked, slapping on the most innocent face he could. "Taj will a'ready 'ave control of da Land, right?"

"It is either then," Master Bragn stated, "or never. By that time Taj will have his power stretched out all over the Land. His foul magic will be weakened and easier to break."

"It will be the perfect time for the ivory dragon to strike," Master Shale added confidently.

"Well, thronge worm," Jaron sighed, "its looks likes ju're goin' back into diapers."

"*This is insane!*" Landon screamed. "*There must be another way. This cannot be the only solution they can come up with. How do they know my body's gone? They haven't found Mazon. He may have saved it.*"

"I trust," Master Orren said, staring hard at Jaron, "that Landon is upset over this decision."

"*Oh, what a* brilliant *deduction, Master Orren. Did it take you all those decades of study to figure that out!*"

"Yes, he's is," Jaron replied smoothly with a nod.

Master Orren leaned forward on the table. "Landon, listen to me. This is what you were born for. This is what you are meant to do. You cannot cast away your responsibilities because you do not like how they are to take place. Only you, Landon, can destroy Taj and save our Land. Does it matter which mundane form you have, so long as your true shape still exists? Is your pride and vanity so deep that you will not sacrifice yourself as you were meant to do?"

"'As he's was meant to do'?" Jaron gaped. "Ju can't 'spect---"

"*Jaron, shush,*" Landon said softly.

"I's will not!" Jaron snapped aloud. "It's bad nuff dat dis is da only way ju can live."

"*Jaron!*" Landon hissed. "*This has nothing to do with you anymore. He's right. This is my duty and what I was meant to do. That's why the Kazimeer's have always been ivory dragons, for this reason.*" His consciousness released a heavy breath and if he had a body, he would be squaring his shoulders and pulling himself up to his full height. "*Tell him I'll do it.*"

"But---"

"*Tell him!*"

"He's do its," Jaron finally grumbled.

"He did not have a choice," Master Bragn sniffed.

Jaron wanted to snap at her for the remark but controlled himself.

"Tell him the rest," Master Merrick said and lifted his head. All the other Masters gaped at him as if he had just broken some unspoken law. "Tell him or I will not participate. And you cannot do it without me, so I suggest you start spilling *all* the facts."

Master Orren gave Master Merrick a cold look, then turned toward Jaron. "There is one more detail." Jaron waited, not enjoying the sound of that. "In order for us to separate the ivory dragon from your mind, both presences must be detached from the host so we can unravel them and place the ivory dragon into the new host, completely separate." Master Orren said no more, but Jaron bargained enough to know when something was being left out.

"And?" he asked.

"And then your presence is placed back, also separate."

"Tell him where," Master Merrick snapped. Jaron turned his head toward him then back to Master Orren, waiting for his answer.

Master Orren breathed deeply before he began. "Your body would not survive with your presence being detached for so long. Therefore, we have prepared a new host for you as well."

"Wha'!" Jaron shouted, getting to his feet. "Ju mean's to tell me   dat---"

"*That you're going to be joining me in diapers, thief boy,*" Landon groaned. "*This is not fair to you!*"

Jaron shouted aloud, "Ju're right!"

Master Orren also got to his feet and said quickly, "Jaron, please. I understand your anxiousness."

"Anckshouness? No dis is not anckshouness. Dis is bloody insane! And I's won't sit 'ere's and listen to ju old bunch'a crazy *feends*!" Jaron spun around, prepared to leave, when he saw four, large students were blocking his exit. They were merely standing there, arms clasped behind their backs, casually waiting, but Jaron had the feeling that if he took one step toward the door he would be ushered back into his chair forcefully. He turned back to the Masters. "So now we's prisoners 'ere?"

"Jaron, please," Master Orren said smoothly as he walked toward him. "This is why we did not wish to tell you. However, Master Merrick has felt it necessary to disturb you with this piece of information."

"Wha' were ju goin' to do?" Jaron hissed, pulling away from Master Orren's outstretched hand. "Jus let me die?"

"Of course not!" Master Orren said appalled. "We found another host so you would not die. There is no reason you should be terminated before your time and after performing the noble act of bringing Landon back to us. This is a chance for you to have a new life, Jaron. A rare opportunity most others would be thankful to receive."

"I's guess U'm jus an ungrateful bastard."

"*Jaron!*" Landon barked. "*Remember, respect.*"

"Bloody forgit respect," Jaron seethed through his clenched teeth.

"*Listen, he's right. You are being given a unique opportunity. You can live your life the way you want.*"

"I's do dat now," Jaron snapped forcefully. "Ifs I's do dis, I's be's dead no matter who's body I's in."

"*You will not be dead,*" Landon insisted. "*You will be you, just in a different form, like I'll be.*"

"Will I's keep me memories?" Jaron asked Master Orren.

"No."

"Will I's 'member anniting from dis life?"

"Not the way you think of it. You will retain your experiences the way the Land knows when to turn the trees green and melt the snow. Your instinct will be retained but the detailed memories comprising those instincts will not."

"Sounds likes I's be's dead to me."

"*Jaron,*" Landon warned, but the boy didn't let him say more.

"Jus da way ju will be's dead, Kazimeer." He said Kazimeer as if he were spitting out poison. "All ju know and all ju are will be's gone. And wha' will be's left is a person who's dey will control and dey will tell wha' to do. Ju will be's someone different and in me mind dat means dead."

"*You're exaggerating,*" Landon stated evenly. "*My essence will still be who I am, as yours will be.*"

Jaron asked Master Orren, "I's 'spose I's don't git da special treatment of growin' up in a couple of years, do I's?

"No. To do so requires great amounts of power. It will be difficult enough to bring Landon where he needs to be. You will be given a new life, with parents, with training for your skills, with love and attention that I doubt were given to you during this childhood. If these gifts are not enough for you, then I apologize but there is nothing more we can give."

"And I's don't 'ave a choice." It was not a question, just a cold statement.

"No, you do not," Master Bragn stated in her flat tone.

Landon immediately felt the boy's mind whirl with rage and such strength that he was certain the boy could have split the ground in two at that moment. He quickly grabbed hold of Jaron's anger and restrained him using all his strength, while trying to calm him down.

"*Easy. That's just how she is. Don't take it personally. Calm down, Jaron.*"

He felt the boy trying to wrestle himself out of his hold and doing a great job of it too. Landon could barely restrain him. He never felt such rage, even in himself, and it was sifting into his emotions, making him feel the same as the boy.

Focusing his mind on one thought, he let it loose with as much power behind it as he could muster. "*STOP!*"

Jaron stopped fighting him and let his mind slump. He was suddenly drenched in sweat as if he'd been physically fighting Landon for hours.

The Masters   183

Master Orren's eyes widen slightly when, in a blink, the boy standing before him was suddenly pouring sweat and looked weak and sick. He reached out and touched the boy's forehead. Jaron was simply too exhausted to stop him. Master Orren's eyes grew wider.

"He is hot with fever," he announced and signaled for the young men in the doorway to come over. "Take him back to the chamber. I believe this was far too much for him to comprehend in one sitting. Let him rest and when he awakes, tell me."

With a nod in response, two of the men took Jaron, who was wobbling where he stood, and escorted him back to the chamber. He was placed on the bed gently, and though his body was exhausted, his mind was alert and kept him awake all night.

Hosting the Kazimeer

DINNER AND A PLAN

Jaron saw the first hint of light streaming through the small window on the other side of the chamber but he didn't move from the bed. When the knock came at the door he didn't answer or budge, much to Landon's distress, and finally forced the knocker, who turned out to be Master Orren, to come in. Jaron remained on his back, still dressed in his clothes from the night before and stared up at the ceiling, not blinking and barely breathing. Master Orren called him, nudged him gently, tried to move him, but Jaron made his body go limp so the old Master was forced to try and lift his dead weight. Master Orren gave up, sighed wearily, and left Jaron alone again.

Landon also sighed, *"Why are you being so difficult?"*

"I's refuse to let dem kill me."

"And you're dramatic. Look, they are not trying to kill you."

"Ifs ju refuse to sees da truth den I's 'ave nutin' more to say to ju."

"The truth is this; I need to survive. In order for them to see that I do, they need to put---"

"Yes, yes. I's 'eard dis all last night. But wha' ju don't sees is dat dey don't give a rat's ass ifs *ju* survive."

"That's the whole reason they're doing this."

"No. Da whole reason dey're doin' dis is so da *ivory dragon* can survive, not ju. And ju won't once dey do dat sor-cer-ee on ju...and me."

"This is what it all comes down to. You don't care about the Land or me. It's all about you. Well did you ever think that if you no longer existed the Land would be better for it? Did it cross this cob-web infested mind of yours that if you made this sacrifice, Taj may not have the Land under his thumb, and maybe other morphers wouldn't be staked up like meat on sale at the market, and maybe you could do something noble and decent with your pathetic life! Did this ever occur to you thief?"

Jaron clicked his tongue. "Now, where was dis att-IT-tude last night?"

"What?"

"Where was dis, 'I's da Kazimeer, kiss me feet's' att-IT-tude last night, when dose fools where decidin' wha' ju should do wit jur life?"

"They didn't decide. They reminded me of why I am the Kazimeer."

"Well den if's all Kazimeer's are as spineless as ju, I's goin' to find Taj and join him."

"You speak of treason so bluntly when I can hear you?"

"Yes. I's speak its 'gain ifs its pleases me. I's shout its from all corners of da Land. Why's should I's care? Ju won't be's 'round to do anniting' 'bout its anniway. And needer will I's."

Landon was silent for a moment, forcing himself to remain composed. Of course this thief had no sense of loyalty or honor to the Land, so he would try to explain it to him. *"I am not thrilled about this decision either. But there is no other way the Land can be helped."*

185

"Dare is no other way *dey* can tink of. Wha' 'bout ju? Oh, wait! Never mind. I's forgit. Ju don't tink."

"*I am not going to be sucked into an argument with you, boy.*"

"Dat's right. I's is a boy and, Kazimeer, ju 'ave disappointed and disgusted dis boy greatly."

Landon felt numb. "*What do you mean?*"

"I's mean I's thought ju were stronger, is all," Jaron murmured. "I's thought ju would be's stronger dan dose fools."

"*I am,*" Landon mumbled.

Jaron snorted loudly, "Ju is not. Ju knelt 'fore dem and asked, 'Who's ass shall I's kiss first?' Likes I's said, wha' 'appened to dat Kazimeer att-IT-tude I's been puttin' up wit fure weeks?"

"*Now even if I agreed with you, which I don't, but how do you propose I get my point across to them? I'm not exactly here to enforce my will, you know.*"

"I's spoke jur words to dem and dey listened. Dey listened real well when ju gave dem no argument and folded to Mader Ass's speech 'bout honor and duty and all dat other manure. Dey 'eard ju quite well, den."

"*I protested.*"

"Once. Only once did ju actually say jur own thoughts, den ju bowed to dem. Wha' kind of Kazimeer is ju?"

Landon heard such statements ever since he took the throne and they always caused some kind of emotional response from him; anger, uncertainty, amusement. But when Jaron said them, they stabbed him like a knife through his heart and it hurt. It hurt because he felt that Jaron was speaking the absolute truth and because *he* knew it was the truth. He did bend to the Masters, because they were his old teachers and they had an answer when he didn't. *He* didn't and *he* should. He should know how to save the Land. He knew if he had a body, he would probably be choked up with anger and frustration. Instead, his frustration came out of Jaron's mouth.

"I's won't fight dem annimore," Jaron whispered hoarsely. "Why's should I's when da Kazimeer won't stand up fure himself. If's dis is da best answer den I's will not fight 'gainst its. But I's don't know if's dis is da best answer since da Kazimeer dinn't bother lookin' fure nather answer. He's dinn't even *try*! Even Nat would never 'ave agreed to jus one answer."

"*What do you know of it?*" Landon shouted, furious that the boy would bring up Nat so casually.

"I's know nuff. I's saw nuff of Kazimeer Natal's rule from a distance and 'ave recently seen him from a closer view. And I's know he's would never 'ave agreed to dis as quickly as ju did. I's don't pretend to be's loyal to annione or to know wha' da Kazimeer is 'sposed to do. But I's tink da Kazimeer should know better den to fold so easily. Da Kazimeer is 'sposed to be's smarter and stronger den da rest of us common folk, 'cause dat's who's us common folk turn to when we's want to feel secure and when we's want to know dat erriting is a'right. Da Kazimeer is not 'sposed to bend so easily but I's tink ju did 'cause its *was* easy. Easier den standin' up fure jurself. Ju asked me if's I's wanted to be's a slave fure da rest of me life. Well, wha' 'bout ju? Ju've been as much of a slave as me."

Landon felt that knife in his heart twist deeper and found he had no words to say in his defense.

"Why's should I's fight, when *me* Kazimeer doesn't even bother to," Jaron spat.

Landon was stunned even more silent. Did he say what Landon thought he said? Landon chose to hear what he thought because those words changed everything for him. Then he forced himself to admit that he had bent too quickly to the Masters and there had to be another solution. Even if there weren't, he wouldn't know until he looked. But in the meantime he was causing a risk to Jaron. The Masters did say that if he weren't removed from the boy's mind, he would eventually take over and push Jaron back. They had to hurry this up.

He realized Jaron rose from the bed and already had placed his hand on the door.

"*Stop!*" Landon cried. "*Wait! Don't open that door!*"

"Who's ju?" Jaron asked. "Do I's know ju?"

"*Don't be cute with me, boy. Just get away from that door and let me think.*"

"Ju...t i n k?" Jaron said slowly, rolling the word around on his tongue. "Do ju's know wha' dat word means?"

"*Shut up, boy. Or are you not finished tearing a new hole for me to defecate out of?*"

"Huh?"

"*Are you finished with your fierce admonishment of me?*"

"Wha'?"

"*Are you done talking!*"

"Oh. Are ju goin' to listen to dose fools?"

"*Not yet,*" Landon finally answered.

"Den I's will not continue wit me fierce admonishwha'ever." Jaron felt the thronge worm already calculating and planning, and smiled to himself as he flopped back down on the bed. "Wha' ju's tinkin'?"

"*How to get out of here.*"

"Dat's easy."

"*Oh?*"

"I's can jus sneak out."

"*I doubt it,*" Landon stated. "*You are probably being watched very closely. I don't think they will let you just take a walk without an escort of many. So I need to figure out how to get rid of the escort.*"

"We's need to figure out. I's doubt ju've had much 'appenings wit dis sort'a ting." Landon had to admit that was true.

The two of them argued, discussed, tossed away, and re-thought several ideas throughout the rest of the day. When the familiar knock came at the door that evening, Jaron opened it and smiled humbly at Master Orren.

"Ma-ST-er Orren, I's wish to apologize fure me tantrum last night and me bes'avior today. I's...I's was jus stunned, is all."

"That is understandable," Master Orren said smoothly, however his face was as hard looking as a rock.

Jaron bowed his head slightly and put on his innocent face. "I's was bein' selfish. I's wasn't tinkin' of da Land or da Kazimeer. I's only tinkin' of me. But I's thought 'bout dis all day and I's know dis is not 'bout me or wha' I's want. I's was jus…'fraid."

"*Easy, boy,*" Landon warned. "*He can see through this dust cloud you're kicking up.*"

"But I's a great dust kicker," Jaron told him silently, while he kept his head bowed and waited. He started to worry that he did pour on the change of heart attitude too much, when Master Orren place a hand on his shoulder and no longer looked like a rock.

"It is understandable that you were frightened. But I promise you this act is not in vain. You will be helping the Land more than you know, along with Landon and yourself. Nothing inside of you will be lost."

"*Oh, you are so right,*" Landon agreed at the same moment Jaron did. Landon chuckled but Jaron had to use most of his restraint not to join him. Instead, he smiled his boyish grin that worked wonders on adults as it did now. Master Orren patted him on the shoulder and his smiled deepen.

"You must be starved," Master Orren said. "You have not eaten since you've arrived."

Jaron had to agree, for he was starved, and allowed himself to be walked down the halls to the dining room where the other students and Masters were already seated.

The first thing Jaron noticed were the many colors worn by the students. The first thing Landon noticed was how few students there actually were. He wondered how many were lost in the attack on the Halls.

Jaron immediately began asking him questions and Landon answered briefly as the boy was led across the chamber. He explained the different colors worn by the students were to represent the different ranks of experience; how the students ranged in age from ten to twenty, how the dinner meal was a very formal and impersonal time, and for Jaron to just hold his tongue as much as he possibly could.

"Isn't ju a bit old to 'ave gone through dis trainin'?" Jaron asked him. He walked slowly by the rows of tables lined up and felt the many eyes staring at him. He was a thief and not used to being observed so closely.

"*I was at the correct age,*" Landon told him, confused as to why the boy asked such a question.

Jaron figured the thronge worm attended many years ago and concentrated on keeping his eyes down, so he wouldn't have to look at any one face for too long. He was led to the head table at the front of the room and seated between Master Orren and Levana. Once Master Orren sat, a bell chimed and other students silently brought in trays of food.

"*Oh, I used to hate to do that,*" Landon remarked.

"*Ju* actually used to serve others?" Jaron asked him curiously.

Landon showed him a memory from when he'd been on serving duty at the Halls and, after a snide remark from his nephew, dumped a bowl of hot portage on Seg's head. Jaron bit his lip to keep from laughing. He didn't like this Seg person any more than the thronge worm did, even though he'd never met him.

His face was turned sharply by Master Levana who then tucked a cloth napkin into the nape of his tunic. Jaron's first reaction was to push her hands away, but Landon told him to just let her do it and not bring any more attention to himself than needed.

"There," Master Levana said with satisfaction once she had finished her near strangulation of him.

Jaron gritted his teeth into a smile and murmured a thank you before he focused his attention to the table, so he wouldn't have to look at anyone. His eyes widened. They had real silver-utensils and crystal plates and glasses! The only ones he had ever seen had been in the hands of other thieves. He could make a small fortune with only a handful of what was here. He was seriously tempted to nonchalantly swipe them under his tunic but fought the urge. No, he must behave himself. He was a guest, however much of an unwelcome one, and he did kind-of represent the Kazimeer, so he must be good. But it was so tempting.

"Do you not know how to use them, boy?" Jaron turned toward the voice of Master Shale, who was looking at him. Jaron was confused by the question and his face must have shown it, when Master Shale grumbled impatiently then held up a spoon. "This is a spoon. You ladle liquids with it, such as soup or cream. But not your wine or water."

Jaron blinked slowly at him with disbelief. "Really?" he asked with over-exaggerated sarcasm. Apparently, Master Shale, and the other Masters listening, had no experience with sarcasm, or if they did, they didn't show it.

"Now this is a fork," Master Shale continued. "You pierce tough food such as meat or vegetables. But do not point it at you. It is very sharp. It is only used for food."

Jaron about had it with this lesson and grabbed his fork in his fist as an infant would, and stared from it to Master Shale. "Wow! And 'ere I's thought dese tings were used only as weapons."

"I assure you, boy, they are not," Master Shale stated firmly.

Jaron noticed Master Levana carefully inching his knife away from him. He ducked his head down so he could stare her in the eye and silently asked what she was doing. When she realized she'd been caught, she merely stared back and said, "You will not be needing this tonight."

Jaron slumped back into his chair and was caught between screaming and laughing. He found he wanted to do both and covered it up by coughing into his fist.

"It's not polite to laugh at the dinner table. Or slump. Don't you have any manners?"

Jaron choked and stared wide-eyed ahead of him at nothing. Just when he was starting to like this person in his mind, he went ahead and said something so condescending it made Jaron want to scream. He made a conscious decision that he had had enough of this. Landon immediately felt the mischief surging through the boy.

"*Thief, what are you going to do? Never mind. Whatever it is, don't!*"

Jaron didn't push the thronge worm away and, in fact, wanted very much for him to see and hear everything he did. He put his elbows on the table, held his face up in his hands, and looked around the room with wide, curious eyes. When the servers placed the several large platters and bowls of meat, vegetables, pickled fruit, potatoes and bread on the table, Jaron nudged Master Orren with his elbow and grinned.

"Dis is lots of food."

Master Orren smiled and nodded as the bowls and platters were being passed down from left to right. When Master Orren held out a platter of meat for Jaron to take a helping, Jaron grabbed a handful, stuffing half into his mouth before he dropped the rest onto his plate.

"Dis is really good," he said, making sure he talked while his mouth was full. He took the platter from Master Orren, whose expression didn't change, and thrust it at Master Levana. "Ju gotta try some of dis," he said as he swallowed his last bite. He placed a handful of meat onto her plate, while her hands were still busy holding onto the platter. She smiled tightly at him, thanked him under her breath, and kept the line of food moving.

The next serving was a bowl of pickled fruits and Jaron noticed Master Orren putting a helping onto both of their plates and then passing the bowl directly to Master Levana. Jaron picked up a handful of fruits, shoved them into his mouth, chewed once, then spat the entire mouthful out across the table, where it landed with a soft squish.

"Tastes likes dung!" he said loudly, so his voice echoed across the room, and wiped his mouth on the back of his sleeve. He caught Master Levana's sharp eye and saw she was glancing from the napkin around his neck then back to his face. Jaron glanced down at his chest, gave her an embarrassed shrug, held the napkin up to his face, and blew his nose into it, making loud honking sounds.

"*Jaron!*" Landon cried. "*Are you insane? Stop it!*"

Jaron let the thronge worm know that he had heard him by giving a quick answer, then busied himself with tossing the napkin over his shoulder and returning to the meal. He noticed the line of platters stopped coming but that was all right. He simply reached across the table, and over the other Master's plates, for whatever suited his mood at the moment.

Leaning across Master Levana's plate, he fumbled around in a bowl of potatoes, kneading one in his hand before shaking his head slightly, and tossing the unwanted potato onto the table. When he found one to his liking he sat back down with a bounce and took a bite too big for his mouth. He opened his eyes wide in surprise and slammed his hand down on the table several times, making the glasses and plates jingle.

"Dis is da best bloody ting I's ever had," he said, spitting bits of food out with each word. "Ju 'ave to taste."

He shoved the half-eaten potato in Master Orren's face. Master Orren shook his head politely, so Jaron turned to Master Levana who was already shaking her head. Jaron got out of his chair, started to offer his food to Master Shale but didn't even give him a chance to decline and turned toward Master Merrick. Master Merrick sat sideways in his chair, Jaron figured so he could see everything going on, had his mouth covered with his hand, and was shaking violently from laughter.

"Want some?" Jaron offered.

Master Merrick shook his head, took his hand away from his mouth, which showed a wide smile, and said softly, "No thank you, Jaron." He gave Jaron a quick wink and shifted himself to sit forward again. Landon had been right; he did like Master Merrick.

He offered his food to Master Bragn, but she slapped it out of his hand before he could speak. Jaron reacted by flinching dramatically and whimpering like a hurt dog.

"*Jaron!*" Landon hissed. "*This is not funny. And if you're doing this thinking it will make me look bad, you are wrong. You're only making a fool out of yourself.*"

Jaron surveyed the students and saw the younger ones giggling quietly and the older ones eyeing him with open disgust. Jaron smiled at the students, food hanging over his teeth, which he noticed made the younger students giggle harder, and returned to his seat.

Master Orren placed a firm hand on his shoulder and whispered, "I think you have had enough fun tonight. Now let us eat like proper people. All right?" Jaron nodded innocently and looked back to his plate.

"Use your utensils," Master Shale grumbled at him.

Jaron smacked his palm to his forehead, grasped his fork in the infant fashion, and studied it closely, as if he had already forgotten how to use it. With his other hand, he snatched at his plate, knowing that if any of the Masters had been able to see the movement, they would have dismissed it. He chuckled inwardly and remembered when he had done this gag before. He enjoyed it, even if no one else did.

"*No!*" Landon shouted, seeing the memory from the boy. "*You will not do that! I command you not to do that!*"

Oh well, he just had to do it now, didn't he? Still studying the fork as if it was some foreign object, he jabbed it quickly at his face, startling Master Levana and Shale, who'd been watching him closely. He screamed, getting to his feet and covering his right eye with both hands.

"Me eye! Me eye! Looks!" He held out the fork in front of him with the olive he snatched at the end of it. At a first, quick glance, and since he already planted the idea into their heads, the Masters and students thought they saw an eye hanging on the end of his fork. Some of the younger students screamed and even Master Levana jumped back in her chair, as if to get away from it.

Jaron uncovered his eye, showing that it was undamaged, and popped the olive into his mouth with a smile.

"Jus a joke," he said, grinning at Master Orren, who was looking like a stone again. He heard the snort and choke from the end of the table and glanced over to see the front of Master Merrick's robe covered in wine along with a napkin he held to his face, while he jiggled hard from laughter. Apparently Jaron caught him at the right moment.

Master Orren grabbed Jaron by the arm and yanked him into his chair. "No more jokes. No more games. Just eat or I will ask you to leave the table."

"It's not me fault," Jaron protested and jabbed the fork into his arm. "Ow! Sees! I's can't control its."

"*Jaron,*" Landon growled warningly.

"Its jus…Ow! Sees!" He made a stab at Master Orren, who ducked back and stared at Jaron in shock. "I's can't…Looks out!" he shouted as the fork made a lunge for Master Levana and caught her arm.

"*Jaron!*" Landon roared. Jaron settled down, hearing the anger in the thronge worm's tone. After a pause, Landon asked calmly, "*May I please have the use of your left arm for a moment?*"

Jaron felt the thronge worm's mood and grinned as he freely gave Landon charge and switched the fork to his left hand. Now he really didn't have control over his movements as his left arm poked Master Orren lightly and any other Master who came near him. Jaron let his left arm have the fun, while he resumed his supper.

The younger students were laughing outright now, while the older, disapproving ones tried to silence them. Jaron chewed a few more bites, took Master Levana's napkin and dabbed the corners of his mouth with it, while Landon continued poking at the Masters and laughing madly in Jaron's head.

Suddenly there was a tight grip on his left wrist and two nails pinched his ear. His head was snapped around and brought up close to Master Bragn's face.

"That will be enough of this," she spat as she twisted his wrist. Jaron and Landon winced together, and the fork fell out of his hand.

"Well what do you expect when you treat the boy like some beast," Master Merrick snapped, moving closer to her.

"If he behaves like one, he will be treated as such," Master Bragn replied stiffly.

Master Merrick snapped back an answer but Jaron couldn't hear him. At first he wasn't even sure what happened but soon made the discovery. Landon had come completely forward. He didn't just have the use of an arm or his tongue; Landon had control of his whole body and Jaron was just an afterthought somewhere in his own mind. However, while he was making this connection, Landon had, in one quick motion, twisted his wrist out of Master Bragn grasp and now held hers in the same fashion. With the other hand he grabbed her chin and pulled her face nose to nose with his.

"If you ever touch me or Jaron or any other student like that again," Landon growled softly, "I will not only have you discharged as a Master but I may also find it necessary to have you arrested, since I know there are many students who have been abused countless times for simple mistakes. Perhaps if you ever had the chance to have copulation in your miserable life, you may not be such a bitter, old, whore who has nothing else better to do than to use her power on helpless children so she can feel grander than a worthless piece of dung." With that, he shoved her away hard.

Hosting the Kazimeer

Just as quickly as he came forward, he retreated, giving Jaron control again over his own body. Jaron slumped back in the chair, breathing deeply, and forced himself not to shake.

"I'm sorry, Jaron. I had to."

Jaron could understand that. He would have done the same thing had Landon not come forward so quickly, though he wouldn't have used such pretty words. But what made him feel so uneasy at the moment was the deafening silence throughout the entire chamber and the way every eye was staring at him, as if he had suddenly turned into some unknown beast right before them. Actually, he did.

"I believe you should go to your chamber," Master Orren said smoothly.

Jaron glanced toward Master Bragn, who was still staring at him with a look of shock and hurt. Jaron thought about apologizing to her, but remembered *he* wasn't the one to say those hurtful things. He got up wordlessly and left the room with three large students following him.

When the door to his chamber was closed, he sank slowly to the bed, allowed himself to breathe again, and shake off the uneasiness he felt.

"Are you angry?" Landon asked tentatively.

"No, not angry. Terrified is more likes its." He dropped his head and gripped the side of the bed tightly. "I's had no control. None at all. Maybes deese fools is right."

"What!"

"Well, maybes dey is." Jaron swallowed and licked his lips. "Maybes we's should jus let dem do dis baby-transfer ting."

"You were the one who gave me grief about it when I wanted to do it. Now you're changing your mind?"

"Its still me mind to change," Jaron grumbled. "Even ifs I's end up in some baby, and even ifs I's not zactly me, I's won't know dare's a difference anniway. I's never know 'bout who's I's is now." He moaned in annoyance and started pacing the room. "But at least I's won't still be's me and trapped in wha' was once me mind. Ju 'ave no idea how's frightenin' dat was."

"Yes I do," Landon answered softly. *"I know exactly how terrifying it was, 'cause I felt it too. Do you think I want to trap you?"*

"I's don't know," Jaron mumbled under his breath. Landon growled in outrage. "I's 'spose not."

"I don't. You were right, boy. There must be another way, but we won't know until we get out of here and look." He made his consciousness release a small wave of quiet disappointment. *"But if you're afraid to try, then I understand."*

"I's not 'fraid," Jaron said defiantly.

"Oh sure you are. I don't blame you. You're the one who has to face all those eye-less things and keep running in every direction. And now you have to worry about me possibly taking over your mind, well, I can hardly blame you for wanting to back out now. It's all right, Jaron. You can break your word to me. I understand."

"I's never gave ju me word," Jaron snapped.

"Sure you did," Landon crooned. *"Remember. You said, 'Weeze need to figure out' when I said I needed a plan. That means you gave me your word that you would help me figure a way out of here so we could find another solution to our problem. Well, at least that's what I thought you meant. I see I was mistaken, since you want to fold to the Master's plans. But, hey, I don't blame you. It's much easier."*

"Ju're usin' me own words 'gainst me," Jaron growled.

"Am I? I didn't think I was. I thought I was just stating the obvious. Anyway, I'm sure...hmmm?" He trailed off and remained silent.

"Wha'?" Jaron demanded. Landon still didn't answer. "Wha'!"

"Oh, sorry. I was just thinking that perhaps when I'm an adult and you're still an infant, I could raise you as repayment. But then I remembered that I probably wouldn't know who you were, unless someone told me and even then I wouldn't care, so I'd probably just end up requesting you."

"To do wha'?" Jaron asked, trying to tell if the thronge worm was serious or not.

"Huh? Oh, requesting? It means that I would order you to work for me, since I would still be the Kazimeer and you would just be a...oh...I don't know. Maybe you'd end up being a girl." Landon felt the boy's utter horror at the thought and continued with it. *"Well the Masters never said you'd be a male, did they? You know, I could end up marrying you."* Jaron gagged. *"Or have you as one of my concubines. That's probably more accurate since I'm sure the Kyriea is displeased with the way you treat women just to add a coin or two to your purse. Yes, that's probably what would happen to you."*

"Da Kazimeer doesn't 'ave concubines," Jaron stated firmly.

"Oh? Well, I guess I'd be the first then. It just seems to be so fitting, is all." He sighed. *"Well, call the Masters. Let's tell them our decision."*

"No!"

"Excuse me?"

"No!" Jaron snapped as he brushed his arms and chest frantically as if they were covered with invisible bugs. "I's not goin' to tell dem anniting."

"Now Jaron, this was your decision. Come on, be a brave boy."

"I's not goin' to say anniting," Jaron stated as he began pulling the top sheet off of the bed. "We's jus go wit our first plan."

"You think so?"

"Yes," he grumbled and shivered as he tried to shake off the idea of being a girl and married to... He shook his head to clear the image, sat on the floor, and began to rip the sheet quietly.

"I suppose you're right," Landon agreed and kept his satisfaction closed off to the boy. *"Now make sure they're thin. That's right. We'll have to get some stuff from the kitchen."*

"Easy."

"And a change of clothes."

"Easy," Jaron sniffed.

"And---"

Hosting the Kazimeer

"I's know," Jaron said firmly. "Jus lemme finish dis 'fore mornin', will ju!"

Landon kept silent, with the exception of a comment every so often, and let the boy finish the first part of their plan.

SHAPES

Jaron finished stuffing away the pieces of his night's work when the familiar knock came at the door. He glanced out the window and saw that it was still dark outside, so he quickly yanked off his tunic and messed his hair. The bed needed little messing, since it already looked slept in, and Jaron opened the door while he fumbled with his trousers as if he had just put them on. Of course, it was Master Orren who was accompanied by two large students. Jaron gestured sleepily for Master Orren to come in and stumbled over to the water pitcher, splashed cold water on his face, and smoothed back his wild hair. He didn't need to pretend that he was tired, he was. Master Orren entered alone and closed the door quietly behind him.

He studied Jaron for a moment then said, "That was quite a performance you displayed last night."

Jaron shot him a glance as he pulled his tunic over his head. "Ju too."

"Oh? How so?"

Jaron mimicked harshly, "'Dis is a fork. Dis is a spoon'." He stared at him flatly. "Why's ju were at its, why's dinn't ju tell me not to piss in me trousers?"

"We thought you had mastered that by now." Jaron rounded on Master Orren ready to explode but Landon quickly told him it was a joke. Jaron bit his tongue hard and said nothing. "You must understand. We are not used to someone of your...background at our Halls."

"Me background? Wha' do ju know of me background?"

"I can only assume, of course, but I am certain you come from a harsh, delinquent environment, with no boundaries in place to keep you from behaving in such an outrageous manner. I can also assume you have had no parental supervision to keep you disciplined and respectable."

Jaron's anger bubbled up again but Landon hushed him. "Ju 'spect me to keep gittin' slapped in da face!" he hissed to him.

"*They're just words. If you don't believe in them they can't hurt you.*" Again, Jaron bit his tongue.

"I can see I am angering you, however, that is not my intention," Master Orren continued smoothly. "I am stating what is evident and why you were treated how you were last evening. The other Masters are simply not used to working with someone as untrained as you are. That will soon change."

Jaron ignored the last remark. "Wha' do ju want of me?"

"I would like you to meet Resh, our shape-seeker."

Jaron's heart stopped when he suddenly remembered what he was. He shook his head. "Dare's no reason fure dat."

"Of course there is," Master Orren replied. "If your shape is discovered now, it will be easier for you to adjust to the new host. Otherwise, you could go through years of not knowing your true shape, which would mean your training would begin later. This way, your training can begin almost immediately when you are of age, and you will grow into an experienced morpher, with discipline."

"Ju mean controlled," Jaron grumbled under his breath.

Landon snapped at him to hold his tongue and added, "*Just do as he asks.*"

"He's tellin' me, not askin'."

"*Do what he says then, so he doesn't become suspicious. Do you want to get out of here or not?*"

Jaron thought if he bit his tongue any harder he would bite clean through and have it fall out of his mouth. Instead, he grumbled under his breath and finished dressing, while Master Orren nodded with approval and waited.

They walked down the hallway with one of the students walking ahead of them and one behind. Jaron became lost by the second turn, but Landon told him *he* would remember the layout of these Halls so long as Jaron continued to let him observe everything. They arrived at a small hallway with only one door. Master Orren knocked once then walked in without being invited and left the students outside. Jaron followed slowly, dragging his feet as much as possible.

They entered in what appeared to be a large sitting room, with pillows in place of chairs and only one small table in the center, with strong, musk incense burning on it. On the walls hung strings of brightly colored beads and rugs, while the floor remained bare. And on every empty spot of the floor, shelves, or walls, there was a lit, scented candle, adding to the sweet odor of the room. Jaron noticed Master Orren shift uncomfortably but he felt completely at ease. He had lived with the Feshare' before and knew of their lifestyle. In fact, he almost wished he brought his ear clip so he could identify his clan. Perhaps this Resh knew where they were and may even be a member, although he didn't recognize her name. But then he remembered why he was here and became tense.

A soft jingling sound came from around a corner and a slim, dark woman stepped into the room. Her face was slightly painted and a red scarf held her long hair back. Her dress seemed to be made up of different patches of bright material, which was modest yet revealing. And any part of her that wasn't covered by the dress had some ring, clip, necklace or bracelet on it, except her feet, which were bare. She nodded to Master Orren with a small smile then swept her rich, dark eyes over Jaron as she glided toward him and took his face in her hands. Jaron flinched involuntarily when he saw those long painted nails coming toward his face, but she merely brushed them across his cheeks and her touch was gentle. She smiled at him, and Jaron couldn't help but smile back and inhaled her scent, which smelled like honey-suckle. His smile deepened.

"*If you don't stop thinking what you are thinking, I will personally stamp the thoughts out of your head myself,*" Landon growled. "*Show an ounce of respect!*"

"Oh, but Landon," Jaron answered silently. "Don't ju know dat da Feshare' women are da best love-mak---"

"*I don't want to hear this!*" Landon cut him off sharply. "*Just remember why you're here.*" That cut down on Jaron's impulses. In fact, it shut them off completely. Resh had pulled away and was gesturing for him to sit on one of those large pillows.

"Tank's a lot, thronge worm," Jaron hissed. "Ju're jus jealous 'cause ju is still chaste."

"*I am not going to discuss my private life with you,*" Landon stated firmly.

"Wha' private life? Ju don't 'ave one."

"*Just sit down, boy,*" Landon snapped. "*We have other things to do today.*"

Jaron sat across from Resh, who never lost her smile but stared at him in such a way that Jaron felt if she could, she would go into his head and take a look around. He tried not to shift under her gaze and held her eyes for as long as he could before he finally had to glance down. He wasn't sure how long she watched him but then she reached under the table and pulled out small pouches along with a mortar and pestle. From each pouch she placed leaves, herbs and small stones into the mortar and began grinding them while she continued to stare at him. When the mixture became a fine powder, she sprinkled some onto the burning incense and it gave off a heavy aroma that made Jaron relax again.

Resh reached under the table once more and pulled out a small goblet that was filled with red wine. She waved the goblet carefully around the smoke of the incense then held it out to him.

"Drink from your family's water line. Drink and become one with the Land and one with your true self."

Her voice sounded like the jingle from her jewelry and Jaron waited to see if she said more. When she didn't, he took the goblet, raised it in a small "cheers" fashion, and then took a sip. It was sweet and tasted like every fruit he ever tried, with not a hint of bitterness to it. He smacked his lips in approval and noticed Resh gesturing for him to finish it. He did so, without much persuading, then handed the empty goblet back to her.

Resh continued to stare at him, but now Jaron didn't seem to mind and actually smiled a little. Resh smiled back but her sharp eyes were not affected by it. Jaron allowed her to watch him while he remained relaxed and tranquil.

"*That's probably why she gave you the wine in the first place,*" Landon commented. "*To relax you so she can find your shape.*"

The words struck Jaron hard and he forced himself to be stiff and alert. He didn't like the idea of someone manipulating him.

Resh jerked her head back and studied him curiously for a moment, before she said softly, "Concentrate." Her eyes snapped back to their probing, but Jaron didn't allow himself to relax this time and did the best he could to avoid her gaze.

"*Would you just get this over with,*" Landon moaned. "*It won't hurt.*"

"How's do ju know? 'Ave ju gone through dis 'fore?"

"*Well no, there was no reason for me to since I come from a line of ivory dragons, but---*"

"Den how's do ju know?"

"*Oh, cut the rope boy and stop being such a coward about this.*"

"I's not a coward!" Jaron growled. "I's jus don't likes someone peekin' into me head."

"Concentrate and relax," Resh said firmly again.

Jaron didn't want to concentrate but found himself relaxing against his will. The heavy scent of the incense plus the wine in his body made it difficult not to relax.

"*Good. Get this over with.*"

"It's a waste of me time," Jaron mumbled to him.

"*Fine. Then let her find out it's a waste of time so we can get out of here and gather the rest of the items we need.*"

"Ju don't believes me."

"*About what?*"

"I's not a merfer."

"*Yes, fine boy, you're not a morpher,*" Landon agreed tiredly.

"I's not," Jaron stated firmly.

"*Fine, you're not.*"

"Don't patronize me."

"*Where are you getting this vocabulary from?*"

"Wha'?"

"*Never mind,*" Landon groaned. "*Just get this finished! I'm tired of listening to your petty thoughts.*"

"I's tired of listenin' to jur big mouf. I's bet ju gotta fat ass too."

"*Oh that's real mature, boy. Why don't you demonstrate some more of that sharp wisdom of yours. You're nothing but a foolish, illiterate mongrel who would steal the milk out of an infant's mouth if the opportunity presented itself.*"

"Only once!" Jaron protested.

"*Why am I not surprised? Look, boy, would you just---*"

The loud, sharp sigh brought both of their attentions back to the situation. Resh was shaking her head and, for the first time since she had entered the chamber, acknowledged Master Orren's presence. "The ivory dragon is interfering," she said as if it was his fault.

Landon blurted out several beginnings of protest and would have been pointing a finger directly at Jaron, if he had a finger, but remembered that his defense would not be heard, so he held his thoughts to himself.

Jaron, still feeling the effects of the incense and wine slurred out, "Ju 'eard da nice lady. Git lost!"

Resh covered her mouth with her hand, but her eyes lost their hardness and she shook her head. Master Orren said nothing, only stared at Jaron in disbelief.

"*'Git lost'?*" Landon repeated, then growled to himself, not wanting to argue anymore. "*Very well, boy. But hurry this up!*"

He withdrew into the thief's mind but had gained enough experience over the past weeks to remain withdrawn yet still able to pick up what was going on around the boy. He was curious about what shape the boy would take and didn't want to miss a single detail.

He remained silent and although he could no longer hear or see, he could definitely feel a change take place in the boy's emotions. There was also a new presence now sweeping across Jaron's mind, probing gently as if it were delicately trying to find something. When it poked at a particular spot, Landon felt another change take place.

At first, Landon wasn't certain what he was seeing, then it all became quite clear, though he couldn't believe it. A stampede of shapes were charging straight toward him with such speed that Landon was certain he would be trampled into the fabric of Jaron's mind. Birds, leer-cats, wolves, jackals, phoenixes, bugs, fish, even dragons and a few beasts Landon knew he never saw or even heard about.

Landon knew if he had the time he would enjoy watching and studying all of these shapes, but all he felt was fear as every creature came dashing straight for him as if they were in a race to see which shape would reach the invisible finish ribbon. Landon screamed and was suddenly caught up in the wave of shapes washing over him. His logical side told him he had no body, and neither did these shapes, so there was nothing to fear. However, his reflexes and instinct told him to get out of the way, which he was having a difficult time doing.

He let out a shriek that came from the most primal depths of himself, and saw through the throng of shapes what looked like a small opening. He didn't bother wondering where that had come from or why it was there now; all he could think about was escape. He dove through the opening…and he found he was alone again. He must have withdrawn further into the boy's mind for he couldn't even feel Jaron now. His fear sparked up again. What if he had gone too far and couldn't come forward? There wasn't even a glimmer of the boy's thoughts. It was quiet and empty. After the sudden burst of shapes Landon thought he would have been grateful for some quiet, but this was too eerie, too frightening, and too alone. Worse, he felt like he was being watched. Not just watched but hunted. This was probably the exact same way prey felt when it was being stalked by something that wanted it dead.

He thought he would start screaming again when a sound reached him. He listened and at first all that answered him was the hum of silence, but then he heard it again.

"Landon?"

He turned in every direction looking for him. He could feel him now and the sensation was becoming stronger, but he was still trapped in the emptiness. He wanted to call back but something inside reminded him that he was the Kazimeer and the Kazimeer didn't call out like a helpless child.

To damnation with the Kazimeer!

"*Jaron!*" he called back, not caring how terrified he sounded. He was terrified. This emptiness was creeping up and threatening to shake him hard. "*Please, Jaron!*" He thought he sounded like a little boy who got separated from his parents at the market, but again, he didn't care right now.

"Dare ju is."

Landon would have wept with relief if he could at the sound of that Granate accent coming from behind him. He spun around, ready to mentally embrace the boy, but stopped short. What had called to him wasn't Jaron and yet it was. Was this the boy's true-shape? Did all morphers have to go through that wild stampede of creatures before their true shape emerged? Was he different because he was an ivory dragon and his shape was already predetermined? He suddenly could think of a dozen other questions he wanted to ask but the shape before him mind-spoke again.

"Wha' da pox are ju doin' 'ere?" The shape looked around the extremely empty area. "Ju shouldn't even be's 'ere. Ju were really lost. I's couldn't find ju. Come on, follow me."

The shape sprinted off and Landon had to use all of his mental strength just to keep it in sight. But it never ran too far ahead of him and soon Landon felt the familiar sensations of what he had become used to over the past weeks. He could hear the muffled voices and once again felt in touch with Jaron's mind. The boy's true shape winked out of sight but not before it changed into at least two other different forms. But that was impossible. A double-morpher was rare, but a triple or quartet one? That just couldn't happen.

The muffled voices became clearer and Landon finally was able to hear what was being said.

"...ver happen before," Resh was saying.

"Perhaps it was too much for him," Master Orren offered.

"Here. Help me get him up." There was a short pause, then Resh's soft voice saying, "Jaron?"

Landon realized for the first time that the boy was unconscious. He poked his mind gently, also calling to him. The unexpected snap and flood of strong feelings let Landon know the boy had awakened.

"Landon!" he shouted silently.

"Yes. I'm still here."

"Wha' 'appened?"

"I was hoping you could tell me?" Landon asked cautiously. Did the boy remember?

"I's don't know. I's tink I's passed out. Dat's wha' I's git fure not sleepin' all night, den drinkin' on an empty stumuk."

Obviously, Jaron didn't remember. Landon agreed mildly but thought it wise to hold the memory of their odd encounter to himself for now. At least until he figured out what had happened.

"Jaron?" Resh was asking softly.

Jaron opened his eyes and smiled sheepishly. "Sorry."

Resh let out a large sigh of relief. "Oh, dear boy, there is nothing for you to be sorry about. It was my fault entirely. I shouldn't have pushed your mind so hard your first time."

"Are you all right?" Master Orren asked, leaning over him. Jaron had a feeling the real question was, 'Is the Kazimeer all right?' but he held his tongue and nodded. He got to his feet unsteadily, after announcing several times that he did not need to see a Healer, and walked with Master Orren to the door.

Resh stopped him before he left and said in her jingle voice, "We will try again when you are ready. Yes?" Jaron nodded, although both he and Landon knew there wouldn't be a next time. Not if they could help it.

When Resh's door was closed behind them, Jaron turned to Master Orren and asked, "Is dare anniting else ju need me fure?"

"No," Master Orren answered politely. "You are free to do as you wish." With that Jaron walked off down the hall, allowing Landon to call out the directions of how to get where they were going, and ignored the two large students trailing behind him.

**   **

Master Orren watched the boy teeter down the hall and shook his head slightly. His two students followed him without being told and he returned to his head-station. The entire way he pondered whether or not he should introduce the boy and Landon to their new parents. They were at the Halls, but it had been decided earlier not to let them have any contact before the Shift could take place. However, Master Orren wondered if that was such a good idea. Perhaps it would do both of them some good to see what new life was waiting for them and what good people their parents would be. Then maybe they wouldn't be so intent on trying to find a way to escape.

Not that there had been any sign of an escape plan taking place, but Master Orren knew Landon well enough, and even from his brief encounter with Jaron, he thought he knew the boy well enough too. They were planning something. Which was why Master Orren had taken every precaution to make sure they stayed where they were now. Students were placed at each entrance and exit, the boy was never left alone, except to sleep and even then there were students placed outside his door. And he'd been placed on the fourth level of the Halls, so it was too far down to jump.

Of course, there had been discussions when the boy first arrived about what they would do if he tried to take his own life. But Master Orren summed up the boy quickly and knew he would never try anything so drastic. Besides, Landon would never let him. He could tell Landon exercised a decent amount of control over the boy, which was to their advantage. Landon would not want to disappoint his old Masters. Not to mention, Master Orren knew Landon well enough to know which rope to yank to make him see reason.

He'd done enough yanking in the beginning, so for now he would let the two of them plan whatever it was they were planning, and even go so far as to let them try and execute it. But when they saw their plan fail, then it would be time for Master Orren to speak to Landon again, push the point to its destination, and show him that this was the only alternative. Landon could be stubborn, and a bit too emotional, but when problems and answers were laid out before him, he would be reasonable.

Still, there was the problem of the boy. The meeting of the parents would be for his benefit mainly. A temptation, a lure to make him docile enough, perhaps even excited to willingly participate in the Shift. It would certainly give him something else to think about and may even disrupt whatever plans they were forming long enough for the Shift to take place without many problems.

After his daily schedule was complete, he made his decision, but called the other Masters together to receive their input. Of course it was met with some resistance, but after Master Orren calmly explained his reasons, everyone, however reluctant some were, agreed.

"Very well," Master Orren said with a nod of approval. "After dinner, I will make the introductions. Until then nothing is to be said about this." He added as an afterthought, "And let us not have a repeat performance of last night." Mouths opened to protest but Master Orren continued before they could speak. "I am sure the boy knows how to eat. Your remarks simply agitated him. We are trying to gain his trust, not make him wary of us. Also, he is not a student here, yet. Until he is, he will be treated like any other guest. Agreed?" It was.

When the bell chimes told them it was the proper hour, they left for the dining hall and stood at the head table as the students filed in. Master Orren waited and looked for the boy. He half expected to receive a message that the boy would not be joining them, in which case, Master Orren would be sure he received an ample helping delivered to his chamber. He couldn't have the boy starving himself, could he?

However since the dining hall was on the first level, he didn't hear the wild commotion taking place on the fourth, but did notice the pale student, who obviously had been sent as the messenger.

The student reluctantly stood beside him, his head bowed, and said feebly, "Master Orren?"

Master Orren could barely hear him over the sound of the students taking their seats and the quiet chatter. He turned toward the student, who was still studying his feet, and said, "Speak up boy and meet my eye."

The student slowly raised his head and swallowed visibly. "Master Orren," he began again, but then muttered into his chest.

"Speak up," Master Orren demanded.

"He's gone," the student blurted out and his face turned even paler as he said the words, "The guest is gone."

THE ESCAPE

The Soil Count was ushered roughly into the back area and released with a shove toward the Second. The Count sneered at the two Defenders and turned abruptly to face Brazet. "I demand to know why I am being treated this way!"

Brazet flexed his hands and forced himself to remain unruffled. "What did you think you were doing?"

"I was trying to get a breath of fresh air. I can't stand the stink of being stuck in this forsaken place any longer."

Brazet took a step closer. "This 'forsaken place' is what is keeping you alive." He grinned. "But I can change that."

The Soil Count scoffed, "Don't you threaten me, Brazet."

"That's Second Brazet to you. And right now, I'm the honorary Kazimeer, so I suggest you be *very* careful what you say to me."

"You are no Kazimeer," the Count sniffed. "No more than Landon ever was."

Brazet grabbed the Count by the front of his jeweled covered coat and raised him off the ground. "Landon is more of a Kazimeer than you or any of those other fools could ever be! I believe I hear treason in your words."

"Brazet!"

The Second looked over to where the Weaver stood and reluctantly dropped the Count. Mazon held in a groan and approached the Count who was getting to his feet. They'd been trapped together for far too long. The longer they were forced to remain in hiding, the more heated tempers would become and soon they'd be at each other's throats, doing Taj's work for him. He was beginning to believe they should attack Taj now, instead of waiting. At least then they could put their anger to good use.

"Martin," Mazon said soothingly, placing a hand on the Count's shoulder. "We must remain patient. It will not be much longer before we're able to---"

"To what?" the Count snapped. "Surrender?"

"We are not going to surrender," Mazon assured firmly. "But we must have a majority of the people's support if we're ever going to---"

"Surrender," the Count finished for him.

"Would you let the man finish!" Brazet growled.

"Martin," Mazon said quickly, before the Count could retaliate. "I know this is hard on you but we can't give up. These things take time."

"What things!" the Count shouted. "What are you doing? I haven't seen any organization of any plan since I've arrived."

"We are doing plenty!" Mazon hissed, beginning to lose his own temper. He got himself under control. "We are doing plenty. The word about Blasdon really being Taj is getting to the people, and they're starting to believe or at least think twice about him. We are gathering those who are in danger from Taj."

"Peasants," the Count sniffed. "Probably the same peasants who drove me out of my home and accused me of murder."

"That's precisely why we want them with us," Brazet jeered.

Mazon spoke loudly over both of them. "We are coordinating our efforts with others across the Land. We are working on an organized strike. Everything must be prepared before we can attack Taj. And we are waiting for Landon."

"Landon's dead!" the Count shouted.

Mazon was beginning to believe that. Anyone they'd sent out to search for him never returned. He'd received no word from him. Recently, he started to wonder if he should continue to spend so much of his power in keeping his body functioning. But the moment he began to think that way, he might as well give up on everything else he'd been working on. Besides, the emotional pain that would surface if he ever truly believed Landon was gone would be too much for him to handle. He practically raised the boy himself, treated him as if he were his own. He glanced over to Brazet and knew the Second was feeling the same way. Both of them had known Landon since his birth and both cared for him dearly. They couldn't give up on him.

But while Mazon chose not to argue with the Count about the matter, Brazet couldn't hold his tongue. "Now *that* sounded like treason."

"What treason!" the Count growled. "I'm stating a fact!"

"You wouldn't know a fact if it bit you on the ass."

The Count took a step toward Brazet. "I know that you and Landon are both poor excuses for Natal. *He* wouldn't have let that fiend get such a hold on the Land."

"Oh right!" Brazet chuckled without humor. "Nat would've known what to do, sure. But he is dead, now, isn't he."

"By Landon's hand."

"No! By Taj's hand."

"You don't know that."

"Well who else could've done it? And before you say Landon again, don't even go there," Brazet growled. "You know damn well Landon wouldn't do that. Even you *have* to know that. But I find it a little too convenient that Natal took ill and then right after Taj shows up."

The Count was silent for a moment, weighing his words. He finally challenged, "If that is the case, then it's obvious that Taj doesn't find Landon to be much of a leader. Why else would he be left alive for so long after the death of the true Kazimeer and his heir?"

Brazet grinned and stood toe to toe with the Count. "Landon was supposed to go on that trip."

The Count blinked in surprise. "He was?"

"It was all arranged but at the last moment Natal changed his mind. Two days before they were to leave Nat told Landon he was staying behind."

"Why didn't any of this come up during the investigation?"

"Maybe because you didn't investigate hard enough. Maybe because you and those other fools wanted to believe what you wanted, instead of actually finding the truth."

The Count considered the new information but then glared at the Second. "Well, it didn't do too much good, now, did it? He's still dead."

"That's the last time you will say that," Brazet threatened.

"Why?" the Count challenged. "What are *you* going to do about it?"

"I'll have you hog-tied, shove an apple in your mouth, and present you to Taj myself! I'll bet he'd just love to carve his name into your hide."

"I warned you not to threaten me, Brazet."

"And I warned you not to leave this area."

"I'll do what I please."

"Not while I'm in charge."

"That can be changed."

"Try it!"

"Don't test me."

"Oh, I'll do more than *test* you," Brazet growled and pulled back his fist.

Ice water dropped down on both of them from above, soaking them thoroughly. When they had finished coughing and sputtering, they looked up together at the ceiling. Then their eyes slowly turned toward Mazon.

"Shall I do it again?" the Weaver asked. "Or are your tempers cool enough?" Neither one said a word; they just grumbled and turned away from the other. Mazon looked toward the Count. "Martin, go dry off and when you are do *not* venture outside again. If you do, I personally will have the doors shut behind you and not let you back in. And before you start threatening to run to Taj and tell him where we are, I'll also personally see to it that you never make it that far. Understood?" The Count stared at him in shock for a moment, then muttered that he understood. He stomped off, making squishing sounds as he went. Mazon turned toward the Second. "And Brazet, just dry off."

Brazet squeezed the water out of his hair and called after the Weaver, "Mazon?"

"Are you going to pick a fight with me now?"

"No." He moved along side of him and whispered, "I've been meaning to ask you."

"What?"

"Well..." Brazet chewed on his thoughts. "Are you sure about Landon? I mean, do you think he's still out there somewhere?"

"I'm positive," Mazon answered after a slight delay.

"Then why didn't Nat or Seg use this...mind-travel thing? They were ivory dragons too."

"I've thought about that," Mazon said. "Brazet, you saw them. They could barely breathe from the pain, let alone use their morpher skills. All their energy was being used just to keep themselves alive."

"But how can you be sure they didn't and aren't out in the Land somewhere, like Landon?"

"Because I didn't feel it happen. I kept waiting for it to happen. I kept asking Natal about it but he couldn't understand me by then. I think that by the time they made it back to the castle, their bodies and minds were so torn apart, that their second half was lost. Whatever killed them decayed their minds first and took the body after. They didn't even know they were ivory dragons by the time they arrived home."

Mazon stared off at nothing, remembering how horrible it had been. Landon didn't know the half of it, since he was kept away, but he'd been there throughout it all. He was there when they died, Maura first, then Segvature, and three days later Natal. He loved all of them, even Seg despite his attitude, and was grief stricken when they were gone. The three days in between Seg's death and Natal's, he pleaded with Nat every moment to mind-travel. But Nat didn't know who he was by then, let alone what an ivory dragon was. Mazon never felt his spirit shift, as he did when Landon was struck. It was ironic actually; with Nat he begged him to travel and he didn't, with Landon he begged him *not* to travel and he did.

The worst part now was he didn't know where Landon had ended up. The most likely person for Landon to mind-travel to, was telling him Landon hadn't, at least, not to him. And even he was telling Mazon how he must have been mistaken about feeling the boy shift. Mazon knew he wasn't wrong about this. Landon was out there somewhere, lost and trapped in someone's mind and they had no clue where to begin to look.

Mazon stared back at Brazet. "I didn't feel them travel. I wish they had but they couldn't by then."

Brazet nodded solemnly. "But are you sure you can still keep him alive. So much time has passed."

"I will for as long as I have to," Mazon stated firmly. He knew there was a serious possibility that Landon could return home but not look like Landon anymore. If his ivory dragon instinct assimilated to the person he was trapped in, Mazon would never be able to put him back into his own body. He muttered softly, "I just wish he would find his way home soon."

**   **

The closest Masters, being Shale and Levana, heard the messenger's words clearly and for a brief second, lost their composure.

"He cannot be!" Master Levana snapped in outrage at the same moment Master Shale grumbled, "That ungrateful little mongrel."

Master Orren was not sure if Shale's comment was meant for the boy or Landon, but he calmly looked from one to the other with an expression that demanded silence. "There is no reason to panic," he stated, and turned back to the student. "Why do you claim this?"

"I was going to bring him down for dinner but when I went inside, there was a duplicate in his bed and he was nowhere in the chamber or the halls, and---"

"Calm down," Master Orren soothed, placing a hand on the boy's shoulder. He glanced back to Master Shale and Levana. "Come with me." He turned toward Master Bragn and Merrick, who hadn't heard the news but could see the tension building. "Nothing to worry about. Begin dinner without us. We will return shortly."

The three Masters walked briskly with the student up to the fourth level, while they plagued him with questions. Were the students who were supposed to be watching him still at their post? Yes. Was there any sign that he jumped out of

The Escape   207

his window? No. Did they search the entire fourth level? Yes. Did they search everywhere the chamber? Yes.

By the time they arrived at Jaron's chamber, the student was even more panicked and tense, as well as the two large students who had been posted to stand guard. Master Orren didn't say a word to them and stopped the other two Masters from giving the boys a verbal whipping. He entered the chamber and saw the figure lying in the bed. He had to admit it was a good duplicate, since he almost believed for a second that it was the boy. However, it was only a well wrapped pile of sheets around a mold of some kind, which matched Jaron's physique and naturally when placed under the furs it could pass quite acceptably for the boy. Master Orren walked to the window and pushed open the shutters, as he asked the students,

"How long before you actually found out it was a duplicate?"

"Only a few moments, Master Orren," the messenger answered.

"He almost left without finding out," interjected one of the large students quite proudly, "until I said we should check to make sure."

Master Orren nodded as he gazed down at the ground. There was no sign of a rope or any other means of climbing down, much to his satisfaction, so he closed the shutters and began searching the chamber.

"We must issue a hunt immediately," Master Shale stated and turned toward the messenger. "Tell Master Bragn and Merrick to halt dinner and have every available person search inside and out of the Halls. You said you found him missing how long ago?"

"Only a few minutes, Master Shale," the messenger answered.

"Then he could not have gone very far," Master Levana said. She turned toward Master Orren. "With your permission…Master Orren?"

Master Orren was on his knees and stared under the bed, looking confused for a moment, and then satisfaction spread across his face.

When he first glanced under the bed, he saw nothing out of the ordinary and began to stand. Then something caught his eye, so he scrunched down again and examined every inch closely. He could understand how the students missed this, since he nearly made the same mistake.

Tucked in the deepest, darkest corner, curled up in a ball with his face turned toward the wall was the boy. He glanced up at both the Masters and hooked a thumb under the bed. The Masters glanced from him to the bed, then at each other, and breathed with relief. Master Shale opened his mouth as he stalked toward the bed ready to pull it away from the wall, but Master Orren held up his hand and shook his head.

"A search is a very good idea, Master Shale," he said loud enough for Jaron and Landon to hear. He got to his feet and brushed off his robe as he addressed the students. "Tell Master Merrick and Bragn to take some of the students and search the hallways and outside. But be sure to tell them that one of them should stay behind and supervise the remaining students."

"Yes, Master Orren," the messenger and the two large students said in unison, then they turned and left.

Master Orren closed the door behind them, walked to the bed, and sat down, pushing the duplicate to one side. "This is indeed a shame. What will we do if we cannot find them?"

Master Levana sat next to him, following his lead, and said with dramatic sympathy, "Master Orren, you must not think that way. This is certainly a prank, for neither child would risk the Land by being so selfish."

"That is true," Master Shale agreed, walking around to the edge of the bed. He kicked the rear left leg, which sent the whole bed shaking and smacked the headboard against the wall. "If I thought either boy would be that selfish, well...I do not know what I would do."

"I would certainly be disappointed in them," Master Levana said softly.

"As would I," Master Orren agreed. "But the true sufferers would be the people of the Land who would fall under that demon's rule."

"There would be no more morphers," Master Shale said sadly.

"True," Master Orren said, then raised his voice a level and spoke deliberately, "They would all be killed like the poor students and Masters back at the Main Halls."

"Or worse," Master Levana added, "they would be twisted by the evil one's power and be made into his...slaves."

"Ah, yes," Master Orren said with a nod. "It is sad enough when one unfortunate person is subjected to that cruelty, but for an entire Land to suffer the same fate..." He trailed off to let the boy finish the thought for himself. He was glad Master Levana remembered the marks on the boy's arm, indicating that he had been part of the slave-Trade at least once. Though, Master Orren figured by the boy's behavior, it had been more than just once.

"*When* he is found," Master Shale said, "perhaps we can try to explain their importance to the Land again."

"If they are selfish enough to run away," Master Orren said, "then there is no point in trying to explain anything to them. The Land will suffer on account of them."

**   **

"Do ju believes dis dung dare throwin' at us?" Jaron snickered silently to Landon.

"*Yeah. It's almost working.*"

"Don't ju even tink of its!" Jaron hissed. "'Member, dare mus be's a better way. Dese Maders don't know erriting and dare not tryin' to find a better answer. Ju 'ave to. Wha' 'bout jur Weaver? Ju said he's would know."

"*I believe he would. But we have to find him first.*"

"Well, dese Maders 'ave to git out of 'ere 'fore we's can do dat."

"*I know, I know,*" Landon agreed wearily. After a moment of quiet between them, the Master's words could be heard again. He spoke just to keep them muffled. "*Did you notice how those students left out a thing or two?*"

"Oh yeah," Jaron sniffed. "Some brave students. Da Maders dinn't hear dem scramblin' all over da place and shoutin' back and forth to each other." Jaron

The Escape   209

mimicked the large student's voice, "'I's was da one who's said we's should check out da bed'."

Landon snorted a laugh at the imitation. *"Now didn't I tell you the duplicate would look all right?"*

"I's know. I's jus wish its kept dem busy fure longer." Jaron wanted very much to shift his position. "I's should 'ave left when I's had da chance."

"No, no! We would have definitely been found then. I'm telling you, this will work."

"I's can't breathe."

"You can so. Just stay still."

"When are dey goin' to git out of 'ere?"

"Soon. They can't stay here forever."

"Dey know we's 'ere, don't dey?" Jaron asked, feeling a lump in his throat.

"No they don't. Just be patient." They listened more to the Masters talking about how the Land would suffer by Taj's hand because they wouldn't do their duty. Landon mumbled, *"The time is now, Master Orren, not in two years."* He said it more to convince himself that he was doing the right thing and only hoped they could find Mazon or Brazet. He was taking a big risk by doing this.

"Oh bloody dung!" Jaron's silent moan snapped Landon's attention back.

"What?"

"I's 'ave da hiccups."

"No you don't!" Landon warned.

"No really. I's do."

"Hold your breath."

"I's am." Jaron tried to keep his body still during the small spasm. "It's not workin'."

"It's mind over element. You do not have to hiccup! Do you hear me?"

"Fine. Tell dat to da hiccup." His body jerked again.

"If you give our position away because you cannot keep in control of your own body, I'll…" However, Landon couldn't think of a threat to follow through with.

It was at that moment they heard Master Orren call out, "All right, Jaron. Fun is fun. Come out."

Now Landon could think of a threat and growled softly into Jaron's mind, *"I'm going to incinerate you!"*

**   **

Master Orren and Levana stood up from the bed and waited. The sound of movement and the soft groan from under the bed while they'd been talking made it obvious their words were having a result. When Master Orren called out to Jaron the movement stopped, as if the boy thought they would be so easily fooled.

Master Orren spoke clearly, "Enough games, Jaron. Come out."

When no response came, Master Orren nodded for Master Shale and Levana to help him, and the three pulled the bed away from the wall. The crumpled figure, now exposed, lulled his head toward them. They all froze and gaped.

It was Master Levana who recovered first and cried out, "Dixson!" She rushed over to her student lying on the floor with the trickle of blood running down his forehead, dressed in Jaron's clothes. She gently sat the boy up and asked, "What happened?"

Master Orren had already gotten a glass of water from the pitcher and handed it to the boy, who drank slowly before he answered.

"I came to bring the guest down to dinner, but when I arrived no one was at the door and there was the duplicate in the bed."

"He must have come after the students discovered the fraud and went to search the hallways," Master Shale said. Master Levana waved him silent as Dixson continued.

"I started to leave to warn you, but when I turned around he was leaning against the door with a knife in his hands and attacked me."

"I's don't believe dis!" Jaron moaned to Landon.

"*It seems he forgot to mention that at the mere sight of you holding that knife, he tripped over his own feet and whacked his head on the floor.*"

"I's was nice," Jaron said. "I's dinn't 'ave to do anniting 'cept switch our clothes."

"*Yes, but the next thing you know he'll be saying that---*"

"He had a murderous gleam in his eye," Dixson continued. "And he said he wouldn't be anyone's puppet. Then he lunged for me and I fought him off as best I could, unarmed as I was, and managed to disarm him. But he knocked me off balance with a hard punch, so I fell. Then he banged my head repeatedly on the floor until I lost consciousness."

"Da next ting ju'll hear is dat I's grew another five feet."

"*And sprouted fangs.*"

"And threatened to kill all da Maders and students."

"*Then chop them up into tiny pieces and eat them.*"

Jaron bit back a laugh and realized that the urge to hiccup was gone. He joked, "Dat boy is such an ass."

"*Completely,*" Landon agreed. "*Now they'll get out of here. Watch.*"

"Do you remember anything else?" Master Levana coaxed.

"No, Master Levana. I am sorry that I failed you, but he was too wild for me to handle. It was as if he'd gone mad."

"This is not your fault, Dixson," Master Orren stated. He nodded toward Master Levana. "Take him to the Healer." He turned to Master Shale. "Double the search. Take every student---" He didn't get to finish because one of the large students came crashing into the chamber.

"Master Orren!" he shouted and didn't wait for acknowledgment. "On the third level, we found a broken window with this hanging from it." He held up a long rope made out of sheets tied together. Master Shale didn't wait for new instructions and hurried out of the chamber, dragging the new messenger behind him.

Master Orren called after him, "Give permission to morph. Have them begin the search in the direction they took." Master Levana had Dixson on his feet and was gently leading him out of the chamber. "When you have brought him to the Healer, you will join the search." She nodded and left.

Master Orren stayed behind, however, because of the odd sensation he was feeling. He could still feel Landon. That was why he couldn't tell that the figure hiding under the bed wasn't Jaron, which could only mean that Landon was still somewhere in the chamber. He started at one end and began tossing aside anything, no matter how small or large, that was in his way.

"Landon," Jaron squeaked. "Someone's still 'ere."

"Don't panic," Landon said, but heard the boy wince at the sound of a table being turned over.

"Dare goin' to find us."

"No they won't. That's why we hung the rope out the window, so they'll be searching outside, not inside. Just don't move and relax."

"So why's is someone tearin' apart dis chamber ifs dey 'sposed to be's searching outside?"

Another loud sound came from inside the chamber and Landon tried to figure out how someone knew they were still here. They were being searched for, but why? There was no reason unless…he suddenly discovered a small problem with their plan. *"They can still feel me and know we're here somewhere."* He thought quickly. *"I'll withdraw. Maybe my presence won't be as strong."*

"No!" Jaron shouted to him silently.

"I have to or they may find us."

"Don't leave me!" Jaron pleaded.

"I'm not leaving you," Landon assured. *"I'm just quieting my presence. I'll still be here."*

"No! Don't leave!" Jaron screamed at him.

"Jaron," Landon began helplessly, not knowing what had gotten into the boy. He felt a tight grip around him and knew it was Jaron holding onto him, preventing him from going deeper into his mind. *"I have to!"* Landon said firmly, hoping that jarred the boy's grip loose. It didn't.

Jaron moaned quietly. He could no longer breathe. The air was too thick, the space was too confined, he couldn't move and he was going to be left alone. He felt as if he were back inside a slave cage again with no way out. He would be beaten, humiliated, anything to break him down. Anything to force him to submit. They would try anything again and again and he would be forced to endure it.

Landon didn't want to withdraw now, not understanding what was happening to the boy, only that it was so terrifying he was starting to feel the effects of it.

"Jaron," he said firmly. The only response the boy made was a soft wheezing sound. *"Jaron, breathe!"* It was a command.

"I's can't." The boy's answer was so hopeless, so heart breaking, that Landon almost let himself be swept up in the feelings. Pure fear streaked across

Jaron's mind, forcing all reasonable thought out. Landon heard him silently screaming for anyone to help him. "I's 'ave to git out."

"*We'll be caught.*"

"I's 'ave to!" Jaron cried.

"*All right,*" Landon told him softly. He still didn't understand what was happening but he would not let Jaron suffer this way. They would find another way out of here. "*Come out of hiding.*"

"I's can't move," Jaron screeched hoarsely. "I's can't sees."

"*Calm down. All you have to do is sit up.*"

"I's can't move!"

"*Yes you can. Here. Close your eyes and breathe for me. Nice deep breaths. Take it easy, you're fine.*" He felt the boy start to relax and no longer sound like he was gasping for air. Landon continued speaking in a soothing tone that he learned from Mazon. "*Easy...relax...breathe. There you go. You're... you're fine. Now, sit up.*"

"No," Jaron whispered.

"*It's all right. You can do this.*"

"No, I's mean I's---"

"Master Orren!" The loud voice startled both of them. The shuffling in the chamber stopped and Jaron strained to hear what was going on.

"Master Orren. You must come. Master Shale sent me to bring you."

"What is the problem?" Master Orren asked.

"Snakes."

"What?"

"Master Orren, there are snakes everywhere outside."

"At this time of year, in this region?" Master Orren asked doubtfully, as he hurried toward the window and threw open the shutters. He gaped at what he saw.

Dozens, hundreds of snakes of every type were slithering around outside of the entire building, and more were still coming across the field. The Masters and students were waving torches at them and the few students who could assume dragon shapes had morphed and were breathing fire on them.

"Stop!" Master Orren cried down to them. He didn't want any of his students to accidentally be hurt by either the snakes or the dragons. He rushed across the chamber and hurried outside.

Jaron waited and listened for any further movement in the chamber. When he and Landon agreed that it was clear, he slowly and stiffly sat up. Had anyone else been in the chamber at the time, they may have been surprised to see it was the duplicate that sat up.

The hands immediately began to unwind the layers of fabric around the head and once unwrapped, Jaron sucked in large breaths of air. The simple act of moving made the mold he was in crack and break. Landon told him how to make it and then he spent the better part of last night slathering the mixture on his arms, legs and chest to make a mold. Thank the Light he had a fireplace in his chamber, otherwise it would've taken forever to dry. The hard part was removing it once it had dried enough so it wouldn't break, and then of course, hiding the damn thing so no one found it. Landon had wanted him to make a mold of his face too but he refused. He thought just covering his face in sheets and odd bits of clothing would work and it did. It fooled the Masters but it still made him feel like he was being smothered the entire time.

He had placed the mold in the bed and hid under a pile of blankets in the corner of the chamber when the first batch of students came in. They didn't search the chamber hardly at all, but Landon had told him they wouldn't. The Masters, though, he knew they would search more thoroughly.

Once the students ran off to tell the Masters, Jaron ran to the third level, broke the window, hung the makeshift rope out of it, and then ran back to the chamber. He was about to climb into the mold of the duplicate when they heard someone coming and that's when Dixon walked in. They hadn't planned on his arrival and Jaron had been ready to attack him, despite Landon's cries of protest. But when the student saw him with his knife, he did panic and knocked himself out cold. That's when Landon got the idea to switch their clothes and shove him under the bed as an added distraction. Jaron was surprised by Landon's sudden switch from 'No, don't hurt him!' to 'Hey, we can use this!' After Dixson had been hidden, Jaron had mere moments to carefully slide into the mold, wrap his head up and then, the really hard part, lay perfectly still. Thank the Light when Master Orren pushed him aside he was able to roll with the motion. It was a good thing no one tried to pick him up. Had they tried, they may have found that the duplicate had grown quite heavy.

The entire plan was not a bad one. Landon had said the makeshift rope hanging out of the window would throw the Masters off and if they remained hidden until everyone else was out looking for them, then they could sneak out amongst the chaos. Landon knew that the boy could not outrun a bunch of morphers and Weavers. If they did actually escape out of the window, the Masters would know exactly which direction they went and be able to catch up with them easily. This way, the Masters *thought* they knew which way they had headed, and they could go in the opposite direction where they wouldn't be looking.

Jaron pulled off the remaining pieces of mold and fabric and looked around the chamber. It had certainly been overturned. Apparently, Master Orren was determined to find them. The window was still open and the commotion from outside poured in. Jaron was tempted to take a peek to see what was going on but Landon told him to get moving. Both of them heard the shouts coming from both Masters and students that every entrance was blocked and the snakes were climbing up inside the walls. That was all they stayed around to hear, then Jaron ducked out into the hallway and trotted along, following Landon's directions and trying to look every way at once.

Landon actually did get them lost once and led Jaron down a dead end. Jaron grunted at him in frustration since he was completely disoriented and spun around to race back up the hall and find an exit. As he came to the mouth of the hallway, there were two students, a boy and a girl, standing in his way. Jaron assumed by their white clothes and their faces that they were probably his age, if not younger. Landon warned him not to underestimate them. They were morphers and with one shout they could bring the entire Hall down on their heads.

The two students stared at Jaron with surprise and the boy called out, "Hey! They're looking for you!"

They advanced cautiously and Jaron's mind whirled for a solution. His instincts kicked in. He wrapped his hands around his throat and dropped to his knees.

"Don't come anni closer!" he choked out. "He's got me!" The two students froze and looked anxious.

"Who's got you?" the girl asked.

"Taj," Jaron squeaked. "He's tryin' to take da Kazimeer. He's killin' me!" He reached out with one hand toward them, while he continued to gasp for air. "Help me!"

The students remained frozen and shot glances back and forth to each other about what they should do. Jaron fell face first to the ground, with his one arm still outstretched and his other tucked neatly under him. The students rushed over and squatted down beside him.

"Hey, are you all right?" the boy asked while he shook him.

Jaron remained silent and slowly reached into his sack. Landon had no idea what the thief was doing but found it amusing. He remained quiet and waited to see where this would go.

"We should get Master Orren," the girl said. "You stay here."

The boy asked, "What if…Taj," the name came out in a whisper, "comes to take him again?"

Jaron didn't give either student a second to think about it, as he found what he was looking for in his sack. With the speed of a viper killing its prey, he attached his hand-crafted manacles to each of their ankles, joining them together. Landon peered at the manacles, never seeing their like before.

They appeared to be what the cooks used to tenderize meat. A circle that the hand could grip, with small spikes lining the outer side. Only, the circle had been turned inside out so the small spikes were pointing inwards now and the clamping devices were locked shut with what looked like a prong from a fork. It seemed to be wedged in tightly and bent at the end, so there would be some difficulty in removing them. And in between the two manacles were three links of chain.

In the time it had taken Landon to study these odd devices, Jaron was on his feet and brushing himself off. The students were still perplexed.

"Sorry," Jaron said, scooped up his sack, and trotted down the hall. He called out over his shoulder, "I's wouldn't try to merf ifs I's were ju eeder." It seemed the students were just finding that out too and yelps of pain followed Jaron down the hall.

"*Why shouldn't they morph?*" Landon asked curiously.

"Dey would slice dare own foot off. Dose spikes are sharp."

"*What if they're small morphers?*" Landon asked. "*What if their shape is a mouse or a rabbit?*"

Jaron considered this. "Den I's jus step on dem."

"*You wouldn't!*" Landon cried.

The Escape   215

"No," Jaron moaned, rolling his eyes. "But I's not as worried 'bout small merfers. I's worried 'bout dose wit big teef."

Landon couldn't help himself and for no reason he could imagine, he started to chuckle. "Wha'?" Landon couldn't answer right away, since his chuckling had turned into laughter. "Wha'?" Jaron asked again, chuckling a little himself.

"*Help, Taj has got me,*" Landon mimicked, once he was back in control of himself. "*I can't believe you got that to work.*"

"Dat's wha' I's do," Jaron murmured. "Which way?"

"*Ah...turn right. And what in the Land are you doing with manacles anyway?*"

"I's made dem."

"*You made them? Why? You just walk around with manacles on you?*"

"Ju's wouldn't believes wha' I's got in dis bag."

After a short pause, Landon asked casually, "*Anything alive?*"

"Possibly"

Landon was still dumbfounded that he had them in the first place. "*And how do you make manacles like that?*"

"It's jus someting I's learned. Its helps to be's prepared fure anniting. Trust me, dats someting else I's learned. I's shows ju how's when ju git back into jur own body."

"*I'd like that,*" Landon said happily, then turned his attention back to what they were doing. "*Make a left. We have to head toward the rear of the Halls. Remember those two large hills I had you look at? If my memory serves me correctly that should be the Twin Crests. Beyond them is the far end of the Fire providence. Now you're going to have to make it up and over the left hill as quickly as you can for two reasons. One, so we're out of sight from the Masters.*"

"And two?"

"*Because the night beasts are all over these parts, but they don't go into the hills. It's too high and cold for them.*"

"But not fure me," Jaron said flatly.

"*It's either that or you can dance around in front of the Masters. The back way is the only way we're going to get out of here unseen.*" It was Jaron's turn to start snickering. "*What?*"

"I's jus had da thought of me dancin' 'round in front of da Maders." Landon picked up on the image of Jaron jumping around before a row of expressionless Masters and had to laugh himself, though he wondered why. It was probably because of the mood he was in. He was finding this to be exciting and exhilarating.

Still chuckling he said, "*All right, all right! Make a right, then a quick left. There's a door down that hall. Come on, hurry up before they come back in.*"

Jaron picked up his pace, rounded the right corner, and made the quick left. He collided into something.

He staggered back, but a firm hand on his shoulder steadied him from falling over. Jaron slowly followed the chest up to the face of Master Merrick. His first reaction was relief, but then remembered that Master Merrick was a

Master and his first duty was to the Halls. And by his icy expression, Jaron had the sinking feeling that Master Merrick was going to uphold that first duty. He glanced around the large Master and saw the door only a few feet behind him. He looked back to Master Merrick and debated if he should try his choking trick again.

"*Don't be foolish,*" Landon warned. "*That may work on a couple of students, but not on a Master.*"

"Wha' do I's do?" Jaron asked him silently.

"*I don't know,*" Landon answered, feeling completely useless and hating it.

Jaron's eyes never left Master Merrick's cold face. He stood there speechless, and waited for him to call to the other Masters. Master Merrick cleared his throat and said coldly, "Do I know you?" Jaron's face twisted in confusion. Master Merrick continued, "Are you a student?"

"No, sir," Jaron said, shaking his head slightly.

"Then if you are not a student, what are you doing in these Halls?"

Jaron was beginning to understand what Landon already figured out. He thanked Master Merrick, although he knew the Master wouldn't hear him. Jaron shrugged in answer and Master Merrick pushed him toward the door.

"If you do not belong here then get out and don't let me catch you around here again."

Jaron trotted to the door, then looked back at Master Merrick. "Tank ju," he said and smiled.

Master Merrick's icy expression melted and he smiled back and nodded toward the door. "Go. Get out of here."

Jaron flung open the door, ready to race across the Land toward the left hill, but Landon's sudden shock stopped him. The snakes were still out there.

"*I forgot,*" Landon moaned. He peered through Jaron's eyes and saw the hundreds of snakes surrounding the door and spreading up into the hills. Why snakes were here right now, he had no idea but they would have to move through them to leave.

Jaron sniffed. "So? Dare jus snakes." He tried to take a step out but Landon's fear pulled him to a stop.

"*You can't go out there!*"

"Ifs ju don't lemme go, we's never git out of 'ere."

He pulled himself free from Landon's grip and trotted on his tiptoes through the snakes, being careful not to step on any. He did step on some, but all the offended snake did was hiss and slither away. Landon watched in horror as Jaron made his way across the snake covered field toward the hills. Once Jaron accidentally stepped on the head of a razor back. Landon knew that one drop of the snake's poison could kill a man. But all Jaron did was cringe in apology and the razor back hissed at him in annoyance, then curled up again. It never once made a move to strike. It was then Landon discovered something else. There wasn't an ounce of fear in Jaron as he walked through the snakes. All the fear was coming from him but as far as the boy seemed concerned, he was walking through a field of daisies rather than poisonous snakes.

The Escape   217

The cluster of snakes finally thinned out as they approached the Twin Crests. Once they were clear of the bulk of the snakes, Jaron turned around to make sure no one was following them. However, Landon saw the small figure standing in the doorway and knew it was Master Merrick. Landon knew what the Master was thinking, because he was having the same thought. How did the boy do that? It was also at that moment the snakes started to slither away from the Halls.

Jaron raced up the hill as fast as he could, dragging Landon away from any thoughts he had about what just happened, and shouted for Landon to tell him which way to go.

Hosting the Kazimeer

THE THIEF BOY AND THRONGE WORM

Jaron continued to climb through the night and didn't stop until the first streaks of dawn started cutting through the distant clouds. No one followed them, it seemed, but that didn't stop Landon from pushing the boy onward. Finally Jaron collapsed on the ground and curled up into a ball. The student's clothes he'd taken were too thin and his cloak wasn't providing much warmth or protection against the cold.

"You have to keep going," Landon urged.

"Ju go den. I's stayin' 'ere."

"You will freeze if you stay here. You must get over this hill first."

"I's can't."

"Jaron," Landon started but Jaron cut him off.

"I's frozen a'ready and I's can't go annimore. I's slept out in weder likes dis 'fore. I's jus need a few hours."

Landon saw no point in arguing since Jaron appeared to be nodding off as he spoke, but he was not going to withdraw this time. He planted himself firmly forward and refused to be budged, even when Jaron's mind tried to push him back. Landon did not want to risk losing the boy while he slept and was determined to wake him at the first sign of his body failing.

Jaron tried to make his body relax enough for him to sleep but with the thronge worm still so noticeable it felt like someone was staring him in the face while his eyes were closed. He rolled over several times on the cold, hard ground trying to find a comfortable position, but no position was comfortable with someone watching him.

He finally grumbled in frustration, "Ju jus 'ave to 'ave jur own way 'bout erriting, don't ju."

"What are you talking about?"

"Go 'way!"

"I will not let you freeze to death."

"It's me body. If's I's want to freeze to death, den it's me choice."

"If you wanted to kill yourself, why didn't you just stay with the Masters?"

"Git out!" Jaron shouted, trying to push him back into his mind.

Landon remained forward and did the mental equivalent of slapping the boy's hands away. *"You're cranky. Go to sleep and I'll keep watch."*

"How's can I's go to sleep wit ju right 'ere?"

"I guess you're not that tired then," Landon challenged.

Jaron cursed under his breath and rolled over again. He tried to think of warm places he'd been to but at the moment they were hard to recall. Then he thought of all the horrible things he would do to the Kazimeer once this was over. His anger warmed him enough to make him forget he was being watched and he began to doze.

Landon observed his own torture with amusement. It probably would have been frightening if not for the fact that the boy had gotten his image completely wrong. Landon knew he was supposed to be watching himself being hung up by his toes and having spikes driven into his fingers, but the image was not of him. Apparently, Jaron thought he was older, plumper, white as a cloud, with no distinguishing features, and weaker. At first Landon laughed at the image until it faded, which meant the boy was probably sleeping, but the more he remembered Jaron's image, the more he started to wonder.

Was that what Jaron really thought of him? That he was some old man who would grovel at the first sign of conflict. Then he reminded himself the boy was in a foul mood, tired, and really had no clear idea of how he looked. That brought up another uncomfortable thought. What if the boy was picking up on what Landon really thought of himself? What if it was really *him* who thought he was a weak, old leader? And if he thought that way, how could he possibly defeat Taj?

"Ju really do care 'bout wha' other people tink of ju."

"*You're supposed to be asleep,*" Landon growled, not enjoying being caught off guard.

"I's would 'ave been but ju keep scramblin' 'round likes a rat in a trap." Jaron wrestled his cloak around him and shifted his position. "Wha' do ju care wha' a thief boy tinks of ju?"

"*I don't,*" Landon stated with confidence.

"Oh. Den would ju lemme go to sleep?"

"*I'm not the one keeping you awake,*" Landon snapped with a sudden burst of irritability. "*All I'm trying to do is keep you alive and I'm starting to wonder why I'm bothering.*"

"Dat's wha' ju're 'sposed to do. Protectin' da Land and all?"

"*Yes. That is what I'm supposed to do,*" Landon sneered. "*Even for a little snot-nosed thief, such as yourself.*"

Before he could stop himself, he conjured an image of Jaron. He vaguely remembered what the fuzzy reflection in the river looked like but he filled in the spots he'd forgotten with his anger. He made the boy three feet tall, with wild, shaggy hair hanging down past his shoulders, gave him a hump on his back, made his nose runny, his clothes torn, his face filthy, and for good measure gave him a blank, slack expression.

"Is dat 'sposed to be's me?" the boy asked. Landon couldn't help but feel a bit triumphant. There was a long pause from Jaron, followed by a sharp cackle. Landon's good feelings were gone when he realized his image had no effect on the boy. Jaron snorted out, "Wait! Wait! Add some puss blemishes on me face and make me mouf 'ang open and drool."

The additions took place and Landon wasn't sure if he put them there or if the boy did, but suddenly the image of Jaron looked twice as ridiculous as it did before.

Jaron exploded with laughter and rolled onto his back, while he held his stomach. Landon snickered himself and realized how foolish and childish he was being. He sarcastically thanked Segvature for making him so self-conscious that the slightest jab at him made his defenses go up and heated his temper. In the

Hosting the Kazimeer

same manner, he thanked Natal for being so indifferent and always choosing his son over his brother.

"Hey!" Jaron called out and his laughter came to an abrupt halt. "I's pickin' up on a bit of saved hostoly---"

"*Hostility,*" Landon breathed.

"Well, ju 'ave a lot of its and I's don't want its comin' over to me."

"*Weren't you going to sleep?*" Landon asked annoyed.

"It's too cold to sleep and I's too tired to move." He shifted his position again. "Ju really do care wha' people tink of ju"

"*So what if I do?*" Landon snapped.

"Nutin' to me. Its jus wastes a lot of energy, is all, but its jur energy to waste."

"*What do you know of it, boy!*"

"I's know I's 'ave more energy den ju."

"*Oh right,*" Landon sniffed. "*Like you never get offended by someone else's insults.*"

"No, not really," Jaron answered honestly. "Why's should I's? Jur problem is ju don't know who's ju is, so if's someone says someting 'bout ju, ju believes 'cause ju're not sure if's it's true or not. But sees, I's know 'bout me. Dat person wit da droolin' mouf and hump on his back isn't me. I's know dat. But ifs ju tink of me dat way, well den, ju don't know me and dare's nutin' I's can do 'bout dat, so why's let its bother me."

Landon said nothing. He noticed that every so often Jaron would have such a clear view of things and it made him wonder why his view was so cloudy.

Jaron growled. He didn't want to make Landon feel worse. "Landon, looks," he said, calling up the image he had of him earlier. "Dis is not ju. I's know dat. But it's sure funny, isn't its?"

Landon stared at the plump, old man and laughed at it again. The image didn't have the punch it had before and Landon felt his anger and hostility drain away. The thronge worm and the thief boy images were placed side by side and the two of them cackled at them until Jaron's body felt warmer and Landon's mind felt lighter.

"Ju made me a wee bit too short," Jaron remarked.

"*Yeah. So did you.*"

Curious Jaron asked, "How's tall is ju?"

"*Over six hands.*"

"Git out! Ju is not."

"*I think I would know how tall I am.*" Now Landon was curious. "*Why? How tall are you?*"

"Forgit its," Jaron mumbled.

"*What? Come on, tell me.*"

"I's don't 'ave to."

"*Baby,*" Landon sniffed. "*And what is with the transparent skin?*"

"Wha'? Ju're 'sposed to be's an ivory dragon, yes?"

"*Yes. Ivory, not see-through. And I do have hair you know.*"

"Someone jur age has hair?"

"*Of course.*" Confused, he asked, "*How old do you think I am?*"

"Wha', I's don't know. Fory, fify."

Was the boy joking? Landon asked carefully, "*Why do you say that?*"

"Ju got all jur fancy words and jur manners and jur da Kaz and all."

"*The Kaz?*"

"Well, yeah. Da Kazimeer. So ju 'ave to be's old."

Landon decided to take the remark as a compliment and wondered if he told the boy the truth, would it make things better or worse. "*Do you always speak to people twice your age so disrespectfully?*"

"Yes," Jaron answered flatly. "Ju tink ju git special treatment?"

"*No, I just figured I'd ask.*"

The boy's remarks, though, caused Landon to think. The boy called him the Kaz; the Kazimeer. The Kazimeer of what? What did he honestly think he could do once he found Mazon or Brazet? Most, if not all, of his army must be gone by now. Even if he did get back into his own body, what was he going to do to that man called Taj, who had the entire Land under his control? Since some people cheered him, what would happen if he removed him? *He* would be seen as the demon, removing the noble, benevolent Blasdon by force. He remembered the conversation back at the tavern. Some supported Taj, others wanted their own rule, but nowhere did he remember hearing anyone mention that it would be great if Kazimeer Landon were back on the throne. People wanted the *ivory dragon* back but not *him*, just like the Masters. Why should he even bother?

"Landon," Jaron called out softly. "Don't tink likes dat."

"*Burn you, I'll think how I want!*"

"People need da Kazimeer."

"*Well they have one. And his name is Taj.*"

"People don't know dat. Dey tink dey 'ave Blasdon."

"*What difference does his name make? He's giving them what they want.*"

Jaron started to become annoyed. "And ju're givin' up!"

"*I'm facing the obvious,*" Landon finally answered. "*I've always said the Land comes first. If Taj can give the people what they want, what they need, how can I compete with that? What can I give them?*"

"Da truth."

"*The truth,*" Landon sniffed. "*Light, I don't even know what the truth is anymore.*"

Jaron growled softly, "Da truth is dat ju is da Kazimeer."

Landon chuckled without humor. "*And this from a thief boy who didn't even know who was in charge of the Land before I dragged him into a tavern. This from someone who didn't even believe me when I said I was the Kazimeer. If I can't even convince you, how can I convince the people?*"

Jaron pulled his knees up to his chest and hugged them, placing his cheek against them. He was silent for a long while before he finally took a deep breath and said firmly, "Landon." He waited briefly for a response but none came. He could still feel the thronge worm listening and continued before he lost his nerve. "I's lied to ju."

"You lied to me?"

Jaron nodded, although he knew Landon couldn't see him. "I's was dare."

"You were where?"

"At da castle."

"At the castle?"

"Wha', is ju an echo! Yes, at da castle. Da day ju were 'sposed to be's... killed."

Landon remembered that day, which now seemed so long ago. Standing there with Taj, listening to the crowd cheer him, trying desperately to make the people see reason. And then... there was the morpher test.

"It was you."

Jaron closed his eyes tightly and nodded again. "Yes."

"You were the volunteer!?"

"Yes," Jaron moaned.

Landon was completely dumbfounded. *"I don't understand? Why didn't you tell me you where there when I asked you?"*

"'Cause I's thought ju were some Weaver messin' wit me head."

"I still don't understand? Why were you there?"

Jaron paused and Landon could feel him thinking deeply. He finally answered in a rush, "I's wanted to sees da new Kazimeer."

"You what?"

"Ju 'eard me," he growled.

"Why? I thought you didn't care?"

"Well, normally, I's don't, but I's dinn't much care fure da old Kazimeer and wanted to meet da new one."

"But why?"

"So I's could sees ifs he's shook me hand. Da old one never did. And so I's could looks into his eyes and sees wha' kind of man he's was." He shook his head in frustration. "I's don't know why's I's went. Its was jus an urge, is all. A stupid urge." He propped his chin on top of his knees and wrapped his cloak around him tighter. "But den I's 'eard ju talk."

"And you left immediately, right?"

"No," Jaron groaned. "Normally, I's probably would but I's liked wha' ju had to say. More suprisin' to me was I's understood its. I's don't tink ju realize jus how's..." he searched for a big word, like Landon would use, but couldn't find one, "...strong jur words sounded. Its even quieted down dose fools up front."

"Which ones?" Landon snorted.

"Dare were lots of people dare dat dinn't know wha' was goin' on. Da ones dat cheered fure Taj, no one from Sevatzer knew who's dey were. No one from Sevatzer cheered fure him."

"Really?"

"When people don't know wha's 'appenin', sometimes dey'll wait to figure out wha's goin' on 'fore dey do anniting. Dey were all jus too confused to react."

"But, apparently, not you."

"No, not me. I's never wait to sees wha' 'appens, I's jus do its."

"Why did you volunteer?"

"'Cause I's believed ju and not him. I's believed in wha' ju said and trusted its." He sniffed a laugh. "'Sides, I's figured ju had to shake me hand den."

Landon was silent, which nearly had Jaron worried, and then he said, *"Jaron, I would've hugged the living piss out of you."*

It was Jaron's turn to be silent for a few moments, his mind running through a variety of ways he could answer that. He finally settled for, "Do I's dare ask why's?"

"I would've been extremely grateful."

"Why's?" Jaron asked again, not sure what to make of Landon's mood. He wasn't sure if he was angry, happy or just…stunned.

"Because someone believed me and not him. And at that moment…" He trailed off and then laughed a little, almost sounding relieved. *"At that moment, I would've been very grateful."*

Jaron sat quietly and after a pause added, "I's tink I's jus settle fure da hand shakin' ifs ju don't mind."

Landon laughed again. *"I would shake your hand at any time."*

Jaron smiled. He wasn't sure if Landon was lying or not, but had the feeling he wasn't. "Well, we's talked 'nuff 'bout ju fure one night. Tell me, wha' do ju really tink of me."

Knowing perfectly well that the boy was deliberately changing the subject, Landon went along. *"I thought you didn't care?"*

"I's don't. I's jus curious. Do ju really tink I's dat dirty kid?"

"No," Landon admitted. However, before he could control it, another image flashed across both of their minds, sending a chill up Jaron's spine that had nothing to do with the cold.

"Wha' was dat?"

"Huh?" Landon asked as casually as he could.

"Wha' was dat ting?"

"Oh, I must have been letting my mind wander."

Landon did not want to be the one to tell the boy of his true shape. Why the shape-seeker didn't was still beyond him. She must have seen it. He couldn't have been the only one, then again, Jaron didn't seem to remember anything that happened. So maybe the shape-seeker didn't see, and it was because he was so entwined in the boy's mind that he saw the… He slammed his mind closed. Jaron had been watching and listening.

"Ju know someting," he said coldly. "Ju don't let jur mind wander. Ju know someting and ju're not tellin' me."

"It's nothing," Landon dodged.

"Why's when ju thought of me dat ting appeared?"

"It's not a thing."

"Den wha' is its!" Jaron demanded.

Landon replied calmly, *"It's called a saxtien."*

"Never 'eard of its," Jaron laughed nervously.

True, he'd never heard of such a beast but the image was still fresh in his memory. The large body standing on all fours, with huge paws and sharp claws poking out of them. The sleek black fur, the long tail, the short muzzle, with those rows of fangs gleaming from inside, and those pointed ears sticking out of the head. He definitely remembered the image and sat up, feeling very frightened. Not because it was so foreign, but because it was so familiar.

He knew what Landon was trying to tell him and denied it outright. "Ju don't know wha' ju're talkin' 'bout."

"I know what I saw," Landon stated firmly.

"Wha' did ju sees?" Jaron snapped. "When did ju sees its?"

"Jaron, I saw your true shape."

"Ju's a liar," Jaron growled and got to his feet.

"Where are you going?"

"I's goin' to find dis Weaver of jurs so ju can git out of me head. Den ju can run from Taj all ju want." He started moving across the hill again, bowing his head into the wind.

Landon ignored the stab, knowing that when the boy was afraid he became spiteful. *"Why are you so determined to deny what you are? You were the one who said you knew who you were, but I suppose that isn't true, is it? Or maybe you only know who you are when it suits you."*

The deep, cold response boomed in Landon's mind.

"Leave me alone!"

Landon jerked back. The last time he heard Jaron use a tone like that, he'd nearly been choked to death. He didn't want to agitate the boy further since he was in this precarious position. He remained silent and watched the Land move by them, while he tried to guess where Mazon would be.

He debated starting their search in Sevatzer or Mazon's hometown of Triple Lake. If he had stayed in Sevatzer, Taj would have killed him by now and if Mazon was dead he had little hope of finding a solution other than that of the Masters. The idea of going back to them and admitting he was wrong was not pleasant. He knew the instant they returned the Masters would rip both of them from Jaron's body and they'd be placed in the infants so fast, they wouldn't even have time to apologize.

Also, Triple Lake was closer and there was a sense of urgency to find an answer. Landon started to feel it after Jaron's prank at dinner and it had grown stronger since. A powerful urge arose in him every so often to shove Jaron out of the way and move completely forward. At first it happened when he lost his temper, so he assumed it was only a reaction to his anger. Now he started to feel it more often, with no provocation at all. He'd been doing well to keep the urge under his control, but he didn't know for how much longer he would be able to do so. They had to find Mazon soon.

He hadn't mentioned any of this to Jaron and wasn't sure if the boy knew of the danger. Jaron, he noticed, seemed to be more panicked about his morphing abilities than the problem at hand. The boy's pace was brisk as he moved across and over the hill then headed into the forest, avoiding the main road. He didn't stop once and Landon felt him lost in his own thoughts, so the Land only appeared as a blur. He wasn't even sure if the boy knew where they were, since he hadn't once asked for directions. He just kept moving, as if by walking quickly enough he could get away from what was inside of him.

Landon couldn't understand the boy's fear, but then again, he didn't really understand Jaron. He wondered how the boy could walk through a field of poisonous snakes without a hint of fear, but found the thought of being a morpher terrifying. Terrified as he was, though, that didn't seem to affect his hunting abilities.

Jaron finally stopped once they were far enough away from the Halls and Landon watched another hare hopping its way into his snare and in minutes, Jaron had it skinned, gutted, and roasting over a small fire. Landon was glad the boy stopped his heated pace, since he knew Jaron hadn't gotten much in the way of sleep in days. Landon figured the boy must be exhausted, though he still felt that fear bouncing around inside of him.

Jaron hadn't said a word to him since he took off again from the hill. Landon felt as if it was his fault for getting the boy so angry with him and decided to make short-talk.

"*How do you do that?*" he began casually. "*Get the hare to just---*"

"Go 'way."

"*Come on, Jaron. I didn't mean to---*"

"I's said go 'way."

Landon sat back in the boy's mind and watched the fire crackle around the hare. It had a soothing effect and Landon could only hope it soothed Jaron enough to make him reasonable again. The boy was still tense.

A connection crashed in Landon's mind. It was enough to make him withdraw, so he could study it from all angles. The boy was tense and there was a hare cooking over the fire. The boy had been really tense when that little Weaver, Jynx, made the ground open up beneath him and then two phoenixes showed up. The boy had been extremely tense back at the Halls and hundreds of snakes popped up out of nowhere. This was all more than just good luck or coincidence. He was missing something, though. He turned the problem over but couldn't find the missing part. There was something more than just Jaron's fear in connection with animals. He could almost grab it but it kept slipping away from him. It had to do with the boy's morphing too, he was certain. All the pieces almost locked together but he felt as if he had them in the wrong order. If he could just look at it from a different perspective he would find the answer. It was like studying a cloud; after a while it takes on the shape of something that is recognizable. He just had to wait until this cloud formed its shape. In the meantime, it was eating away at him.

"Why's should ju care if's I's a merfer!"

The sudden outburst snapped Landon forward. "*What?*"

"Yeah, ju don't tink I's feel ju doin' jur calculatin' and analysis." Jaron paused for a moment, then growled softly, "Wha' in da name of da Guardian's back-side does 'analysis' mean?"

"It means to study or examine. To break down all possibilities."

"Uh-huh. And wha' am I's doin' wit dat word in me head?"

"I don't know. You used it properly, though."

"I's don't care if's I's used its properly," Jaron said as if he was explaining to an infant. His words picked up speed as he continued. "It's not 'sposed to be's in dare. So ju jus git its out right now or I's will rip its out along wit ju, and I's don't care if's ju's da Kazimeer or if's da Land is dyin' or if's dis Taj takes over, I's jus want to be's left alone!"

Landon had to stifle a nervous laugh. The boy was borderline hysterical. He kept his tone cool. *"Jaron."*

"And I's don't want ju to call me dat!" Jaron spewed out. "Dat's me name and I's won't 'ave ju sayin' its."

"Then what shall I call you?" Landon asked as seriously as he could.

"Nutin'."

"Fine. Well then, Nutin, might I suggest that you maybe get some sleep and we can discuss what we're going to do tomorrow, when you're feeling a little better."

"I's feel fine."

"Ah...no you don't." Landon couldn't help but chuckle slightly. *"You don't feel fine. You feel like you're about to explode."*

Jaron dropped his head in his hands and kicked his foot angrily at a rock that had been in his way. "Dare's too much at once," he whispered.

"I know."

"No, ju don't. Ju keep sayin' ju know wha' I's mean when I's know ju don't. Ju don't know how's simpel me life was 'fore ju came."

"Life never stays simple," Landon said, knowing all too well how true those words were.

Jaron stayed quiet, while the fire crackled. He raised his head and took a deep breath, blowing it out as he spoke. "I's 'sposed not. I's jus 'fraid."

"So am I," Landon admitted. *"Everyone's afraid of the unknown and we don't know what's going to happen. So let's pretend like we have some control over this situation and head toward Triple Lake."*

"Jur Weaver?"

"Yup, my Weaver. He's either there or maybe he left word about where we can find him. It's better than doing nothing." He realized Jaron had snorted out a laugh. *"What?"*

"Ju said, 'Yup'."

Landon thought about it. *"So I did,"* he answered casually. *"And you said 'Analysis'."*

"So now we's swappin' words?"

"Yes, we're trading. So far it's your 'Yup' to my 'Analysis', and we'll just go from there."

"Wha' 'appens when we's run out of words? Wha' den?"

Landon could hear the undertone in Jaron's voice and knew what else he was asking. He answered for both questions. *"We'll figure something out."*

**   **

It had always been a rare talent to be able to tell a morpher from the real beast. Most morphers couldn't do it, let alone common people. So the large gray wolf sniffing around the outskirts of the village was practically invisible. If any of the villagers caught sight of it, they simply headed in the opposite direction. No one wanted to mess with such a large wolf, although Dapp never stayed around any one village for long. He remained just long enough to sniff the air trying to catch a whiff of the boy. If it turned out to be a dead end, he'd move on. So far he'd run into nothing but dead ends.

Then again, he'd only started a few days ago. Still, he didn't want to disappoint Taj. The sooner he found the boy, the happier he would be. Taj's anger at someone else was one thing; Taj's anger directed at him was something he didn't want to be around for. But for all of Taj's quick temper and tantrums, Dapp truly believed in what he was trying to do. The boy would believe in it too, once Taj set his mind straight.

The scent of the village told him the boy hadn't been through this way, so he darted off into the forest again. He was making excellent time in his wolf shape, considering his wound was still tender. Plus it was bitterly cold and if he'd been in his regular shape, he would've been too frozen to move as quickly as he was.

Normally, he would have had another reason for wanting to find the person who had inflicted such a wound on him, but not with that boy. Dapp found he couldn't stay angry at the boy who used to call him Bapp, then press his nose, to which Dapp would make a honking sound that always made the boy giggle. How could he stay angry when all the boy was trying to do was protect himself? Dapp thought he would have been disappointed if all the boy did was stand there and not fight. However, he'd been sent to bring him back, and though he didn't want to use force, he would drag the boy back by his hair if he gave him an ounce of trouble. Taj did not like those who made mistakes.

He'd been running the entire time he was thinking and stopped to find his location. Where was he? He walked slowly, sniffing the air as he did, finding it filled with pungent odors. He came to a frozen ravine, found a small hole in the ice, and took a drink. When he was finished he sniffed the air again and followed the smells of dozens of animals. He stopped when he came to a clearing and saw the large building, which seemed to be in some kind of frenzy as all sorts of people were scurrying around outside. The more he sniffed, the more they smelled like morphers to him, and he made a mental note to mention this place to Taj. He remained still so he blended into the Land, and watched as groups moved off further away from the building. He sniffed deeply and caught the scent. It was faint, very faint, but definitely there.

He moved carefully around the building and realized that they were all looking for the same person. The difference was, Dapp knew what the boy smelled like. He'd gotten a good whiff of it when he was restraining him and remembered it from when the boy was a child. These fools would be going around in circles, while he knew what to smell for. He let the scent guide him around the building and up the hills behind them. He was on the right path now.

TIME GROWS SHORT

"So, why are you afraid of morphing?" Landon asked out of nowhere as Jaron moved through the trees toward Triple Lake.

"I's not 'fraid," Jaron finally answered.

"Right. Who are you talking to?" Landon asked dryly. *"I say the word and your fear nearly shot out of your ears. I don't understand why, though."* Jaron did not respond. *"It's an asset,"* Landon tempted.

"It's a danger."

"But you're denying half of yourself to be expressed." Jaron said nothing again, although he was curious. *"You've been doing it already. How do you think you've survived your stunts of dropping down four levels of stairs? Or reaching a tree branch more than ten feet over you? You just don't want to commit to the full shape."*

"Why's do ju care?" Jaron asked annoyed.

"I hate to see any morpher's talent wasted because of unreasonable fear." He paused then said confidentially, *"Besides, I know how you feel."*

"Ju don't---"

"I was just as terrified as you," Landon stated firmly.

"Oh?" Jaron slowed down to a lazy pace and pondered asking a question. He finally released it at Landon. "Wha' was its likes?"

"Different. Odd. Terrifying. Fun."

"Fun? How's can losin' jurself be's fun?"

"Is that what you think happens? You think you lose yourself to the shape of the creature you become? It's not like that at all. In fact, you must have discipline and control to morph into anything. That's why we go to the Masters. No, you don't lose anything; you gain."

He felt Jaron's interest climbing, although he wondered why he should care if this boy morphed or not. Perhaps it was because he felt the boy's excitement and panic, the same way he felt when he began his morphing only there wasn't anyone to explain anything to him. Maybe he just didn't want the boy to go through the mistakes he made on his own.

"Imagine how fast you could move and how flexible you would be in the shape of a saxtien. Imagine all you could sense with enhanced sight, smell, and taste. You would learn to understand the language of the ground, the way I understand the language of the sky."

"Ju really fly?" Jaron asked skeptically.

"Of course I do! A dragon just isn't a dragon if it doesn't fly."

"So wha' so great 'bout dis...wha' did ju call its? Saxtien? Well, wha' is so great 'bout its?"

"A saxtien is a hunter. It has great speed, strength, and intelligence."

"So," Jaron sniffed.

"Jaron, you don't seem to understand you have a shape that a lot of other morphers would give their right eye for. You've been given a great gift. Don't waste it by being afraid of it."

Jaron considered his words but said nothing more on the subject. He was thankful that neither did Landon. He didn't want to talk about shapes and morphers. He just wanted to find this Weaver of Landon's. However, he found his uneasiness about the whole morphing idea starting to lift a little. He continued to move briskly along, since he wanted to travel as much as he could before dark. When he finally did stop for the night, he discovered he was more exhausted than he thought and didn't even feel like eating. He curled up on his cloak, thankful that the further away they got from the Halls the warmer it was, and listened to the sounds of the night creatures. As he drifted off to sleep, he thought again about what it would be like to morph and found the idea becoming less frightening and almost having an appeal to it. Maybe it was the reassurance he received from Landon or perhaps he was just getting used to the idea. In either case, he fell asleep wondering what it would be like to be that big, furry, black animal with the pointed ears on its head.

Landon listened to the boy's quiet thoughts for a while, not commenting, or rather, keeping his own opinions and enthusiasm to himself, and thought over what he was to do once they reached Triple Lake. He remembered a few people Mazon had mentioned in passing who he could have Jaron try to find. But the uncomfortable thought kept coming back to him. What if Mazon was dead? There was Brazet, but he wasn't a Weaver. Still, Brazet had experience with strategies and siege plans. He would know how to organize an attack…but Brazet was his Second, probably battling in his place when Taj and his army took the castle. He was probably gone too. What was he going to do if all he had on his side was this boy? Muddling over what the next step should be, he scratched his nose absently.

He froze mid-scratch, remembering that he didn't have a nose. Turning his eyes down, he saw his hand positioned next to his face. No wait; Jaron's eyes were seeing Jaron's hand next to Jaron's face, but *he* was in control of them. Unsure of what to do next, he remained still, swallowing hard, (he could swallow again), feeling terror run up his back. If he was here, in control of the body, where was Jaron? Afraid to call out to him because he wasn't sure if he would get a reply, he frantically tried to recall how he did this and how he could undo it. There had been no barrier this time, no resistance, he simply had moved completely forward without even wanting to.

A stabbing pain, like a knife's blade, was in his mind, jabbing at it fiercely. He almost fought it until he realized it was Jaron and allowed the boy to remove him from his control. There was a moment of resistance from himself as his instinct held onto the body, but he forced his grip away and let Jaron rip his way forward. The boy was attacking him frantically, as if Landon was somehow smothering him. But Landon let himself be torn apart like a piece of parchment until Jaron finally ripped him completely out and shoved him back into his bodiless void. Landon felt white horror, not sure who it belonged to, and remained quiet.

Jaron sat up, resting his throbbing head in his hands, breathing deeply to calm himself. He might as well have been fighting the eye-less the way that battle went. It was like trying to remove an oak tree from the ground using only his thumbs. Opening his eyes and making sure he still had control of them, he let out a jagged breath.

"Wha' ju do dat fure!" he finally snapped at Landon.

"*I didn't do anything,*" Landon insisted. "*It just happened. I was thinking--*"

"Don't tink!" Jaron screamed. "In fact, don't do anniting annimore. Ah, bloody Light! If's I's dinn't wake up, ju would 'ave taken me body, wouldn't ju!"

"*I could have fought you, but I didn't. I don't want your body. I want mine.*"

"Jur body is a pile of ashes, Landon," Jaron moaned. "Did we's jus make a big mistake by leavin' dose Halls?"

"*No, we didn't,*" Landon answered confidently, though he didn't feel it. Jaron began feeling his uncertainty, so Landon forced himself to believe in his own words. "*We didn't make a mistake. There is another solution and we will find it.*"

"Please don't do dat 'gain," Jaron whispered.

"*I didn't mean...I won't. We should arrive at Triple Lake by tomorrow evening. Git some rest.*"

"Ju said 'Git'," Jaron said lightly. "So wha's me word?"

Landon did the mental equivalent of a smile. " *'Patronize'. You already used it.*"

"Oh, right," Jaron chuckled uneasily and lay down on his cloak again. Neither one got much rest that night.

Jaron said little to Landon the next day as he traveled toward the town. He was afraid if he started a conversation Landon might do the same thing he did last night. He really didn't believe the phronge worm did it on purpose, but the experience had been too terrifying to tempt again, so he only asked Landon for directions and kept his thoughts to himself. He couldn't tell if Landon minded the silence between them or not. He would answer shortly and never once tried to talk to him, so maybe he didn't want to tempt fate either.

Jaron came out of his thoughts and glanced around him, having a sinking feeling in his stomach. The path Landon put him on a few hours ago had long since run out and he was surrounded by trees with no sign of a town nearby.

He growled to himself and asked, "Where am I's?" Landon didn't answer and he couldn't even feel the sensation of him coming forward to peek through his eyes. "So wha' now? Ju're not talkin' to me?" No response. Jaron's patience snapped and he shouted, "Fine! Stay buried!" He stalked deeper into the trees and figured if the phronge worm wanted him to go in the right direction he would come forward and tell him so.

"Hello."

Jaron spun around and searched for who had spoken, since it hadn't been the phronge worm. He breathed with relief when he saw the small boy sitting on the ground off to the side of him. He studied the boy closely and recognition suddenly struck him.

"Ju helped me git 'way from dose eye-less tings." The boy smiled and nodded once. "Ju're one of Jynx's kids."

The boy's smile never wavered but he answered clearly, "No." Jaron narrowed his eyes in confusion. "She's one of mine."

Jaron pulled his head slowly back and licked his lips. "Oh," he said, slapping on a fake smile. "Well, nice to sees ju 'gain." He turned on his heels and continued walking.

"Jaron," the boy called out. Jaron stopped short and turned slowly to face the boy again. He couldn't remember if he told this child his name or not. The boy chuckled, which sounded like birds singing. "Where are you going?"

"Dat's really none of jur 'usiness," Jaron said and smiled politely. "Run along now."

The boy approached him. "You're going the wrong way."

"Yeah, well I's jus keep goin' da wrong way."

"The castle is over there," the boy said and pointed off in the distance.

"Ju sees. Dat's not where I's goin'," Jaron stated. He wanted to walk away but his legs wouldn't move.

"No. You *do* want to go there."

Jaron was becoming tired of this prank and said sarcastically, "And wha' does a little boy likes ju know 'bout its, eh? Go run along now."

The boy stood about two feet from him, still wearing that sweet smile. "This is the form you gave me, Jaron. I only came to you like this because I didn't want to frighten you."

Jaron sniffed, "Really? I's don't frighten easily, so why's don't ju go ahead and frighten me."

The boy raised a brow then winked out of sight. In his place, towering over Jaron, was a being of no shape. Jaron couldn't keep his eyes on it and when he forced himself to stare, didn't know what he was looking at. The more he looked at it, the more his mind whirled and snapped until he thought he was going mad. But the one thing he was certain of was the raw power coming from the being. It was so intense and strong that Jaron couldn't think of any comparison, including what he thought the entire, combined power of the Land might be like. This was far stronger.

In the few seconds since the being appeared, Jaron thought of all of this and it was far too much for him to understand or stand against. He shrieked, fell to his knees, and covered his head with his arms, even though the being had done nothing more than appear. A few moments later he felt a hand smoothing back his hair and tentatively raised his head. His whole body was trembling, he'd been crying, and he was almost certain he'd wet his trousers. The boy smiled his sweet grin at him.

"See. I told you." Jaron nodded, since he didn't believe he had a voice at the moment. The boy breathed heavily and wiped the hair out of Jaron's eyes. "You are not ready yet. That is why you don't remember. You won't let your emotions interfere with your judgment. I wanted you to have the best, but you decided to put yourself through the worst. I didn't want that for you. Please understand that." Jaron heard the words, recognized them but still didn't understand a thing this being said. Apparently it didn't matter to the boy because he continued.

"And I had such hope. I actually had hoped you would reunite my other children but they have made that impossible. That's why I helped you hide from them. You decided to hide from yourself." He smiled sadly at Jaron. "Now I know who is sincere. You always want to believe your children. Even when they tell you one thing and do the opposite, you still have faith in them and want to trust them. But I never let my love for them interfere with your wellbeing. So I have waited and now I know who truly cares for you and loves you. Oh, both have sworn they did, but only one really understands and admits that you aren't some prize to hold over the other." He held Jaron's face in his small hands.

The boy clicked his tongue. "He screamed at me but it was only because he cares for you so. He misses you, he needs you, he wants to make it up to you." The child smiled warmly. "He cried for you. I bet you never thought anyone would ever cry over you, did you?" Jaron shook his head numbly, though he didn't understand the question. "It's time for you to go home, Jaron. I don't like to interfere like this but you need a push. Your memories have been aching to come out and succeeded several times. Explore them, savor them. For they are who you are. Go home. Go to the castle and begin your self-discovery." The boy disappeared.

Jaron stared ahead of him for a long moment and tried to think clearly. He wiped his nose with the back of his hand but couldn't remember what made him so upset. He felt confused and light-headed, which made Landon's shout nearly unbearable.

"*Jaron!*"

"Wha'!" Jaron winced and rubbed his head.

Landon sagged with relief. He'd been calling to the boy for several long minutes but the boy never responded. First he asked him for directions, then pushed him back and kept him there so he couldn't answer.

"*What happened?*" he asked and searched the boy's feelings, but all he found was foggy confusion and fear.

Jaron didn't know what happened. He felt like he'd been in a dream and now that he was awake it was slipping away from him. He was certain of one thing, though. "We's 'ave to go to da castle," he said slowly.

"*What! Did you hit your head?*"

"I's don't tink so," Jaron mumbled and rubbed his head, looking for a bump. There was nothing there, so he repeated his sentence.

Now Landon felt confused and asked carefully, "*Why do we want to go there?*"

"I's don't know."

"*That's the last place we want to go.*"

"No. We's need to go dare," Jaron said surely.

Landon sighed and would have run his hands down his face if he had either. "*I'm trying to understand this, Jaron, so please explain it to me. Why would we want to go where Taj is?*"

"I's don't know," Jaron admitted.

"*Then we don't go there.*"

"We's 'ave to."

"*I feel like I'm running around in a circle with you. Give me your reasons and I'll be more than happy to entertain them. But we can't just walk into our death trap.*"

"I's don't know why's. I's jus…dat's where we's need to go."

Landon grumbled irritably and was about to snap the boy's head off, when he felt the uneasy feeling and heard the sound through Jaron's ears.

"*What was that?*" As he asked the question, Jaron was already looking over his shoulder. They both stared at the gray wolf standing behind him.

"*What's a wolf doing so close to a person?*" Landon asked uneasily.

"It's not a wolf," Jaron answered silently. To prove him right, the wolf transformed itself into a man. Jaron recognized him immediately. It was Tirell, the supposed brother of the phony Darrell. And since Darrell turned out to be Taj that could only mean that he had sent this man.

"It's time to go home," the man said confidently to him.

Jaron also recognized the voice belonging to the same man who had nearly squeezed him to death when he discovered who Darrell really was. His eyes slid from his face toward the spot where he plunged his knife. The area was red and looked sore, but the man chuckled when he saw him looking.

"Think nothing of it."

Jaron swallowed and his breathing increased along with his heartbeat.

"*Run!*" Landon commanded.

"I's can't," Jaron answered him.

"*Burn me, you can't! You're a bloody saxtien! Run!*"

"Wha's da use. I's jus be's chased down 'till I's can't run annimore. We's 'ave to face dis ting." He remained on his knees and turned his head away from the man, who seemed to be waiting for him to make some type of move.

"*What are you doing!*" Landon screamed.

"We's need to go to da castle," Jaron said plainly.

"*Jaron, please!*" he begged, feeling more terrified than the boy.

"We's need to Landon," Jaron told him calmly. He was not surprised when he felt the arm wrap around his neck and cut off his air, though his instincts took over and his hands grabbed the arm and tried to pull it away.

"Just relax," the voice in his ear whispered.

Although he tried he couldn't, even though he knew the man was not trying to kill him; he was merely cutting off his air until he became unconscious. He supposed it was better than being knocked in the head or something worse, but he couldn't control his frantic reaction to having his air cut off from his lungs.

"*Jaron!*" Landon cried, trying to force his way completely forward the way he did last night. However, now that he wanted to he couldn't. In fact, Jaron's panic was pushing him further back and he could barely hold onto his current position. He heard Jaron's raspy breaths come to a stop and the Land blackened out of sight. Landon was thrown back into the darkness of Jaron's mind along with the boy.

Jynx watched anxiously from her perch in the tree as the thief collapsed into Taj's minion's arms. She bit her lip, drummed her nails against the bark, and glanced toward the figure standing a foot away from her. The image was that of a girl maybe two years older than her. Ever since she was a small child this same image had always come to her. And she needed no introductions to know who it was.

The image of the girl watched what happened to the thief without expression and didn't acknowledge her stare.

"Let me help them," Jynx nearly begged. The image of the girl shook her head slowly. Jynx felt her anger flare and asked stiffly, "With all due respect, great one, why not!"

"It is no longer your concern," the image answered, still watching what was going on below.

"Not my concern!" Jynx cried quietly. "You drag me into this, told me not to let anything happen to him, which I have done without question---"

"Without *too* much questioning," the girl injected.

Jynx continued. "I've risked your lost children's spirits and now you're willing to let *him* have them? Forgive my ignorance but I do not understand this."

The image slowly turned its head toward her. "You have done what I have asked. For that I thank you. Now you are no longer needed."

"I see," Jynx said tightly. She crossed her arms over her chest and glanced back down at the thief, whose hands and feet had already been bound, while Taj's minion dug through his sack, pulled out the thief's clothes, and dressed quickly. Jynx clicked her tongue. "So I'm free to do as I wish, then?"

"Of course," the image said. "So long as you do not interfere."

Jynx smiled and answered sincerely, "Great one. I would never go against your wishes." The image nodded and watched as Taj's minion scooped the boy up over his shoulder and hurried into the forest. They remained there in silence for a long while before the image nodded to her and winked out of sight. Only after Jynx was certain the presence was gone did she finish her sentence. "Until now."

She bounced down the branches of the tree as if they were made of rubber and summoned her sprites as she quietly followed behind Taj's servant. She called out, "Forgive me, great one. But you cannot bring me into this then not expect me to stay through to its end." She gathered her sprites as she went, no longer giving the image girl another thought.

The image of the girl, however, reappeared in the branches just as Jynx landed on the ground and scurried off. It heard her silent plea and a broad, gentle smile spread across its face as it answered her.

"I knew you could not. I counted on it." The being disappeared.

THE ACCIDENT

Dapp stood with his legs slightly apart, hands clasped behind his back, and waited. Taj walked in a wide circle as he did when he was either furious or deliriously content. Dapp could tell by Taj's expression that it was the latter and couldn't help but feel beaming pride, though he showed none of it in his face. If Taj liked to do anything, it was to cut people down when they assumed they had done right by him. Besides, Dapp knew he'd done well. He did what the Mytocks failed to do, although he didn't mention to Taj how easy the boy made it for him. He didn't think Taj needed to know that the boy just sat on his knees talking to himself or probably with that ivory dragon thing, and never once made a move to run. Also how easily the boy succumbed to him, as if he had no desire to fight him. It had gone better than Dapp expected but there was no reason to let Taj know that.

Taj stopped his circling right in front of him and his black eyes gleamed.

"You deserve a rest," Taj said with a grin and slapped his arm in a friendly gesture. It had taken much practice and control not to flinch when Taj touched him, but it was a talent, Dapp found, worth learning. He knew Taj hated people cowering from him when he was being nice and a cringe or flinch could lead to pain or death.

Dapp bowed his head respectfully. "Thank you, my lord."

Taj, still grinning and practically dancing, nodded then walked over to the Captain and whispered quickly to him. Dapp was not going to leave, though, until Taj told him to. Suddenly, Taj seemed to remember that he didn't dismiss his Second and glanced over his shoulder, smirking.

"Do you not require the rest, Dapp? I have plenty for you to do if you don't."

Dapp shook his head. "No, my lord. Thank you, my lord."

Taj turned back to the Captain, and Dapp gratefully headed for his chamber but not before he gave a sneer to one of the Mytocks standing there. He'd gotten less than an hour of sleep when the shouts snapped him awake.

**   **

Taj heard Dapp leave and smiled to himself. That young man had no idea just how thrilled he was and how rewarded he would be for this. He addressed the Captain again.

"Now remember, no sentries in or outside his chamber. I do not want him to be hindered in any way. I want to see what he does. Understand?"

"Yes, my lord." The Captain saluted and hurried off to carry out his orders.

Taj dismissed everyone else in the Justice Hall with word to have his personal servant come to him at once. He sank down into the new throne he had just put in and stared up at the new stained glass ceiling, with its new image imprinted on it. He hadn't felt this good in years. The boy was back in his possession again. The ivory dragon would soon be gone. The Land was back

237

under control, since he convinced the people nothing was wrong and of course, they believed him. He half-expected Abbnar to be taken by his Mytocks and brought before him, so he could destroy him slowly. He chuckled aloud. Now that was a fantasy he could only dream of, but perhaps one day he would make it happen.

He checked his timekeeper and tapped it impatiently. Where was that boy? He called for him minutes ago. He drummed his fingers on the arm of the throne for a moment, then got up and began pacing again.

He wondered what would happen when he and Jaron were reintroduced. He imagined this scenario dozens of times in the past, but now that the moment had come, he wasn't certain which way it would lead. For the longest time, he pictured the boy recognizing him immediately and the two of them having a joyous reunion. However, that image was dashed when he showed the boy his regular form back on the cliff and the boy didn't recognize him at all. There were other scenarios he could imagine, though.

Once he showed the boy his past, he would remember and then they could begin their reunion. He had no idea what happened to the boy after he wandered off all those years ago, so he was curious to find out. Although there was that one time when he nearly caught up with him but because he didn't supervise the acquisition himself, it got fouled up and he lost track of the boy again. But surely, once Jaron knew of his past, he would remember him in a favorable way. As far as he could recall, Taj never appeared to be anything other than patient and loving with him, although that wasn't exactly true. Patient, yes; loving, never. He couldn't afford to love the boy, not then and not now. If he did, the boy would just be a liability and that's not what Taj wanted him for.

Oh, but it had been so easy to let himself sink down into that sweet smile he remembered so well on that little round face. He recalled how the boy used to crawl into his lap and go to sleep. He enjoyed those few moments more than he admitted. Even now, even with the boy's hot temper and distrust, he could still feel that parental twinge inside of him. But always, *always*, he pushed it down.

The image of the boy sleeping peacefully in his lap stayed with him for a moment. He tried to push it away but the more he did, the more details came back to him. Such as, how he would hold the boy for hours while he slept. The boy would squirm in his arms to find a better position but never would he want to go to his bed. He wanted to stay within the protection of his arms and Taj was more than delighted to let him.

Taj found himself smiling at the recollection and snapped back to himself. What was the matter with him? There was no room for love when the Land was at stake. Still, the frozen image of him and the boy stayed in his mind. Why couldn't he shake it?

What were you feeling then, Taj?

Taj heard the question clearly in his mind. It was so clear he looked around the hall to see if he was alone. When he discovered he was, he realized it must be his conscience at him again. He refused to answer.

What were you feeling?

Taj knew he had to answer himself or else the image would continue to haunt him. He murmured under his breath, "Control."

That was the last thing you were feeling.

"Power, then."

Why won't you admit that these two ideas were the furthest from your mind at that moment? For one brief, incredible moment all you cared about, all you wanted, was to hold that child close to you. To feel his approval of you, to feel his love for you. For that one moment you no longer cared about what he could do for you, you wanted to know what you could do for him. You would've killed anyone who tried to take him away from you, not because you wanted to keep his power, but because you wanted to keep his love.

Taj was too stunned by what his conscience had to say that he couldn't find an argument. It rang too true to him and it bothered him greatly that it did.

Your brother couldn't find his love for him at the time. I was hoping he could bring it out in you. And he did...briefly. But you smothered it, extinguished it, and buried your feelings so you could have his power.

The voice in his mind let out a soft noise, as if on the border of tears. Taj was not used to feeling such regret and shame and it made him extremely uncomfortable. But still, he couldn't seem to break loose from the power forcing him to stand silent and listen.

Total strangers have fallen in love with this child for no other reason other than that he is kind, gentle, and loving. The two people he needed to love him for who he was, only saw what advantage he could have, only saw ways to use him. In a way, I seriously regret letting either of you have anything to do with him. I should have kept him separate from you both. I should have waited before I brought him back. Your brother, at least, understands but you...Taj, why do you wrap yourself in hate? Why do you push away any form of love I try to give you? Why do you insist on being miserable? What can I do to make you understand?

Taj felt his rage bubble instantly. What didn't he understand? He understood perfectly what he wanted and what was important. Taj knew this was not his own conscience speaking to him. With renewed confidence he spoke aloud to the voice, "I understand perfectly what is happening here...*Abbnar!* Such feeble tricks will not get me to release the boy. What can *I* do to make *you* understand that, old man! He's mine!"

The voice in his mind sighed sadly but it said nothing more. Taj listened closely but no further comments came from it. He smiled and nodded knowingly to himself. Abbnar could not contend with him once he knew what the old man was up to. And despite what the old man said, he knew exactly what would happen once he and Jaron came face to face again.

The boy would be distrustful, angry, and even dangerous. Ah, but those were qualities Taj wanted to encourage in the boy; bring to their full potential. Once those emotions had been trained and developed, he and Jaron would have a most pleasant relationship. Taj would be everything to him; teacher, friend, maybe even father. But always, *he* would be in control.

He glanced at his timekeeper again. At the same moment, Webben came trotting into the Hall.

"Ma'lord, forgive me," the boy said quickly.

Taj studied the boy's face. It was red and sweaty, as if he had just run across the entire castle. He smiled. "That's perfectly all right, my boy. I understand you have duties you must attend to. However, I wanted to inform you we have a guest."

"We do, ma'lord?"

"Yes and I want you to tend to him." Taj placed his hand on the boy's shoulder and walked with him across the Hall. "It seems he claims to contain the Kazimeer."

The boy stopped short. "But the Kazimeer is dead."

"Yes, I know. Strange, isn't it?" Taj smiled down at the boy. "But we will treat him as we would any other important guest. Perhaps if he does somehow manage to have the Kazimeer with him, I will finally have a chance to speak with him peacefully, as I wanted to the first time." He patted the boy's shoulder. "Now, get yourself cleaned up and bring him something from the kitchen. Soup, perhaps. And remember, Webben, be respectful."

"Yes, ma'lord." The boy nodded and trotted off.

Taj watched the boy leave with a smile. Now he would see who this child was loyal to. He planted the seed and all he had to do was either watch it grow or wither. He sat down on the steps of the dais with his face in his hands and waited. Something had to happen soon and he could hardly wait.

**   **

Jaron woke with a jerk. He sat upright and blinked several times before he was sure he was seeing clearly. He stared around at the chamber he was in and felt his jaw drop. He'd never seen any place so beautiful before. Everything was so polished, so shiny; the entire chamber sparkled. Silk tapestries hung from the windows, an elaborate wooden table was next to the bed, and the bed itself was made of rich, dark wood, polished to a high shine. Jaron thought it was simply amazing that so much beauty, and wealth, could be contained in one chamber.

"*I'm home.*"

"Home?" Jaron mouthed out slowly. "Dis is jur home?"

"*Yes. This looks to be a guest chamber. Question is, which one?*"

"Dare's more chambers likes dis?"

"*Of course,*" Landon answered absently, while trying to figure out what part of the castle they were in. "*See if you can peek out... Jaron! Would you listen!*"

Jaron snapped out of his wide-eyed daze from all the splendor he was staring at and shook his head to clear Landon's shout. "Wha'!"

"*Pay attention, boy. Now, take a peek out the door and look around. See where we are.*"

Grumbling under his breath, Jaron got out of the warm, cozy bed and noticed for the first time he was only dressed in his oversized nightshirt.

Someone had taken off his boots and trousers and he didn't see them anywhere in the chamber nor did he see his pack. *That* didn't make him feel too comfortable. He slowly tiptoed to the door and pressed his ear against it. He heard no sounds coming from beyond but that didn't mean someone wasn't there.

"*Open it,*" Landon commanded.

Jaron winced. "Stop shoutin'. Me head a'ready 'urts."

"*I didn't mean to be loud but you're moving too slow.*"

"Slow?!" Jaron cried softly and clicked his tongue. "Fine."

"*No, no, no!*"

But by then Jaron had already flung open the door and marched out into the hall. He stopped short when he didn't see anyone. No one, it seemed, was watching him. He felt more nervous than before.

"I's don't likes dis."

"*Be thankful for the little breaks we get,*" Landon said, observing the area. "*I know where we are now. If you head right you'll...your other right...you'll come to a back stairwell the servants use.*"

"And wha' do I's do when we's git dare?"

"*We'll figure that out when we do get there.*"

Jaron was inching his way down the hall, constantly looking over his shoulder to see if he was being followed. "I's don't understand someting. Why's is we's leavin'?"

"*Because Taj is here.*"

"But don't ju want to face him? Ju know, fight him?"

"*Not like this. Look, thief boy, this was not* my *idea. This was yours and Light only knows why!*"

Jaron was starting to wonder why too. "I's guess its seemed likes a good idea at da time."

Landon held back a remark and let the boy make his way down the hall. The wall on one side of the hall ran out and was replaced by a banister, with a stairwell leading down around the other side. Jaron peeked over the banister but saw no one coming up the stairs and pressed himself back against the wall.

"Well, now wha', thronge worm?"

"*Go down.*"

"Half naked! I's 'sposed to go outside likes dis? I's freeze!"

"*You won't freeze, although you may stub a toe. If there's no one around you can take a horse from the stable.*"

"Oh, tank ju very much," Jaron sneered.

"*Just get moving!*"

Jaron carefully moved toward the stairs when he heard someone coming up them. He froze, unsure of what to do. He began to back up and looked desperately around for a place to hide. By then it was too late. A young boy reached the top of the stairs, carrying a tray with a steaming bowl on it, and nearly dropped it when he saw Jaron. The two stared uncertainly at each other until Landon broke the silence, at least in Jaron's mind.

"*Webben!*"

"Webben," Jaron echoed.

The boy's eyes grew larger. "Kazimeer?" he whispered. His face was suddenly strained and his voice sounded as if he'd break into tears at any moment. "If you leave, you'll ruin everything!" He quickly looked down the stairs then back at Jaron, his small face twisted with indecision.

"Webben, what are you doing?" Landon asked, knowing full well what that look could mean. Could the boy actually have been mesmerized by the lies Taj was spreading? Webben appeared to make up his mind and his expression hardened. *"Webben, no!"*

Webben deliberately and forcefully threw the tray down, while he shouted, "You're not supposed to be out here! Stop!"

Jaron instinctively backed away from the shouting boy.

"Jaron wait! Call him by his name. Tell him it's me."

"I's tink he's a'ready knows its ju!" He picked up his pace.

"Stop!" Webben screamed. "Ma'lord Blasdon! He's trying to leave!"

Jaron sprinted down the hall back the way he came but skidded to a stop when three eye-lesses stepped out from three separate doorways. He scrambled back toward the shouting child and shoved Webben out of the way, rounding the corner to rush down the stairs. Coming up the stairs were two more eye-lesses and behind them was an armed man, shouting commands.

Jaron was grabbed from behind and shoved roughly back against the banister, so there was nowhere he could run. He was surrounded by white, pasty, snatching hands, all reaching for him at the same time. He kicked, punched, and snapped his teeth at them, no sooner getting loose from one grip, then being held tight by another. He thrashed around like a caged beast, not caring who he hurt. For one brief moment he felt no hands on him. Then he realized why.

In the process of whipping himself back and forth, while trying to back up, he managed to push himself over the edge of the banister.

During the span of those few seconds, he saw the pasty faces of the eye-lesses staring down at him and for the first time since he learned he was a morpher, he actually wished he could morph on command. But everything was happening too fast and his mind was not prepared.

No sooner did he think about morphing when he felt his back hit the edge of the stairs and snap his spine. He rolled down the stairs like a doll, his arms and legs flinging in all directions, slamming hard against anything they came in contact with. Having no control over his limbs, he was unable to slow his fall and tumbled into an awkward, backward somersault. His head supported his full body weight and when it was no longer able to sustain the strain, his neck snapped. He continued to spin out of control, until he landed face first against the stone floor, shattering the front of his skull and his entire face in the process.

"JARON!"

Jaron hardly heard Landon, despite the volume, and felt very tired.

He hit the ground the same instant Taj came skidding to a halt at the bottom of the stairs.

Taj stared at the bleeding, broken boy lying on the floor, then slowly shifted his gaze up. The Mytocks had already begun to scramble down the stairs, perhaps trying to stop the boy's fall. The Mytocks stood frozen once he came into view and waited for him to speak. Only Taj couldn't speak. He was too furious to speak. Out of the corner of his eye he saw the fighter scoop Webben up under his arm and run out of sight.

Shrieking, Taj threw out his left hand and a fireball, measuring the width and length of the staircase, erupted from it and smashed into the Mytocks, splattering them like melons. Before the debris could hit the ground, he rested both hands onto Jaron's broken head. He never had to work so quickly in his life to heal another, but managed to stay ahead of the damage. He grabbed hold of Jaron's essence and restrained it from leaving. He stopped the blood flow, reconstructed bones, muscles, organs, fusing them to their proper shape. His power coursed through the boy's body like new blood, making him jerk and spasm, but healing him. When Taj was finished, he let his body slump and gently turned the boy's head, waiting anxiously for him to open his eyes.

Jaron remembered hearing a horrible scream and being in horrible pain, but after that everything was fuzzy, until now. There was a sound in his ears, like a hundred horses stampeding, but soon it faded and he no longer hurt. He opened his eyes carefully and pushed himself up on his palms. The first thing he saw was the blood that had been where his face was. His body shook, knowing it had all come from him, and absently wiped his face.

He looked away and tested his jaw, rolled his tongue around his mouth, and shook his head to see if it was all in one piece. Confused, he glanced up, then cried out in fear. Those black eyes were studying him, then closed in what looked like relief, and the man he'd once known as Darrell let out an unsteady breath. Jaron felt Landon recoil slightly but then come forward completely.

"*Are you all right?*" he asked anxiously.

Jaron was too terrified to do more than give him a quick "Yup", and continued to stare at that face.

Those black eyes opened and Taj shook his head. "You scared the piss out of me, boy." He placed a reassuring hand on his shoulder.

Jaron swallowed hard and forced himself to turn away from the pile of blood and Taj. He couldn't help but notice the stairwell, now black and burnt, with pieces of flesh and insides hanging on the walls and ceiling. The stench that filled his nose made him wish he couldn't breathe. He couldn't take his eyes off the charred pieces of bodies and felt his stomach turn over several times. Also, that this man called Taj was not only right next to him but was also touching him, made him want to vomit. He held onto Landon tightly and Landon held him back. Both too afraid to do anything other than see what happened next.

"*Why did we come here?*" Landon asked weakly.

"I's don't know," Jaron answered just as weak. Far too much was happening at once and it made his head spin. He rolled over onto his hands and knees, feeling his stomach lurch forward and came within an inch from the red, sticky puddle again. He saw bits of bone and a few teeth floating around in it.

Taj caught him before he landed face first in his own blood.

REMINISCING

Poke, poke, poke. Jaron wrinkled his nose and grunted as he rolled over. Poke, poke, poke. He waved his hand in the air as if he were brushing away a fly. Poke, poke, poke. He growled sharply and woke up enough to know that the poking was coming from inside his mind.

"Wha'?" he asked Landon sleepily.

"*I have been more than patient, boy.*"

"Huh?"

"*You've slept long enough. Wake up now.*" Poke, poke, poke.

"I's up! Leaves me alone." Jaron rolled over and buried his face in the head cushion.

"*Did you forget where you are?*"

Jaron's eyes flew open and he jerked his head upright. "So we's 'ere 'gain?" he asked.

"*Looks that way.*" After a pause, Landon asked tentatively, "*How are you?*"

"Fine. Why's wouldn't I's be's?"

"*Did you forget?*"

Jaron thought hard for a moment and realized he didn't forget. He remembered clearly all that happened to him. Falling over the banister, down the stairs, the horrible pain, the blood pouring from him, and then there was...

"Do not be frightened."

Jaron flipped over and did a double take when he saw who was sitting next to the bed. He shrank away from those black eyes, pulled the blankets up to his neck, and brought his legs up to his chest, while Landon ducked deeper into his mind.

Taj leaned closer and studied him, his face set with genuine concern. He leaned forward and felt Jaron's forehead. Jaron tried to move away from his touch, but couldn't back up any further with the large, wooden headboard behind him. He shivered when he felt that warm hand brush against his skin. Taj smiled down at him and rose to his feet.

"How are you feeling?"

Jaron opened his mouth to respond but nothing came out.

"*Answer him,*" Landon urged. Jaron tried to respond to him too, but all Landon received was a flood of incoherent thoughts and feelings.

Taj's smile deepened. "I bet you're hungry." Without waiting for an answer, he went to the door and told the person outside to have some broth and tea brought up immediately. He returned to the chair next to the bed, still wearing his pleasant smile, and stared at Jaron.

Landon inched his way forward again. He noticed instantly what Taj was doing. The man's body language was opened and relaxed. He leaned forward toward Jaron, made direct eye contact, spoke gently, with almost a singsong quality to his voice. He was trying to break down Jaron's barriers and was beginning to succeed. Landon planted himself forward in the boy's mind, keeping

Jaron alert and on guard while he watched carefully. He realized he was in a unique position; to study his opponent without having his opponent studying him.

"Almost twelve hours," Taj said casually. "That's a long rest."

His voice sent chills up Jaron's spine. "Landon," he pleaded silently. "Do someting!"

"*I am,*" Landon replied levelly.

"Wha'? Wha' are ju doin'?" Jaron demanded.

"*Shush! I'm watching.*"

"Watchin'! Dat does not help me git out of dis."

"*Quiet!*"

"No! Ju git me---"

"*Jaron, shut up!*" Landon snapped. He noticed the way Taj was cocking his head slightly as if he were listening to their conversation. Could he hear him the way Jynx could? He didn't want to risk saying more to the boy, but thankfully didn't have to since Jaron also seemed to notice what Taj was doing. He said nothing more to Landon.

"Are you feeling better?" Taj asked as he moved from the chair to the edge of the bed. Jaron forced himself to nod. Taj chuckled, which startled Jaron and Landon, and shook his head slightly. "I can't believe you're sitting right here." He brought his fist to his lips gently and shook his head again. "It's been a long time and I have missed you."

It took much effort for Jaron to keep his face neutral and not have his expression twist with confusion at what this man was saying. Was he mistaking him for someone else and if he was, what did that mean for him? Would Taj kill him? Landon grunted in frustration since the boy's thoughts were whirling around so quickly he could barely concentrate. Jaron forced himself to calm down and let Landon do his watching.

Taj's eyes narrowed slightly as he watched Jaron, then he brushed his hands on his thighs and took a breath before he said, "You are uncertain of me. I understand that and must apologize for my behavior when you last saw me." Jaron started to ask what he was talking about but Taj's face quickly grew hard, so he said nothing. Then Taj's expression returned to its serene, passive expression and he continued. "It was not my intention to frighten you so. I wanted to acquaint myself with you again before I told you the truth. I had no idea what rumors you heard and wanted to be the one who told you what was true and what wasn't. But when that demon child started attacking you...well I could no longer keep my distance."

Jaron started to protest about Jynx, then thought better of it and kept his mouth closed.

Taj continued. "I had to protect you from that demon, but unfortunately, my coming to your aid only made things appear more suspicious to you. I would like to set everything straight now." He smiled warmly at Jaron, but Jaron kept his face neutral and tried not to gag.

"*He's lying,*" Landon said more to himself than to the boy, but Jaron answered him.

"Oh really? Ju tink?"

"There's no reason to get so touchy, boy."

"Ju're not da one sittin' 'ere an arm length 'way from dis man."

"Yes, I am." Jaron actually felt better, knowing that he wasn't alone in this. *"Now be quiet."* Landon noticed Taj doing his head tilt again.

"I suppose you have many questions and I hope I can answer them all for you," Taj said. "But let me ask one of you first. Do you remember me?" Jaron blinked at him with confusion and shook his head. Taj sniffed a laugh, "I know you can talk. I've heard you do it."

Jaron swallowed gingerly and forced his knees down, though his grip on the blanket was still tight. "From when would I's know ju?"

"From a long time ago, from your past. Any recollection?"

Jaron shook his head slowly and mumbled, "No."

Taj looked disappointed then smiled at him. "It's all right." He reached out to pat Jaron on his arm but, unable to help himself, Jaron jerked away from his touch. He saw a darkness wash over Taj's face just for an instant, then the smile was beaming at him again. "It's all right," Taj repeated, leaned back, and said nothing more.

They just stared at each other in complete silence, so when there came a sharp knock at the door Jaron cried out before he could stop himself. Taj didn't seem to hear his outburst and let the servant in with the tray of food. It was set down on the table next to the bed and with a bow to Taj, the servant quickly scurried out.

"What is my servant doing bowing to that man?!"

"I's tink he's be's dead ifs he's dinn't," Jaron answered. "'Sides, wha' ju care? Ju don't even know his name."

"Of course I do."

"Den wha' is its?"

Landon paused for a moment and then snapped, *"I'm trying to do something very important here. Be silent and let me concentrate!"*

"I's knew ju dinn't know his name," Jaron said smugly. Landon growled but didn't respond.

Taj uncovered the bowl and set the tray down on the bed next to Jaron. "Eat. You must be starved. You look so thin." He smiled and gestured to the tray.

Jaron took the tray, placed it on his lap, and couldn't help but find the smell of everything to be so tempting.

"Careful," Landon warned, but Jaron had no need for any warning. He knew how to pretend to eat without ever taking a bite and proceeded to make sipping sounds as he ate, never taking any of the broth or tea into his mouth.

"Good, eh?" Taj asked.

Jaron nodded, took another sip and then set the tray aside. He cleared his throat, and asked carefully, "Why's would ju know me?"

Taj's brow came together in confusion. "You really don't remember me?" Jaron shook his head. "Granted, it was a long time ago but...oh, I guess all I can do is try to help you remember. Now, what else would you like to know?"

"Landon!" Jaron cried humbly. "Wha' do I's do?"

"Ask him about the castle. What happened to the people that were here?"

Jaron didn't bother mentioning just why *he* would want to know such a thing, so he started a little less directly. "Where am I's?"

"*Good point.*" How would Jaron know he was at the castle?

"This is my home," Taj said pleasantly. "I hope one day you will come to think of it as yours too."

Jaron looked around the chamber. "It's big."

"Yes, I suppose it is," Taj chuckled.

"Anni towns nearby?" Jaron asked casually.

"One," Taj responded, not offering the name of the town.

Jaron backed away from the castle subject, since Taj didn't seem to want to say much about it, and started on another topic. "So, wha' do ju want wit me?"

"I need your help," Taj said sincerely, then raised his brow slightly. "And I think you could use mine."

"Me help?" He looked around the chamber again. "I's don't tink ju need anniting stolen."

Taj chuckled and Jaron looked back to him and smiled a little. He knew how to play the darling, shy, little boy role, which often provided him with more information than if he beat someone over the head with questions. Besides, he had no idea who this Taj person really was. He didn't know his strengths or weaknesses, so it was best to play naïve until he found his footing.

"Yes, I know of your vocation," Taj said with a grin. "I may just have a need for it, but that's not the help I'm referring to."

"Den wha' help do ju need?"

Taj studied him briefly then answered, "We'll get to that in a bit." He said no more.

Jaron waited a few long moments before he asked, "Well, if's ju needed me help, why's dinn't ju jus ask?"

"You didn't remember who I was," Taj said. "If I walked up to you and said, 'Hi Jaron. I need your help.', you would have told me to go bury myself. I wanted to be sure you had all the facts, which was why I lied about who I was when we last met." He spread his hands. "I was feeling you out before I invited you to rejoin my family."

"Uh...Landon?" Jaron asked silently.

"*Be...very...careful,*" Landon warned. "*He's stacking up all the blocks and just waiting for you to knock them over.*"

"He's a cow short from 'avin' a full farm, isn't he?" Jaron asked him, while he kept his eyes on Taj.

"*That's a good guess. But do not underestimate him, as I did.*"

"Ju 'ave a family?" Jaron asked Taj, making his face show innocent curiosity.

"Everyone has a family. Mine is a big one, a happy one. We have loyalty and trust between our members. We help each other. We're there for each other in times of trouble. And we're in trouble right now."

"Wha' kind of trouble?"

"One involving the Land, which I think you would be interested in." He offered no more.

Reminiscing   247

"Wha' is its?" Jaron pressed.

"Soon," Taj said patiently. "We'll discuss that soon."

Jaron was starting to feel like he was walking in thick mud and not getting anywhere. "Wha' do ju want of me?"

"I told you, I need your help."

"But ju dinn't say wha' help dat was. How's do I's know ifs I's can give its to ju?"

"Oh, you can," Taj answered with a short nod. He said nothing else.

Jaron growled in frustration to Landon, "Wha' do I's do now? He won't answer anniting."

"This is his instrument and he's playing it however he wants. So give him a sour note and see if he can make it sound as pleasant as this other dung he's been playing."

"How's do I's do dat?"

"Try to catch him off guard. Give him a question he has to answer."

Jaron thought about it quickly, then carefully tiptoed into the question. "I's don't know, but ifs I's needed someone's help, I's wouldn't bring dem to me house den...ah...try to 'ave dem killed."

Taj shook his head sadly. "I can't apologize enough for that, but believe me when I say that I didn't wish any harm on you." He leaned closer and Jaron braced himself in case Taj decided to touch him. He didn't but stared straight into his eyes. "My Mytocks were trying to keep you from hurting yourself. I suppose they should have addressed you properly, instead of just reacting, but they are like children. They think with their hearts, not with their heads. Their only concern at that moment was your wellbeing." Taj dropped his head and shook it. His voice was barely a whisper. "I can't tell you how sorry I am for that horrible accident."

"But ju killed dem," Jaron said slowly.

"Yes." Taj shook his head in regret. "Out of mercy. They were so upset having indirectly caused your injuries they could no longer function. They were in pain and I could not heal them, so I eased their misery."

Jaron's expression never changed but he knew what he saw and knew he was being lied to. He didn't imagine all that blood and insides on the walls and ceiling. When you put someone out of their misery, you do it quickly, painlessly; you don't shred them down to nothing.

"Well, I's don't 'member much, but its sure was messy. I's guess dare was a lot of misery ifs ju had to grind dem down likes dat." Taj's expression darkened slightly. Feeling a jolt of panic from that look, Jaron quickly asked, "Den its was ju who's healed me?"

"Of course I healed you," Taj answered smoothly. "I told you, I want you to be a part of my family."

"Don't back down, Jaron," Landon encouraged. *"You were going to snap the trap close before and lost your nerve. Don't let him frighten you. I believe him when he says he needs you or you wouldn't be here now. So use that to your advantage and force him to tell you the truth."*

Jaron hoped the thronge worm was right and said as casually and with as much self-confidence as he could muster, "Yes, ju want me to be's a part of jur family, which is why's ju brought me 'ere, but I's tink jur plan got pissed on. Ju wanted to sees wha' I's did so ju dinn't 'ave annione standin' watch at me door. Oh, I's sure ju wanted me to tink dat its was 'cause ju trusted me, but I's pretty sure ju wanted to sees ifs I's would try to leave. Which, of course, I's did. But when I's tried, and jur eye-less tings tried to stop me, its got out of jur control. Instead of bringin' me back to dis chamber, dey knocked me over da banister and nearly killed me. Sees, I's tink ifs dey did git me back to dis chamber, ju would've been 'ere in seconds tellin' me how's sorry ju were fure 'avin' dem treat me so rough, and ju probably would've yelled at dem or someting, to makes its looks good fure me benefit. But wha' 'appened was I's a'most died and ju had to heal me or else I's wouldn't be's able to give ju dis help ju need so badly from me, and den I's tink ju lost jur temper and killed dose eye-less tings. Or maybe ju killed dem first, I's don't 'member. Me head was split open at da time." Jaron smiled boyishly at him. "At least, dat's how's its looked to me."

Taj's face never changed and he continued to hold that semi-dark expression. Then he sniffed a laugh and patted Jaron lightly on the cheek. "No more talking to that beast, all right?"

Jaron was momentarily frozen and didn't know how to respond. He whispered to Landon, "Its dinn't work."

"*Yes, I can see that,*" Landon answered calmly, though he was just as panicked as the boy. Could Taj really hear him?

"But wha' do I's do now?"

"*Hold your ground and don't let---*" He stopped because Jaron let out a muffled cry, when Taj slipped his hand behind his neck and grabbed a handful of hair.

"*I said!*" Taj shouted, then his voice dropped down to a low tone and he continued calmly. "No more talking to that beast." He released Jaron's hair and pointed a finger in his face. "I am tired of watching you two plot against me while I'm sitting right here. Oh, at first it was amusing, but from now on you pay attention to me. I will tell you all these things you've been so cleverly working your way around trying to get me to answer. And when I am finished, your outlook on everything will change. We will deal with the ivory dragon beast later." He withdrew his finger but remained next to Jaron, who forced himself not to back away and not to talk to Landon. He also lost his innocent, little boy routine.

"I's tink ju got da wrong person," he said flatly.

"For your sake I hope you're wrong, but *I* don't think so." He smiled again and said lightly, "But let's find out for certain."

Jaron immediately felt a grip on his mind and panicked. He thrashed his head back and forth, trying to shake loose from the hold and automatically reached inside of himself to find a weapon he knew was there, though he never remembered using it before. He was slammed up against the headboard and held there by an invisible force. His eyes went wide with fear when he saw the even, calm expression Taj wore.

"Please, Jaron," Taj said with a sigh and checked his nails absently. "Let's not embarrass ourselves anymore, shall we? All of this is just making you upset and me tired. So let's just settle this matter right now and find out for sure."

Jaron felt icy fingers sliding across his mind and wanted to retch. It was an uncomfortable, sick sensation that made his skin itch and his insides feel as if they were on fire. But he couldn't do anything other than let it happen.

Landon ducked down deep into Jaron's mind the second he felt Taj moving in. His fear was also mounting, since he was certain Taj could find him easily and remove him permanently. However, Taj didn't seem to be looking for him. He was slicing into Jaron's mind, looking for something specific; something very specific. And it was something that Jaron blocked out so completely that even with Taj's fierce persistence, Jaron still managed to fight him. Apparently, Jaron didn't want whatever it was to be revealed to him.

However, Taj's persistence overshadowed Jaron's resistance, and the memory clearly unfolded before both of them.

Jaron was a little boy again. The perspective was odd, since he was seeing out of his childhood eyes and yet he had no control over what happened. He was being forced to relive this. He felt his young self pout and twist his head away from the spoon being held in front of him by a young woman.

"You have to eat," the young woman said, but young Jaron shook his head back and forth, while keeping his mouth tightly closed. "Come on. Here's the horsy riding into the stable." She made the spoon bounce up and down like a horse's gallop, but young Jaron twisted his head away again. The woman dropped the spoon into a bowl and grumbled, "You're being difficult on purpose, aren't you?" Young Jaron didn't understand the meaning behind the words so he hummed loudly in protest. The woman imitated him and the two of them hummed at each other until young Jaron broke up with giggles.

"What is going on in here?"

Young Jaron swung his head toward the opening of the tent and called out happily, "Bapp!"

Jaron watched as the wolf morpher, who looked much younger, probably only a few years older than Jaron was now, approach his younger self. Jaron wanted to recoil but the young Jaron seemed happy to see him and allowed Dapp to roll him onto his back and tickle him.

"He won't eat," the young woman stated.

"That's because he's being bad!" Dapp grinned. "Aren't you?"

"Nooo!" young Jaron squealed.

"Yes you are!" Dapp teased as he picked him up by his feet and hung him upside down playfully. "You're going to be in so much trouble."

Young Jaron twisted and giggled, until the cool, smooth voice from the tent's opening broke up the fun.

"Put him down before you drop him." In one quick motion, young Jaron was flipped over and set on his feet.

"I'm sorry," Dapp mumbled. "I was just playing."

"If his head was cracked open, I would have 'just played' with you," the voice snapped. Young Jaron pushed his way around Dapp's legs and beamed, although Jaron and Landon both watched horrified.

Taj, looking exactly the same as he did now, squatted down and held his arms open. "Where's my good boy?" he asked with a smile. Young Jaron raced over and embraced him freely.

Jaron felt his head spin and his stomach tighten. He remembered none of this and yet remembered all of it. He felt like he was drowning in his own mind and couldn't find his way to the surface.

"Landon?" he called out silently, wanting to hear some reassurance that this wasn't happening. Landon opened his thoughts to answer, but didn't know what to say, so he said nothing.

The memory continued.

Taj ruffled young Jaron's hair, then stood and placed a protective hand on his shoulder. "What is going on, Grec?" His voice was as cold and hard as ice. "I'm gone for one day and he's already thinner. Have you been starving him?"

"No. He refused to eat," Grec stated. She seemed less affected by Taj's presence than Dapp did.

"That's because you didn't think of bribing the boy," Taj spat. Young Jaron was oblivious to the entire, edgy mood of the tent. Taj picked up a sack he dropped on the floor when he entered and dangled it before young Jaron. "I have something for you," he tempted. Young Jaron reached out for the bag but Taj yanked it out of his reach. "Uh-uh. You have to eat your supper first."

"It's icky," young Jaron grimaced.

Taj shrugged. "Oh well. I guess I'll just have to give this to another little boy who eats his supper."

Young Jaron's face went white. He rushed over to the bowl of porridge and gulped it down without much help from the spoon. Taj turned a satisfied glance toward Grec and Dapp.

"See how easy that was? Don't let me find him like this again." Both nodded and, with a quick jerk of Taj's head, they left together. Taj sat behind Jaron once he was finished and cleaned him off.

"I said to eat it, not bathe in it."

Young Jaron grinned happily as if he had done something marvelous, then glanced at the bag next to Taj. After a short wait, Taj reached in and pulled out a ridiculous looking stuffed rabbit. Its ears were so long they fell over, and its arms and legs dangled almost to the floor. Its stitched face wore a permanent smile and two X's for eyes. But young Jaron squeezed it tightly and cried out in a shrill voice,

"A bunny!"

Taj winced from the volume the boy used and nodded. "Yes. A bunny."

"For meee?!"

"Yes, for you." Young Jaron squeezed the bunny again then squeezed Taj. Taj embraced him and asked, "Who's my good boy?"

Jaron pulled back from the memory and dozens more started flowing into his mind. He remembered that stupid looking rabbit and how he had it with him when he was in the slave-trade. He also remembered when one of his Masters finally found and burned it in front of him as he screamed and cried, although he didn't know why at the time. Then he had been beaten for his deception and tears.

Another memory with that rabbit popped up. He remembered having it tucked under his arm as he followed another little boy into the forest.

"Where are we going?" he remembered asking.

The little boy leading the way turned to look at him and smiled sadly. "You'll see."

Jaron knew that little boy was familiar but from when? He couldn't think of it and yet he had the distinct feeling this same little boy was somehow responsible for making him want to come to the castle in the first place. He also recalled the little boy disappeared when they wandered into a town and left Jaron alone to be snatched up by the slave-trade.

Memories of the slave-trade came pouring into him. Things he was certain he had forgotten about now were fresh and just as painful as when they first happened. The beatings, being sold to new heartless Masters, having the age-lines cut into his young flesh with a rusty knife, and being locked away for hours, sometimes days, in a slave cage.

Jaron shrieked and ripped his mind away from the memories and felt the icy fingers withdraw. His mind came back slowly to where he was. He shivered, his head clutched in his hands, and his eyes stared wide at nothing. He slowly turned his eyes toward Taj, who was still sitting on the edge of the bed, looking passive.

Taj's emotions were anything but passive. Some of his questions were now answered as to what happened to the boy after he wandered off. In a way, he was glad the boy had lived such a hard life. It made him strong and thick-skinned. Now Taj could use those defenses and skills he learned while he was in the slave-trade to his advantage. He would have liked to tell Jaron his life of pain hadn't been for nothing and that his misery would help Taj to control him more. Somewhere deep inside of his mind, though, there was a part of him that cried for the boy's pain. A part that wanted to run out and find all those bastards who hurt this boy and pull their hearts out. But that part was quickly buried beneath the rest of his agenda. He had no time to waste on pity.

"It's a lie," Jaron croaked finally and ran his hands through his hair. "Dat was a lie."

"Oh it was? Why? Because you refused to believe it?" Taj leaned forward and dropped his voice a level. "You know it was true, just as I do. Just because you wish it wasn't, doesn't change the fact that it happened." He leaned back and smiled. "Now that you know we have met before and you *are* the one I need, we can go further."

"No!" Jaron cried and leapt out of the bed, getting as far away from Taj as he could. He wobbled and felt dizzy, but somehow remained standing. "No furder!"

Taj got to his feet, though he didn't approach Jaron. "I meant, we can go further about how we can help each other."

"Wha' do ju want?" Jaron hissed and felt the chamber grow steadily warmer.

"Oh, the utmost would be your love, your admiration, your friendship. But let's be realistic, shall we? I would only require the following." He counted on his fingers with each remark. "Your loyalty, your respect, and your power."

Jaron blinked in confusion. "Wha' power?"

"Is that also lost in your complicated mind? No matter. I can show you how to use it."

"Wha' are ju talkin' 'bout?"

"I am talking about your power at my disposal," Taj snapped as he started to lose his patience with the boy.

"Ju are mad," Jaron whispered, shaking his head back and forth and moving further away.

Landon cried out for the first time since the memories appeared. *"Jaron, I really hope this is going somewhere, because calling this man mad is not what I would call being careful."*

However, Taj merely smiled at the remark. "I'm glad you think so." He casually walked around the bed. "Now, let us discuss that thing inside your mind." Jaron shook his head in confusion. Taj growled, "That thing! That abomination! That festering sore on the face of the Land!"

"I think he means me," Landon mumbled.

"Don't flatter jurself," Jaron told him.

Taj's face snapped with anger and he stalked toward Jaron so quickly, Jaron barely had time to register that he was moving closer. Taj pushed Jaron up to the wall and spoke softly but sharply.

"Didn't I tell you to pay attention to me?" Jaron could do nothing more than nod. "You see, this is what I mean by loyalty and respect, and obviously, you have no intention of giving me either. Yet!" He leaned his face so close to Jaron's that he could see each pore, each hair in his face and had a feeling he would wake up screaming from this image. Taj's voice was nothing more than a fierce whisper.

"You see, Jaron, loyalty and respect come with time. Power, however, does not. Not with me, anyway. And luckily for me, I don't have to wait for it. Just because you don't know what I'm talking about, doesn't mean I can't use your power. I can pull it from you minute by minute, hour by hour, until..." Taj spread his hands. "Well, until it's just mine. I could pull it all from you and leave you so empty you'll be too confused about how to take a piss without me telling you how."

"But," he continued after a short pause, "I don't want to do that. I want *you* to use your power. I just want you to use it for me. Is that such a terrible thing?" He didn't wait for an answer. "And the thing in your mind I'm referring to, although I suspect you already know, is called an ivory dragon. Do you know how unnatural that beast is? Do you?" Now he waited for an answer and Jaron could only shake his head numbly.

"Of course you don't," Taj said softly. "No one does. That's what I'm trying to change, Jaron. I'm trying to make everyone see just how ruined this

Land is and that it needs help. It can't be ignored any longer. If it is, the Land will die and so will everyone else. The morphers, Jaron. The morphers are eating away at the Land's strength, especially ones like the Kazimeer. It's the unnatural ones that drain the most energy because they were never meant to exist. If they don't exist any longer, the Land can heal. That's all I'm trying to do, Jaron. I'm just trying to heal the Land, the way I healed you.

"Imagine that you are the Land and remember all that pain you felt just a short while ago. Didn't you want it to just stop? Weren't you glad, maybe just a little, when you saw those eye-less things dead? Because you knew they could never hurt you or come after you ever again. Can't you understand what I'm doing?"

Jaron swallowed and felt a pang of fear rise in him because he could understand. What Taj was saying made perfect sense. The only problem he had with it was it *felt* wrong to him. Landon sagged with relief. For an instant, he was certain he had lost the boy to Taj.

"But all dose people?" Jaron asked.

Taj nodded sadly. "Yes, I know what you're thinking. All those innocent people, innocent morphers, who have no control over what they are or what they're doing are the ones who are going to suffer. But Jaron, is it fair to let them live, because if they are living they are sucking more energy away from the Land. So eventually, they will die anyway. And their children. And everyone else who isn't a morpher, who are just as innocent as the morphers are. More so, because they have nothing to do with what is happening. Is it fair to save a handful of people at the expense, the extinction, of an entire Land?"

"*Yes and an entire Land of non-morphers and non-Weavers, with just a few select morphers and Weavers, would be very easy to control,*" Landon commented. "*Don't answer me, Jaron. Just think about this. A population of non-morphers and non-Weavers would fall very easily under the rule of morphers and Weavers because they would be defenseless. Jaron, he doesn't want to save the Land; he wants to own it.*"

Jaron listened to Landon and kept his face neutral so Taj wouldn't have another fit. It occurred to him that maybe Taj couldn't so much as hear Landon as he could pick up on *his* expressions when he talked to him. Maybe he could feel Landon's presence the way the Masters could, but when Landon spoke, Taj didn't respond. It was only when Jaron talked back that somehow he picked up on it. So far, it seemed to be working, since Taj was still staring at him, waiting for an answer, although Jaron wasn't sure how to respond.

Taj's plan made him uncomfortable and Landon may have hit upon what it was. Up front, it made the common people seem like a first priority and they would follow such a person who would stand up for them instead of the morphers and Weavers. Then they would be slaves to that person, constantly in debt and fear. However, Jaron didn't know what to say to Taj, who had taken his hesitation negatively.

Taj took a step back and smiled. "You need to think about this, I can tell." His smile faded and his expression grew fierce. "But let me make two things *crystal clear!*" Jaron flinched at his shout and wanted very much to melt into the floor. "The ivory dragon beast will be killed. It will be destroyed, gone, no more! So don't think you can protect that thing by standing in my way when I come for It. With or without your consent I will take It and the only thing you will get by fighting me is a very unpleasant experience.

"The second thing is this; I will use your power. Again, with or without your consent, I will have it when I want it! Now I am going to give you some time to think about this. I want you to think very hard about what I am saying. I don't want to hurt you, Jaron. I honestly don't, which is why I'm giving you this time. But I'll rip you apart if you fight me and leave you wondering why you were born. You think the slave-trade was horrible? I'll make it seem like a romp with a whore if you decide to be your father's son. Just remember, the only one you'll be hurting if you fight me, is you." He shouted over his shoulder, "Dapp!"

The door opened and Dapp marched in. Taj's dark expression was gone and he spoke pleasantly, "Take our young friend to a nice, quiet place where he can think clearly."

Dapp approached Jaron, who tried to press himself into the wall behind him. Moving like a sharp wind, Dapp grabbed Jaron's arms and twisted them up behind his back. He forced Jaron to walk before him and Taj called out happily, "Think well, my boy."

Jaron barely heard him. All he could think of as he was being marched down the hall was that he had no choice. However, Landon was already calculating and thinking. Neither one was very surprised when they entered the dungeon.

MORPHING

Jaron was given a shove from behind and fell into the hole of the dungeon cell. He just landed with a hard thud and was pulling himself up to his knees when he heard the creaking moan of seldom used hinges. He looked up to see the heavy iron grate slamming closed above him, and quickly turned his face away as flakes of rusted metal and dirt slipped down through the darkness into his hair and onto his shoulders. He heard the final snap as the lock fell into place.

Jaron craned his neck up and met Dapp's eyes for a moment. Dapp regarded him briefly then strode away, leaving Jaron to stare at the black bars high above him.

He dropped his head on his knees and groaned, "Dis is me fault."

"*No. It was inevitable.*"

"Wha' do I's do?" Jaron begged. Landon felt the boy's fear climb higher as he continued to speak. "I's 'ave no choice. He's insane and I's don't tink dare's anniting I's can do to git out of 'ere. He's left me wit nutin'."

Landon was wondering about something else, though. "*Why am I still here?*"

"Wha'?"

"*Why am I not dead or banished or something? Why did he let you walk out of that chamber with me in your head and put us down here together?*"

"I's dinn't 'zactly walk out of dare, more likes shoved."

"*But he knows I'm here, why didn't he just finish me?*"

"Ju sound disappointed dat he's dinn't."

"*I'm just confused.*"

Landon let Taj's words race through his thoughts again, looking for those little slips of the tongue or clues that may give him an idea about what this man was thinking. He could've just taken him at any moment and yet he was giving Jaron time to think. Could Jaron block Taj somehow from simply taking him? Did he need Jaron's cooperation? That didn't make sense; Taj seemed powerful enough, why would he need Jaron's cooperation? Although he did say something about Jaron having power. But that really made no sense. Granted, Jaron was a morpher so there was power there but certainly not enough to overcome a Weaver of Taj's caliber. Or maybe if Taj tried to take him out of Jaron's mind by force, he could end up hurting or killing Jaron too. And since Taj just made it clear he wanted Jaron for...well, for something... then maybe he didn't want to risk it. It was obvious he was trying to win the boy over. If he couldn't do it through kindness, he'd do it through fear. Perhaps the entire process would just be easier if Jaron agreed. Still, it was just strange. Taj wanted him dead, that much was certain. So why give him any chance to come up with a plan? Unless he was just overconfident and assumed there wouldn't be a chance to come up with a plan.

His mind was spinning with questions and it became worse when he felt that sensation act up again.

The entire time Jaron had been asleep he'd been fighting the urge to come forward. Even while Taj was talking and showing those memories, Landon had

256

still been wrestling with it. It was constant now. It never eased up for an instant and it took much of Landon's concentration to keep it under control. So naturally, his nerves and patience were stretched and when he spoke it was short and heated.

"*All right, enough of this.*" Jaron jerked from the sudden response. "*We have to get out of here. You're a thief, aren't you?*"

"So?"

"*So, boy, I will bet that you've been in worse situations than this. Don't you know how to pick a lock?*"

"I's never been in a cell likes dis 'fore."

"*Can you pick the lock?*" Landon asked again, trying to keep himself composed. The amount of energy he was using to keep his instinct at bay was great and causing him pain.

"I's don't 'ave anni of me tools wit me." He heard Landon grumble with annoyance. "But I's 'spose I's can takes a looks."

"*Then get up there. You might even be able to pull out one of the bars. They're nothing but rust practically.*"

"Ju want me to wha'?!" Jaron gasped and automatically glanced up at the cell door. "How's ju want me to git up dare? Dat's at least fifteen feet over me head!"

"*Then it's no higher than that branch was.*"

"It's a lot higher den dat branch---"

"*Jaron!*" Landon yelled. He dropped his tone to a low growl. "*Just get up there.*"

Jaron got to his feet and stared up at the bars. Murmuring something about how impossible this would be, he took a series of quick, short breaths and sprang up, missing the bars by several feet. He tried again and this time his fingers managed to brush against the bars before he dropped back down. He started circling the small cell a few times to build up a little speed, then took a short running start, leapt into the air, and finally grabbed hold of the bars. He wrapped his right arm around them, and using his left, tried to fiddle with the lock, while Landon happily praised him.

Jaron was feeling pretty good too, until the staff whacked his left hand and sent a shooting pain up his arm. He glanced up in time to see an eye-less raising its staff, then bringing it down with such speed he didn't have time to unravel his arm before the staff made contact. He fell to the ground again and bit back a wince as he hit bottom. When he got back the breath he lost from his fall, he stared up into the black, empty sockets that were watching him closely, then the eye-less moved away.

Jaron dropped his head, suddenly finding it too difficult to hold up.

"*It's time you learned.*"

"Learned wha'?" he asked, not really caring.

"*Morphing.*"

Jaron jerked, feeling a wave of panic grip him. "I's can't---"

"*There's no time for this,*" Landon snapped. "*You must learn. Now.*"

"Wha' difference will its makes?"

"As a saxtien you could reach and break through those bars before those eye-less things ever knew what happened. Those bars are old. You should have no trouble breaking through them." Jaron's indecision made him take a softer tone, though his pain made it difficult. *"Jaron, you must do this. When I say there is no time, I mean, there is NO more time. I'm losing control. I don't know how much longer I'll be able to stop myself from moving forward."* Jaron's dread echoed his own. *"Trust me."*

Knowing if he didn't try they would both be trapped down here just waiting for Taj, he reluctantly agreed.

"Take off your clothes."

"Wha'?"

"Don't argue with me, just do it. Once you morph you'll split them apart and I doubt you want to roam around naked if you change back." Jaron stripped the nightshirt off quickly, keeping a watch out for the eye-lesses. *"This is hardly the time to be modest. Tie it into a loop and be sure to take it with you after you morph."*

"How's do ju even know I's will merf? I's thought its took years to learn?"

"You've been doing it already, just not committing to the complete shape. You're actually over the hardest part to learn, which is letting your body recognize the powers of your morph and acting with them. Now all you have to do is go further into that power and surrender to it."

Clenching his teeth so they wouldn't chatter, Jaron stood awkwardly and waited for Landon to instruct.

"Kneel down. A saxtien moves on all fours." Jaron did, feeling the stone floor dig into his knees and shivering the entire time. *"Now, forget about your physical state."*

"I's freezin'!"

"Forget about it," Landon stressed. *"Concentrate on the saxtien. Close your eyes. See its shape, its strength, its natural power. Feel yourself becoming one with it."*

Jaron's shivering slowed down as he concentrated and listened to Landon's soft tone. He thought about the beast he'd seen in Landon's mind. How it looked, how he thought about taking its shape, and instead of being frightened away by the familiarity of the beast, he embraced it. He tried to remember what was familiar about this animal but finally gave up when he was covered in sweat and the throb in his knees brought him back to where he was.

He opened his eyes, sat back on his heels, and growled with frustration.

"I's can't do dis." Landon did not respond, although Jaron could still feel him there and got the impression he was disappointed in him. "I's tried and I's can't."

"You've already done this," Landon finally told him in his matter of fact tone. *"I've seen you do it."*

"When?"

"In your dreams. I've seen you running through the trees, climbing mountains with ease, experiencing a sense of freedom you've never felt before.

Commit, Jaron. All you have to do is commit." Jaron licked his lips and rubbed his eyes tiredly. *"Again. And this time, try to remember your dreams.*"

Grimacing, Jaron pulled his legs out from under him and tried once more. He went beyond his uncomfortable memories and looked for something to latch onto. He didn't know how long he searched before finding a quick memory and holding onto it before it disappeared. He wasn't sure if it was a fragment from a dream or a faded recollection but he put all of his concentration into that vision, forcing it to become clearer.

He was that small child again. A saxtien, although he didn't know what it was at the time, was sitting in front of him. Young Jaron reached out with childlike curiosity, wanting nothing more than to touch the soft, black fur. The saxtien allowed him to and purred under his touch while it stared down at him, since he was so small it towered over his head. He pushed its black, wet nose, for no other reason than that it was there. The saxtien opened its mouth, not to attack, but to emulate a smile. He giggled, pushing the wet nose again and again, until the saxtien nuzzled its face against his.

There was another voice coming from above young Jaron's head. It was a soft, sweet voice that tried to bring back a flood of other memories but Jaron held tightly onto this one and this one only. Young Jaron turned his head up to look at the face that spoke but all he saw was a pair of bright, gray eyes and a warm smile. Jaron tried to lean forward to see more but his memory didn't allow for that. The sweet voice spoke to the saxtien, and although young Jaron couldn't understand the words completely, Jaron did.

"You're gettin' him too excited. It's his nap time." The saxtien sniffed and turned its head as if it had been insulted. Young Jaron giggled and the sweet voice continued. "See. He'll never go down now."

"Yes he will." It was a gentle yet firm voice that spoke and seemed to be coming from behind him. Strong arms lifted him into the air and placed him over a broad shoulder. Young Jaron immediately stuck a thumb in his mouth and rested his head on the shoulder. The gentle voice spoke to the saxtien, "Go practice elsewhere."

Jaron desperately wanted to see the face belonging to that voice. It didn't make him feel sick the way Taj's memory did. This felt perfectly comfortable and relaxing. Plus this memory was so vivid. It wasn't so much his sight, since young Jaron seemed to be dozing off, but it was more of what he felt and smelled. The smell was the most powerful of all. Musk, sweat, dirt, wind, leaves, water, all seemed to be coming from this person holding him. It was so peaceful, Jaron wanted to lose himself completely in it, but somewhere in his mind he remembered why he was doing this.

As the memory continued, young Jaron was carried into a tent and was placed down on a pile of soft furs.

"There you go, funny face," the gentle voice soothed and a blanket was pulled over him.

He was only left alone for a moment then the saxtien crept in and lay down next to him. It put its nose in between its front paws and closed its eyes. However, young Jaron suddenly forgot to be tired and started giggling again.

The gentle voice spoke testily from behind, "Would you leave him alone!"

Only this time the saxtien answered. Jaron heard its voice as clear as if it had spoken with its mouth. *"But he's almost got it. You of all people don't think that's interesting? At his age? Come on, Pop, even you gotta be curious about this."*

"Yes, I'm fascinated," came the flat response. "And there will be plenty of time for him to 'get it'. Right now he needs to 'get' sleep. Out." The saxtien slumped away and young Jaron was getting up to follow but those strong arms placed him back down on the furs and that soothing voice whispered, "It's time for funny faces to go to sleep."

Young Jaron turned his head toward the voice and Jaron felt as if he had willed it to happen. He never felt such a dramatic urge before but there was a definite need to see that face. Young Jaron stared up at the face and grinned, but Jaron felt all the blood drain from his body.

Black eyes. All he saw were those deep, black eyes staring at him.

"Hey! Hey!" Landon called to him quickly. *"You had it!"*

Jaron opened his eyes and was shivering again, though he knew it had nothing to do with the cold.

"Do it again, go ahead."

"I's can't," he answered in a crackled voice. The image of those black eyes stayed with him. It had always been Taj. Even when the memory was pleasant, that darkness somehow wiggled its way in, making him want to cry out.

"You just had it! Come on, we don't have much time."

"No," Jaron mumbled.

Landon felt the boy's helplessness and wasn't sure what caused it. He didn't actually see the memory, since he had been mainly trying to keep himself at bay, but he thought it was a good one, until now. Still, he couldn't let the boy's uncertainty get in the way of this.

"Either do it or wait for me to take over completely; then I'll do it."

Jaron remained quiet. Landon felt his hesitation and overwhelming grief but still that couldn't stop them now.

"Do it!" he screamed at the boy, tempted to control his body briefly to get him started. Jaron must have sensed that, because he snapped his eyes shut and concentrated again.

He tried not to picture the memory itself but the feeling he received when he thought of it. That calm, serene, peacefulness he experienced and enjoyed. He let his thoughts slip away, going wherever they wanted, and focused on the feelings only. The sensation was different, odd, terrifying, all the things Landon said it was, but Jaron was still waiting for the fun part to come. It didn't.

He forced himself to stay with it, not retreating like he did before, and felt his body grow heavier, larger, and stronger. Not knowing how long it took, it seemed like minutes and hours all at the same time, he remained perfectly still and tried to push down his terror. The sensation stopped. He waited and wondered if he lost it again. He listened for Landon to say something but never heard a peep from him. He opened his eyes slowly, saw that nothing had changed around him, and slumped in frustration. He did lose it again.

He reached up to rub his suddenly itchy face when he noticed he no longer had a hand, but a paw. He shouted, only it came out like a snarl, and he skidded back against the wall, trying to get away from himself. Landon's voice hit him like a punch.

"*Stay with it! You are in control of yourself and can lose your morph at any time.*" A thousand thoughts raced through Jaron's mind at once, none of them coming out intelligible. Landon kept himself from laughing, knowing what the boy was going through, and said calmly, "*Don't go insane on me now. Just relax.*"

Jaron took the advice and snapped his eyes shut again, trying to soothe his pounding heart. Landon was actually curious as to what a saxtien would feel like. He'd only been able to morph into the dragon shape so this was really a treat for him. Not to mention since Jaron had morphed, the urge to come forward had dissipated slightly.

He encouraged eagerly, "*Let's try to break out of this prison. What do you say?*"

"Wha' ifs I's 'urt someone?"

"*You're worried about the eye-lesses?*" Landon asked flatly.

"No, I's mean a normal person."

"*I think you'll know the difference.*" Out of nowhere, an urge gripped him and tried to force him to grab Jaron's body. He pushed it down with much effort and said breathlessly, "*No more time, thief boy.*"

Jaron opened his eyes and noticed how bright the cell suddenly was. He looked up and saw the bars waiting for him overhead, but now they appeared much clearer and didn't seem as impossible to reach or break open.

He took a cautious step forward, not knowing exactly how to work four feet, however his body seemed to, naturally moving opposite legs together. He pushed the loop of his clothing around his thick neck, then glanced up at the bars again and knew for certain that he could reach them with no problem. He knew he could break right through them.

Feeling something of a smile on his face, he gathered the strength he felt pulsing through him and channeled it. He pushed himself off the floor and flew to the top of the cell so quickly he barely had time to open his mouth. His fangs tore through the rusted bars like parchment and he exploded out of the cell. He spat out the fragments of rusted, old iron and turned toward the eye-lesses, suddenly wanting nothing more than to gnaw at their throats.

**   **

After he sent the boy away with Dapp, Taj headed for his chamber feeling exhausted. He normally needed very little sleep but had been neglecting that small bit lately and it was catching up to him. He flopped down on the bed and ran his hands hard through his hair to make himself relax, while he stared up at the dark ceiling.

That had not gone exactly as he planned but it still would work. He knew the boy and that beast were sitting in the dungeon right now trying to come up with a way to either escape or trick him. Neither would happen. His mind was connected directly with the Mytocks guarding the cell. If anything happened, he would know about it immediately.

He wanted Jaron's cooperation on this. It would make things so much easier if he did. If he continued to fight him, Taj would have no choice but to rip the ivory thing from the boy's mind but that would have dire consequences. For one, he may kill Jaron and then where would all that boy's wonderful power go? True, a portion would come to him but a portion would also go to Abbnar and that he did not want. It would just make life so much easier if he agreed.

He didn't think he fell asleep but he must have, because he bolted upright, feeling as if something was wrong. He listened for the Mytock's report but there wasn't any. He sat on the edge of the bed and tried to shake the uneasy sensation gnawing at his stomach, when he glanced up and saw his mother standing across the chamber. Now he knew this must be a dream, since she had been long dead before he was ever sent to the Pit.

"Hello," came the husky voice; too husky for the delicate face that contained it. But it was the same voice he remembered so well from his past. He couldn't help but stare at the dream and wonder if he really looked so much like her. Their hair was the same blonde color, his eyes were once like hers, clear blue like a lake, before the power filled him. Even his features were similar to hers, sharp yet curving.

He had forgotten, or rather blocked out, that he ever had a mother. However, the longer he stared at the image, the more he remembered about her. How she was sweet, kind, loving, everything a son could want from a mother, she was to him. She supported him almost blindly, gave him whatever he asked, and was the one person he'd come to depend on at the time. Until one day he accidentally peered into her mind and found out why she was such a wonderful mother. She was afraid of him and his power. She didn't give all the support and kindness out of love; she gave it out of fear. She would have killed him if she didn't have some moral objection to destroying her own child.

Discovering all of this nearly crushed him, until he decided that being feared was better than being loved, even from his own mother. He didn't destroy her or even so much as mention what he had seen, although he was certain that she knew. Instead, he never contacted her again. He never even heard of her death, just assumed it took place at some point, and after that day never really gave her much thought.

Now she was standing only a few feet away from him, looking as he remembered her and smiling at him as if nothing was wrong. He'd had enough of this dream and told himself to wake up but he didn't. He remained on the edge of the bed and stared at the woman before him.

"What is it?" the vision of his mother asked.

Taj shouted at himself to wake up but again nothing happened. So he was to stay in this dream, was he? He leapt up from the bed and stalked away from the vision toward the door. It also did not respond to him and remained tightly closed. He spun around to face the vision and growled, "What is this?"

The vision tilted its head slightly. "I simply want to talk to you."

Taj studied the image as a thousand thoughts raced through his mind. Could this be Abbnar's doing? But Abbnar never met his mother…or did he? Abbnar had a way of being terribly sneaky and clever when it was most inconvenient to him. Was he using her image to unsteady him? Could this all be Abbnar?

"I just want to talk to you," the image said sweetly and moved closer.

"You just stay right there, whore," Taj replied evenly. If this was Abbnar he didn't want any of his magic coming closer than it had to. He would wait and see what the old man had in mind, then counter it. He did, after all, hold the ultimate trump in his dungeon.

"All right," the image replied with disappointment and remained where it was. "But I will talk now and I want you to listen."

"You do that."

"Still so distrustful, aren't you?" the image asked, shaking its head sadly. "Still so hateful. Why? Where did I go wrong with you?"

"Somewhere in the womb," Taj grumbled flatly.

"You weren't supposed to be like this," the image said sadly again. "You were supposed to use your gifts for the Land."

"I am," Taj said confidently. "Come on, if that's the best you can do, I suggest we end this game right now."

"Taj, you are so confused. You are so misled, as your brothers and sisters were but I could not save them. I have been trying to save you. Why do you continue to block me?"

"This has gone far enough," Taj hissed and tried the jammed door again. When it wouldn't budge, he rounded on the image and snapped, "You must be desperate to try a stunt like this. Admit it, you've lost Abbnar."

"Abbnar has nothing to do with this," the image responded calmly. "At least his actions I can understand, but yours? Why do you hate the Land so? Why do you hate me?"

"I am trying to save the Land!" Taj exploded.

"You are killing it," the image said levelly. "You were doing it before and you're doing it now. I thought if you had time to think about what you were doing, you would understand why your brother was fighting so fiercely to stop you." The image's face grew long and sad. "But nothing has changed."

"You just made your final blunder, Abbnar," Taj growled as he stalked toward the image, no longer caring what magic Abbnar used. His anger and hate fed him his strength. "Your stunt of dropping me into the Pit *did* change me. I'm ten times stronger than I was before. Strong enough to break out of your little trap and---"

"You didn't break out," the image interrupted, as it stared up at him. "I let you out." For some reason, the words struck Taj hard and he found he had no air to speak with. "I thought enough time passed to cool your heated blood but it only grew hotter. If I put you in there again, you would just get worse and worse until finally you would destroy everything in your path." The image sniffed a laugh then smiled weakly. "Besides, I love you too much to hurt you like that again. Before I thought it would jostle loose your hate, but since it didn't, I won't do that to you anymore." The look of sadness was replaced with gentle desperation. "But I don't know *what* to do for you. You won't talk to me, you won't listen…what can I do for you?"

"Suck sweat off a dead man's back."

The image seemed amused by his remark. "I don't see how that will help you, Taj. Please let me back into your life. You and I used to talk…a lot. Then you didn't like what I had to say and closed me out. You're still a good child." The image reached up to touch Taj's cheek but Taj grabbed the wrist and… gasped aloud.

A powerful surge, more powerful than anything he had ever known, rippled through him. It moved through his body like a fire, consuming him, dragging him into it. It filled every fiber of him until he wanted to scream. He even felt the tears begin to well up in his eyes but blinked them away fiercely. However, the image was not forcing pain on him; it was forcing love. Pure, untainted, unconditional love…for *him*!

He could stand it no longer and with a snarl, snapped his hand away and took a hasty step back.

The image smiled weakly. "Misled, but still a good child. I suppose all parents are blind to their children's actions and keep seeing what they wish, but I know who you were once. Taj, remember that time."

The image winked out of sight and Taj barely heard the door THUNK open.

"My lord!" the voice from behind him cried out at the same instant a flood of shrieks and visions came into his mind from the Mytocks.

At first, his whole head and heart ached too much to receive their visions, but as they played out and he saw what happened and what was happening, his pain stopped. Somehow, Abbnar managed to block off his reception to his Mytocks. Furious, he screamed to the empty space where the image had been standing, "*YOU WHORE!*"

Taj Transferred to the dungeon.

**   **

"*Careful,*" Landon warned as Jaron stalked toward the eye-lesses. "*Don't start playing with them, just get us out of here.*"

He saw through Jaron's eyes the blurred surroundings of the dungeon, with eye-lesses in every direction. He noticed none of the other prison holes were occupied, with their lids swung open ready to encase the next victim. That actually made him feel slightly better. Perhaps Mazon, Brazet and the rest of his Defenders and servants had gotten away. Or the empty cells may mean that they were dead.

A low growl coming from Jaron brought him back to the situation at hand. Three eye-lesses were blocking their path and Jaron's new saxtien sense told both of them that there were more behind him. Deciding to deal with what he could see, Jaron sprang forward and knocked down all three at once. His moment of surprise and cockiness were brief as the eye-lesses began to stab him in his side. He swatted the lot with one fierce stroke, slashing all of their pasty, thin necks.

He recoiled when the black blood oozed out of their wounds slowly and wrinkled his nose at the scent, suddenly very glad that he didn't bite them. A sharp blow to his lower back made him spin around to find more eye-lesses that were beating him repeatedly with their staffs and jabbing at him with their spears. Growling and swatting uncontrollably, he tore open several more thin necks with his dagger claws. He managed to hear Landon's voice shout to him over the commotion.

"Just run! They can't possibly catch you if you just run!"

Jaron began backing away from them, snarling with a swipe every few seconds, trying to keep them at bay. He saw the staff out of the corner of his eye a split moment before it cracked against his head, which sent his mind spinning and made him lose his balance. He quickly crouched, as another staff just missed his head, and slammed his paw against the eye-lesses side, causing it to falter. That gave him enough time to scramble out of the dungeon and down the dim hall, trying to listen to Landon's directions while attempting to keep his body cooperating with him in this new form.

"Go left! No left! LEFT! Damn you, I said left! Go back. Good, now follow this to the end and make another L-E-F-T! Good! Now keep going. Faster! Go, go, go, go!"

Jaron picked up speed and charged through the halls as Landon directed. He was moving so fast, he barely felt his paws touch the ground and it felt like he was flying. This must be the fun part Landon had been talking about.

"Make a right!" Landon shouted.

Jaron did so with ease, then bounded onward with renewed energy, glancing down at his graceful and powerful saxtien limbs. When he looked up, though, he slid to a stop. Dapp was standing alone at the end of the hall. Jaron remained frozen, not knowing what to do, although some instinct inside of him was urging him to attack. Landon felt the instinct too and couldn't help but feel a little wicked.

"Do it."

"Wha'?"

"Kill him."

"I's can't," Jaron started to protest, but Landon quickly cut him off.

"Look at him. He's been sent to kill you or at least hurt you real bad. And he's one of Taj's closest people. He's the one who brought you here. He's the one who's been dragging you around like some rag-doll." He felt the boy's anger increase. *"He's the one who Taj depends on. If you kill him, you may unbalance Taj."*

Jaron growled warningly at Dapp, but all he did was unsheathe his sword and hold it ready.

"Look at that!" Landon cried. *"He's asking for it! He's not even morphing because he knows you'll tear him apart if he does. He needs a sword to fight you, Jaron."*

Jaron's pride and saxtien instincts were filling his blood. He revved his hind legs while remaining still so he built up more power and speed. Dapp, his face hard and cold, held the sword ready for his attack.

Landon shouted out the final words to make Jaron move. "*Get him*!"

With a deep growl, Jaron sprang forward with such speed that the entire hall was just a blur. Dapp was the only thing that remained focused and seemed to grow larger the closer he came. Growling and snarling as he raced down the hall, Jaron was ready for a fight.

At least fifty Mytocks and sentries stepped out of everywhere and surrounded Dapp completely.

Landon shrieked, "*STOP!*"

Jaron tried to but he was moving too fast. He couldn't stop; he didn't have enough control. Panicked, he put all of his paws together in a bunch and stuck out his claws, but all that did was leave scratches along the polished wooden floor as he continued to sail straight toward the mob waiting for him.

He tried reversing the movement of his front paws, forcing them to walk backwards, but they slipped out from under him and he sprawled out on his belly as he continued to skid ahead. He gradually did come to a halt, directly in front of Dapp's feet. He had enough time to glance up before he was surrounded by spears, swords, and knocked arrows.

"*A saxtien's a big creature. Roar! See if they back off enough for you to get out of this.*" Jaron sucked in a breath, then let out a noise that sounded like a kitten's cry. "*Oh well. That was good. I can see them trembling in their boots. Try licking their hands next time.*"

"Wha' do ju want from me!" Jaron hissed silently to him.

Landon didn't answer since Dapp had knelt down and was speaking evenly.

"I suggest you morph back. My men are in the mood for some hunting and a nice saxtien pelt would be just the thing for the upcoming cold months."

"*Don't you dare!*" Landon threatened.

"I's 'ave no choice."

"*He's trying to scare you.*"

"And doin' a really good job of its."

"*Taj wants you, remember?*"

"Oh, I's feel so much better now," Jaron spat sarcastically. "And do ju 'member dat he's wants me to join wit him and to 'ave ju destroyed?"

Landon felt his mind twist and wanted to scream in frustration. Was the boy right? Did they have no choice?

As if answering his question, another twenty Mytocks came moving down the same hall Jaron just raced across and stood behind him, with their spears added to the many other sharp blades already surrounding him.

"Well, boy?" Dapp asked sternly as he rose to his feet. "Shall I give the order for them to strike? It'll be less painful then what Taj will do to you."

"Oh Light! *Landon!*" Jaron silently pleaded.

"*All right, all right,*" Landon said as steadily as he could. "*Morph back. We'll figure something out.*"

"Likes?"

"*Likes...I don't know yet. But it's obvious you're not going anywhere in this form, so you might as well morph back.*"

Jaron slowly got to all fours and reluctantly started to release the form he'd grown quickly attached to.

Swords, spears, arrows, eye-lesses, sentries, and Dapp went flying everywhere. Stunned and confused, Jaron held onto the saxtien shape and spun around, fearing it was Taj. He and Landon stared in shock.

"Would you two come on!" Jynx snapped at them as if she had been waiting there all day.

"Where she's come from?" Jaron asked.

"*Who cares! Go!*"

Jaron ran in place for a second as his paws slipped on the slick, wooden floor. He saw a slight wrist movement from Jynx then heard the thud and clang of someone and their sword going down right behind him. That inspired him to move forward toward the girl, who was already racing down the hallway.

He followed her blindly and Landon didn't bother shouting out directions. If this girl was making the attempt of getting them out of here, he would trust her. Light! He would trust Jaron's backside if it made a suggestion at this point.

Jynx led them down the halls toward the library. Landon knew that the library hall was a dead end and also spotted the small figure waving to them frantically. It was Webben. Landon shouted for Jaron to stop, thinking that the girl and his former servant had betrayed them. Jynx halted her running and pointed at the stone wall near the library entrance, where Webben was also pointing.

"Go!" she shouted to Jaron and waved him to move forward.

Jaron had stopped his running when Jynx did, and now looked from the wall back to the girl in confusion.

"Wha' does she's want?" he asked Landon.

"*I have no idea. I think she's as mad as Taj.*"

"I'll smack you later for that insult, Kazimeer," Jynx snapped. "Now go!"

"Please, Kazimeer," Webben begged. "Hurry!"

The sound of pounding footsteps were coming closer, along with the cries of commands and the unmistakable shouts of Taj. But Jaron still didn't know what the girl wanted him to do.

With a sharp breath from Jynx, she threw her arms over her head and Jaron suddenly felt invisible hands grab hold of him and shove him toward the wall. He tried spreading out of his paws to stop but the hands pushed him harder and faster, until nothing but the stone wall was in his view.

He and Landon screamed together and Jaron snapped his eyes shut, not wanting to see when the wall smashed against his face.

THE DRAGON RETURNS

Jaron gradually slid to a stop. His eyes remained closed and he wondered how close he'd come to getting his face bashed in by that stone wall. Slowly he opened them and blinked to focus. The space they were in was almost completely dark, except for a few hints of light far off in the distance. Remaining in his saxtien shape, he turned around carefully and made out the wall only a foot or so behind him. Was that the same wall they had been heading straight for?

"Landon?" he asked, only Landon didn't know what the answer was either.

"Try going back through it again."

Jaron took careful steps forward as if the floor would fall out from underneath him and, out of instinct, started sniffing the air, trying to find any familiar scent. No sooner was he standing in front of the wall ready to walk through it, when Webben and Jynx came bustling through, which sent Jaron scurrying backwards.

Jynx stood with her hands on her hips and one foot tapping. "Are you two mental or is this just how you always act?" And she was actually waiting for an answer.

Jaron replied with the only question on his mind at the moment. "Where are we's?"

Jaron saw Jynx roll her eyes as she answered, "Kazimeer, you tell him. I have to hurry. My sprites will only keep them busy for a little while. Now." She continued in one long sentence, not stopping once for a breath of air or long enough for either of them to interrupt her. "I'm going to go back out there, say a few nasty things to Taj, then I'm getting out of here so while I'm stalling him I suggest you two get as far away from here as you can, since he will be able to feel you hiding back here." She shifted her gaze back to Webben. "You too Tiny. I think your service to Taj has just ended."

Webben blinked slowly and clicked his tongue. "Tiny?"

"And when I'm done," she continued over him. "I'm out of here 'cause I have other things I have to take care of, so go find the others and don't mess anything up."

"Tiny?" Webben asked again.

Jynx stared at him flatly. "What didn't you understand?"

Webben stood toe to toe with her, making Landon realize just how much his young charge was growing. He glared down at her. "Just you see to it that ma'lord remains safe or I'll take it out of your hide, wench!"

Landon would've done a double take if he could. Webben was always so quiet and shy around him. He never would've imagined the boy could sound so sharp and…mean.

Jynx smiled. "What a delightful challenge. I just may take you up on it." With that she turned and ran through the wall again.

Jaron remained where he was for a moment and Landon didn't bother to tell him to move yet. They were both too confused. In a few seconds they heard her muffled voice calling out,

"I knew I smelled something foul around here. At first I thought it was a rat or a snake but now I see that it's just you."

"Cursed wench!" Taj's voice roared. "I warned you about interfering with me."

Landon saw Webben flinch at the sound of Taj's voice and the boy slowly backed away.

"So you did," Jynx's voice answered. "But I thought you were just flirting."

Jaron mind-whispered to Landon, even though he knew Taj couldn't hear him, "He's sounds angry."

"*I bet he is.*"

Webben faced Jaron, his expression back to the innocent one Landon was used to seeing. "Come on, ma'lord." He spoke so softly, only Jaron's saxtien ears were able to pick it up and just barely. Webben was already trotting down the dark tunnel, waving for Jaron to follow.

Jaron needed no more encouragement when he heard Taj roar at Jynx again. He sprinted down the dark tunnel, trying to keep the running figure of the boy in sight.

"So where are we's?"

"*I don't know.*"

"But she's said---"

"*I know what she said but I haven't the slightest idea where we are. Just keep going.*"

Jaron continued to run, though his brief conversation with Landon caused him to lose sight of the boy. Neither of them had any idea where they were going now and Landon didn't offer any suggestions. Jaron simply ran steadily through the maze of dark tunnels, turning corners whenever the mood struck him. He was being led, he realized, by a feint scent of something his saxtien senses connected with security. He didn't fight them and allowed his ears and nose to lead him, finally catching the whiff of water. Now knowing where he was headed he called to Landon, who had fallen strangely quiet since they entered the dark tunnels. When he didn't answer, Jaron decided not to bother him and figured he was thinking about what to do next. He continued running toward the sound of water that now reached his ears.

A shriek exploded in his mind, making him lose his shape completely. He crashed down on the hard ground that tore at his exposed skin. He rolled over a few times, recovering from the speed he had reached, and clutched his head tightly, realizing it was Landon who was screaming. He didn't even have time to form a question before he felt him pushing forward. Jaron pushed him back, feeling as if he was trying to push back a mountain, and shouted aloud to be heard over Landon's wails.

"Stop!"

"*I can't!*"

The terror in Landon's voice struck every nerve in his body. He felt Landon trying to fight against the advance and joined him but neither was having any success. Breathing roughly, he started to crawl down the pitch-black tunnel and thought desperately that if he kept moving he could delay the inevitable. Without any warning, he could no longer feel his arms and fell, smacking his face against the ground.

Landon did not say anything but Jaron still felt him wrestling madly with himself, trying to prevent the possession from taking place. Jaron felt a new sensation building up inside of him. It felt like a volcano had suddenly sprang up within him and his entire body broke out into a sweat. There was something growing inside of him and it began to move. If he had to name a direction, he would say it was moving directly for Landon. He wasn't even sure what this was, let alone how to control it, but he tried feebly to stop its advance. It was not deterred by him and almost seemed to gain speed. Whatever this was, it was most certainly unhappy about Landon's takeover and seemed determined to stop him.

A dim light was coming from directly ahead and Jaron barely managed to raise his head to see a tall figure approach him. His instinct told him to move back but the control over his body and mind were becoming hazy, so all he could do was stare. His terror over Landon's moving forward was replaced by a new horror when he pieced together who this figure must be; Taj. He made out the silhouette raising an arm slowly and could guess what was coming next…pain.

He called to Landon, pleading with him to hold on for a little while more, but he no longer heard him. His mind was silent.

Power rushed from the figure straight at Jaron, who snapped his eyes tightly waiting for the pain to come. It struck his mind first, ripping through it like parchment, then sent wild tantrums throughout his entire body. He collapsed, allowing his mind to drift and leaving him oblivious to everything around him.

He awoke feeling stiff and sore, and blinked at the darkness around him, not knowing how long he'd been unconscious. He was tempted to morph but felt too exhausted to try, and groped around for his large nightshirt, thankful that he took it with him because Landon had said…suddenly he remembered.

"Landon!" No response. "Landon! Answer me!" He knew it was futile but continued to call to him for long minutes. No one responded. The figure he saw must have been Taj because Landon was completely gone now. Then why was he still alive? Or maybe he wasn't and this was what death was like, black and silent. And cold, he discovered, finding his rolled up nightshirt a few inches away from him. He pulled it over his head, glad he had control over himself again but feeling unbelievably empty.

Shuffling slowly through the tunnels, he felt his way along the rough walls and searched for any sign of an exit. For what felt like forever, he tried to find the water he sensed in his saxtien shape and continued to hear the bubbling off in the distance, but he never came near it. He gave up trying to locate it and blindly searched for a way out.

After stumbling around in the dark for an endless amount of time, his throat became dry, his hands were cut from the scratches he received from the walls, and his feet were bruised and sore from walking without protection. His

Hosting the Kazimeer

legs moved without him feeling them and he feared that if he sat down he would never get up again. He moved as if he were walking through a dream until he started to believe that he really was dead.

He wondered why he was even bothering trying to find a way out. What would he do? Face the eye-lesses again? Face Taj again…alone? His shuffling slowed down to the point where he took a step, debated moving, then took another. A helpless, dismal feeling crept over him, the kind that keeps an old man from leaving his burning house.

He finally tripped over his feet and felt a rush of tears well up in him as he hit the floor face first. He wanted to cry. He felt useless. He was not smart enough for this sort of thing on his own. He admitted to himself that he needed Landon only Landon wasn't there. Jaron could swear that he still felt him, though. It was probably because they'd been connected for so long…how long? Honestly, Jaron lost count of the days, the weeks they had been together. He also realized something else; he missed that arrogant thronge worm.

He sat on his legs, feeling miserable and pitying himself to the point where he threw his head back and screamed so loud his throat burned. He didn't care who heard him.

****   ****

Sounds drifted slowly to his ears though he could barely understand what was being said. Something hurt, but then he discovered that everything hurt. Every muscle, every bone, even his hair cried out in stiffness and agony. Was he dead? It was possible but to prove if he was right or not, he opened his eyes.

Landon immediately squinted against a bright light in his face and cringed, though the quick movement made his face muscles and bones twist with pain. He blinked until his eyes focused and stared at the face hovering above him. He slowly remembered who it was.

"Brazet!" Mazon called out over his shoulder and in an instant the Second appeared at the Weaver's side.

"Oh Light!" Brazet breathed, then looked up and repeated, "Oh thank the Light!"

"Yes, yes," Mazon said irritably. "It was the Light. I had nothing to do with it."

"What…" That was all Landon got out before he winced in pain from talking. His mouth tasted like something had died in it and even his teeth and tongue hurt from the effort of speaking the one word. Mazon shushed him immediately and Brazet already had a cup of water ready. Mazon took it and gently lifted Landon's head. Landon drank down the water greedily, nearly sucking the drops off the side. Mazon asked Brazet to get more as he rested Landon's head back down and waited until the Second was out of sight, before speaking softly to him.

"You really had me worried there for a while." Landon found that he could only ask questions with his eyes, since his mouth and throat weren't working yet. Mazon smiled. "You mind-traveled before I could stop you. You were hurt but not beyond repair. By the time I had gotten you back here you were already gone. I've been keeping your body alive by spells but that would only keep it for so long. Time was running out and we couldn't find you. We sent scouts to the Training Halls, only two of the five returned and said the rest had been destroyed."

Landon nodded stiffly in response.

Mazon studied him curiously. "Did you find the Masters?"

Landon nodded again.

Mazon jerked his head back a little in surprise. "And they *didn't* get you to do some fool thing like Shift your essence?"

Landon mouthed out slowly, "Almost."

"Damn fool Masters think they know everything," Mazon spat heatedly. "They never believed any Weaver's magic could reverse an accidental mind-travel but their own. I wish they would've thought to contact me."

Landon didn't have time to ask the dozens of questions buzzing in his head, as Brazet was back with a pitcher of water and handed a cup of it to Mazon, who lifted Landon's head again. Landon drank another three cups and had several coughing fits before he could speak without wanting to tear his throat out.

Mazon mumbled, "It's a good thing you didn't let those fools ply their quack magic on you."

Landon spoke slowly and found that his own voice sounded strange to him. "I almost did. If it hadn't been for…" He trailed off and instantly sat upright, suddenly realizing who was missing from this reunion. The action of sitting up made his head spin but that didn't stop him from trying to stand.

"Landon!" Mazon cried and pushed him back down. "What's wrong?"

"Jaron," he croaked and pushed Mazon's hands away, trying to sit up again. "Where's Jaron?"

"What?" Mazon asked the same moment Brazet asked, "Who's he talking about?"

"Jaron!" Landon said, raising his voice as strong as it would go. "The boy! Where is he?"

"Is he delirious?" Brazet asked quietly of Mazon.

The Weaver shook his head and answered, "I don't know." He turned back to Landon. "Come on now. Lie back down and tell me what---" Mazon didn't have time to finish as Landon shoved him away with more strength than he thought he had and got to his feet. His knees immediately buckled and it was Brazet who caught him from crashing to the ground.

"What has gotten *in*-to you?" Mazon asked as he gently forced him to sit down and knelt in front of him. "Now tell me, calmly, what do you want?"

"Jaron," Landon began hoarsely. "The boy. The one whose mind I was in. Where…is…he?"

"The one attacking you?" Mazon asked.

"No." Landon swung his head back and forth. "I was attacking him."

Mazon glanced up at Brazet. "Find out where the Defenders put him. I asked that they bring him back for questioning."

Brazet took off around the corner in a wink and Landon felt the ice ball in his stomach melt with relief that Mazon didn't kill him.

"Who is this boy?" Mazon asked once Brazet was gone.

"I couldn't have come this far without him," Landon mumbled. "It was his idea to come to the castle. I wanted to go to Triple Lake."

"Triple Lake?"

"Yes. I thought you might be there, but he said we had to come to the castle. It was his idea to get away from the Masters and he was the one who made the plan happen, and he, somehow, kept Taj from taking me and---"

"All right," Mazon said soothingly. "Calm down."

Brazet came back from around the corner, looking slightly distressed. "They said he wasn't there when they went back."

"What?" Landon asked, trying to get to his feet again.

"They searched all around the area but he was gone."

"I have to find him," Landon said, struggling against Mazon to stand.

"We will find this boy," Mazon assured. "He couldn't have gone far."

"You don't know Jaron," Landon mumbled. He met the Weaver's stare firmly. "I can't let Taj have him. He's my friend."

"We will find him before Taj," Mazon said with a reassuring smile. "But your body hasn't been used in nearly three months, Landon. You can't go wandering around these tunnels in your condition."

For the first time since he awakened, Landon noticed where they were. The area they were in had better lighting but it was still the same tunnels he and Jaron had been running through.

"Where is this place?" he asked.

"Under the castle," Mazon answered, with just a hint of amusement.

"I never knew about this," Landon said, looking around.

"It's old," Mazon stated. "It was built during the *Second Land Bloodshed.*"

Landon nodded, remembering his history. Four hundred and sixty three years ago, the Land had been fighting with itself, so naturally the Kazimeer would have been a prime target for assassination.

"So these were made to protect Kazimeer Mirima?"

"She insisted, or so the history says," Mazon said. "They've been used mostly for storage. Until now."

"But what are you doing here?"

"We had to leave and quickly," Mazon explained. "There was no way to get out of the castle, Taj made sure of that. I knew this place still existed and knew the spell to open the hidden door. So Brazet and I gathered everyone we could and made a dash for here."

"All while carrying you over his shoulder," Brazet added.

Mazon waved him silent and looked back at Landon. "Once you were struck down, I knew the ivory dragon instinct would look for a stable body, but I couldn't stop it before we got to safety. By then it was too late."

"Well it wasn't like we could just stroll down here," Brazet grumbled. "It took a while to slice through those madmen of his."

"And for some people to admit that we were beaten," Mazon added under his breath.

"We were not beaten!" Brazet growled. "Just outnumbered."

"And out powered."

"How many," Landon began, then swallowed to moisten his throat. "How many people did we lose?" Both the Weaver and Second were silent and exchanged glances. Landon looked from one to the other. "How many!"

"More than three quarters," Mazon answered softly. Landon closed his eyes tightly and let out a long breath. So many people who were counting on him that were gone now. "There just wasn't enough time to save them all. We gathered as many as we could and brought them down here. Town's people too. Not many are safe anymore."

"Don't forget the Counts," Brazet added with a sneer.

Landon opened his eyes. "The Counts are here?"

"We brought them here," Mazon answered.

"Why?" Landon asked flatly.

Mazon spread his hands. "You need all the support you can get, Landon."

Landon nodded, knowing Mazon was right but also wishing that Taj had found a way to destroy them. Perhaps they would be respectful to him now, after seeing what another man's rule could be like.

"Ma'lord?" Landon looked up at who spoke and his eyes widened. Webben bit his bottom lip and looked close to tears. "Ma'lord, please don't be angry with me for deceiving you."

"I put him up to it, Landon," Mazon said quickly in the boy's defense.

Landon stared at him. "You?"

The Weaver nodded. "I know a bit of Taj's weaknesses. He's partial to children. I knew he'd take to Webben like a pig to mud."

"How did you know?" Landon questioned.

"I'll explain when we have more time," Mazon dodged. "The point is, without Webben we would never have known half of what we do about Taj's plans. We have an advantage. He doesn't know we're here but he will soon. We have to act now."

"That will still be a neat trick," Brazet hissed. "Landon can barely stand, how can we send him in to attack?"

"Don't tell me you've been waiting for me to come and end all of your problems," Landon said, eyeing the Weaver.

"No one expects you to end them all by yourself," Mazon answered. "But we do expect you to be the major element in bringing Taj down."

Landon laughed hoarsely, "My entire army, with all of my skilled Defenders and Weavers couldn't make a dent in Taj. Now most of them are gone, the rest are in hiding, and *I'm* going to make a difference?"

Three faces stared at him with shock and appall.

"You are the ivory dragon," Mazon said sternly. "You are the only one who can 'make a dent' in Taj. Even with all my skills and power, I couldn't break through his magic, especially with that accursed piece he wears. Only you can bring him down."

Landon was struck with a thought he somehow managed to forget. That necklace. Granted it wasn't the whole of Taj's power, as Jynx pointed out, but it was a portion of it. If he could somehow manage to remove the necklace... But how was he ever going to do that?

"My lord," Brazet said softly. "Are you thinking of surrendering?"

"Of course not," Landon hissed.

"Then why do you look as if you're considering it?"

"I'm thinking," Landon spat and stared levelly at his Second. "And if I want to sit here and think, I will do so with whatever look on my face that pleases me and if you don't like it you can eat me bones!"

Landon nearly choked when he realized what he'd just said.

"Ma'lord?" Webben asked. "What happened to that big, fuzzy cat? Surely you could use a big beast like that?"

Jaron; he needed Jaron's help if he was to ever catch Taj off guard. He looked at the Weaver. "Yes, what did happen to that big, fuzzy cat, Mazon?"

"Big, fuzzy cat?" Mazon asked in utter confusion.

"I have to find Jaron," he said to himself. He began calculating, planning, thinking. After a moment he looked at Brazet. "Gather the remaining Defenders and have them stand ready. Ask the town's people, morphers or not, if they want to join this fight. If they do, warn them of the dangers. If they still do, put them with the Defenders. *Order* the Counts that they *are* going to fight even if they have to use their tongues as weapons. If they give you any grief, tell them the Kazimeer will look upon any refusal from them as treason."

"Isn't that a bit harsh?" Mazon asked.

"I've been out of my body for three months while a madman destroys the Land and everyone in it. I'm not happy."

Brazet was smiling ear to ear. "Anything else, my lord?"

"Yes. Do not pressure a single town's person to fight if they don't want to. *Ask* them and let them know I am only asking because I need their help if I am to defeat Taj. Those who don't wish to fight, make sure they are in a secure area and...I hate to do this but leave no Defenders wit them. I can't spare anyone wit fighting experience."

"'Wit', my lord?" Brazet asked curiously.

"And when my command comes, probably from Mazon," Landon continued not hearing Brazet's question, "tell everyone they are to fight against Taj's army with their last breath if need be. They are not only fighting for the Land...their Land...but for their right to exist. If Taj wins this, they may not have that right any longer."

Brazet nodded and headed off quickly. Webben began to follow.

"And where do you think you're going?" Landon asked.

The boy turned around slowly. "To suit up."

"Into what?"

"Armor."

"You're not going to 'suit up' into anything. You're going to find a nice corner somewhere and hold a shield over you until this is over."

"But ma'lord!" the boy protested.

"Webben," Landon stated firmly and wagged his finger. "Come here."

The boy reluctantly and cautiously moved toward him. Landon squeezed his shoulder gently. "You have done more for the Land than you will ever realize. You have done the most dangerous of all tasks and managed to keep yourself alive and safe without a stitch of armor. And even the strongest of Defenders take a rest after completing such a critical assignment."

"Defender, ma'lord?" It was a question but it was a hopeful question.

Landon smiled. "Honorary Defender. Besides, if you go running out there and get yourself hurt, how will I ever be able to place the Medallion of Valor around your neck?"

The boy gasped and his eyes went wide. The Medallion of Valor was the highest award a Defender, or anyone, could receive from the Kazimeer. Only a handful ever received such a tribute, and never a young boy. Webben was speechless and continued to stare at Landon in shock.

Landon's smile deepened and he squeezed the boy's shoulder again. "Your father would be so proud of you and I'm proud of you too." Webben flushed and shifted his gaze toward the ground. Landon patted his shoulder. "Now go find yourself that corner. I expect to find you there later."

Attempting to hide a wide grin, Webben answered, "Yes, ma'lord." He was beaming as he hurried off.

"That was very nice of you to say to him, Landon," Mazon said once Webben was gone. "He'll appreciate the thought."

Landon stared at him. "I meant every word." The Weaver blinked at him in surprise, never believing for a second that the Kazimeer was actually serious until now. Landon ignored the look. "I must find Jaron."

He got to his feet unsteadily, with Mazon's help, and grunted with frustration. His body was so weak that he could barely hold himself upright. How was he to fight Taj in this condition?

The thought beat him over the head. How did he overlook the obvious answer? He wasn't supposed to fight Taj like this. He reached into himself and found the familiar sensation he had missed. It took a few tries before he managed to morph into what everyone was waiting for…the ivory dragon.

He instantly felt additional strength surge through him and mind-spoke to Mazon.

"Let's go find him."

**   **

Jaron's scream came to an end. He panted and stared up into the darkness, wondering if Taj heard him. He hoped he did. At least he wouldn't be trap in this dark maze by himself. He hated to be alone. Even when he was traveling by himself, there was still the life of the Land all around him. But this place was damp, dark, and lifeless. Not even the sound of the water reached his ears any more.

He pushed down his self-pity for a moment and concentrated again on how he was to first, get out of this eerie place and second, get away from Taj. Curse Landon! He'd gotten him into this and now when he really needed him, he abandoned him. He was steadily becoming more furious the longer he thought about it. Landon probably left him alone here to rot while he went on as

Kazimeer...*if* he really was the Kazimeer. Jaron started to doubt anything Landon ever told him and then started to blame Landon for anything that ever happened to him in his life.

The slave-trade was his fault; Allaendra's death was his fault; the bad nights he had spent out in the snow was his fault; the fact that he was short was his fault. Anything, no matter how unreasonable, that he laid his mind to was Landon's fault. By now his anger reached a peak he never thought possible and he screamed again into the darkness to release some of his tension. When the echo of his scream died down, he heard it.

Someone was behind him. Spinning around and peering into the darkness he saw nothing but was certain someone was there. He reached down, picked up a clump of dirt, and flung it hard into the empty space. He listened as it fell to the ground, not striking anything. He began to think he really was losing his mind to the darkness, so he got to his feet and started to feel along the walls for guidance. He'd only moved two more steps before he stopped and spun around again. Someone was definitely behind him. Perhaps it was Taj coming back to deal with him. That was probably why he was down in this maze; being kept busy until Taj had time to destroy Landon.

A fury built up in his throat, pushing its way out. He heard his cry of frustration bouncing off the tunnel walls, but no one answered him. His anger mounted, knowing he was being followed and wanting to fight whatever it was. If only he could see.

"Duck." The voice came to his mind as it always had. Confused and startled, he gazed into the darkness. "Duck, thief boy."

Taking the advice, he fell onto his stomach in time to see the blaze of white fire streak over his head. When the sound of the flame had died down, he glanced up and saw the old man with the flowing white hair standing there, holding a lit torch. Then Jaron looked at what was behind the old man and gaped openly.

How something so large could move without a sound he had no idea. He also wondered how it didn't get wedged in between the walls, since it looked like it could just barely squeeze by. Instinctively he leapt to his feet and backed away. The ivory dragon squirmed closer and swung its head down so that it was only inches from him. The length of its face was the same size as Jaron's body. Jaron could smell the fire on its breath and couldn't look away from the piercing green eyes staring into his. A voice filled his head.

"Shall I eat your bones now?"

Jaron knew when he first saw the beast that it was Landon but his mind didn't make the connection until now. He had no idea Landon would be so...so big!

Keeping his voice steady, he replied casually, "Ju can wait. Don't rush jus fure me." Landon's huge jaw opened slightly, mimicking a smile, but all Jaron saw were the long, pointy teeth. Landon pulled back, making Jaron breathe quietly with relief. "Um...how's did ju...ah...?"

"Mazon."

Jaron could hear the satisfaction in his voice and briefly wondered why he was still hearing him in his mind. He didn't bother asking such questions now, as the tall, commanding figure behind Landon stepped closer.

"Forgive me, Jaron," the Weaver replied, smiling sheepishly. "I had no idea who you were. When I felt Landon so close by, and you were screaming so…well, I thought you were attacking him. I hope I didn't hurt you."

"No, ju dinn't," he said absently and shook his head slightly.

"Of course you didn't," Landon said lightly. "His head is made out of wool. I know, I've been there."

Mazon smacked his massive leg, making Jaron wince. "Hold your sarcasm," he snapped then gestured toward Jaron. "He's obviously overwhelmed by all of this."

"Confused mostly," Jaron admitted.

"All the time, in fact," Landon teased, receiving another hit from the Weaver.

Jaron smiled at him and found himself feeling a little giddy. Maybe this was just a hallucination and he had lost his mind. But if this was an image concocted by him, he had a better imagination than he thought. Still, he didn't care if it was or wasn't. At least he wasn't alone any more.

"Actually, da confusion came from ju," he retorted.

Those green eyes widened slowly. "From me?"

"Well, its was ju who's never knew wha' to do."

"Excuse me but I always knew exactly what to do."

"Ha!" Jaron sniffed. "Ju a'most let dose Maders turn ju into a baby. Ifs its wasn't fure me, ju would be's pissin' in jur diaper right now."

"And you'd be right beside me."

"No I's wouldn't."

"Oh that's true," Landon said with mockery. "They would never put common folk next to me."

"And ju is fat!" Jaron sneered.

If a dragon could look smug, Landon managed. "And you are short."

Jaron's eyes blazed and he snapped, "Ju is a big, old, fat dragon, jus likes on da sign of dat tavern."

Mazon cleared his throat to break up the argument. "Excuse me," he said softly and looked curiously at Jaron. "Do you know he's the Kazimeer?"

"Oh, yeah," Jaron said and nodded casually. "I's know dat da thronge worm is da Kaz."

"I'm sorry?" Mazon asked, as his eyes bulged.

"Never mind, Mazon," Landon said and let out a heavy breath, which blew back both the Weaver's and Jaron's hair. Jaron started to wonder if maybe he shouldn't have teased so. Those big teeth! Landon fixed his gaze on the boy. "Now, shall I tell you what's been going on?"

Jaron knew he should just let the thronge worm go on, but he had to add, "But I's not done wit me fierce ad-mon-ish-ment of ju's."

Landon snorted loudly, watching the boy stand there, beaming with pride at using the new and large word. He didn't give the boy a chance to go on further and explained quickly what happened. How Mazon kept his body safe while he was trapped in Jaron's mind. How they were gathering the people down here and he also briefly explained where 'here' was. Then he delicately tiptoed into the real matter.

"Mazon and any other Weaver's magic have had no effect on Taj."

"Wha' 'bout Jynx?" Jaron asked innocently, but both immediately heard Mazon wince aloud.

"She's here?" the Weaver asked, looking around the tunnels.

"Not annimore," Jaron said at the same moment Landon asked, "You know her?"

Mazon answered Landon. "Of course I know her," he said with a hint of frustration. "She tried to get me to teach her my best spells. Such a young girl, with great power but quite undisciplined. When I refused she stomped off. I should have taught her. She probably just learned them somewhere else and badly too."

"When was this!" Landon cried in shock.

Mazon waved his hand at him, as if waving away the entire issue. "Oh, you were at the Halls and our meeting was brief." He addressed Jaron. "But you say she could counter Taj's magic?"

"Not well," Jaron admitted, rubbing the back of his neck. "A little bit."

"I think," Landon added, "that had more to do with Taj's frustration of dealing with her."

"Ah yes." Mazon nodded and grumbled under his breath, "She does that to everyone." He stared sharply at Jaron. "But she was here?"

"She helped us git into dis place," Jaron said, gesturing around to the walls of the tunnel and then nodded. "She helped us a lot."

"How did she know…?" Mazon asked himself, then shook his head firmly. "Never mind. Anyway, don't depend on her help, especially if Taj is involved. She's not reliable. If she helped you it was because she wanted something. She's a swindler, that one."

Jaron glanced toward Landon, who did his best to imitate a shrug and continued to explain to the boy where his thoughts were going.

"Now I have to find a way to get back into the castle without being seen by Taj first and find a way to remove him, permanently if possible."

Jaron narrowed his eyes in deep thought and Landon let him. That's what he wanted the boy to do; come up with one of his clever, odd ways of handling the situation. Perhaps they were still on the same mind-track.

Jaron rolled the thought around in his head for a moment then wrinkled his face in serious concentration at Landon. "Wha' zactly did Jynx say 'bout dat necklace he's wears?"

Landon nodded his large head ever so slightly. Yes, Mazon indirectly reminded him about that black stone necklace. He'd forgotten about it with everything else going on, but now that he was back in his own body, the memory of that piece stood out. "I doubt Taj is into fashion." Landon turned his large head toward Mazon. "Does that piece truly increase his power?"

"The legend of Taj," Mazon said slowly, clicking his tongue, "said that the black stones made him an impossible enemy to defeat. They add to his own power, making him a strong opponent."

"Its only enhances his power, den?" Jaron asked the Weaver. Mazon nodded.

Landon gave him a dragon smile. "What's my word?"

Jaron narrowed his brow for a second, then remembered. "Ju gave me dat one fure free."

"Burn you! I did not!"

"Yes ju did. Now shut up and lemme tink."

Landon cocked his head slightly. "A bit touchy, aren't you?"

"I's 'ave a right."

Landon got back to the subject. "If the stones are only for enhancement, he still has his power."

"But maybes it's not dat strong," Jaron suggested.

"Do not fool yourselves," Mazon said. "Taj's power is quite strong, even without the necklace." He thought something over briefly. "Although he does rely on the stones heavily."

"Den ifs we's could git dat necklace," Jaron began, "he's might be's easier to defeat."

"No, wait. If anyone could have taken off that necklace, he would've been defeated already."

"Do ju tink Taj will let annione git dat close to him to take its off?"

"Actually," Landon began casually, "there's only one person, I believe, that he would let get that close."

Jaron slowly blinked at him and took a step backwards. "Oh, ju do not mean me."

"I think I do."

"Oh no ju don't, thronge worm," Jaron chuckled nervously. "Ju do not means me, 'cause…" He thought rapidly then said with false confidence, "I's ain't goin' to be's 'ere."

"And where are you going?"

"'Way."

"'Way?" Landon mimicked. "There is no 'way', because there will be no Land to 'way' to."

"Dare might be's," Jaron mumbled.

Landon let out a long breath and then leaned down again so his face was next to Jaron's body. "Jaron, I need you."

Jaron grunted in frustration and stamped his feet. "Why's!"

"Because you are the only one who can get that close to Taj and not be suspected of anything. He wants you, remember?"

"Yeah, but he's mad!"

"Yes, but if we can just knock him off balance a little, I might be able to stop him."

"How's do ju tink I's can git dat close to him? I's left, 'member? He's goin' to be's pissed off."

"Yes, he'll be pissed and then he'll forgive you."

"Whiles I's bein' forgiven, where's ju?"

"This is where I'll be," Landon said and enlightened Jaron of the plan he worked out in his mind. Jaron moaned and grunted, saying how it would never work, but finally and reluctantly agreed.

The trap was set and all they had to do now was invite Taj into it.

SAVING THE BAIT

Landon stood at the entrance of the false wall and watched Jaron soundlessly trot down the hallway and around the corner. He then started counting to himself. This entrance, Mazon said, was not near any main areas, so there was little chance of Taj's troops being nearby. Still it didn't make Landon feel secure, especially since he was alone now. He sent Mazon back to Brazet about twenty minutes before, according to his internal timekeeper. He hoped that gave Mazon enough time to relay his message and for his army to get into position. He was fairly certain it did, but there was always some doubt rumbling around in his mind, probably due to the overwhelming fear and nervousness he was experiencing.

He continued to mentally count evenly and was almost ready to venture out into the hallway, when a thought occurred to him. If he remained in his dragon form it would be quite obvious. A big dragon lumbering down the halls would certainly draw attention, though he was hesitant about returning to his regular shape because he wasn't sure if he would be able to morph back. However, the whole backbone of this plan was surprise and if he was caught or killed everything would be ruined.

He reached the end of his counting and made the decision. Slowly, he morphed back to his regular shape and nearly collapsed to the floor. He'd forgotten how weak he still was and, on top of that, how naked he was, but this was the better choice so he stayed with it.

Already too much time had passed since Jaron left, so gathering all of his strength, which wasn't much, he steered himself into the hallway. His body did not wish to cooperate with him just yet, which left him weaving from one side of the hall to the other, smacking up against the walls and already out of breath. How could three months totally wipe out the good shape he'd been in?

When he came to the end of the hall, he leaned up against the wall for a short rest. He started to follow the path he told Jaron to take, when he caught the sounds of muffled voices. He froze, straining to hear better, but they were too low and incoherent that he wasn't sure which direction they were coming from. If he waited until they became louder and more distinct, he could run the risk of being caught before he even started. It would take time to morph into his dragon shape, a few seconds, but those seconds could cost him the entire Land. If he retreated back to the false wall, he'd never make it through before they spotted him. He hated being so unsure of himself and the situation, and nearly gave in to his dragon instinct, then thought better of it. His dragon instinct was extremely sensitive to his surroundings and sometimes knew before he did if there was danger. Though, it would undoubtedly demand that he waltz up to the enemy and breathe fire on their heads and that would not do him any good right now. Then again, if he could just resist the urge to stampede into battle…

He reached inside of himself and submerged into that hot, bubbling pool that was the dragon. Sometimes he would have sworn there was another creature living inside of him with its own agenda and goals, but it was certainly reliable because he felt what he needed to know. Also, as he guessed, that impulse was encouraging him to morph and stomp all over the threat. He forced himself to withdraw, feeling more exhausted than he did before, but now knew which way he should go. The instinct let him know the danger was to his right, so naturally he went left.

His intuition was confirmed a moment later when the mumbled voices grew louder. Landon quickened his pace, though he was certain that if anyone spotted him now they would wonder what a naked, drunken man was doing careening his way through the castle. He knew where he was headed, though, and soon came upon the small alcove. It indented the wall, recessing three feet in, with a door that led to the wine cellar. He stumbled into it and figured he could duck into the cellar until whoever was coming went by. He turned the handle.

Locked. He suddenly remembered they kept it locked because all that wine would be too much temptation for a couple of bored, off-duty Defenders. But he needed it to be open now! Feebly, he pulled on the handle again, however his need did not impress the door. It was still locked.

Those mumbled voices were coming his way. He didn't believe he had time to morph or to run out into the hallway and get further away. Doing the only thing he could, he pressed himself face first into the far corner of the alcove and hoped his pale skin made it possible to blend into the white walls. Although he remained perfectly still, his breathing sounded as loud as beating drums to him. Even the sweat from his pours suddenly sounded like a waterfall. All of it was too loud. So were the voices he could now hear clearly. He squeezed his eyes shut and instinctively put his arms over his head.

The voices were coming from two men, talking about nothing in particular and laughing at crude jokes they made. Their voices grew louder until, without even looking, he knew they were walking right past the alcove. Then the voices faded slightly, enough for him to peek out from under his arms and see that they were not standing there calling for an intruder capture. They continued to grow softer and Landon pulled himself away from the wall and started to relax.

"Is this what you call patrolling?" someone asked calmly.

The voices immediately became silent and Landon was twice as tense as he was before. He knew that voice. Even though he only heard it once before while in his own body, he knew who was speaking.

"No, my lord!" the men spoke in unison.

"You just thought that if you walked around the halls you could call it patrolling and I wouldn't ever need to know, is that it?"

"No, my lord!"

There was a moment of silence, then Taj's voice snapped, "Get back to your posts."

The scurrying of feet immediately followed and Landon thanked the Kyriea that they didn't come back passed the alcove again. He squeezed himself up against the opposite wall and heard the slow footsteps start to walk away. Then his breath caught when they came to a stop. Slowly they scraped against the floor as if someone had turned around while standing in the same spot. Landon remained frozen and knew what was happening. Taj could feel him, which was part of the plan but then, where in the name of Light was Jaron?!

One footstep echoed off the walls, then another, then another, then they stopped again. All that water Landon drank earlier was threatening to come out but he didn't think his absolute fear would allow it to. There was no time to morph, and even if he did, a part of him would be sticking out of this alcove before he was complete and then Taj would definitely see him.

Two more slow steps came closer, followed by a loud tongue click. Landon felt a small amount of hope. Maybe Taj was confused. He might be able to feel him but probably didn't think he was hiding right around the corner. Where was Jaron! Did he leave him? Did he get cold feet and decide to just leave? Then he reminded himself that this wasn't the spot they planned to meet. Jaron didn't know he was here and didn't know he needed to come…now!

The sound of a short, frustrated sigh lightly bounced off the walls. Landon suspected what Taj was trying to do. He was trying to flush him out by doing nothing, thinking if he remained quiet enough Landon was bound to make a mistake. Because of the hesitation, Landon knew Taj wasn't absolutely certain about his location. If he had been, he would have just walked up to Landon and destroyed him. No, Taj wasn't sure and wanted Landon to make a mistake to confirm his suspicions. Landon didn't think he could flinch now if he wanted to, so he wasn't going to be moving anytime soon.

The echo of the slow steps took on a different sound, which made Landon want to relieve himself right there.

The footsteps no longer bounced off both walls, they only bounced off one. Which meant Taj was right up against one of the walls, Landon guessed it would be the further one, so he could peek around into the alcove. Maybe Taj didn't know what to expect from him and was being cautious. All of the history Landon read said that Sulan had beaten Taj quite easily. Maybe Taj thought he could do the same thing. Landon nearly blurted out a laugh of fear when he thought about what Taj would find if he did peek into the alcove; a terrified, naked boy, close to tears, ready to relieve himself on the floor. Some threat.

"Taj!" The voice made Landon jerk despite his terror.

The feet scraped the floor again as they spun around quickly. Taj didn't answer and the voice didn't speak again. Landon was on edge, dying to know who was out there, and found himself leaning toward the opening of the alcove so he could hear better. He forced himself to remain still and waited for someone to say something more.

"So," Taj finally answered with a hint of amusement in his voice. "There you are."

"Yes," the voice answered. Landon strained to hear, since the voice was speaking so softly.

"Why are you back?" Taj asked lightly.

"Its was inevitable," the voice said. Only 'inevitable' came out as 'inEEvetable'. Jaron? "I's can't be's runnin' from ju me whole life." Jaron!

Landon was stunned. When he was in Jaron's mind, he didn't actually hear Jaron speak with his voice. When Landon heard him in dragon form, he sounded tiny and weak but so did everyone. Now that he was in his regular shape Jaron just sounded young. Landon had no idea how accurate he was to call him "boy" all the time. And he was the one who asked this boy to be a decoy for him. Oh Light! Was he insane to send him out there to stand before Taj? Then he remembered Jaron was not as innocent as he sounded and, in fact, could be quite deadly. Besides, this was the only way they could make this work. He just hoped the boy would be all right.

Landon's evaluation of Jaron took place in a few seconds time and now Taj answered the boy.

"A wise decision. Come, let us discuss your future." He paused. "And your mistake."

Jaron didn't answer and the next thing Landon heard were the two sets of feet walking back down the hall. He would have sunk to the floor in relief, only he was afraid that he wouldn't get up again. But one thing bothered him. How did Jaron know where to come? He was in the complete opposite direction from the spot they'd agreed on earlier, so how had Jaron known to come there right then? The answer was so simple and obvious Landon didn't recognize it at first. Then he put his finger on the familiar sensation.

He could feel Jaron, as clearly as he could when he was inside his mind. Which must mean Jaron could feel him as well. Since they seemed to still be linked, he would be able to locate Taj by his connection to Jaron, so long as the boy stayed close to Taj.

Landon slowly and carefully peeked out of the alcove, relieved that no one was around, and staggered down the hall, following his connection with the boy.

** **

Mazon watched Taj's troops bustling around the hallway through the false wall illusion. He couldn't believe how many people that Dark Master corrupted and glanced over his shoulder at the loyal Weavers, fighters, and town's people waiting anxiously behind him ready to fight. He stared back toward Taj's people and debated. Not yet. This timing had to be perfect or else he could seriously jeopardize Landon's plan. He couldn't help but smile a little with pride for Landon. What also added to his pride was the way all the people, with the exception of the very old, the very young, or the sick and crippled, rallied immediately to his call. Brazet told him that when he relayed Landon's words about needing the people's help and telling them they were fighting for *their* Land, not just the Kazimeer's, not a single person refused. Mazon wasn't sure if it had to do with their fear of Taj or their faith in Landon. Either way, this was the moment when Landon would prove to the people that he was indeed the right choice for Kazimeer. He wished the boy could have seen their reaction and all their hope and faith in him.

"We should advance now," a sharp voice whispered in his ear.

Mazon growled inwardly. How kind of Brazet to place two of the Counts in his charge. Mazon knew the former Captain did it just so he didn't have to deal with all four at once.

Without looking at which Count spoke, he answered softly, "Not yet. We need to give the Kazimeer time."

"They are not expecting our attack!" It was the Fire Count that spoke and he pointed firmly toward Taj's people walking back and forth before the false wall, unaware of who was hiding behind it. "If we wait it may be too late!"

Mazon turned his head slowly toward the Count and whispered calmly, "If you do not hold your tongue, I'll turn you into a mushroom." With that, he stared back out through the wall.

The Count retreated angrily but Mazon did not let it affect him. Instead he turned his thoughts toward the upcoming battle. He'd been in his share of fights and battles when he was *much* younger but that didn't alter his memory or his growing, wicked excitement. He was actually looking forward to showing everyone that the old Weaver could still kick backsides from one end of the Land to the other. Mazon the Mad was what he'd been called. A title he still thought of with pride, though not many people around now would know to call him that. But back then he was mad because he took risks and never cared what others thought of him. He'd do things other Weavers wouldn't even fathom, do them well, and get away without a scratch. He'd been so sizzling that ice melted in his presence. Now he was seen as an old, paranoid man with 'poxed up' magic.

Enough time had passed and if Landon wasn't ready by now, then he wouldn't ever be. He raised his hand to signal the advancement and waited a few moments to let the crowd behind him close in tighter. He wasn't that old, was he? Could he still be Mazon the Mad? A smile played on his lips; yes, perhaps he could be. He snapped his hand down and charged out through the wall, spraying his magic all over Taj's unsuspecting troops.

**   **

When Jaron felt Landon's fear, he dashed through the castle in a matter of minutes, which was a considerable feat since he was also avoiding being seen. At the time, he had no idea what caused the flow of panic or even where Landon was. He'd been waiting where Landon told him to when the overwhelming terror exploded in him. It took a few moments to realize it wasn't his terror but Landon's, and followed that sensation which fortunately or unfortunately, led him straight into Taj. Jaron knew Landon had been somewhere in that hall but hoped Taj thought the feeling was coming from him, since Taj didn't know Landon was no longer residing in his mind. He just hoped Landon would hurry up.

He followed Taj into what was once called the High Room, though he didn't know that. Surrounding the entire perimeter of the hall were those eye-less things, just standing there looking lifeless. Jaron's fear couldn't stop the awe he felt when he looked around. It was a breathtaking sight. The silk tapestries hanging throughout the room, the elaborate carvings all over the walls, and the domed ceiling with the multicolored glass center arranged to form a picture of a man. Jaron didn't need to get a closer look to know who that man was. Even the white, shiny floor looked too stunning to walk on, but since he had to, he walked very carefully so he wouldn't smudge it. The most awesome sight was the golden throne placed toward the back of the far wall. The jewels set along the arms, legs, and back sparkled and Jaron thought that just a piece of the chair would let him live in comfort for the rest of his life.

"Beautiful, isn't it," Taj whispered in his ear. Jaron jumped, unable to help himself and nodded feebly. Taj continued casually, "I just had it put in. Made by the finest craftsmen in the Land. I'll soon have the whole castle redone but I wanted to start where it counted. Why did you run away?"

Jaron was slightly caught off guard by the sudden question and fumbled briefly for an answer. "I's 'fraid," he mumbled.

Taj nodded, never taking his eyes off the throne or moving away from him. He even wrapped an arm around Jaron's shoulders. It took much restraint from Jaron not to flinch or move away.

"I can understand that," Taj answered. "So why did you come back?"

"I's told ju. I's wasn't goin' to spend da rest of me life runnin' from ju."

"Well," Taj said with a tight smile and glanced down at him. "That was a well rehearsed answer. I doubt I could've come up with a better one myself." His eyes strayed across the hall and one narrowed slightly. "Well…yes, I could." He stared down at Jaron again and squeezed him closer. "But that was a good try."

"Why's else would I's come back?" Jaron asked, feeling a little unnerved by Taj's sense of humor.

"Oh, there are plenty of reasons. I don't care, actually. I'm just impressed that you did. But honesty, Jaron, is what I'm looking for here. Honesty about why you returned. I don't care if it was because you wanted to shove a knife in my back or because you may actually be tempted by this power I speak of. Or maybe you just had nowhere else to go, but honesty is what I want to hear from you. Not some half-cracked answer that you think I want to hear."

Jaron thought his answer was believable enough and, in fact, it was partially the truth. But he had to give Taj more or else he was in serious trouble. He didn't know what to say, though. If he quoted any of the reasons Taj just gave him it would make things worse. He thought quickly, trying to outguess this man standing so close that he could see the insanity whirling around in those black eyes. Black eyes he remembered from his childhood. One thought collided into another until he found his answer. It wasn't that far from the truth had the situation not changed.

"'Cause he's tryin' to take over me body and I's won't let him. I's jus got dragged into dis. I's don't tink it's fair dat I's 'ave to lose me body 'cause he doesn't 'ave one annimore." His answer was more heated than he expected but the memory of Landon's take-over was still too fresh in his mind.

Taj cocked his head. "You want me to remove him so you can have control of your body." Jaron nodded. "Even though your power will be mine?"

Jaron swallowed and said softly, "I's can say dis honestly. I's really don't know wha' ju's talkin' 'bout wit dat."

Jaron's eyes widened a little and he thought his imagination was playing with him, but discovered it wasn't. Taj's expression softened and he actually looked sad. He leaned his face closer to Jaron's and stared him straight in the eye.

"I'll teach you," he whispered, with what Jaron figured was as much affection as Taj could show.

Jaron didn't know how to answer so he said nothing. They stood like that for several long seconds before the voice from the door called out anxiously, "My lord?"

Taj backed away from Jaron and turned around, while Jaron glanced around him and felt his insides knot. It was Dapp, which could only mean something had gone wrong. Jaron also knew he missed the perfect opportunity to grab that necklace, but with Landon nowhere to be found, he was not going to pull such a stunt without backup. There was no telling what Taj would do to him. He wanted to moan aloud but kept it inside. Where was Landon?!

Taj approached Dapp, who remained at the door and looked nervous. Taj leaned close so his voice would remain low. "What is it?"

"I'm sorry to disturb you---"

"*What* do you want?"

Dapp hesitated for a moment. "We're under attack."

"Oh?" Taj asked. "By whom?"

"They are the former Kazimeer's Defenders. Their uniforms confirm it. And also the people. They're coming out of the walls. Literally!"

Taj appeared to be in deep thought for a second, then he put on a twisted smile. "So that's where they've been. Hiding right under my nose. Clever." He glanced at Dapp and narrowed his eyes. "What are you waiting for?"

"Your orders, my lord."

"My orders? What do you think my orders are? Kill them."

"Forgive me, my lord, but I did not know if you wanted any prisoners."

Taj considered it, bobbing his head back and forth as if he were weighing the idea on his mind, but then he shook his head. "No, too much trouble. Just have them all destroyed and clean up the mess. Here." He nodded toward a few of the Mytocks near the door. "Take some of them." He began to walk back to Jaron, already hearing the shouts of battle coming from the halls and through the windows. He stopped short. Through the windows? He rounded on Dapp.

"I thought you said they were coming through the walls?"

Dapp, half way out the door with the Mytocks, turned back to him. "They are, my lord."

"Then what are they doing outside!" Taj immediately stalked to the closest window and pushed the tapestry out of the way just enough so he could see. At least a hundred morphers were crawling all over out there. Those were not the Kazimeer's Defenders.

"Abbnar," he hissed under his breath. That man had the most excellent timing Taj ever encountered. He spun around and glared at Dapp. "The morphers outside are the first priority. The Defenders inside are second. And there is only one person you are to capture alive." He sent Abbnar's image directly to Dapp's mind, causing him to jerk back a bit. "If he is killed, you are responsible." Dapp nodded once and hurried out of the hall with several Mytocks right behind him.

Taj didn't believe Abbnar would be out there with the rest of them but he could hope. He knew Abbnar was too smart to put himself at risk by joining the ranks. No, Abbnar was tucked neatly away somewhere, waiting to see the result of this battle and based on its outcome would then either raise a new army or dance on Taj's ashes. And Taj did not relish the idea of Abbnar dancing on him.

He walked away from the window back to the boy, who seemed rooted to the spot where he stood, and turned an idea over in his mind. How did Abbnar and the Kazimeer's Defenders coordinate this attack? Jynx, that little wench, could have acted as liaison between them, but then he would have definitely felt her coming and going from the castle. Could it simply be coincidence? Taj didn't believe too much in coincidence. No, there was something more to this.

Could the ivory dragon have contacted Abbnar somehow? But that made no sense, because Abbnar would have snatched the boy or at least made contact with him. Taj would certainly have felt the old man's presence if he tried that. Unless… Taj studied Jaron carefully. Unless…He walked purposely away from him, then slowly back.

It was gone.

He hadn't bothered to check the sensation since they'd been in the hallway and he took for granted the supposed obvious and let his emotions get the better of him. He wanted the boy so badly that he let his guard down and the little bastard used it against him! He checked again just to be sure. He was correct. The ivory dragon was gone from the boy's mind.

Something else struck him. That thing *had* been in the hall! With Jaron's appearance he thought the strong sensation of the ivory dragon was because of the boy. How mistaken he was. He watched as the boy's face turned white, then green. Yes, he knew this little plan of theirs had failed. This was why Taj never let his emotions come out because someone always turned them against him. He approached the boy with ice in his heart.

**　　**　　　　　　****

Although he didn't know it, Brazet and his Defenders came spilling out of the walls on the opposite side of the castle the same instant Mazon did. Though he was not a Weaver, Brazet did have his fighter instinct which was sometimes more reliable than magic. That's what he was…a fighter! Not some Second who involved himself with politics and governing. He would always be Captain of the Defenders and charged into battle as one.

His sword plunged into Taj's sentries quickly and he was pleased to see his Defenders doing the same without any hint of reservation. They'd been trained by him and an enemy was an enemy, no matter if it was a man, woman, or thing, whatever those eye-less beings were. However, the battle was tough since they were greatly outnumbered.

He decided to use a trick his father taught him to quickly raise morale. He ripped his blade across one of Taj's people and shouted loudly, "For the Kazimeer!"

The cry was quickly taken up. With each kill the Defenders shouted out, "For the Kazimeer!" It just as quickly became a chant, which seemed to unnerve Taj's people. It seemed they had no such loyalty to their leader and their faces showed it. The only ones not affected were those eye-less things, but then, as if by some silent message, they left the battle and hurried down the hall.

Saving the Bait　　　　　289

Brazet was not about to let those creatures get away. As he sliced his way to follow them, he felt the sweet pain of a blade being sunk into his side. To him, it was almost a caress. With one spinning motion, he swung his sword around, imbedding it into the face of the sentry who attacked him. The rest of his body finally caught up with his sword and he saw that he'd sliced deeply into the man's head. He had to brace his foot against the man's chest to dislodge the blade. His attacker fell backwards, screaming wildly but Brazet had no time to finish him. With a few of his Defenders directly behind him, he darted down the hall to destroy those beings.

When he came to the door leading outside, he skidded to a halt. "What in the Land?"

Surrounding the castle were dozens…no, hundreds of animals. Or maybe they were morphers. Brazet could never tell the difference. But what were they doing here and where in the name of the Guardian did they come from? He saw a dozen shapes he recognized and a dozen more he didn't. They were attacking and being attacked by those eye-lesses along with a few of Taj's people. So that's why they left the other battle. Somehow, the eye-lesses were called upon to deal with the threat outside of the castle.

If these animals or morphers were considered a threat by Taj then Brazet was determined to help them. He plunged into the battle, suddenly surrounded by ten blades. He called out as he ripped his sword through the mob, "For the Kazimeer!" Once again, the chant was quickly taken up.

**   **

Landon inched his way along the wall, constantly looking over his shoulder. The cries and shouts of the battle sounded as if they were coming from all directions, while he, the Kazimeer, naked and unarmed, was sneaking his way around his own castle like a rat. But he reminded himself he only had one task and that was to deal with Taj.

He followed his link to Jaron, which led him to his High Room. He made his way to the rear door and leaned up against the wall, while trying to make out the conversation taking place inside. He could hear both Taj and Jaron speaking but couldn't make out what they were saying. The talking stopped and then a few moments later Taj was called. Landon held his breath, wanting desperately to make out the sharp low tones but soon heard Taj growl something about dealing with the morphers first and his Defenders second.

Morphers? What morphers? Did Mazon have a stash of them he didn't mention? Landon didn't dwell on it too long and was simply grateful for the added distraction.

It became quiet in the High Room, so quiet Landon was concerned about his breathing being heard. Then Taj started talking calmly and Jaron began dancing around with answers. Landon swallowed hard; the game was over. Taj knew he was no longer in the boy's mind. His body tingled with panic. If Taj knew then he could no longer stay here hiding. He was too close. Surely Taj would be able to feel him soon but he couldn't leave Jaron alone.

Hosting the Kazimeer

'Soon' didn't accurately describe the speed in which Taj located him. 'Instantly' was more like it. First he felt Jaron's frantic warning to him, a moment later he heard Jaron cry out his warning aloud. Then he heard the boy scream.

Landon was momentarily frozen with indecision. If he ran in there now, without any type of protection, he and everyone else were finished. He could try to morph once he got into the High Room but he'd never be able to do it in time to stop Taj. If he morphed out here, he'd never be able to get inside the hall. His mind whirled, searching for a solution that would enable him to face Taj in his dragon form. Jaron's scream was cut off abruptly. There was no more time, he had to act now and did.

He ran down the hallway as fast as his weak body could move him. As he rounded the corner he felt a blast of energy whip by just missing him, and heard the loud crash as it made contact with something. Once again, he heard the boy's screams but now knew how he could get inside. The problem was, he'd have to leave in order to do it.

He reached a set of stairs and tumbled down them. Taj wouldn't follow him, he was certain. Instead he would hurt Jaron in an attempt to make him charge without thinking. Landon knew better, though, and only hoped the boy would forgive him. Once he hit the bottom of the stairs, he saw a door ahead of him leading directly to the outside. He lunged for it.

He viewed the battle outside the instant he opened the door and wished again that he had some type of protection on him. But since he'd run out of time, he had to improvise. Puffing hard, he threw himself outside, dodging and moving as fast as he could away from the battle. The only thing he allowed himself to see was the forest beyond the rear of the castle. If he could just reach it, he could morph. He didn't dare risk morphing in the middle of this battle without armor or protection. And since morphing took time, if he stopped where he was to do so he'd be dead in seconds. He headed straight for the trees, shoving everyone out of his way whether they were his own people or Taj's. He knew how this must look and soon heard his Defenders cry out,

"The Kazimeer's retreating! He's leaving us!"

Landon wished he could've explained his plan to them but would have to settle for telling them later. He reached the edge of the forest and ran deeper into it, looking behind him for any intruders. He could still hear his Defender's cry out that he was a coward and betrayed them, and felt his heart cringe with pain. He stumbled to a stop, breathing hard and feeling every inch of his body ache and throb. He leaned on his knees, trying to catch his breath, while he forced his mind to focus on only one thing. His body protested loudly when the change began but he couldn't let that affect him.

He had to face Taj.

SPELLS, FIRE, AND BLOOD

"Do you think I'm that big of a fool?" Taj spat.

"No," Jaron answered. He couldn't move from where he stood and didn't think it had to do with any of Taj's magic. "Actually, I's surprised its took ju dis long." Taj's eyes narrowed sharply and Jaron continued. "I's don't mean dat as an insult. I's really dinn't tink its would take ju dis long to figure its out."

Taj stopped his advance and studied him. "Now you try flattery?"

"It's not flattery. I's bein' honest."

"You wouldn't want to continue being honest and tell me where that *thing* is, would you?"

"I's don't know," Jaron said and shrugged helplessly.

"I see your honesty only goes so far, though." Taj lost his patience completely and hurled the boy back, smashing him against the wall.

Jaron's air was knocked out of him but he staggered to his feet as quickly as he could and repeated hoarsely, "I's don't know."

"Maybe you don't," Taj replied with a sharp growl. "But you're going to help me find it."

Jaron shook his head slowly. "No."

Taj tilted his head thoughtfully to one side. "Really?"

He debated bonding with him right now but decided against it. He did not want to have a bad connection with this boy, no matter how furious he was with him. Perhaps he could incapacitate him just long enough for him to finish the ivory dragon, its army, and Abbnar's, then he could turn his attention to using him fully. He was a bit pressed for time at the moment.

He was reaching out with his power to seize the boy's mind when he felt it. The sensation sickened and excited him. It was here. That accursed thing was right here! He looked around the chamber slowly and his eyes zeroed in on the rear door. It was just outside!

Tensely, he stalked toward the door when Jaron jumped him. Taj was knocked to the ground and Jaron landed on top of him, calling out a warning to the beast. In his excitement and fear, Taj forgot that Jaron was still mobile but was somewhat amused by the boy's attempts to stop him. Jaron swung his fists madly, making contact everywhere he aimed, and Taj did not try to stop him. The boy's punches had no affect and with a soft chuckle, Taj encased him in a web of energy and raised him into the air. Jaron struggled wildly against his power but Taj simply hurled him across the chamber. Taj got to his feet, brushed himself off absently, then wrapped a tight grip around the boy's mind…and squeezed.

The boy screamed and held his head as if that would stop the pain ripping through his mind. Actually, all Taj wanted to do was cause enough pain to make the boy pass out but much to his surprise Jaron fought him. He increased the pressure briefly then released the boy, who fell to the floor and was silent. Taj stalked toward the rear door, building his power with each step.

A white blur raced by the door. Taj ran and skidded out into the rear hallway. A black wave of pure energy erupted from him and chased the white figure down the hall. The figure veered around a corner and his power hit the wall, causing a large hole to form in the stone. Taj began to pursue but stopped himself. He looked back into the Justice Hall and stared at the boy lying on the floor. He was not going to go chasing after that beast like some hound. He'd make the beast come to him.

Taj casually walked toward Jaron while ordering his Mytocks to guard all entrances to the hall. There would be no way that creature could get to him, in his dragon form or not, without him knowing about it first. Besides, he wasn't too worried about that creature morphing. There wasn't nearly enough space for that thing to get through the door and if that mutation was foolish enough to try to morph while in *his* presence, then it would be making a serious error in judgment.

Jaron slowly raised his head and stared at him in fear. Taj grinned happily and sung, "Oh Jaron!"

The boy was once again entangled in his power and squeezed steadily. Jaron cried out instantly, which made Taj's smile broaden. He'd *make* that thing come to him one way or another, only he would have the advantage. He lifted the boy off the floor and threw him against the far wall. The boy didn't even have time to slide down to the floor before Taj grabbed him again. This time he went straight for his mind, tearing into it the way a starving man tore into food. Not only would he finish that miserable creature's existence for good *but* he'd also take control of this boy's power. He never felt more delighted in his life.

**   **

Jaron wanted to rip his own head off. His eyes felt as if they were on fire, his mouth and throat were raw from his screams, and never in his life would he have believed that such agony could be lived through. Taj had been correct, because at that moment Jaron would have begged to go back to the slave-trade if only the pain would stop. He would've cut out his own heart and eaten it; delivered Landon tied up with a bow to Taj, if only the unbearable agony would just stop. But it didn't and, in fact, grew worse, if that was at all possible.

He could no longer scream, not only because of his raw throat but because he had no more air left in his lungs. He couldn't even cry; all he could do was endure. Endure until his brain popped like a bubble and oozed out of his ears. Even then he wasn't certain the pain would stop. He was shaking violently and didn't realize that he was lying face first on the floor until the torture did cease.

His mind felt like an open sore and a roaring sound filled his ears. He could barely raise his head but when he did saw Taj staring up at the ceiling with a look of shock. Slowly Jaron looked up too and was only able to watch in awe.

**   **

Mazon never felt more exhausted or more insanely alive. Taj's sentries were everywhere. Light! How many people *did* that demon corrupt? Although they were poor spirits and ultimately misguided, he had no choice but to destroy them before they destroyed him and the Land. However, he was using his power too quickly. He didn't grasp this until a man swinging a mace at him came too close and he cast a spell that should have been the equivalent of having a large fist fall on top of the man's head. But since his power was so drained, he only managed to give the man a slap on the cheek.

The attacker grinned and swung the mace confidently now. Mazon did know how to fight without the aid of his magic but it had been so long since he had to. Still, he never let his worry show in his face and sneered deliberately at the attacker, ready to fend off the blows as best he could.

The mace swung downward, aiming directly for his head and despite his will to remain strong, he instinctively threw his arms over him. Without warning, the mace swinger snapped into flames and within seconds, he and his weapon were a pile of dark ashes. Mazon uncovered his head, blinked at the mess, and then glanced around, looking for the Weaver with such power to activate a spell so quickly and deadly. His eyes grew wide when he saw who it was and, unable to help it, he groaned aloud.

Jynx grinned at him and shouted over the battle, "There's more where that came from, great Weaver."

Mazon looked beyond her and for the first time noticed the dozens of sprites aiding his group.

Jynx shouted to him again, "We'll take care of these fools. Go outside and help the morphers. They need you more than I do."

Mazon hesitated. He did not trust this girl for a second. As if she read his mind, she shrugged at the same instant one of Taj's sentries advanced on her, bringing his sword down on her head. With a glance toward him, Jynx flicked her hand and the man sucked in on himself, becoming nothing more than a pile of clothing. She shrugged again.

"Suit yourself. But your suspicion will be Landon's downfall." With that, she returned to her casting and ignored the old Weaver.

Mazon sneered openly and wanted to lecture her. Actually he wanted to put her over his knee and spank her, but Landon still needed his help. Going against his better judgment, he ran down the hallway and out the first door he came to and saw what the girl spoke of.

The morphers were everywhere and, much to Mazon's surprise, Brazet and the Defenders were already out there fighting alongside of them. Feeling his energy recharged, he too joined the battle.

**

When Landon rose out of the forest all sound below him came to a halt for a moment. He briefly looked down at the faces of his Defenders, then flew higher into the sky, the only sound being his wings flapping against the air. The cheer that erupted from his Defenders was sudden and unlike anything he'd ever heard before. It thundered across the entire area and filled Landon with pride. When he climbed high over the crowd, he hovered and stared down at them again, as if to say, "I did not abandon you. I merely had to change into *my* armor."

Arrows came for him but he was too high for them to reach and besides, his Defenders immediately went into action again. Another wave of salute reached his ears and Landon wished he had the time to bask in it. He flew over the roof of the castle, hovering when he saw the stained glass ceiling below him. He cocked his head and stared at the image now placed where the ivory dragon's used to be. His anger boiled instantly. Taj's image now stared back at him in a triumphant pose.

Landon breathed heavily, pumped his wings hard to build up speed, and began to feel the burning sensation at the back of his throat. He turned snout first toward the stained glass ceiling and dove straight for it, beating his wings against the air current. When the glass ceiling was directly in front of him, he folded his wings against his body and blew a streak of white fire at the head of Taj's image. The glass shattered from the heat a second before he crashed through the ceiling and now he was no longer staring down at the image of Taj but at Taj himself.

As soon as he felt his tail clear the jagged glass, he righted himself, placing his hind legs on the floor first then slamming his front claws down so hard the chamber shook. He whipped his neck down so his face was directly in front of Taj and snarled, being sure his pointed teeth showed. For a moment all he and Taj did was stare at each other. Landon saw the gleam of the silver chain and glow of the black stone hanging around Taj's neck. Jaron never got it away from him.

Landon's confidence faltered slightly and he snarled louder to reassure himself. For a moment he couldn't believe what he saw but then allowed the idea to sink in. Taj's expression was perfectly calm up until he snarled again. Then his eyes grew slightly wide and the color began to drain from his face. He was afraid of him. Taj, the Dark Master, was actually afraid of *him*; a twenty two year old boy who was thrust into a position he never wanted and couldn't even make a thief boy obey him. *That's* who Taj feared. Landon would've fed deliciously on the thought if it weren't for the fact that he was terrified about who he faced too. But he was also filled with such anger and hatred he thought he was going to burst. He never considered himself violent but at that moment he wanted nothing more than to chew off Taj's head.

Landon's snarl rapidly increased in volume and he whipped his head forward, his jaw wide open to bite Taj in half. His head shook slightly from the amount of force he used when his teeth clamped down on nothing. Taj wasn't there. Landon spun his head around in time to see Taj materialize behind him. He pulled back his tail and heaved it at Taj. It struck the Dark Master directly in the side and sent him flying backward, crashing into the wall. Ten eye-lesses were suddenly upon Landon. At least, he counted ten in front of him. The stabbing pains in his tail and lower back let him know there were more behind. He didn't dare blow fire, since he caught the sight of Jaron lying helpless on the floor. Instead, he struck out with his front claws, striking seven of the ten eye-lesses at once, while he swung his tail back and forth, whacking aside a few of the eye-lesses behind him.

Landon attempted to turn around to deal better with what was behind him but soon found there was no way he could do so easily. He was stuck the way he faced. He did have a bit of room above him, though, so he reared up on his hind legs and positioned his claws directly over two of the eye-lesses. When he came down they were flattened under his claws and dark blood spurted all over his white scales. He felt tiny shocks throughout his hind legs and backside and attempted to get a better look, but the eye-lesses were well hidden from his sight. Becoming frustrated and annoyed, he slammed his tail down hard, jostling loose a few of them, while he opened up his wings and swept them backwards. Despite their delicate looking nature, his wings were actually quite strong and tough. They acted like a broom and pushed away the stray eye-lesses, lifting a few off the ground and smashing them into the wall behind him.

Landon still felt the small shocking sensations but was more interested in locating Taj. He whipped his head around awkwardly, trying to find him. He saw Jaron still motionless on the floor and wished he could somehow get the boy out of here. Aside from the fact that the boy was hurt, Landon was restricted in his attacks. He could've set the whole hall ablaze and would have never been affected by it but Jaron would burn with everything else. He also couldn't stomp around too much, fearing the boy would get squished under him.

Damn Taj! Where was he! Landon didn't have to wonder too long.

A tremendous, searing pain struck him at the nape of his neck. It felt like lightning had found its way through his scales and into his flesh. He threw his head back and forth, trying to shake loose whatever was causing the unpleasant sensation but soon realized no one was sitting on him. Taj was hovering in the air above him and Landon saw the black ray of light coming from his hands and attaching itself to his neck. The pain was horrible, making Landon's vision blur and his head pound.

Landon sat up on his hind legs, attempting to close the distance between him and Taj, but Taj winked out of sight and reappeared on the opposite side of the chamber. The black light continued to cut into Landon's flesh and he felt blood dripping down his scales, as the pain moved along the circumference of his neck. He realized in that brief moment that Taj was trying to cut his head off. Without even thinking, Landon spat a fireball straight at Taj. The fire made a direct hit but all it did was throw Taj back until he was stopped by the wall. The flames didn't even touch him. But they did touch the tapestries, instantly setting them ablaze.

Taj shook his head to clear it from the impact and vanished again away from the fire. He reappeared behind the dragon and kept low, making it difficult for the thing to find him. He commanded the black stone to release *all* of its power to him and combined his own with it, doubling the force of his magic. He held his hands out in front of him and a sphere of electricity instantly sizzled between his fingertips. He sent it coursing up the ivory thing's spine where it reached the open wound in the neck and dug deeper into it. He blocked out the deafening roar from the creature and continued to keep an eye on that long tail, knowing how unpredictable it was. The beast's body shook from the pain and twisted back and forth, trying to free itself. Taj saw that white tail come swinging around for him and quickly glided out of its way. A great wind blew his hair wildly as the tail whizzed by him but he was in the clear. Taj began to smile and turned his attention back to the thing.

He had time to shout, "OH POX!" He threw his arms over his head instinctively as the large claw batted him down to the ground like a ball. He landed hard on his back and gasped for air, barely registering that the white claw was bearing down on him. He rolled out of the way as the claw smashed into the floor where he'd just been. When he stopped flipping over, Taj opened his eyes and felt as if the entire hall was spinning. He held his head with both hands to steady himself and noticed how dim it was. Blinking hard he looked up and realized where he was, directly under the dragon. How perfect!

Instantly Taj surrounded himself with a web of light, strong enough to keep him safe in case this thing decided to lie down on him and enclosed the creature's body in an invisible net. Then he grabbed his power to form the ray of black light again. He heaved it upward directly into the beast's gut, and began to move it up and down, slicing into the scales and flesh underneath. He would cut clean up to the beast's throat and there would be nothing it could do about it.

Landon felt the hideous pain in his lower abdomen and tried to lie down on top of what was causing it, only he couldn't move. The pain increased rapidly and he frantically tried to swat at the cause, but his tail and claws wouldn't react to his command. He felt something leap onto his back and soon felt small shocks tearing into his open neck. His first attempt at turning his head didn't succeed. Panic raced through him and he madly pulled at the restraint. He felt his head twitch and increased his effort, slowly tearing his head loose from the entrapment. With a final yank, his head was free and he painfully craned it around to see an eye-less sitting on him. With a quick snap, Landon grabbed the eye-less in his teeth, shook his head violently, and threw it across the chamber where it landed with a thud and was soon consumed by the flames moving along the wall. Landon spat several times, not liking the after taste in his mouth, while his body screamed for him to move away from the agony beneath him.

But he couldn't. Only his head could move back and forth but the rest of him was still trapped. He roared, hoping that it might shake him loose or at least relieve some of the pain and pressure. It didn't. His mind whirled trying to find a solution to his dangerous problem and his eyes fell on Jaron. The poor boy, Landon couldn't even tell if he was alive. He silently begged the boy to forgive him for getting him into this mess. Another wave of agony struck his stomach. He could feel his body shaking but couldn't get loose from whatever was holding him still. It felt as if thousands of bugs were eating away at his insides and the overwhelming pressure made it worse.

Some threat he turned out to be. Everyone expected him to just stomp all over Taj, even Jynx.

"Can you imagine what this one will do to him?"

Allow himself to be carved into tiny dragon bits; that's what *this* ivory dragon would do to Taj.

The thought crashed so loudly in his mind that he winced. He stared at the boy on the floor and would've smiled if he could. He forced himself to relax which wasn't as easy as he first thought, since the pain was difficult to ignore. But he closed his mind to it and focused on only one thing. After a moment, he felt his bladder loosen.

He didn't just piss on Taj's head…he pissed on *Taj*. The flood of urine washed the Dark Master out from under him and sent him through Landon's front paws and half way across the hall. Landon wished he had the ability to make an image crystal because he would have loved to keep that look of humiliation, shock, and disgust on Taj's face for the rest of his life. Taj leapt to his feet and stared at him, his eyes wide, his mouth twisted in a sneer, holding his arms out as if he didn't want them to touch the rest of his soaked body.

Landon felt the hold on his body vanish and the stinging in his gut from the deep wound. Without warning, without even inhaling, he blew a streak of white fire directly at Taj. He surprised the Dark Master, who spastically blocked the flames but hurled a dense cloud back at him. The cloud surrounded Landon's head and soon the rest of his body, once again holding him still and infecting his mind. He thrashed his head back and forth, feeling as if a hundred swords were stabbing his brain. He opened his mouth, ready to incinerate Taj but the cloud moved down his throat and began choking him.

Landon managed to focus his eyes long enough on Taj but the man wasn't smiling as he thought he'd be. Taj's expression was hard, his eyes blazed with fury, and the black stone was glowing brilliantly. Landon squinted against the white light that shot from the stone and then felt his head erupt like a volcano. Taj's power burrowed into his mind, like worms into dirt.

**   **

Brazet pulled his blade out of his opponent's chest and spun around, looking for more. But all he saw standing were his own Defenders, town's people, and those animals. During the battle he caught a glimpse of Taj's people retreating, being led by a man who wore the uniform of a Second, Taj's Second. Brazet wanted very much to kill him but unfortunately he'd been engaged the entire time and they squirmed away before he got the chance. He witnessed briefly, though, that the animals wanted a bite of that man's flesh too, but he moved with speed and grace, getting as many of Taj's scum away as he could. Now that the immediate frenzy was over, Brazet dispatched a group of Defenders to track him and Taj's sentries down and destroy them.

Breathing heavily he walked carefully around the dead and dying bodies on the ground. The people and some of his Defenders helped the wounded, while the rest took those still alive from Taj's army and quickly bound them, not being too careful about their wounds either. Brazet scanned the battle area, finding some dead faces of his Defenders and town's people. He did not show his grief in his face, though, and pushed it down while he scanned the rest of the area, finally finding who he was looking for.

The Weaver was bent over, his hands on his knees, breathing just as hard as Brazet. He glanced up when he felt the Second's eyes on him and smiled weakly. Brazet returned it and moved toward him.

"How are you?" he asked.

"Fine," Mazon gasped and nodded. "But feeling my age, I'm afraid. And you?" Brazet opened his mouth to answer, but at the same moment noticed Mazon's expression change. Brazet looked over his shoulder and stared also confused, as the animals began to move away.

Brazet leaned down and whispered to him, "Where are they going?"

"I do not know," Mazon answered, shaking his head slightly. "I don't even know where they came from."

"You didn't call them?" Brazet asked.

"Me? Oh no. I don't have the power to call the animals of the Land."

"They are animals, then?"

"Half are. The rest are morphers, who I knew about, but where…?" He didn't finish and turned toward the castle. "We should see who else is---"

Every person, including the retreating morphers and animals, either ducked or grabbed hold of their heads as the windows of the High Room exploded outward. Flames licked the outside of the castle and smoke poured out from the inside. However, it wasn't the explosion or the falling shards of glass that made everyone wince and cringe. It was the deafening dragon roar, which shattered the windows in the first place.

Mazon and Brazet stared at each other briefly as the roar subsided rather quickly. Without words, they dashed into the castle with most of the remaining Defenders and town's people behind them.

**   **

Jaron had been in and out of consciousness since he saw the ivory dragon crash through the ceiling, when the roar exploded in his ears and snapped him awake. His eyes flew open but immediately began to water from the fire. He coughed violently, not only from the smoke but also from a hideous stench that filled his nose making him want to vomit. He briefly saw some of Landon's quick, thrashing movements through the dense smoke but mostly he felt the floor shake and heard his friend's cry of pain. Jaron tried to stand but his body protested loudly and didn't budge. He buried his head in his arms as a series of coughs took hold of him. He kept trying to get a breath but couldn't and felt his head start to spin. He closed his eyes to steady himself, waiting for the dizziness to pass. It didn't and instead of opening his eyes again, he left them closed and dropped his head to the floor. He began to drift, the sounds from the battle fading in his ears and soon saw nothing but darkness in his mind's eye.

He wasn't sure how long he drifted along the quiet, emptiness of his mind, but soon collided into a barrier that knocked him out of his drifting. When he was able to think straight, he raised his mental head and saw the little boy standing before him. He remembered him clearly this time. He *was* the same little boy who led him to the slave-trade and to Taj. This was all his fault! Furious, Jaron screamed with rage and slapped the boy across the face as hard as he could. He immediately was sorry for doing it but the child seemed unaffected.

Jaron's eyes were pulled away from the boy and rested on what was sitting behind him. A violent whirling of enormous, raw strength took over the entire section beyond the child. There was no end to it; it just seemed to go on forever. Jaron didn't know what he was looking at but knew it was the answer. He took a step toward it but the little boy held up a hand and stopped him.

"No. Not yet."

"Wha' ju mean 'not yet'!" Jaron cried and tried to move forward again.

"No," the boy said firmly but gently.

"But dat's wha' I's need!"

"You'd never be able to handle it," the child said smiling. "Not now, anyway."

"So wha' do I's do?" Jaron pleaded.

"Well, I can't hand you a monsoon but I can give you a rain drop. I think you can control that on your own." The boy gestured off to the side and Jaron watched as the familiar shape strolled toward him. The boy smiled. "You already have."

"But dat's not 'nuff," Jaron protested.

"It's enough for now," the child stated. "Now, get back out there." Jaron shook his head defiantly. He needed…wanted…what lay beyond the child and wouldn't leave without it. The boy raised his brow. "Jaron, you're not going to get it and you're not going to talk me into giving it to you. Take what you can control."

"I's can handle more."

"No, you can't," the boy stated. "You don't even know what that is."

"So!"

"Jaron," the boy chuckled and took his face into his small hands. "Don't be greedy. Soon enough you'll learn all about it."

The boy kissed his forehead and Jaron never felt so loved or secure in his life. He wanted to stay there and bathe in the feeling, never letting it go. The boy stepped back and the wondrous feeling began to decrease in intensity but part of it still lingered.

The child patted his cheek lovingly. "Now, get back out there or I will carry you."

Jaron was actually curious to see how this child intended on doing that. As if he read his thoughts, which he probably did, the little boy took his hands and whispered gently, "You keep surprising me."

One moment, Jaron was staring into that sweet face, the next he was being pulled through the darkness at an amazing speed. He tried to pull his hands away from the child's but couldn't so much as twitch them. He was being dragged along whether he liked it or not. Suddenly there were sounds echoing from everywhere and the boy came to an abrupt halt. Jaron's hands were released but he had enough momentum that while the child came to stop, he didn't. He continued to race forward, sailing through the darkness, completely out of control, while he screamed. He crashed through some type of boundary in the darkness and his body jerked awake.

His eyes flew open and he sucked in a much needed breath. Not much seemed to change where he was. The chamber was still thick with smoke and stench, and Landon was still fighting furiously against something Jaron couldn't see. Then he spotted Taj standing there stiffly, staring directly at Landon, with a bright light coming from his hands and chest. Jaron remembered that he didn't fulfill his part of this plan. He never got the necklace away from Taj even when he had the perfect opportunity to do so. He wouldn't let Landon suffer for his mistake and reached into himself.

It was right there, as if it had been waiting patiently for him to call it forward. The image of the saxtien that he saw only a few moments ago bounded

Hosting the Kazimeer

toward him and Jaron held open his mind to embrace it. He caught the image as it leapt upward and held onto it tightly as he pulled it deep inside of him. The change happened so effortlessly, so easily this time, he wondered what made him so nervous about morphing in the first place.

He felt his strength and size increase, but during the process, he ripped through his clothing and saw them fall to the floor in shreds. He looked up and focused on Taj instantly. He sprang forward, a bit surprised that the smoke no longer bothered his eyes or throat. He charged straight for him and for a brief moment thought that Taj hadn't spotted him. He soon changed his mind when, without even looking at him, Taj shot out his hand toward him and a rope of energy tangled around his paws. Jaron crashed face first to the ground and slid across the wet floor, stopping just short of Taj's feet.

Jaron strained his neck around and for an instant caught Landon's eye. His friend seemed to be fading right in front of him. When he searched those green eyes, he felt their minds connect more strongly than ever, and for one brief moment he was also experiencing Landon's terror, despair, and anguish. The feelings almost overcame him, until Landon snapped his mind closed and released him.

Jaron twisted aggressively against the binds on his legs but they didn't loosen. He even tried to chew through them but all he succeeded in doing was biting into his own flesh. Through the smoke he saw dozens of eye-lesses speeding their way toward Landon and surrounding him, while Taj's power continued to dig into his friend's mind. Landon roared again but it wasn't fierce, it was mournful. Jaron knew Landon couldn't break free from Taj's power and was beginning to fold under it. Jaron's heart broke and he cursed himself. Why didn't he grab that stone when he had the chance! This was all his fault! Landon would die and the Land would be Taj's because he didn't have enough courage to do what he said he would. He was just a miserable, feeble-minded thief.

Growling in self-hatred and frustration, Jaron kicked madly at the invisible rope, but all he managed to do was spin himself around in a circle. His bunched legs whacked hard against something and the next thing he heard was a smash on the floor next to him. Jaron looked up and saw the glow from Taj's necklace had stopped. He craned his head around and saw the Dark Master flat on his back.

Jaron rolled over quickly until he felt Taj's body under him. He flipped himself over, pushing the air out of Taj's lungs, and sank his fangs deep into Taj's shoulder. Taj screamed and punched at Jaron's head but he didn't release his hold and in fact, got a better hold at the curve where Taj's neck and shoulder met. Suddenly Jaron felt a current of air under him. It started to lift him off of Taj but he held tightly onto his spot, refusing to be moved. The current shoved him away violently but not before Jaron raked his fangs across Taj's neck.

Jaron landed on his back but was able to move his limbs again and got to his feet. He felt something stuck in between his fangs and started to shake his head to dislodge it when he realized what it was. With wide eyes he stared at Taj, whose face was twisted in fury. Taj screamed a curse that shook the walls.

The eye-lesses that Landon hadn't torn in half, vanished once freed from Taj's power, leaving behind only their rank odor and weapons. Landon was now free to turn all his attention toward Taj and took a step forward. He stared down at Taj and roared with everything he had, making his own ears ring. He wasn't going to stomp, bite, or even tear Taj in two; he was going to burn him to a black crisp. He inhaled deeply, smoke already rising up out of his nostrils.

Everything for Taj was happening as if he were in a dream. He knew he made a mistake; a serious one he'd overlooked. When he combined his power with the stone they acted as one, so when the stone was torn away from him, so was his power, however briefly. It was only for a few seconds, but in those seconds, every spell he'd ever used the necklace's power for was gone. His creations, his wards, his protection, his death grip on the ivory dragon, all vanished, all lost.

He stood helpless for those few moments, as his power slowly began to rebuild. The ivory beast roared at him and moved in quickly. So he was going to die now, was he? Or would he be returned to the Pit? In either case, he could leave the Land without a tantrum. However, he wasn't going to leave without some company.

His eyes darted across the hall and glared at the boy. Well, he wasn't a boy at the moment; he was a huge saxtien and the one responsible for him being in this predicament. In one quick movement, Taj scooped up a spear left behind by a Mytock and hurled it at Jaron with such speed, Jaron could only register what happened after the spear tore through his fur and sank deep within his body. Jaron collapsed, his saxtien shape lost, and heard Landon roar with rage. Then he heard nothing else.

Taj turned smugly toward the ivory thing and stared defiantly into its green eyes. The dragon thrust its head forward and released the thick stream of white fire. Taj suddenly felt the familiar sensation of his power slowly flowing back into him. He snatched at it wildly and left through the first opening he could conjure, just as the white flames poured completely over where his body should have been.

Landon continued to blow his flame until he could breathe no more. He wheezed to a stop and stared at the black, charred spot on the ground in front of him. There was nothing remaining of Taj.

Mazon, Brazet, Jynx and their combined odd armies came crashing through both front and rear doors. Instantly magic from all Weavers was deployed to stop the fires burning down the High Room, but Landon barely registered that they were there. He could only stare at Jaron, wanting to lose his shape and go to his side, but knowing his own wounds were too severe to withstand in his regular form. So he stiffly lied down on his side and put his large face directly next to the boy, while he mind-spoke encouragement to him.

Jaron didn't respond and remained unconscious on the floor, with the spear sticking out of his body and Taj's necklace still clenched in his teeth.

CONFIDANT

The four Counts rose to their feet when Landon walked into the chamber. He walked slowly with his head held high. He had no choice but to keep his head high since his neck bandage didn't allow for much else and his stomach stung with each step. His wounds were healing but slowly and Landon didn't have time to wait until they were completely mended. He was the Kazimeer, after all.

He lowered himself carefully into his chair without wincing once. He found it amusing that this was the same chamber, same chair in fact, where he'd sat so many months before accused of murder. The Counts no longer stared at him as if he were some mongrel. Now they watched him anxiously, waiting for him to speak.

Landon waited for the Counts to be seated before he began. "Gentle sirs, it seems we have a lot of work ahead of us. Report on each providence; how do they fare?"

Four "Well, my lord," answered him.

Landon's eyes widen and he checked his timekeeper. "That didn't take long, did it? I guess we can all go home." The Counts began to stand. "Sit... down."

They did so unhappily.

"My lord," the Water Count stated. "What is it you want to hear?"

"Details. For instance, how goes the rebuilding in the northern providence?"

The Water Count spread his hands. "It continues."

"Continues? Well, how much has been restored? Most, half, a quarter?"

"I'd have to say a quarter, my lord."

"Why is it going so slowly?"

"Rebuilding takes time," the Count answered stiffly. "There are not enough workers to go around."

"To my knowledge, hundreds of people no longer have work. Farmlands were wiped out, shops and mills burned; where are all the people who no longer have these places to depend on for pieces?"

"But they have not volunteered."

"Volunteered!" Landon leaned slightly forward. "You pay them."

"We do not have the pieces to pay all of them," the Wind Count hissed.

"You don't have the pieces because you don't have the businesses to provide the resources that normally would be bought and sold to produce the pieces." Landon leaned back and smiled tightly. "But we are no longer in a normal state, are we?" The Counts grumbled in agreement. "No, we are not. Therefore, we must start from the beginning again, which means you pay the people first and then worry about profit."

"How are we to *pay* the people," the Soil Count sneered, "if we do not have the pieces to do so?"

Landon stared directly at him. "A very big, very heavy, very ugly throne was just removed from the High Room the other day. Once it is melted down and

303

the gems removed and appraised, the gold will be distributed equally among the four providences. *That's* what you will begin with. And everyone is to be paid the same amount, no more or no less than anyone else is. That includes the four of you."

Instant outrage filled the chamber. The Soil Count rose to his feet and slammed his hand down on the table. "This is an insult!"

"I agree!" the Wind Count stated. "I do far more than any of these… peasants. I should be compensated."

"You want to be compensated?" Landon asked, pointing a finger at him. "Fine. Then let's discuss Aman and we'll base your 'compensation' on that, agreed?"

The Wind Count seemed to be searching his memory and his eyes slowly went wide. He stared back at Landon's cool expression and swallowed. "But Aman is just one town."

"Yes. One town that should never have reached the condition it's currently in. Are we agreed on your compensation based on the condition of Aman?"

The Count dropped his eyes. "No, my lord."

Landon ran his eyes across all four faces. "Anyone else wish to express grievance with my decision?" No one said a word and the Soil Count slowly dropped back into his chair. "Then it's settled. Everyone will be paid equally."

"Including you, my lord?" the Soil Count growled.

Landon smiled. "No, not me." He waited for the looks of hatred to reach their peak before he continued. "I will be paid nothing until the Land is restored. Now, shall we proceed?"

"My lord," the Wind Count said. "If I may speak freely?"

"You will whether I give you permission or not, so go ahead."

The Count scowled but continued. "You should not concern yourself so deeply with such…unimportant matters."

"Unimportant?"

"We have each submitted reports to you on our plans for restoration of each providence. We can handle the minor details and all that is necessary for you to do is to give your written approval."

Landon smiled and rested his face in his hand. "Oh yes. The reports." He called out over his shoulder. "Webben?" Instantly the boy entered with an armful of parchment. He placed the pile neatly next to Landon. "Thank you, Webben."

"Yes, ma'lord," he said with a wide grin.

Landon held in a laugh seeing the boy's expression. He was still beaming over the upcoming Medallion award. Landon didn't know how he would have ever gotten through the first few days of his recovery without him. The boy never left his side. He tended to him, kept him informed, even made him laugh once or twice. The boy was a rare jewel that Landon had forgotten about and overlooked, and only recently remembered the splendor and value of such a gem. Landon waited until Webben bounced out of the chamber before he acknowledged the Counts again. He flipped through the stack of parchment.

Hosting the Kazimeer

"Yes, your reports. I've read them." He pulled out a handful and began separating them neatly, making four piles on the table. "I've never received more timely or orderly reports. Not a single word misspelled or a drop of ink spilled, and *excellent* penmanship. By far the most organized reports I've ever seen." The Counts exchanged proud glances and smiled at him. Landon smiled back. "Laughed my ass off when I read them."

The Counts gaped at him with shock.

"My lord?" the Wind Count finally asked.

Landon didn't answer him directly, simply took one report off the top of one of the piles and began reading. "'Hold public executions of those captured who were convicted of treason'." Landon stared up at the Wind Count. "And that will do...what? Raise morale?"

"It will send a warning," the Count answered firmly.

"Ah, a warning." Landon nodded slowly in understanding and then stared questionably at the Count. "To whom?"

"To those who are still loyal to the...false Kazimeer."

Landon chuckled, "The false Kazimeer? Say his name, Taj."

The Count clicked his tongue, "To...Taj."

"So it will be a warning then?"

"Yes."

"But if you've captured and convicted all of these treasonous folks, then whom is the warning for?" The Count opened his mouth but Landon held up his hand. "Don't tell me there are some still loose in the Land because if there are, *I* will convict *you* of not performing your duty. I ordered every one of those dangerous people to be rounded up two weeks ago." The Count snapped his mouth shut. Landon eyed him sharply. "If I hear of any person, any morpher, *anyone* being assaulted or killed by some fool doing it in the name of Taj, I will hold you personally responsible. And that goes for each providence. As for the matter concerning the captured prisoners, perhaps making them repay their debt to the Land is more suitable. I understand Botin was destroyed." Landon looked over to the Water Count. "Correct?"

"Yes."

"Then have the prisoners work to rebuild the town their Master destroyed. Also, I think it would do them good to spend a bit of time with the families who lost someone during this Bloodshed. Morpher families, especially."

Landon shuffled through the reports again, while the Counts remained silent. "Ah! Now this...*this* is my favorite. 'Increase levy on the people by twenty percent to improve current conditions'." Landon stared at the Soil Count. "And how do you propose we do that?"

"Tell the people they are to pay the increase."

"Ah, I see," Landon said and nodded. "*How* are they to pay it?"

"Everyone will have to dig deeper into their purses."

"Most don't *have* purses, let alone a single coin to put in them. What will you do if they don't pay? If they *can't* pay?"

"It will just have to be ordered that they do."

"Orders don't suddenly make pieces appear."

"It will be enforced," the Count growled.

"What will you do? Take away the rubble that was once their home? Or perhaps you will take their children as payment? Maybe you're thinking of executing those who can't pay the increase, is that it?"

The Soil Count blew out a sharp sigh, "Landon."

"Martin," Landon answered in the same tone. The Count's eyes widen. Landon never had used any of the Counts personal names before. "If you refuse to show respect, don't expect to receive any from me. What is your complaint?"

"I don't think you've thought this matter completely through."

"Well I *know* you haven't. Think about what effect a levy increase will have on the people. Most cannot pay so their morale's will be even lower than they are now. If you 'enforce' this act then people will do some Kyriea awful thing to get the pieces and if they can't, will have to face your consequences. Promoting and enforcing such an act is asking for rebellion. And if rebellion is brought on by this, I, for one, will be standing on the side of the people." Landon leaned back in his chair and folded his hands on his stomach. "However, as I explained earlier, each providence will be given the same amount to start with. From there the people will be put to work, earning a living, and the shops they are rebuilding will be able to sell items to these same people, who can now purchase products with their newfound pieces. The shopkeepers will have to purchase more supplies from the mills and farms, thereby giving them an opportunity to hire more people to supply the demand. Do you see the process and how easily it will work if you are willing to be patient?"

The Counts said nothing. Landon leaned forward again. "There will be no levy increase, or public executions, or reorganizing of the masses placing them with others of their own wealth, or any of the ridiculous suggestions I have seen in these reports. It will be done as I said and there will be no deviating from the plan set in place until further notice."

The Soil Count was the first to speak. "Will there be anything else, my lord?"

"Yes," Landon said pleasantly. "The schools Taj began---"

The Wind Count interrupted. "Arrangements have already been made to take them down."

"You will do no such thing."

"My lord?"

"I want them completed as soon as possible and I want to see a list from each of you of the best Masters from each providence. I want a variety of talents to be shown at each school; reading, writing, computation, history, and any other subject that would be beneficial to the children... and the adults."

The Water Count cleared his throat. "My lord that will take time."

"I want the lists by next week and the schools completed by the end of the month." The Counts all opened their mouths to protest but Landon spoke calmly. "I will dock the pay of anyone who does not perform their duty in a timely fashion, starting with the four of you. Any questions?"

Each Count opened his mouth to argue but Landon stared down every one of them until they finally sat silently.

Hosting the Kazimeer

Landon smiled broadly. "Good! I'm glad to see we're getting along so well. Now, I want each of you to take whatever informers you have…don't tell me you don't have any, I know you do, and have them discover all they can about two people. The first is named Jynx; she's a young, talented Weaver who helped me out quite a lot, but knows just a bit too much for someone her age and seemed to know a lot about Taj. Find out where she lives, her background, anything and everything. Someone like that loose in the Land can be more of a danger than an asset.

"The second person is named Abbnar. I can't tell you anything about him but Taj mentioned him, and it seemed whoever he was referring to bothered him. Anyone who could cause Taj any bother is someone I would be honored to meet and form an alliance with. Also, I want an investigation regarding rumors I've heard that the slave-trade is in operation."

"My lord," the Soil Count groaned wearily. "That would be a complete waste of time."

Landon eyed him coldly. "*I* do not think so. See that it is done. I want weekly updates on these matters." Landon didn't mention that he would have his own investigations being performed by people he trusted far more than the Counts. "The next point of business I want to discuss---"

A rapid knock at the door caused Landon to pause. "Yes?"

Webben came bustling in and whispered something quickly into Landon's ear. Landon stared at the boy in mute shock.

He was brought out of it when the Water Count asked, "Are you all right, my lord?"

Landon jerked his head toward the Count, winced, and nodded feebly. "Yes, thank you." He began to rise to his feet unsteadily. "If you will excuse me gentle sirs, there are some important, personal matters I must attend to." He allowed Webben to guide him out of the chamber.

"But…my lord!" the Soil Count protested. "We have not finished."

Landon didn't hear him. His mind was spinning too much for him to know anything other than what Webben just told him.

Jaron had remained unconscious for over two weeks and much of Landon's spare time was spent at the boy's side, including some sleepless nights. According to his Healers and Mazon, that spear ripped him apart on the inside and had done much damage. Although they could supply herbs and spells to heal him, it was just a matter of waiting to see if his body could repair itself. Mazon assured Landon that sleep was the best thing for him.

Landon spent his time either reading to the boy or simply talking to him, but he never knew what to say. It was weird trying to hold a one sided conversation, but he knew that Jaron didn't like to be left alone. However, it was rare that Jaron ever *was* alone.

Every cat in the castle was determined to stay in the boy's chamber. Landon hardly ever noticed the cats before this. They were there to keep the mice and rats out, since rodents didn't care if they inhabited a shack or a castle. They were workers, just like the guard hounds, and he never saw much reason to treat them as pets. But no sooner was Jaron placed in his own chamber to heal than every single cat had to be in there with him. No matter what the servants did, they couldn't find a way to keep them out. Landon would've thought that with all the cats off duty keeping watch over the boy, the rodent problem would become unbearable but that was not the case. For it seemed the rodents also had to be at Jaron's side. The strangest part was the cats never once attacked them. They all sat peacefully together either on or around the boy's bed, until someone shooed them away. And it was more than once when Landon caught a guard hound scratching outside Jaron's door with a frustrated Defender forcefully pulling it along.

It was another peculiarity about the boy that Landon couldn't figure out, although the answer always felt as if it were just within his reach.

The oddest thing, though, was that he could still feel Jaron and he finally went to Mazon to find out why. Mazon gave him his speculations. He believed they were mind-bonded, which meant that each would always be aware of the other's feelings and presence. They would always be connected to each other. Landon wasn't so sure he liked hearing that and knew Jaron wouldn't be thrilled either, but when the boy awoke he would find a way to tell him.

Landon often stressed the word "when" even to himself. The longer Jaron remained asleep, the longer he feared he would never get the chance to say, "Thank you" and have Jaron actually hear him. Then again, he did feel the boy's connection to him constantly and Jaron's presence was not something one could ignore easily.

Still the waiting had been eating him up inside.

Webben's sudden interruption caught him completely off guard. He knew he should not be surprised and had braced himself for this moment, but he suddenly wasn't sure how to feel or react. He continued to walk slowly to Jaron's chamber and felt numb.

**   **

He was comfortable. He was *sooo* comfortable that he never wanted to move again. Honestly, he didn't think he could so he didn't bother. He heard the door open, soft shooing grunts, and then what sounded like a dozen feet moving across the floor quickly. But he didn't open his eyes to see who it was or what was happening, and nestled down against the pillows and pulled the soft blankets up to his chin. He heard someone walk to the foot of the bed but didn't even want to speak. *That's* how comfortable he was.

After the silence stretched out, he began to doze until he heard someone ask, "Comfy? Cozy?"

He smiled slightly in response and began to drift off again.

"*Jaron!*"

The happy shout jerked his eyes open and startled his whole body. He opened his mouth to spit a curse at the person, then stopped himself, narrowed his eyes to a squint, and stared. The voice didn't match what he had become used to. For one, it was spoken aloud. Secondly, it sounded lighter, softer, not as strict or heavy as it used to sound. And finally, he'd never actually seen Landon before, up close anyway, so he wasn't sure if he was staring at the right person or not. Then again, who else would be standing at the foot of his bed, smiling as he was? He supposed his mental image had been mostly correct. Landon was tall, pale, and held himself like a Kazimeer...but he was so young!

Landon also experienced a strange moment as he stared at Jaron now awake. Granted, he'd seen him while in dragon form and while the boy had been unconscious all this time, but seeing Jaron alert while he was in his regular shape was almost awkward. He wasn't sure how to feel. He had to admit his first reaction after staring into those big, round, bright eyes and that smooth, young face was to pat him on the head and give him a coin. However, Landon knew Jaron would most likely distract him somehow and take his whole purse.

Jaron, wincing now and then, slowly pulled himself to a sitting position, propping the many pillows up behind him. He carefully smoothed out the blanket, folded his hands on his lap, met Landon's stare levelly and cleared his throat.

"Ju lied to me."

"I never lied to you," Landon stated, walking around to the side of the bed.

"Ju made me believes dat ju were an old, fat man," Jaron said in the same level tone.

"I never led you to believe that. You just assumed," Landon said, lowering himself slowly onto the edge of the bed. "You never asked, you know."

"And ju never told," Jaron growled, losing his dignified look. He shook his head. "I's was polite to ju, too."

"When!" Landon cried, leaning forward. "When was that! Oh, I missed that part."

"I's dinn't say many tings dat I's wanted to." He grinned wickedly and opened his eyes wide. "But now ju gonna hear dem."

"I'm glad to see you're feeling better."

"I's glad to sees ju 'ave a body." He looked Landon over as if he was buying a horse. "Is dat da original one?"

"Yes!"

"Oh." Jaron shrugged, unimpressed. The motion from shrugging made his side scream and he winced.

"How's your wound?"

"Its bloody hurts," Jaron growled, rubbing his side gently to ease the pain. Then he remembered where he had gotten it. "Where's...ah..." He looked around the chamber as if maybe Taj was hiding somewhere in there.

"Gone."

"Really?"

"Completely," Landon said and smiled.

Jaron let out a sharp laugh, which also made his side hurt but he ignored it. "And dat necklace ting?"

"I have it. Mazon's cast a protective spell on it while we figure out what to do with it. There's an inscription around the edge that says we shouldn't destroy it." Jaron cringed and Landon nodded. "I know but we'll figure something out."

Then the silence grew steadily between them. They simply stared at the other strangely, as if still trying to find all the details they had missed before.

Landon broke the silence. He grew humble and serious as he met the boy's eyes levelly. "Thank you." Jaron smiled shyly as he looked away, and actually flushed. "Those words sound pretty hollow I'll admit after what we've been through but there are no other words to express how grateful I am to you. I couldn't have done any of this without you."

"Well, 'corse ju couldn't," Jaron answered, then became a little humble himself. "Anniways, I's likes to tank ju too."

"For what?" Landon asked, blinking in surprise.

"Fure stickin' up fure me," Jaron mumbled, as he picked at invisible fuzz on the immaculately clean blanket.

"When did I do that?"

Jaron grumbled under his breath, shifted uncomfortably, and pushed the conversation in a different direction. If the two of them continued like this, it would become sappier by the minute. He pulled himself up straighter and asked, with just a hint of amusement, "So is dis when ju arrest me?"

"What?"

"Ju wanted to arrest me." Landon shook his head in confusion. "Fure bein' a thief and a traitor."

Landon blinked in surprise again. How did the boy remember that! Even he had forgotten. "Ah…I'll do it after you've healed up."

"Oh, well, tank ju very much," Jaron said and grinned.

"Are you hungry, *thief boy*?"

"Why's yes, *thronge worm*, now dat ju mention its."

Landon got up from the bed, walked to the door, and said, "I'll have the servants dig up some bugs for you."

"Ju is jus too kind."

"I know," Landon said grinning and opened the door.

He was startled for a second when he saw the crowd gathered. The two Defenders were supposed to be there, but Mazon, Brazet, and Webben were there as well. They were waiting outside of Jaron's chamber when he first entered but he never thought they'd stick around. Brazet and Mazon smiled sheepishly at him but didn't move along. Webben casually peeked around him to catch a glimpse of Jaron but Landon gently pushed his head out of the chamber. He addressed one of the Defenders, asking if he could go to the kitchen and bring up some broth.

Jaron suddenly snapped out, "Wha' ju lookin' at, piss face!"

Landon whirled around and stared wide-eyed at the boy with the deadly look, then realized he was talking to the other Defender, who apparently had been staring. Webben's cackle could be heard half way across the castle, which didn't help matters much. The Defender began to stalk into the chamber when Brazet's large hand came down on his shoulder.

"Easy, man," Brazet said calmly. "He's just a boy."

Landon waited until the Defender settled down and turned back to Jaron. "What is wrong with you?!"

"Well, he's was lookin' at me funny," Jaron grumbled and crossed his arms over his chest.

Landon stared at the Defender. "Don't look at him funny. Trust me, you don't want to look at him funny." The Defender dropped his head and said nothing. Landon rested a hand on his shoulder. "Perhaps you could go to the kitchen. Please."

The Defender glared coldly at Jaron for a moment, then nodded pleasantly to Landon. "Yes, my lord."

Webben snorted loudly as the Defender walked by him.

"Webben!" Landon warned.

"Honorary Defenders do not snicker," Brazet said firmly.

The boy quieted down but as Landon began to close the door, Webben pushed it open wide enough for him to stick his head through. He smiled at Jaron and whispered, "That was great!"

Jaron's eyes went wide with amusement and he chuckled softly. Landon growled warningly and the boy quickly ducked out of the chamber, almost slamming the door behind him.

Landon sat on the edge of the bed again. "You really are too wound up *and* are a bad influence."

Jaron nodded. "Yes, I's know."

Landon smiled and after a moment, offered his hand. "We've never been introduced properly. My name is Landon."

Jaron stared curiously from the outstretched hand to Landon's face. He suddenly realized what Landon was doing and sniffed a laugh. "I's Jaron," he said, taking his hand.

"Owner of the Four Seas. I've heard of you." Landon pumped it gently. "I'm very pleased to finally meet you, Jaron."

A slow smile spread across Jaron's face. "I's pleased to finally meet ju too…Kazimeer."

"Ah-ha! So you finally admit it!"

Jaron quickly took his hand back and said coolly, "I's admit nutin'."

"You called me Kazimeer," Landon crooned wickedly.

"Well I's sorry ifs ju *'eard* Kazimeer but I's clearly 'member sayin' thronge worm."

Landon wagged his finger at him. "I's know what I's heard and you called me Kazimeer."

"Wha's me word?" Jaron grinned.

Landon just realized what he had said and came up with the perfect exchange. "I'll trade you. Your 'I's' for my 'confidant'."

"Huh?"

Landon smiled. "It means friend."